Romance Under Wraps

ENDORSEMENTS

This is a slice of chocolate cake morphed into Chinese takeout, that leaves you feeling empty and wanting more. More of this couple and their adventures! It was a pleasure from beginning to end, and I'd recommend it to anyone.
—Rodney Likes, author

These were two complex and believable characters with plenty of twists and turns, who finally made it in the end. Enjoyed reading complex plots, beautiful descriptions, woven with good dialogue and action. I don't usually like humor in fiction, however, I found myself laughing at Cade's predicaments.
—'Sly Jones', author,

A big shout-out to Claire O'Sullivan, grande dame of new romantic thrillers! Claire's debut novel was released by Elk Lake Publishing, October 2020. She's used her medical and forensic background, along with a few diabolical FB mentors (!!), to craft an unusual (translated: forbidden) romance between a female con artist and the detective pursuing her. Of course, a murder is involved (won't say who), along with ambushes and assassination attempts (won't say where), and an ending that will blow you away (won't say why). You'll need to read this book. Seriously! Congrats, Claire!
—Rebecca M. White

Hey friends! I just finished an advanced copy of Claire O'Sullivan's *Romance Under Wraps*, and it has more twists and turns than the roller coaster, Steel Vengeance. Keep an eye out for it!

—**Linda K. Rodante**, author

If I'm yawning today it's because I stayed up late reading Claire O'Sullivan's soon-to-be-published Christian Suspense-Romance, *How to Steal a Romance*. Great book. I recommend snagging it as soon as it's released. Deadly twists and turns, an innovative plot, and characters that pull you into the pages with them. By the time I got through reading *How to Steal a Romance*, I had to figure out on which side of the pages I lived.

—**Stephanie Parker McKean**, author

I read *Romance Under Wraps* and found it full of suspense, great characters, and a plot that had many twists and turns. The love story takes a while to start to become a romance but it and the story keeps you engaged until the end. I found it hard to figure out who the killer was and the reason why the victim was murdered. Catherine Cade did not know who she was, and she always felt like running until she meets Rick Calhoun who takes her under his wing and trains her to help solve cold cases. This is non-stop suspense that has many plot twists. This book will keep you on the edge of your seat. I received this book as a gift, and all the words are strictly my own. If you love Christian Suspense and Romance you will enjoy this book.

—**Rory Lemond**

Romance Under Wraps

Claire O'Sullivan

ELK LAKE PUBLISHING INC
PUBLISHING THE POSITIVE
Plymouth, Massachusetts

Cover and Interior Design: Deb Haggerty, Derinda Babcock

Editor(s): Mary W. Johnson, Deb Haggerty

PUBLISHED BY: Elk Lake Publishing, Inc., 35 Dogwood Drive, Plymouth, MA 02360, 2020

Library Cataloging Data

Names: O'Sullivan, Claire (Claire O'Sullivan)

Romance Under Wraps / Claire O'Sullivan

394 p. 23cm × 15cm (9in × 6 in.)

Identifiers: ISBN-13: 978-1-64949-087-2 (paperback) | 978-1-64949-088-9 (trade paperback) | 978-1-64949-089-6 (e-book)

Key Words: Mystery, Suspense, murder, police procedural, romance, con artists, amnesia

LCCN: 2020948350 Fiction

DEDICATION

ACKNOWLEDGMENTS

First, I cannot say enough about my husband, Pat, for his patience, for letting me write without time limits or complaining. For cooking when I didn't feel up to it, and for shopping. God bless him. Seriously.

To my family for knowing I am an introvert and still love me, thank you Dave, Steph, Travis, Trisha, and Matt and Jessica.

To Rebecca Macomson White who has been walking this journey of writing with me for eight years—from "that is the worst copy I have ever read" to "I really, really like this." She's cracked the whip all along from horrible writing to my utter apathy, distress, or simple angst. Her critiques can be scathing, her wit, acerbic, but her love (you know, the tough love that we really appreciate 'after' the fact) abounds. And her grammar and editing skills have been gifted to her from above, not to mention her patience. Thankful that you are part of the Elk Lake Publishing team! I just don't want to swell her head too much, so let's not tell her!

And many thanks to Deb Haggerty, Elk Lake Publishing, for taking a chance on a new author, for her encouragement and explanations (with a great deal of patience) of those teeny details I didn't understand, and for her great purpose in fulfilling God's will in her life. And to the rest of the Elk Lake Publishing team for every ounce of love, care, and encouragement they give.

I have had a plethora of alpha and beta critiquers—perhaps around forty or more, who have given me a vast amount of great information. I cannot tell you how absolutely essential you have been in this process. For those names I can't recall, I apologize. For those I do, thanks to Sharon McLittle,

Richard Bryson, Rory Lemond, Stephanie McKean Parker, Linda Rodante, Kara Kelley, Tina Chan, and Rosi D'Amber.

Thank you to my 'dear readers,' because without you, well, I'd have to go cook or do something relatively boring in comparison to writing.

First and last, thanks be to God.

CHAPTER 1

CATHERINE CADE
0700 MONDAY

Another week passed, and I still had no idea who I truly was. I stared at patient charts and their familiar name tags with a pang of regret. I knew their names, but I didn't know mine. There it was.

If only I knew mine.

Whiskey River, my new home, was tucked in the mountains. Cherry trees and pine surrounded my office, scattering leaves and cones like fast-food trash. The pine trees, baking in the August heat, smelled like Christmas in the middle of summer. I was thankful to be working in an air-conditioned office on such a day.

In the back office, my medical assistant, Teresa, swung around, a green lollipop bobbing in her mouth. She spoke in a mumble. "Miss Catherine, check those charts. The city commissioner, Mr. Thompson, ditched his annual physical, and his file isn't digitized. Want him to come to the clinic?"

For the past few years, I'd been Catherine Cade, nurse practitioner. I was all for joking around, but this was serious, and I adopted a stern tone. "Yes. Can't have our good politicians fall ill. I'll call him."

"Got it." She clicked her pen and disappeared into the hall. I should've mentioned the lollipop still in her mouth. She'd figure it out.

In the meantime, I turned the retro Star Trek chair toward an old x-ray light box, now antiquated, checked a couple of digital images, and pressed the smartphone to call Thompson's home number. While on my third "please give him the message" to Thompson's home, I saw another patient's emergent x-ray result. I swore under my breath, thumbed the phone off and called the ER.

Twenty minutes after my frenzied morning routines, my eyes drifted shut as I breathed out the anxiety I lived daily. Whatever my name was, my license and my life—all things Catherine Cade—were fake. Pulling off a PhD and working as a nurse practitioner in Whiskey River was the scam of scams. If the cops found out about my recent felonies, well, they would land this identity thief in prison.

RICK CALHOUN
0700 MONDAY

Homicide Detective Rick Calhoun stepped under the crime scene tape, pushed up his ball cap, and asked God for wisdom as he glanced at the wall.

It was difficult to tell blood from brain matter.

He stood in Thompson's home and figured the body belonged to City Commissioner Stephen Thompson, or at least someone wearing the victim's pajamas. Surveying the spatter, it could be anyone. Other than the body and blood and the crime scene unit, the house appeared lavish with massive wood doors, high ceilings, and vases filled with flowers in the spacious living room. The body lay on a Persian-style rug near a large leather armchair, and tables topped with black Egyptian marble dotted the room. Not a home appropriate for a poor rural town. Calhoun turned his attention to the ordinary busyness attending death.

The rookie ride-along, Tristan Phillips, vomited in the bushes, and Calhoun shut his eyes. If the kid kept it up, he'd have to bust him back to work Vice—not Homicide—for the kid's health. He moved to the door and howled at him. "Hey, Phillips, when you're done there, don't use the garbage. Could be brains in there, too." Aw, maybe egging him on was a bad idea. Time to tuck away the bout of sarcasm.

As he had a migraine dogging him, Calhoun itched to do the walk-through, file the paperwork, and go home. He tipped a finger salute to Kim Pierson, the crime tech working the scene, then reminded himself silently to be polite before he spoke to the medical examiner. "McCloud, what've we got?"

"What have we got? Let's see. We got a nightmare for the cleanup crew. We'll need lunch bags to get him to the morgue. City Commissioner Thompson most likely, and half his head is on the wall."

Calhoun ground his teeth. Seeing McCloud was never on his list of Things I Want To Do Today. "Who found the body?"

"Victim's wife."

Calhoun turned a half-circle. "She call 9-1-1? Is she here?"

"Yeah, she did. No, she's not. You were late, so Mike picked her up and drove her to the station. You got a hangover or something?"

"No." Calhoun crossed his arms. "Cause of death?"

Then McCloud grunted. "Did you leave your brains at home? 'Cause this guy sure did. Over there, and some over here. Watch your step. Gunshot wound, most likely. Won't know more 'til we get the parts back to the forensic lab."

"Weapon?"

Dr. McCloud grunted again and pointed to a .45 caliber pistol with a spent casing, while Kim, the CS tech, busied herself photographing the evidence.

Calhoun examined bottles on the kitchen counter. "What are these bottles for?"

"Insulin."

"Huh. Isn't insulin quick-acting?"

McCloud leaned an elbow on his knee, turned his head, and yelled, "Pack it up, people, Sherlock's solved the case. Don't worry about the finger painting and bone fragments on the wall."

Calhoun fought the urge to roll his eyes and ignored McCloud, directing his gaze toward the tech. "It's a wonderful day, Kim." He grasped her shoulders and grinned. "Even a dead body. Did you find evidence of forced entry?"

"No, sir, and I might add you have an unusual notion of wonderful."

"Homicide is very boring in Whiskey River."

"Well, when you live here long enough, you'll see we really are dull as toast." She tipped her pencil toward Calhoun and whispered. "Detective, I know it's none of my business, but the last time you and Dr. McCloud had a fight—"

Calhoun held a hand up. "I know, I know. Making him cry like a little girl is not my job."

Kim pressed her lips together and hesitated. Finally she asked, "What happened between you two?"

"It's ancient history."

"The Hatfield and McCoy families are getting a run for their money."

He spoke a low, stern, "Kim ..."

"Yessir." She cleared her throat. "Back to your questions. I found no unusual marks on the lock." She checked her notes. "I didn't find broken glass or forced windows. The alarm didn't go off, so no break-in." She leaned toward him and whispered. "Think it's an inside job?"

Stroking an imaginary beard, he sighed. "Someone has exceptional lock-picking skills. Or a housekeeper with keys and codes."

"Spoilsport."

"Who has access to the alarms? Has someone tampered with the alarm or switched off the device? Give me that, and I'll buy you lunch."

Kim's professional camaraderie gave way to smiles. "Thank you, Detective. However, Groucho is picking up the tab today. Want to join us?"

"Not a chance."

"A rain check, then."

Calhoun studied the room. "Do they have a safe?"

"Yes, unopened." She lifted her pen in the air. "Oh, there were three phone calls to the house, Detective. Same woman each time."

Calhoun pivoted. "Did you answer?"

"Yes. I kept her on the line, and it's evident something irritated her. Said she needed to see him today, and with each call, she became more agitated."

"What time was this? Did she leave a name?"

"Yes, and a number. The first call was around seven this morning. Catherine Cade, that was her name." Kim handed over her notes.

He read them. "Outstanding. You're a godsend, Kim." Calhoun kissed her forehead. He moved about to assess the blood loss, the position of the body, and the arc of brain matter along the wall. He saw a void in the splatter where someone else had stood, a phantom outline. The medical examiner had checked, but Calhoun dug into his pocket, gloved, and grabbed his measuring tape. He scribbled and measured.

Interesting.

Calhoun stepped outside in time to watch a familiar banged-up silver Honda Accord as it pulled away from the curb toward town, one that belonged to journalist Leo Smart, ambulance chaser. Calhoun eyed the car as Leo pulled away. The news was quick to find the dead.

CHAPTER 2

Calhoun arrived back at the Police Department and moved through the bullpen past the vice detective and the dispatch officer. He rapped on Chief Greg Dumont's door, keen on starting the interview with the wife of the deceased.

"Commissioner Thompson was murdered—what happened here?" He goggled at the sight. The Chief fidgeted with paperwork, and his dark skin glistened with sweat. No coffee. *National Institute of Justice Journal* tossed on the floor. Something odd was going on. The Chief didn't fidget or sweat under pressure.

"Nothing." Dumont handed over a packet. "I need you to—" He coughed. "Run an errand for me as a favor. Take this to the doctor at Whiskey River Family Practice. Dr. Jonah Riley."

"You gonna tell me what's got your knickers in a knot?"

"Nope."

"So, running dry cleaning across town?"

Greg's head snapped up, and he lapsed into his Louisiana accent. "Listen, Rick, when I tell you to get my dry cleaning, I 'spect you'll be driving across town. Hear?"

Now was not the time to figure out the Chief's state of mind, nor was this a battle worth fighting. "Yup. Will do."

"Make sure you bring it back signed. Dr.—"

"Riley. Later, Greg."

Time to interview Thompson's widow. Calhoun stepped into the observation room and checked the note from Detective Mike Tanaka. She had not yet lawyered up.

He read the notes on the spouse. Sarah Thompson, the dead man's wife, had an age difference worth taking a gander at, as the dead man was seventy, and she forty. Calhoun stood behind the two-way mirror. She didn't appear to be a day over thirty ... or grieving. She was a platinum blonde, but on closer scrutiny, she had darkened roots. He rubbed his right thumb against his forefinger. History of plastic surgery? He poured a paper cup of coffee from the office pot, ambled into the sparse room furnished with two metal chairs and a white table, and presented his badge.

"Mrs. Thompson, I'm Detective Calhoun. Horribly sorry for your loss, ma'am. This is a difficult time, I understand, especially for questions, but I have to ask. Thought you could use a cup of coffee, unless you prefer something else." He sat down. "Can you tell me if anything in the home was disturbed, or the safe tampered with?"

She reached for the cup and hesitated. "I didn't look. I wasn't thinking, I guess."

"I understand, Mrs. Thompson. We'll need the combination to the safe. Do you know of anyone who might have held a grudge against your husband, or wished to cause him harm?"

Sarah scribbled the combination on a napkin and leaned back in the chair. "The editor of the *Whiskey River Medallion*, Marcus Stewart, shared words, unkind words with my husband. He promised to end him. I don't know if the editor meant to destroy his political career—or worse." She stopped and pressed a tissue to her eyes.

Calhoun noted her lack of tears. "Did your husband appear depressed? Changes in his behavior?"

"No." She wrapped her hands around the cup and peered into the coffee. "Sometimes he mentioned vague issues with board members. I was not encouraged to pursue answers."

"Do you know the names of any of the board members?"

"Yes."

Calhoun scratched the names of committee members on his pad as she listed them. Maybe he could catch them before lunch.

"Tell me about his diabetes."

Thompson's voice was tremulous. "He kept it controlled. That was him, always in control."

He placed paperwork on the table, faced her, and leaned forward with elbows on his knees. "Did you have any marital troubles?"

"No negatives in our marriage except his snoring. I wore miners' earplugs." The widow wiped non-existent lint from the table. "Funny, I used to joke with him about it. I said the earplugs kept our marriage together." She twisted her fingers. "Not funny—not anymore."

"You're certain you didn't hear the gunshot?"

Sarah shook her head again. "People who work with explosives wear this brand of earplugs. I grew up near Hibbing, Minnesota. Mining country."

"Forensics will pick them up, you understand that, correct?"

"Of course."

"Any idea what might have happened?"

Thompson's leg bounced. She picked at her jacket. "No."

"Tell me about the gun we found. It's registered to him."

"What's to tell? He owned the pistol. He took potshots at obnoxious birds sometimes."

He scribbled a note. *with a .45 caliber.* "Big caliber for birds."

She pulled her coat close around her. "I know nothing about guns."

"What time did you set the house alarm?"

She blinked rapidly. "Oh. My husband always did that. He stayed up late, and midnight was his usual bedtime."

"Does anyone else have the alarm code? Service workers, family?"

"No. We don't, well, we don't have family, and I supervise help in the home."

"We saw CCTV cameras. Do they work?"

"Yes. The setup is terrible, and the pictures are grainy."

"We'll check those, too. What about the alarm's code?"

"Oh," she said, slipping an errant strand of hair behind her ear. "It's his birthday."

"Were you home all night?"

She glowered. "If you're suggesting I'm having an affair, you're wrong."

"I wasn't, but interesting you brought it up. You're an attractive woman, and he was elderly."

"He wasn't old. His brain was sharp. Loving." Mrs.

9

Thompson pushed her chair away from the table and crossed her arms. She slipped her jacket over her shoulders.

"Worried about something, Mrs. Thompson?"

"No." She bit her lip. "It's obvious. You think I did it."

"Did what?" He kept his eyes on her.

"Killed him. You think I killed him."

"Did you?"

"No." Her eyes flashed. "I loved him. Am I a suspect? Do I need an attorney?"

"Mrs. Thompson, I know you want to find out what happened. An attorney advocating for you is your choice."

She swallowed. "I think I'll make that call."

He scratched a note: *Crosses arms and leans away. No direct eye contact. Leg bouncing. Nervous or ready to run?*

Sarah Thompson's eyes flashed. "I loved him." Almost in a whisper, she repeated it. "I loved him."

He scrawled a note: *She talked about him in past tense. She's already transitioned from present to past within an hour. Grief takes different forms. Not incriminating, but curious.*

Put together, Sarah Thompson's defensive posture, vague answers, hiding her face, and questionable profession of love led Calhoun to sum up the interview in two words: *Suspect One.*

Plugging in names on his computer, Rick obtained information on each member from the council website. He grabbed a pad and tucked it into his back pocket. Standing, he left the ringing phones of the bullpen and walked two blocks to A Street. It was Coffee with City Council day. He hoped he'd catch them all there.

Calhoun stepped to the counter and ordered black coffee to go. He watched the group huddle around tables. Five minutes left according to his watch.

Several people joined them. Some were old-timers, others in their mid-thirties. Each sported attire which seemed a statement of their political stance. A tall, underweight man with blond dreads, jeans, and sandals spoke animatedly about the marijuana restrictions on dispensaries in the city limits.

Brian Jackson. The first commissioner on his list. His picture had changed from the past two years, now hitting for somewhere between generation Y and Z. Considering that he was born in the early 1960s, Calhoun wondered if it fooled or offended anyone.

His coffee break ended at the conclusion of the meeting, and he walked out to meet Jackson and slow-jogged the cracked sidewalk to him. "May I have a moment of your time?" Jackson turned, and his face soured. "Nah, man, I gotta get to work. Shoulda spoke up in the coffeehouse."

Calhoun presented his badge. "Then let me put it this way. This isn't a request. Rick Calhoun, Whiskey River Police Department. This has to do with Stephen Thompson."

Jackson chortled. "Why, what's he done now?"

"Sir, he's dead. I have some routine questions."

He stopped, and a flip-flop came off his foot. "Dead? When?"

"Early this morning. Can you tell me anything about the relationship between the members and Thompson?"

"Hard to believe. The man was a machine." He laced his fingers behind his head and gazed at the sky, showing off sweat that had already soaked his shirt's underarms. "If you read the paper, he and Marcus Stewart went at it all the time." Brian hee-hawed. "Man, Marcus got so mad at him he even said he'd end Thompson's career."

Calhoun turned a page on his notepad. "Were you on friendly terms with Commissioner Thompson?"

Jackson closed an eye. "I've never much cared for the life-styles of the rich and famous, if you know what I mean. Plus, we have kids, and they don't." He winked. "With demograph-ics changing, I've reinvented myself."

Rick pointed to his dreadlocks. "I don't remember those before."

"Election year, man. Gotta stay ahead of the curve, grab those kids just voting." He placed a hand on Rick's shoulder. Calhoun glared at Jackson, and Jackson removed his hand. "Anyway, once I get home, off comes the wig."

"Uh-huh. Did you two ever argue?"

"We're politicians." Brian guffawed donkey-like again.

"Outside the ring."

"Not me. You might talk to Andy Denmark. Then again, he's impatient with everyone. Say," he pointed a finger, "reminds me, Thompson and John Murray clashed, but ..." Brian said. "You'd have to ask."

"Thanks, Mr. Jackson, for taking time out of your schedule."

"Anytime."

Calhoun walked away with few answers, other than Brian Jackson was an ex-car salesman still up to his slick ways, and who never even asked why he was being questioned or how Thompson died. And the only board member at the coffee klatch. Maybe everyone else was working.

CHAPTER 3

CATHERINE CADE
SAME DAY, 1130

Early and throughout each day, the radio supplied faint background chatter in the back office I shared with Teresa. After lunch, I slid ChapStick across my lips. I peeked at the clock. I wanted to see the commissioner before he could make an excuse, but my phone calls were diverted with a "we'll get back to you."

On the radio, the sultry voice of a woman reporter said, "Whiskey River Board of Commissioner Stephen Thompson was found dead in his home this morning. No foul play is suspected."

The ChapStick fell from my hand. I did not see that coming. And I'd left messages with the family. *Oh, no.*

He was my patient. Nurse Practitioner Catherine Cade's patient. Death certificates normally landed on the doctor's desk, but Jonah Riley, MD, wasn't here. If he didn't come in tomorrow, I might have to deal with officials, since the dead man was a VIP.

I breathed a prayer to a God I wasn't sure I believed in. No answer. Maybe God ran in the same social circles as Santa Claus.

The quietus of a VIP in this hamlet could throw a huge monkey wrench into my life.

Stephen Thompson, dead. Seventy years old and the cops declined to state a simple deduction. Why? I mean, he wasn't fossilized, but if he died from natural causes, an announcer would say, "So-and-so died in his home this morning from an apparent heart attack," or some other malady chosen from a menu of more-or-less natural causes. So, "declining to speculate" meant someone did speculate, and officials weren't talking.

One had but to read between the lines. I suddenly had a million questions about his past, his larger-than-life presence in the district.

Paranoia, my constant friend, found me, and the thought threw me back in time. How did his death affect my thinking? Did I miss the con? Did I lose the mark? Would I catch a beating? Should I run? It always took me three shakes to rid myself of the dread of my old life. I still ran from him—Jerry, the ex-husband and criminal partner. He'd proved his specialty of grifting not to be exclusive.

But with Thompson, the medical examiner would have to do the autopsy and determine the cause of death, and it wouldn't pop up on the paperwork radar for at least a day. I could pass the job on to Dr. Riley. Scrambled nerves that had laced through my muscles at last disentangled.

Just to be safe, I threw another prayer into the cosmos.

Not quite five minutes after my impromptu prayer, Teresa appeared again. I ate lunch at my desk. My sandwich shed crumbs, and I brushed them into my hand and tossed them into the trash before stuffing the rest of my PB&J in my mouth.

"Hey, can you listen?"

Unaware she'd returned, I focused. I held up a finger and swallowed the last bite of the PB&J. "What? Didn't catch what you said."

"Someone's in room two. He came to talk with Dr. Riley, but since he's out—"

"He's stuck with me. What does he want?"

She straightened her ponytail. "He's a cop. Here about Thompson's death."

Oh, no. *How could you, God?* I even prayed. *C'mon.* The peanut butter stuck to the roof of my mouth as I zeroed in on her face.

"I think he has a hangover. He's a looker, though."

"Is he blond? Young? Accent?" A quick peep at the back

door might give my concern away, but if Jerry or his goon showed up, how fast could I outrun him? I'd grab my keys, knock Teresa off her feet, and make it to my car with my go-bag already packed and in the trunk.

"Southern accent, darker hair than yours, maybe a foot taller, five years older than you, give or take. Forty-ish. Easy on the eyes. Looks like a defensive linebacker. Unlike your muddy ole eyeballs, he's got serious blue."

"Muddy?"

She smirked. "Okay, brown. Why?"

"No reason." I stacked prescription requests with a vengeance. Jerry, a malicious con, became the Feds' paid informant in a convenient twist of fate. They made a sweet deal for him but left me out. Funny how that worked. He pocketed cops everywhere. Now one waited for me in an exam room.

I stood in the hall in front of the exam room door. Steeled myself. Checked my pistol, a SIG Sauer I carried under my lab coat. Donned my reading glasses. Gulped water to ease the cottonmouth.

Thompson's chart showed nothing of interest. Without his information in the electronic medical records, reviewing his loose papers took longer than expected before I went into the exam room.

I wrapped my hand around the knob. Instead, the door opened and yanked me in. I yelped as my forward motion caused a collision, and the documents flew. He caught me and apologized.

"Ah ... ah ..." I noted an angled jaw, salt-and-pepper hair, and grizzled stubble. "... I'm Catherine Cade."

"Apologies, ma'am, but I'm in a hurry." He helped gather the papers. "I'm Detective Rick Calhoun with Whiskey River PD." He presented his ID, thrust out a big hand, yet grasped mine gently. "Needed to bring you this." He closed the door and rested his back against it. "Got questions about Thompson."

Big man, armed, leaning against the doorframe and my one way out. Jerry had sent him. My internal freak-out meter shot straight to nuclear.

CHAPTER 4

"M—move away from the door."

A wrinkle creased his forehead. He ambled to the counter where he plopped a manila envelope. I resisted the urge to flinch. He leaned against the stand. "The mayor's office wanted this delivered. You new here?"

"No." Still nervous, I steadied my hand on the counter, monitored him for movement toward me, and removed paperwork from the envelope.

"Jonah's out for the day?"

"Yes. Hospital rounds." I lifted my head. Well, what a surprise. He knew Dr. Riley.

"Okay." He rubbed his face. "Tell me why you called Stephen Thompson's home three times this morning and swore at the woman who answered."

I hesitated, surprised. "Skipping appointments is a no-no. Swear? Oh, I was looking at an x-ray and had to drop everything to call the ER." I stopped. "Thompson's dead."

He straightened. "How did you know?"

Here was the exact ballgame I wanted to avoid. "I heard it on the radio. If you don't believe me, ask Teresa."

"Uh-huh. I'll check with her. You arrived at the clinic at what time?"

Was he accusing me of murder? "I suppose I got here around six-thirty. Jonah was making early rounds at the hospital, a patient emergency. He called me. I can give you his number if you need it." Even if I could reach the door, he was bigger, faster, stronger. Being stuck in a room alone with a cop asking me pejorative questions was worrisome.

"Okay, you're fine. You're looking a little nerve-wracked, and I just want you to deal with the stuff in this envelope."

"Not nervous. I just don't understand. His healthcare was my responsibility, and it makes me testy when folks skip exams. Also, Jonah drops patients who don't show up, and when mine do show, he takes my scheduled patients, and it shortens my hours, thus my paycheck."

An understanding nod followed. "Like budget cuts. I think we started off wrong. I apologize for rattling you." He stuck out his hand. "Friends?"

I grasped his. "Friends." I glanced over the paperwork. "Hold it. You'd better wait on that concept. You can't bring me this paperwork and expect me to do anything with it."

"Excuse me?"

"This is a death certificate. Thompson died this morning, and it's still morning. I can't sign this."

"Death certificate? What?" He paused. "You're a doctor. Can't you sign it?"

"Nurse practitioner, and in Oregon, yes, I can, but not this one. Did you read its contents?"

"No, ma'am."

A contemptuous snort escaped me while my feel-good attitude melted. "The note attached says 'natural causes' and a list of disorders he didn't have. Must have been one fast autopsy. Not signing."

He fished in his shirt pocket and out came a pair of reading glasses. He snatched the papers from me and put his hand over his mouth. A burst of hot-whisper words escaped him.

A diamond-bit wet saw couldn't slice through the concrete silence which followed. Speechless. Surprised.

Good. I scanned his blue eyes as they flicked my way.

"You read my mind, didn't you, Officer? No one attaches a note to an unsigned death certificate, and he died at home. So, Officer—"

"Detective Calhoun." He looked away.

He needed time to process the information, and I gave it to him. His plight was unmistakable. Cops.

"Thompson was healthy for his age. Why would a cop bring me the certificate when it should come from the funeral home?"

He put a hand to his head. "I don't know why this is buggin' me today, but I'm a detective, not a cop. Detective

18

Rick Calhoun. Please try to remember that."

Jerk. Yeah, dirty cop, and here I almost liked him. "Are you with Vice? Sure, 'cause this has corruption written all over it."

"Homicide."

Homicide. I held up a hand. "Wait. A homicide detective comes to my clinic as a delivery boy the same day the commissioner dies, and someone wants me to sign off on natural causes. So somehow Thompson overdosed on lead? You were at the scene. You hadn't read the contents of the envelope, and it was a beat too long when you saw it, meaning homicide."

He rubbed his forehead.

Information he didn't want to share?

He pushed away from the counter. "Interesting answers."

"Death certificates list the manner of death as natural, accidental, suicide, homicide, undetermined, and pending. After observing you, there's only one option. Homicide. I can't sign this. Let me explain how the death certificate process works in Oregon. Keep up." I launched into the regulations. His eyes glazed over, and the muscles in his jaw tensed. I finished with, "Clear?"

"Huh? Sure, if you can remember I'm a detective, I'll remember whatever you said."

A *tsk* came from my mouth. "These circumstances say something is worth looking into. A cryptic note, officer. Someone pulled one over on you. Imagine my shock. Well, Mr. Tall and Handsome, you must think you're all that. Guess what? Someone did a number on you, and you tried to play me with the whole 'let's be friends' business."

I didn't want to add, you can't play a player.

His behavior gave him away. I had lived with a lying thief. Well, to be honest, I was one too—but only for self-preservation. Cop, Detective—whatever his name was—tugged on his earlobe, touched his mouth, and stared at the counter. His small movements were a drunken man's poker tells and more, his obvious anger shouted in silence.

"Lady, I could do without your attitude." He grasped the death certificate and pushed it into his jacket pocket. "Not asking you to sign—"

"You don't seem ... well. Want me to call an ambulance? I see all the signs of Dengue fever." A slow walk around him allowed me a clinical assessment of his jeans, tee shirt, and how he filled them out. Great shape for a forty-ish man. Almost lost my train of thought.

Beyond the malfeasance, something about him bugged me. Couldn't quite put my finger on it, but I stopped assessing his physique. There. Better. Focused.

"I'm not bleeding from my eyes or anywhere else. Lady, he took insulin. I found bottles and needles at the scene. He might have injected the wrong dose. Maybe you missed critical info because your reading skills are dulled." He managed a disarming half-grin.

I gaped. "He didn't receive insulin from me, and I read just fine, thank you." He tried to throw me, and how did he know about Dengue fever? More importantly, how did the commissioner die? Who wanted his death muzzled?

Calhoun circled around me and moved to the door, his hand close to the butt of the service gun at his hip. Still, this guy might be another one of Jerry's moonlight requisitions, and I slid my palm to the small of my back and my SIG Sauer.

He took a step forward and cocked his head to one side. "Miss Cade, you're aggravating my headache, and you're more stubborn than I—than—" He stopped, pressed a thumb to his temple, and finished the sentence. "More stubborn than I expected."

"Don't." I raised my empty palm. "I'm not stubborn. I'm right."

"I promise, you will see me again." He punctuated his words in a growl.

"The anticipation is overwhelming." I narrowed my eyes. "You look familiar."

"I probably arrested you." He tucked his reading glasses into a shirt pocket.

Anger heated my chest, and my teeth clenched. But it was my practice never to let a good insult go unslung. "Now I know you. I found a brain tumor on your prostate exam."

My phone camera would've snapped a great picture of his face. Brows raised, eyes wide, and mouth open. Classic expression of shock.

He didn't say a word. I studied his hardened face as he scrutinized me. Did he see the plastic surgery scars from the wreck that left me empty of old memories?

I noticed little crow's feet at the corners of his eyes, lines around his mouth, producing a serious glare. Silver scattered through his pepper-dark hair gathered at his temples. Muscles tensed in a strong jaw.

Without warning, he shook my hand gently and walked out the door.

I followed him to the lobby. The bell above the glass door rang as it closed behind him, and he glimpsed back. Mystified, I stood there and gawped.

CHAPTER 5

RICK CALHOUN

His skin tingling, Calhoun stopped just outside the door and made eye contact with Catherine as she stood near the entry, a hand to her cheek.

Who does she see?

His back straightened, and with shoulders squared, he trudged to his cruiser and sat in the driver's seat. She'd been so near, yet a lifetime away. Still no hint of recognition in her eyes.

Lord, please help me. You know I'm a disaster, and that I've just insulted the one woman I wanted to pursue. Vice Detective Tanaka claimed Rick remained single because of social ineptitude, and the rumor lingered without dispute. He groaned. Why couldn't he be upfront?

He gripped the steering wheel and gently bumped his head on his hands. Calhoun half-hoped Cade would follow him to his cruiser and continue her diatribe. He closed his eyes and pinched the bridge of his nose.

Mike Tanaka warned rookies, "Don't question him; the man shaves with a blowtorch." Things hadn't changed. He felt like a blithering idiot. Calhoun could never come close to communicating with Catherine Cade like a normal person. She didn't recognize him. It was like starting all over.

Asking Sarah Thompson if she killed her husband was a cakewalk compared to working up the nerve to ask Cade on a date.

Melanie had taken the initiative and talked him into dinner and a movie, and later, hauled him to church each week until one day, he prayed for the first time. Later, he—a mere twenty-one-year-old—stuttered through a marriage proposal to her. Now he scarcely recognized her faded, wrinkled picture in his wallet.

Then, without warning, Melanie was gone. And now, thinking about asking Catherine Cade took him back twenty years to the petrifying memory of a young soldier desperate for a date with a beautiful woman.

He bumped his head against his hands again and mouthed a prayer. Cade had the audacity to insult him with her acerbic wit, and the guts to stand up to him when she was right. He squeezed his eyes shut. She said he seemed familiar. Could be good. Or bad.

Perhaps the search engine, SeekIt, offered expertise in dating advice for men his age. He lifted his head and tapped a finger on the steering wheel. He knew just enough about Cade to wonder if he should dig into her background. There had to be an angle.

Dumont had involved him in a murder and cover-up. Twice Calhoun hit the wheel, angry he had played the fool, and worse, appeared to be involved in corruption, and to Catherine of all people. It could have been a simple, easy introduction. But no. Regardless of Dumont's Cajun temper, Calhoun planned to light into his boss.

Calhoun drove the mostly empty streets to the police department in silence, his ire cogwheeling up as he parked. He skipped two stair steps at a time to get inside, then back down another set of stairs to arrive at Dumont's office. He strode through the bullpen doors, through the office, and into Dumont's sacred space, slamming the Chief's office door behind him.

Dumont's eyes widened. "What?"

Calhoun kept his voice low. "Why the blindside, Greg? She refused to sign, and what a surprise for me." He plopped the manila packet on the desk. "What made you do this?"

Dumont stood and paced, ranting. "The doctor refused? Bring him in on charges for obstructing—"

"Doctor wasn't there. I got the nurse practitioner. And what is she obstructing? A murder investigation? But you attached a note, telling her what to write, and she went into orbit. You sent me on an errand meant to fail. It's not like you to leave out key information. You left me hanging there with a bogus death certificate, and me looking like I have rocks for brains."

"Can't talk 'bout it." Dumont sat and shuffled papers.

Calhoun leaned forward, teeth clenched. "You understand what happens if a murder cover-up drops in your lap, right? Does someone have something on you?"

"Not even lint. Explain what happened."

He jabbed a finger Dumont's way. "She read your note, put it together fast, and recited the law. You cannot argue with a woman with the law on her side. Or me."

"Did she threaten you?"

"She gave me a migraine."

A moment passed. Calhoun could see Dumont's wheels turn.

Dumont said, "Fine. Take the death certificate to Jack McCloud. It's between you, me, and Jack. We've been gagged."

Rick gritted his teeth. "You really want a murder on your head?"

"Mayor Guy Mahn and his assistant threatened my girls, sideways."

Rick pressed his mouth in a tight line, holding back a tirade he now wanted to unleash on the mayor. Instead, he said, "Feds?"

"Feds tossin' crap around how rural cops need a manual to flush a toilet? You're not thinkin', son. Out."

Calhoun left the Chief's office. Bottom line, he figured the Chief wanted an investigation under a gag order, giving him a shroud of reasonable deniability.

The medical examiner, Jack McCloud, wouldn't want to sign the DC either, and Calhoun bet he'd hit the ceiling. Worse, Catherine Cade had nailed it, assigning venality to him.

He slung his ball cap on the old steel desk, squeezed his lower lip with thumb and forefinger, and parsed out information before he entered notes into the computer.

His head throbbed. He closed his left eye to focus and typed notes with his forefingers.

"Dagnabbit, stupid computer." Calhoun mumbled, hitting DELETE over and over. Everyday occurrence. "Zoe, you make coffee?"

"Not my job," Zoe Carter, the dispatcher/receptionist, said. "Mike, make coffee."

Mike stood and walked toward the coffeemaker. "Need help, Calhoun? How about giving dictation a whirl?"

"Nope." Calhoun put his reading glasses on. He opened the closed eye, peered at Mike, and scowled. "I prefer pen and paper. Dictation? Who would appreciate my fine sense of humor?"

Zoe said, "In a homicide report. Besides, you never smile anymore, much less laugh."

He frowned. "I smile."

"What happened?" Mike asked. "I should've eavesdropped when that walrus-stuffed-into-a-tux mayor of ours and Darren Hughe showed up. They held a quiet powwow in there."

Calhoun said, "What they talked about is none of our business 'til Chief makes it our business."

Mike turned. "If I'd listened in, stealth-like ..." He shrugged. "And you know my people are thinner, faster, and quieter than yours."

Zoe covered her mouth. "Your people?"

"Who made you boss, Calhoun?" Mike swung his head back to the dispatcher. "Yeah, my people. Jet Li, Jackie Chan. Japanese."

"They're Chinese," she said.

"What do you know? You're Latino."

"I'm black." Zoe put a hand to her head.

"Whatever." He pushed the button on the coffeemaker and walked to a dry-erase board.

Calhoun said, "He's yanking your chain again, Zoe."

"Ahem." Zoe played with the phone cord with an upside-down file in her hand.

Mike moved to his desk and idly twirled a quarter. "Where'd you tear off to?"

Rick walked to Zoe and righted the file. "Hightailed it to see my doctor."

"You burst outta Dumont's office, rush to the doctor, and a half-hour later you're back. For what?" Mike asked.

"Saw the nurse practitioner."

Mike shot Zoe a *this is gonna be good* look.

"Shut up," Calhoun growled.

"We didn't say a thing," Mike said.

"Yeah, I know all about those furtive glances."

"Explain. A nurse?"

"Nurse with a PhD, like a doctor."

Mike unwrapped a candy bar, bit into it, and spoke with a mouthful of chocolate. "I've dated nurses."

"Three, and they all slapped you."

Zoe snickered. "Big surprise."

"Tell Dumont I'm running an errand. I'll be back." Calhoun tucked his wallet into his pocket and left.

CHAPTER 6

CATHERINE CADE

My receptionist avoided looking at me. "Three no-shows and two cancellations." Ray raised his palms in the air.

My evil eye passed unnoticed. "And a partridge in a pear tree. Lovely. I could've taken a nap."

Rest had its benefits. So did running prison data banks and morgues.

My fingers traced my necklace. Figurative or literal, everyone has a bullet. I'd etched Jerry's name on one. Kind of hoped he would find me, because he needed a solitary push, at about 1250 feet per second into his open grave. It seemed charitable. Better him than me, at least.

He wanted something from me, something he'd never earned. He'd made it clear to what lengths he'd go to retrieve it. So working a legitimate profession using new skills helped me keep a step ahead of him. For now, I dodged from one town to another, always keeping an eye on the road behind me.

I was a quick study, armed with a great skill set. I could steal anything from diamonds to internet secrets, and if need be, shoot a threat. None of that fit well on a résumé. A little piece of identity theft came in handy. How oxymoronic—grifting for honest labor.

I didn't like my history, hated Jerry, and despised myself for all my shortcomings I remembered every time I thought of him. And me? A throwaway. A woman forgotten. Shattered, I ran and vanished.

Ray Lopez set down the remains of his lunch. "Hey, why so tense? Wanna go for a drink after work?" His upturned lips parted, showing a chipped front tooth that added to his Latin machismo and charm.

"Nope." I turned my back to him and walked down the hall toward my office. "I don't drink." At least in the present. I didn't know about the past.

"You need some fun, *chica*."

I liked my receptionist. He truth-bombed my emotional doorstep on schedule.

I ached for a life like Ray's, but instead, I hopped from one city to the next, avoiding the ex. Often worked as a server. Utilized financial bootlegging, what I called "funds acquisitions," to obtain papers for a PhD as a nurse practitioner.

I possessed an aptitude for the medical field. A healthcare provider seemed the natural choice for me. So, as a nurse practitioner, I could theoretically perform a thorough exam, pick a credit card from the chair where the patient's jacket lay, and the unfortunate rube would never know what hit him or her.

"Ray, why didn't Stephen Thompson show up for his last visit?"

He raised his eyes. "I'll check. Chica, you got your crazy face on, what's wrong?"

"Nothing, no worries." I turned and waved him off with a hard-edged smile, dropping it once his back was turned. Heck yeah, I was worried. A VIP dead, a corrupt cop in my office, and my ex's whereabouts unknown.

RICK CALHOUN

Calhoun pulled into the *Medallion* editor's driveway. The Japanese maples and rock garden stood in stark contrast to the raked and patterned sand surrounding the two-story Tudor. He parked and walked along the curved sidewalk over a covered bridge above the rocks.

He did a double take. Nothing but colored granite made up this garden. Pondered some. What did this say about a man? The usual cottage gardens were too pedestrian for Stewart. Eclectic, what with an unlikely combination of a Tudor home and a Japanese garden that shouted to the world he was a firebrand, and clever enough to know a real raked-sand garden would wash down the street after one good rain. Paid good money to make it look real. What else might he change to suit his needs? What else might he buy? The truth?

Calhoun pushed an insistent finger on the doorbell. A short wait followed, and he presented his badge. Editor Marcus Stewart answered the doorbell, and he and his wife ushered Calhoun into their living room. Mrs. Stewart offered Calhoun a cup of coffee.

"Thank you, but no." He held a hand up. "I've had my coffee quota for the day."

Stewart was tall and lean, impeccably dressed, with a cleft chin and bottle-brush eyebrows. His wife, Blondie, had teeth bright enough to shine a light on her husband's bush country over his eyes. Both, Calhoun figured, were obviously frequent visitors to the gym and tanning stations which were stretching and tanning their leather just fine.

Stewart twirled his mustache between two fingers. "Does this have to do with the death of Stephen Thompson?"

"Yes, sir, it does. Did you know him personally?"

"Via the board and our banter." Marcus sat. "If he died of natural causes, why talk to me?"

"The devil is in the details, I hear, and I am just closing final questions."

"I see. And you wonder how I'm involved?"

Rick said, "Did he communicate anything to you about his politics?"

"Politics only, and he never insulted me directly. Just a backhanded compliment on TV."

"That must have made you mad."

Marcus's thin smile failed to reach his eyes. "All in a day's work. Journalism is entertainment, not news. People follow for the back-and-forth. Won't affect me a bit, except this is going to affect sales—until I find another politician to pick on."

"Did you know of any of his businesses?"

Stewart's eyes widened. "He never spoke about businesses, at least with me. Are you suggesting a conflict of interest? That would be huge!"

"I'm not. I wonder if you know anything about his wife."

"Nothing. She's a recluse, I think."

"Thank you, I think that's all." Rick handed the editor a card. "If you think of anything, please call me."

"Sure."

Calhoun left, frustrated he hadn't been able to hit hard with pertinent questions. He felt like a trained Belgian Malinois K-9 locked in the back of a police cruiser while his handler fought with a bad guy.

He drove to the newspaper's headquarters. The *Medallion*'s employees reported the editor usually arrived around seven a.m. In the editor's favor came his love-hate relationship with Thompson. Stewart hated Thompson's politics and loved to disparage his conservative political stance, but Thompson's wife had suggested a malevolent conversation. Glancing up, he noted that reporter Leo Smart, ambulance chaser, stood near. *The same Leo Smart as at the crime scene earlier.*

Whiskey River covered two miles. Even at a stroll, the editor could have wound his way to Thompson's home, killed him, and returned to *Medallion* HQ by seven a.m.

Suspect one was Thompson's widow. Stewart took a noteworthy second place as he may well have known about Thompson's businesses. Records were public information, and once Stewart blew the lid of corruption, he'd go for a new guy. Thompson's death would make him fair game. And the dead can't object. Brian Jackson was low on Calhoun's list, having an alibi, but that didn't mean he might not have had a hand in Thompson's death.

Back in his car, Calhoun twisted the keys, and the engine turned. The question remained. *Why did you die, Commissioner?*

He arrived at the bullpen, searched different databases, and ran a superficial background check on the widow. He got nothing from Hibbing, Minnesota, where she'd claimed to grow up. A check of public records showed her maiden name as Granger. Still nothing. He could only go so far without a warrant. What about Stephen Thompson? Public records were available, including online net worth of both the newspaper editor and Thompson.

The alarm company was local, and Calhoun requested logs and timestamps sent via secure email.

His interest floated to Cade as he tented his fingers. Should he check her bank account? Yes.

Catherine Cade wasn't a real suspect, and there was no need to examine her life. In fact, it was downright unethical. Yep. Unethical, all right. A quick recon of the office, and a few taps on the keys later, information on the elusive Cade unfolded. Her history was born three years ago, and the fancy PhD was pure air.

He straightened. No substantial income and no significant other. Calhoun wished he hadn't checked. Another tap on the keyboard. He saw from the business applications database that she was in the process of opening a doughnut shop and rocked back in his chair.

Back to SeekIt. How much did it cost to open a bakery? *No way.* Anywhere from ten thousand to over fifty thousand dollars. With a three-year existence, where'd she get the money? He read on. To set up a pastry shop would be time consuming. Would anyone else have noticed this behavior? Red flags everywhere. Twice today he'd stumbled over something curious about Cade. She had the means to open a bakery and a solid backstory. Of all people, he knew what that meant.

He ran her Social Security number and learned it had actually belonged to one Lucille Corrina, an African American seventy-nine-year-old grandmother of seven who'd died from a fatal aneurysm five years ago. But the con in Whiskey River opened an account using Corrina's number, keeping little money there. A poor working stiff, so to speak. *Catherine, what are you trying to hide this time? Confidence artist or contract killer?*

Reluctant, he wrote *Suspect Three* in his notes, leaving the name blank. He tucked his notes in his pocket.

Calhoun picked up the handset and dialed the morgue to get some details. He reached Kim Pierson.

"Kim, I've got a question. Anything on those prints in the house?"

"Not much, but this is interesting. The handle on the refrigerator was wiped clean. So were the insulin bottles."

"Great. Hope we catch some kind of break." He paused.

"Hey, can you do something for me?"

"Sure, Detective. Name it."

"Between you and me. I want you to befriend Catherine Cade. Here's her address."

"You mean show up at her door?"

"That would be it."

"You like her or something?"

"Or something. Is Dr. McCloud done with Thompson's autopsy?"

"He's just finishing up." Her voice became muffled for a moment. "Yes. He wants to see you."

Calhoun drove to the hospital's morgue. After Jack's long-ago advances toward Melanie, Rick still struggled to speak to McCloud without a starting a fracas.

At the least, he set up Kim and her penchant for gossip while he worked out how to do his interviews in secret.

"Heard the gag order." McCloud removed his gloves, tossed them into a hazardous materials basket, and returned to the slab where the dead man's body lay.

"Yup." Calhoun's back muscles tensed at McCloud's voice.

"So, this is between you an' me. I can't risk working the case."

"Can you send everything to an independent lab, make sure the puddle on the table is Thompson?"

"That, prints, gun, blood, and vitreous humor are all on their way to Portland. Already ran a preliminary vitreous. High in potassium, but without toxicology there's nothing to check. I ran a rifling report before the mayor quashed it, and it's uploaded." He leaned against a counter.

"What's the vitreous—?"

"Gooey eyeball stuff."

Calhoun scratched his head. "Thompson was a diabetic?"

"That he was. The vitreous can show the potassium and glucose levels, both of which can be DOA depending on their levels. Both can hint at a murder, but they can't rule out any other cause of death." He lifted a shoulder.

"Sign the insulin from his house out, and I'll take it to another lab. Can you get me some blood for toxicology, and I'll deal with the fallout?"

McCloud looked askance. "Yeah."

"Good. Find anything on CCTV or the alarm?"

"A quick check of the CCTV showed this. Poor quality, though." He keyed the digital feed on the computer and stopped when a figure appeared at the front door. "No other cameras installed."

Jeans, ball cap with head down, long sleeves, tennis shoes. Someone knew what they were doing. "Prints?"

"Prints were too smudged to tell, but the system revealed no hits on IAFIS ."

"Huh."

"Okay. This is all I can do, and I'm denying anything else. Won't know squat 'til ballistics finds its way back. Problem is, we've nothing for comparison." McCloud withdrew a pencil from his pocket and pointed at the remainder of Thompson's head. "See this? It's stippling. These marks on the remainder of the decedent's skull prove my theory. Gunpowder tattoos indicate distance, at the minimum, six inches. Not impossible for a suicide, but unlikely. My guess, your boy here is a homicide, pure and simple."

CHAPTER 7

CATHERINE CADE
0900 FRIDAY

I walked toward the police department, concerned by the big parking lot with its sparse cover of three cherry trees and several unkempt juniper bushes. I knew my plan was fraught with little details. Breaking into the evidence room of a police department was reckless and unrealistic. I might get caught, but the corruption in the department needed exposure.

I refused to be a crook—except for the upcoming break-in. My gut relentlessly growled the question: *Who killed Thompson, and how?*

If I could reveal a murder, perhaps the act would redeem my life, and I'd be worthy of something. Maybe. Light up the truth, regardless of the outcome, and I'd be one step further in the right direction. The prospects of going to prison or falling straight into Jerry's hands didn't suit me. At the moment, I'd plunged from confidence to a nauseating near panic attack.

My job allowed me anonymity. Rural Whiskey River gave me the ability to see anyone coming my way. Someone had tried to drag me into a cover-up. The cop and his report needed evaluating by an unbiased eye, namely, mine. I refused to let this go, and I would not brand myself as immoral as the cops. It was a paradox, yet this was different.

Checking out the proof turned into a plan, outlined four nights ago on Monday. The issue was time, but I didn't have the luxury of waiting.

Tuesday morning was a day off, and my derring-do required scoping out the police station. Wearing a ball cap, I strode toward the office in question. I filled out an application to work at the County Clerk's office, and lingered, drifting along the hallways and noting the security cameras and the evidence room. If anyone stopped me, I'd tell them I was looking for a place to sit and fill out the application.

I slowed. The frosted glass on the door showed an outline of a desk officer. I didn't doubt Abraham Lincoln installed the old, near-rusted lock himself.

Check one.

I meandered to the smoking area outside. Haphazard cigarette butts stood in a sand-filled can. I figured there would be three times for breaks, and right on cue, at ten a.m., noon, and two p.m., people filtered in and out of the smoking area and lit their cigarettes.

Check two.

Back inside, tucked in a nook out of sight, I waited to get more information on the evidence holding room.

An older man left the evidence office twenty minutes before noon and headed for the bathroom and lunch, securing nothing behind him in his haste. That gave me maybe fifty minutes to get in and get out of the evidence locker. No officers arrived except a man ten minutes after noon. I would move in early and check the bolt on the cage.

Plan one: wear a wig, slip on the fake tag, go in unnoticed, and get pictures of the files if they were not locked up. Easy in, easy out. Plan two: in disguise, ask for records, and run for my life if scrutinized. I wasn't crazy about plan three. Slip inside the cage, lock myself in, and if the guard returned, stay until his next bathroom trip or the end of the shift.

Check three.

Simple as pie.

At home, I put my plan into action. Now, for a badge, outfit, and a wig. On Thursday, at home, I situated a realistic lanyard and badge-holder with my photo on my counter, then employed a little inspired laminating to get the job done.

Friday came and I called in, needing a mental health day. *Oh, boy, did I.* Dressed in a blue blazer and pants. I added an inch in height to my five-foot-four height with a pair of cream pumps. I drove to the police station, stepped from a car I'd temporarily stolen, and swore to myself I'd return it in the same shape I took it. Transformed into a blonde with sunglasses and a floppy hat, I was ready for action.

With a cigarette to puff while waiting, I checked my watch. Three minutes max until the next smoker. Not long, and the back door opened.

The cop, or whatever his title was—the one I'd had a run-in with at my clinic—pushed it outward, with a bag of trash in his hand. He tossed the garbage into the bin and eyed me. I tugged my coat around my neck. "You must be new."

"Yeah," I answered in a low voice, shocked. "County Clerk's office."

"Quit smoking. It'll kill you."

My floppy hat hid most of my face, and holding the cigarette helped. Sunglasses covered many sins. Then I inhaled and suffered an explosive coughing fit.

He smirked and opened the door. I snuffed the smoky butt out, and before the door shut behind him, I slipped my credit card between the lock and jamb, stepped in, and wound my way through the halls toward 102 EVIDENCE.

I checked my watch again and took a big breath. Go time.

Confident, I nipped the rim of the hat that hid my face from the CCTV units. I sauntered along the hall. The guard ambled from the office and wandered toward the restroom. So much for plan one.

Darn it. Plan three.

I pushed against the office door as it squeaked. My heart pounded. A quick survey of the room indicated no cameras. Weird. Now for the pen. I picked the latch and stepped inside years of imprisoned boxes. The cage door shut behind me. I clicked the lock and yanked a string hanging from an old swinging bulb.

Four aisles from the cage door, I found the box labeled "Stephen Thompson." I gloved and jerked the pack close, my heart hammering. *A felony by any other name* ... I pressed my forearm to my face and wiped sweat away. I opened the files. Pursed my lips and let a slow breath out. It felt like pinching diamonds in the old days.

One picture brought a curse to my lips, and each photo thereafter, the same. The note attached to the death certificate verified my suspicions, but the reason became clear—these were images of a gruesome murder site. Pictures showed a horrific gunshot wound to an unrecognizable man with at least a .45 caliber gun. I tugged on my cellphone and photographed everything.

Homicide. The detective at my clinic. A cryptic note. And I sat staring at the proof of the cover-up. Stephen Thompson, to be specific. Deep, deep doo-doo.

The medical examiner reported in his autopsy notes, almost illegibly, natural causes. A careful look showed where the medical examiner hesitated mid-signature. The pressure was notable, even on the copy. Clearly he did not want his signature on this. No surprise someone sent me a message, but who? The question appeared again. *Why did you die, Mr. Thompson?* Here was the "what and where." Now I needed the "who and why."

The knob turned, and I jerked my head toward the exit. Footsteps came my way. I pushed the box back, dashed to switch off the bulb, and hid behind the packed rows of shelves. A man stopped at the desk. Bile rose in my throat.

"Who's here? Dutch, you left the door unlocked again."

I knew the distinctive baritone with a hint of the South. It was the cop from my office. What was his name?

Calhoun.

The rankling of the chain raised the hairs on my neck.

"What the heck? You locked this backward. How did you even manage this? Next, you'll be waiting for your bathroom break in the cage. You'd better not be mummified back there."

A drawer opened and slammed shut. A key in the lock turned. The cable played against the wired entry. The door squeaked.

I put a palm over my mouth to quiet my breathing and peeked around the corner. His hand stopped the bulb from swinging and remained on it. Certain it would feel warm, I bit my lip as he pulled the string.

The crisp clicks of Calhoun's dress boots struck the concrete flooring. Footsteps came my way, louder with each step. He turned a corner. I evaded him as he roamed each aisle of stacked shelves.

I yanked off my pumps and caught one mid-air. The click-click neared, and I tiptoed away and bumped into a mountain of magazines already threatening to fall. Where did my criminal acumen go? Poised over the journals, I held my breath and steadied the stacks, with pumps in hand.

"Who's here?"

I prayed to God to get me out of this jam.

The unmistakable sound of a gun sliding from a hard-shell holster came next. The metallic racking of the slide turned my mouth to cotton. I closed my eyes in cold terror. Even blood spurting from arterial wounds had never caused this kind of fear crushing against the inside of my rib cage.

The click of his steps resumed, slower this time, and he closed our distance. My hat and wig slipped from my head to the floor with a soft plop. His footsteps stopped, and I squinched my eyes shut. He neared the corner where I clutched the load of periodicals to my breast.

"Calhoun, the phone's for you," a male voice yelled.

"Hang on, I'm not done."

"It's urgent."

He didn't answer. The light clack from his shoes started again, slower.

One chance. I shoved the mountain of magazines over and plucked my hat from the floor. Dropped a shoe by accident. Grabbed it. Heard him hurry his steps. I dashed toward the exit and ran through, turned, and locked Calhoun in the cage. Then I plopped the sunhat on my head and fled out the back door, wishing I'd been able to grab the wig.

I hustled to the car, hopped in, revved the engine, and floored the gas pedal. Before I cleared the corner of the building, the back door swung open. Calhoun stood there, my wig in his hand.

I steered the car, careening around the corner, yelling at myself the entire way. "Go, go, go—!"

A mile later, my breathing calmed after my clean getaway. I'd have time to think over the evidence during the looming weekend.

CHAPTER 8

RICK CALHOUN
SUNDAY 1300
After church, Calhoun spent Sunday under the radar, gave the duty officer in the evidence locker a break, and rummaged through boxes marked CLOSED. A sign-out sheet was available, and he ran a finger along the names.

Zilch. No one's signature.

A note attached to the death certificate on Thompson had stunned him. How Dumont wanted it filled it out, a remark so illegal that Calhoun could barely comprehend it, three words. *Write Natural Causes*. Now Thompson's files no longer existed. Worse, Calhoun's personal journal locked in his armory said murder, but handwritten notes attested to nothing without evidence. The woman he almost grabbed must have taken everything.

The bullet casing, packaged evidence, and pictures were gone. Someone wiped the drawings from the computer. For once, he didn't own that technical disaster.

Now the physical evidence, everything, gone. He fumed because he hadn't taken his own set of pictures at the homicide scene.

He checked his watch. The officer's break bought him time. Someone had made this a hands-off case. What did the pillars of the community fear? High-powered corruption crept over the valley, encircling Whiskey River in a python-like grip.

Calhoun's angry fist banged against a box. Thompson's file was empty. "Natural causes" was the only note, corroborating his point. Nothing else exuded from the confidential corridors of politics but corruption and fraud, with murder the end result. The threat to Chief Dumont hailed from the mayor's office.

He possessed the unidentified woman's wig with dark hairs caught inside. *If only I'd caught her!* He would have had trouble getting the hair tested, anyway. Rural backwater towns did not have extensive forensic labs.

Calhoun leaned, hand on the wall, thrumming his fingers. When the duty officer returned, he hustled from the basement to the security desk on the first floor, taking two steps at a time. If someone had tampered with the PD's digital security videos, the case for murder would be dead-on-arrival.

"Hank, right?"

"Yeah, Detective. What can I do for ya?"

"Show me how this works. I need a peek at the security feed for the past few days."

"Which ones?"

Calhoun scratched his head. "I could be here a while. Give me the rundown."

"Okeydokey." He jotted on a piece of paper.

"Thanks."

He read the directions and found the videos intact. The day in question rolled up, Friday. Video of him taking the trash from the PD to the garbage. He toggled to the outside camera and homed in on the woman with the wig.

She came in as a platinum blonde and left as a brunette, a hand holding a floppy hat while she tore out of the building. He rested his chin on the palm of his hand, ran the video back to Thursday, and found her casing the station. Baseball cap. Shorter.

He rumbled a gravelly growl. Catherine Cade. How had he not known her? Keystone Kops. A week ago, at the clinic, she'd given him a truckload of trouble with a sprinkling of anatomically impossible insults. She alluded to corruption. His. Now, this.

The digital feed advanced to Friday, and he leaned forward watching as she slipped into and illegally entered a police evidence room. The hallway camera captured the action as he sauntered in, and minutes later, as she exited at a dead run, with him behind her.

He pushed his reading glasses to the bridge of his nose. She didn't ransack the locker but went straight to Thompson's file.

The cameras' eyes fed her images into the digital wonderland. He had almost caught her, until she had fled empty-handed. She was a one-woman disappearing act. He shook his head and spoke aloud. "Unreal."

Worst criminal ever.

Saturday morning's feed appeared. A skeleton crew manned the PD. She wore a hat and coat, careful to hide identifying features. He swallowed hard. She'd entered and left with a file in hand. His heart tanked.

He ran the feed backward. *What is that*? Color of her skin was pale between her gloves and her coat sleeve. Catherine's skin had an olive tint. Was it the lighting? He watched it again and scribbled a note.

Calhoun fumbled with a thumb drive, found a USB port, and downloaded a copy of those three days.

Reconnaissance was required on Cade. And he'd search more databases. He rubbed his knuckles. Not the irascible nurse practitioner who refused involvement. Far worse, she tainted his picture of her and exhibited the same maliciousness as anyone in the mayor's office.

Catherine, who made you do this?

Sleight of hand was legal, and he hoped to find the missing reports in Cade's possession.

He keyed DONE after downloading the information and winced as he inched the thumb drive from the computer. A message, OK or CANCEL, blinked on the screen. Faced with a technical decision not scribbled on Hank's cheat sheet, Calhoun hovered one finger over the ENTER key and pushed it. DELETION SUCCESSFUL, the new message read.

"Oh, no." He gaped at the message and tapped keys with determined repetition. "No, no, no." He rubbed his temples and paced.

The officer returned with his Gomer Pyle grin.

"I don't know what took place, but it's snow."

"No problem, Detective." The lanky man motioned Calhoun to move. "What days? Wait a sec, what happened?"

"Um."

"Did you touch anything?"

Define touch, was what Calhoun wanted to say.

"Oh, man, this computer is a mess. Detective, I must have hit DELETE before you sat. I need to write a report on what hit the system." His face drooped into embarrassment.

"I—I—"

"Yessir?"

"My fault. I'll fill out the forms." Calhoun put the palm of his hand on Hank's shoulder and faced him. "This is my specialty."

He thanked him for saving his job, and Calhoun headed for the office. Yet another computer disaster he'd caused. Calhoun entered the bullpen and reviewed his notes. He popped a mint in his mouth and thought what came next. It was time to confront Cade, a job he didn't relish.

Calhoun eased his cruiser into the dirt driveway, muddying his wheels with the first rain of fall. A folded newspaper substituted for an umbrella, and he strolled along the rain-soaked sidewalk as his eyes followed gnarled roots of pine, oak, and yew trees.

Nearby, her vegetable garden was winding down, while early September's fruits were ready for harvest. A Bartlett pear tree loaded with ripe fruit shaded the driveway, and daisies waggled next to roses and some purple flowers. *Lavender, that was it.* Lavender had been Melanie's favorite. So, Cade was more than a thief. An astute, assiduous, busy nurse practitioner, baker, gardener ... and thief. A tall redwood filtered misty daylight as light refracted in the downpour. He inhaled cleansed air and scanned the oatmeal-colored sky and said aloud, "Help me, Lord."

Rick gave the old house a cursory exam. Smaller than expected, white with new trim. Rain from the muggy September storm sounded tinny plops on her faded green pickup. Peering through the driver's side window, he noted keys. Glancing around, he opened the door and quietly removed them.

He ambled by the window and peeked in, admiring her concentration on a book while she missed the *cop* who stopped there and peeked in. *Detective,* he chuckled. He readied his service gun.

She was armed.

CATHERINE CADE
SUNDAY

Normally, I spent the better part of my free time after work during the week at the YMCA rock climbing or the weekend at the shooting range on the weekend. However, I had to scratch the itch to put information together on the murder. Time was short or the case would be cold, and I'd lose leads.

Friday after my caper, I drove to the homes of the suspects listed on Calhoun's notes and scribbled some notes of my own. He had jotted the names of committee members. On Saturday, I pored over the journal and pictures again. Attached them with tape to a corkboard. Wrote a timeline and the alibis. I added the mayor, the police department, and the collective panel of commissioners. I thought out scenarios and re-read my notes until I figured my eyes would fall out from fatigue. Last, I photographed all my information.

When I awoke Sunday morning, I was not ready to tackle the project. After finding out Thompson was dead, I'd had a long week working for Dr. Riley. I reflected on all I had accomplished in the short time since the murder. Broke into the police department, and indeed, my patient's death was murder and the cops dirty. Completed hours of theorizing. Then I put the information together.

I lazed about in pajamas and slippers on the rainy early autumn day with a full box of candied popcorn. A new paperback sat in my lap. The back flap read "true FBI story."

Relax, relax. I bobbed my head side to side, loosening tight muscles, needing to read. Then post more on my board or pack to run. I hadn't decided which.

The book's tension level ramped up in each chapter, and I bit a nail almost to the quick as I turned each page. And I only just finished chapter thirteen.

FOURTEEN

Special Agent Carrie Hartley tugged the cargo bin door open and searched for the cache of cocaine. Instead, she found teenage girls in varying stages of panic.

She grabbed her mic. "I need backup. We have a sit-u-a-tion. James, where are you?"

Behind her, feet skittered to a stop, and the spin of a revolver sounded behind her. She turned to see her partner.

"Hello, Carrie." James pointed his Taurus, and—

A loud knock on my front door jolted me back to reality. My book plummeted. I fumbled my candied popcorn and dropped from the chair to my knees. I holstered the SIG and crawled to the kitchen. I peeked from the bottom corner of the window to make certain Jerry hadn't found me. Who would interrupt my Sunday and mangle the calm I'd worked so hard to achieve?

Not Jerry. I could shoot him. I couldn't shoot a cop.

Calhoun.

My chest tightened. I'd met him when he seemed a bit disheveled. Today he wore a suit and tie, dark glasses perched on his nose. Head topped with a cowboy hat.

He knocked again. Storm Center's Keith Carson dictated a report for my imagination's inner TV.

"In the news tonight, scientists have uncovered the mystery of global warming. This phenomenon has been traced to"— dramatic pause—"Rick Calhoun."

The weather report was dead-on despite my whole "I hate cops" concept.

I gazed too long. Calhoun turned and stared right back. I ducked.

"Whiskey River Police Department, Detective Rick Calhoun. Miss Cade, I know you're hiding in your kitchen."

A loud whack hit the glass. I slowly peeked. Calhoun pressed an envelope against it and rapped his knuckle against the window.

"Warrant, Miss Cade. Warrant to search the premises."

CHAPTER 9

At the entry, I chewed on a knuckle and realized his suspect number three was me.

"You can open the door, or I can kick it open. Your choice, lady."

"Wait a second," I yelled, and hurried to clean as much as possible. I pushed the corkboard into the spare room, ducked into the bathroom, and grabbed a brush in an attempt to tame my hair. I checked my teeth, brushed them at an Olympic gold medal pace, pinched my cheeks, and took one last glimpse in the mirror.

I skittered from the bathroom, half slid to the front door, and opened it. Hand on hip. Very chic.

"Well, if it isn't John Wayne. Come here to insult me again?"

"Afternoon, Miss Cade." He grasped the rim of his hat, giving it a tug. He hooked a finger on his dark glasses, drawing them down his nose as his gaze meandered. "Hadn't planned on it. Although I have to give you credit for the element of surprise."

"Whatever do you mean?"

"Big comfy chair, reading a romance novel, and eating popcorn. While wearing your sidearm strapped to your flannels at three in the afternoon. In pink bunny slippers."

A muscle tic annoyed the corner of my eye. So much for chic. "It's not a romance novel. Why are you here?"

"Gun. Handle first." He held out his hand. "Don't want to get shot today."

I glared at him and handed over my SIG.

Calhoun popped the gun's magazine into his hand, emptied the round from the chamber, and gave me a subtle and disapproving head shake. He pocketed my ammo and picked up a sack on the porch.

That can't be good.

The space closed between us as he tucked the warrant into his jacket pocket and dropped the bag onto my couch. He pushed past me, brushing my side. Weren't cops supposed to say something before barging in? What was in the bag? He removed his hat and turned in the living room. The popcorn was scattered across the table and floor. The novels he stared at were my pile of books to read. The popcorn was his fault. Still, he frowned and scanned the room.

He asked, "Any other weapons? Like an Uzi? Throwing knives? Revolver strapped to your ankle?"

I felt my face shape itself into a sneer. "Don't be ridiculous."

"Well, Miss Cade, I don't trust you, so, turn around, raise your arms."

"What?"

I complied, then lost it. Felt a bit foolish as I giggled, instinctively squirming during the pat down. "Stop, I'm ticklish!"

When I turned, there was a twinkle in his eye, and the same procedure produced the same results. It was finally over.

"I have more questions about Stephen Thompson."

"Right," I said. "You figure it out, Detective."

"Fine by me." He thumbed his phone. "Forensics will go through everything you own while we chat at the police station."

"Wait—no, hang up the phone, please. What's the charge? What kind of flimsy excuse did you give a judge to sign—" Before I requested to see the warrant, he spun me about. My throat almost closed with panic.

"Miss Cade, you have the right to remain silent—"

Handcuffs clinked, coming from wherever he kept them.

"Hey, hey—on what charges? What about the Constitutional right to know, amendments four, five, eight? C'mon!"

"You want to talk here?" Calhoun put the cuffs away, turning me back toward him.

"I'd prefer it."

"Okay, go on, change."

Alarm bells went off in my head while my threat level rammed all the way to red. I knew it. He intended to haul me to the police station. My mouth dried. "I—I—"

"Can't concentrate with those staring at me." He pointed to my slippers. "You've got three minutes to change. Don't go out the window."

The keys to the truck jingled as he held them up. I glowered at him for taking them from the truck, slouched my way to the bedroom, and mocked his words under my breath like a ten-year-old.

I snatched jeans and a tee shirt and got dressed, then peeked from the hallway as he manhandled everything in my living room. His hands coursed over my hearth as he pushed and pulled. A copper teapot on the woodstove enticed his consideration. He turned it upside down, giving it a vigorous shake. Then he used his flashlight on the inside, and pressed gloved fingers around the edges.

I walked into the room and stood by a table topped with a desk lamp. With my toes I straightened a corner of the rug beneath the stand, so he wouldn't see the loosened wooden boards.

He cleared his throat and returned the vessel to its place. Gravity played havoc with his eyes when confronted with my shirt. Great, the tee with inflammatory words on it—"The voices are back. Excellent."

Proving an unbalanced state of mind. Thanks, Jules, terrific Christmas present, I'll remember this in jail.

His hand covered the hint of a smirk, and he coughed. "Your shirt answers a whole bevy of questions." He grabbed books from my floor and flipped through pages.

This invasion of my home made my hands clammy. "What do you want?"

He didn't answer, but he raised his head toward the spare room.

"What's in there, Cade?"

"Nothing, it's a junk room."

"Show me."

I stood against the door and batted my lashes in an attempt to con him out of finding my hard work. "You got me, Detective." Add in bedroom eyes and I was an artist.

Calhoun, smiling, put an arm around me. Delighted, I thought he would fall for the kiss of distraction as he pulled me against his chest. His head dipped, and his words were a soft, slow whisper in my ear. "For once, you're right."

I tingled, looking forward to a con's trick on a detective, and lifted my lips toward his. My eyes popped open instead when I heard the knob jiggle as he pushed the door open.

"Excuse me, Miss Cade." He swept into the room and moved against the corkboard, did a double-take when he saw my work, and said, "Miss Cade, you have made my day. You have no idea the gift you just gave me." He stepped back and took a picture with his phone.

So, so busted. "He was my patient. Someone murdered him and wants it covered up. I won't let that happen."

Calhoun paused after ripping off the printed pictures and notes. "Give me a break. Every piece of information I need to put you in prison for breaking and entering, felony theft, and obstruction of justice is here. Your junk room, my treasure trove. Got ya."

He pulled me into each room and tossed my closet and my cabinets, and overturned the mattress in the bedroom. Then he dragged me to the living room, grabbed the paper bag, and upended it, dumping my wig onto the couch. He opened his hand to show me a thumb drive. "You took pictures that don't belong in your hands. What made you commit this crime? Who paid you to steal evidence? You're a thief, and I'm recommending you for the Worst-Thief-Ever medal. As far as I know, you killed Thompson yourself."

My jaw tightened. "I murdered no one, and you know nothing about me."

He pointed a stern finger my way, and his eyes flashed. "Actually, I know almost everything about you. You'll fill in the blanks. Over here, Miss Cade. Computer. Open it."

The detective fixed an unrelenting gaze on me. I didn't like this icy, judgmental Calhoun and swallowed a hard lump.

I clenched my teeth as he grabbed the last of the candied popcorn off the coffee table, made himself at home in my chair, and opened my laptop. He crooked his finger in the universal *come here* gesture.

"Over here. Make yourself comfortable."

He checked all angles of the computer, mumbling to himself. "Where is—where's the ESP port?"

"The ESP port? They don't have those on these computers."

A hard stare came my way. "One of these here's a port. You tell me which, or I'll shove this thing into each one 'til I destroy your computer. I'm talented that way." He held the drive between his thumb and forefinger and fixed his eyes on mine. He handed me the memory stick.

"It's called a USB port." I leaned toward the computer and pushed in the thumb drive.

"Were you aware they make cameras the size of a small screw?"

Thankfully, I was facing the computer when my mouth fell open. *No way.* Not expecting minuscule cameras in the little cage room, I fumed at myself. What kind of diabolical engineer would make CCTV cameras so tiny?

The offending pictures from the evidence room flickered into view, and he offered me the popcorn that remained in the bowl. With his mouth full, he narrated the summation of my felony.

"Here's Thursday. You cased the entire courthouse and evidence lockup. Here's my favorite part—with your derriere in the air on Friday. And here's Saturday where you took everything in the files."

"Hey, hey. I don't even own a trench coat or a fedora, and I wouldn't go anywhere dressed like Inspector Clouseau."

"So, you stole the evidence on Saturday. Where did you stash it?"

"What? I didn't steal anything. Show me that again."

He ran the feed backward again.

"Detective, that person is *not* me. I was there Thursday and Friday and took pictures only. Thompson didn't die of natural causes. If he wanted to commit suicide, insulin would be much easier. No muss, no fuss. Someone murdered Thompson. You know it, too."

"Why? Then who do you believe stole the evidence and killed the commissioner?"

"I'm not doing your job for you, but I promise you, that's not me."

"Which is why you broke into the police department. Just on a photo tour."

I broke eye contact and whispered. "Give me the keys."

"Not on your life."

"All the evidence is on the memory stick." I put my hand out. Reluctantly, I removed it from the key fob and plugged it into the USB port. My personal autobiography came into full view instead of the evidence, and I gasped. I jumped over him to close my therapeutic work, a novel based on my known life.

Calhoun jerked to the side. "Hey—ow—"

I had miscalculated and tumbled against him. Awkward, but I would have crawled over him like Spiderman before I'd let him see.

He groaned. "Assault and battery. You're writing *Smile, You've been Caught in the Act?*"

I had never had a homicidal bone in my body until he walked through my door. I sat on the chair after successfully securing my novel. "And what's on that drive is none of your business."

"We'll see. You're a flight risk and a safety hazard." He looked more closely at my neck. "What's this? Why don't you tell me about this unique necklace?"

"How should I know?" I snapped. "I've had it as long as I can remember." I hoped he didn't latch onto my memory loss slip up.

Each page came onto the screen, revealing the evidence. "You saw the scene. These pictures prove my point—murder. Corruption as usual." A quick flick of my finger keyed a copy to my hard drive while my hair swished in front of the computer.

Calhoun gave me a stern look, and I felt out of sorts with his eyes on me. "What's your angle? You're a grifter. You've been here for three years. Catherine Cade doesn't exist."

"I'm right here."

"Yes, you are. Except Lucille Corinna is dead."

"Who?"

"Instead of finding a woman who was your age's Social Security number and resemblance, you generated one that brought up a dead woman. Either you didn't think it through, or you were moving fast."

I evaluated my hands. He was right. That method was a layer of anonymity. I needed time and knew Jerry would see a random number as sloppy. He'd never figure it out. Or it would take him a long time.

"What is it? Are you hiding something?" He peered at my neck again. "Interesting, you're wearing a bullet for a necklace."

I gazed out the window, unsettled. Long ago, Jerry had threatened, "if you leave, this bullet is the caliber I'll use to put you into the ground." But I did leave, and I wore the necklet with pride.

I clenched my fists. "I'm done with corruption, and I'm not walking this time. You wanna keep me quiet? You'd better kill me now before I go public with uncomfortable questions about Thompson."

Calhoun chuckled. "That's dramatic. So you have a bee in your bonnet, and if it's not a what, it's a who. Someone … an ex after you?" He waited, and I didn't answer. "I see. Now you're running like the devil's chasing you. You're charging into flames with a bucket of gasoline. I don't know what you've been through—"

"No, you don't." I turned and hurled words laced with venom. "What do you want from me? You don't know me, and you come here, judging me like I'm a crook." I scowled at him.

"You are a criminal." He drew a finger across his upper lip, and his eyes warmed. "Want to stay out of jail? You work for me, I keep an eye on you, and in the meantime, you tell me why you're running. Until I let you go, you belong to me."

"I knew you were dirty. Involuntary servitude. Amendment thirteen—" I couldn't remember for the life of me if I was right. "What about the warrant?"

"That? That was my electricity bill."

"You poser!"

He revealed a lopsided grin.

I felt my eyes widen. "There's a conspiracy and a gag order. You want my help."

"No. I work within the law. You don't. But you can thank God I need assistance, and I'm willing to keep you out of jail."

"God wouldn't blackmail me." *Or would he?*

"Try mercy. You're not getting what you deserve, which is time in prison for the crimes you've committed."

"I refuse to do anything illegal for you."

Calhoun sputtered. "You? Do anything illegal? Why, Miss Catherine, you misjudge me. Does Dr. Riley know you're a bogus nurse practitioner?"

My jaw fell open. "I am not bogus." Just my identity and the PhD, and of course, the time put into the class.

We walked toward the door. His whisper, only a soft breath in my ear, raised the hairs on my neck in what sounded like a threat. "Don't run from me, Catherine."

He leaned over and snatched the book I had been reading off the floor. He shook off the popcorn and laughed.

"*Sex Detective*? Cade, you need Jesus."

CHAPTER 10

Rick Calhoun
Wednesday, September 10

Rainwater cascaded along the marble steps of the courthouse. Calhoun avoided the rivulets with a measure of futility. Bits of the polished granite shone like diamonds when sunlight pierced the clouds. Inside, he wound through the halls to the law enforcement department.

He strolled through the doors to greet Zoe and Mike. Calhoun suspected Mike Tanaka wore the Vice detective badge, the emphasis on vice, with pride.

Zoe held a note in the air. Calhoun snatched it and rapped his knuckles against the Chief's door.

"What's up, Greg?"

Chief Dumont slid paperwork across the desk. "Did you ever get around to doing a background check on the volunteer you want?"

"Yeah."

"Well?"

"Squeaky clean," Calhoun crossed his fingers behind his back. "She's ready to start."

"Is she single?"

"Excuse me?" Calhoun asked.

"Keep her away from McCloud."

"Agreed. She doesn't need to be another notch on our medical examiner's belt."

"Is she going to be a distraction to you?"

"No." He shifted. "Mike would be the problem. He's still hitting on Zoe."

"Uh-huh, I find it interesting how you picked her. I checked. She's your neighbor. And she is single. Downright thought-provokin'." Dumont touched tented fingers against his lips. "We'll need her fingerprints on file."

"Understood."

"One more thing." He removed his reading glasses. "Remember, the woman's a civilian. She had better be able to fend for herself. As Resident Training Instructor, you get her ready in case a suspect goes off the wall. No skimping your regular job."

"Not a problem."

"She got enough time in the day to do this?"

"I'll work with her during the evenings. Weekends should be quiet."

"When she's finished training and passes the test, we'll swear her in. Then you get your much-coveted and *bona fide* volunteer deputy."

"This will be a relief."

"Relief? Be careful of personal entanglements." Dumont leaned forward with fingers laced.

"Greg, it's been so long, I wouldn't see one coming." He left the office, his back muscles tightening as he closed the door.

"You're forty. Time you get a wife."

"Later."

"What did Dumont want?" Mike grimaced as he struggled with a cardboard package.

"We're getting help with cold cases from a civi. What's the box?"

"Think I'm opening your mail. Overnighted, must be important. You're bringing in a what? Have you lost your mind?" His eyes widened. "A civilian will destroy our feng shui. I don't like having them around. They're always in the way."

"Feng shui is Chinese."

"No, it's not, Zoe. It's Japanese. Who's the outsider?"

"Knock it off, Mike. Zoe needs your humor like ... no one. The volunteer's name is Catherine Cade."

"What? A woman? What's she like? Is she attractive? Available?" Mike gritted his teeth as he struggled with the last strands of tape on the box.

"Down boy, you'll meet her soon enough." Calhoun turned. "Don't you have scissors?"

"Mm-hmm," Zoe mumbled, "but he never gives me my stuff back."

Mike pulled a book from the package, squinted at its contents, and turned the cardboard box over. He raised widened eyes.

"What?" Calhoun eyed the box.

"*Sex Detective*?"

Zoe pivoted. "Who?"

Calhoun grabbed at the novel while Mike usurped it. "We've lost our homicide detective to the ways of the world. Is this porn?"

"Gimme my mail."

Zoe and Mike guffawed.

Dumont came from his office. "What's going on here? I don't hear the clickety-clack of computer keys. Mike, don't you have vice to chase?"

Mike sputtered. "Evidence is right here, Chief. And the worst kind."

Zoe raised her eyes, cocking her head at Dumont, unable to contain herself. "*Sex Detective*, sir. Calhoun is reading—"

"I studied it. Accurate. Enthralling." Dumont kept walking.

Both detectives and the dispatcher gaped at the Chief.

"A true story. You might learn something new." Dumont poured more coffee into a mug that said, "I can't fix stupid, but I can cuff it," and he headed to his office. "Back to work."

"Why are you reading *Sex Detective*?" Zoe rested her chin on the heel of her hand.

"Research. Our volunteer is reading this." Calhoun snatched the book away and moved toward his desk.

Mike mumbled. "He keeps Melanie's picture in his wallet. Maybe he's interested in dating again."

Calhoun spun and shot him a hot glare.

Mike put his hands in the air. "Man, I meant no offense."

"You idiot. He's fifteen feet away," Zoe whispered.

"How many years? He needs to move on."

"Let him be. People grieve in different ways."

"You know I can hear a flea fart in a whirlwind," Calhoun said. "Say it louder, Mike, not like I can figure it out without my hearing aids turned up. I've never shown you her picture. You been in my wallet?"

"No. It's 'cause you look at it every day. You say her name a lot." Mike became quiet. A few seconds later, he brightened.

"What's the civi's name again? I bet she's beautiful. When does she start?"

"I can't believe you," Zoe said.

Mike stared off into the distance. "So if she's not available, will you marry me, Zoe?"

"No."

"Think about the beautiful babies we'd have. Me, Japanese, and you with your beautiful dark skin."

She snorted. "You sound like we'd have a litter of chocolate pugs. Why am I even acknowledging you? I'm married."

CHAPTER 11

CATHERINE CADE
WEDNESDAY

No sooner than Calhoun had taken off on Sunday, I'd blabbed to my friend, Jules. Just the basics. In response, a loud lecture on illegal activities came from her directed my way, and how peeved she was at being left out of my little escapade.

Oh, the contradictions.

Calhoun. What a jerk. Why blackmail me? What did he want? A cop. And after all, those encounters never ended well for me.

But by Wednesday, my concentration still fled, and I nibbled a nail while pacing my office. A migraine threatened. What if his digging didn't stop, then what? The palms of my hands stung where my fingernails dug.

Until my botched job at the police station, stealing identities kept me safe. His discovery jeopardized my next persona, not just the bakeshop. What if he was another round of suffering?

I needed to establish a solid identity and a handwritten reference as a pastry chef for the new personality in Portland. With elaborate execution, I ordered and waited for appliances, signed a rental agreement, had recipes, and was ready to start.

Calhoun.

Heated with embarrassment, even my neck burned. The hottest guy ever at my house, and here I am with my cherubic face, a little too chubby, clambering over him in my stupid shirt about the voices.

At last, work ended, and kick boxing at the gym relieved my anxiety. I was worn out, and finally, the familiar wood-and-concrete bridge over the river came into view as I drove home.

Autumn, in an unapologetic, almost intimate public affair, kissed summer farewell. The pines' earthy, pungent scent formed a background for the eye candy of orange and red leaves waving dreamy farewells.

Whaam—!

My head thrust forward and hit the steering wheel. *Great.* Someone slammed into my truck's back left bumper, pitching my vehicle's nose toward the wooden bridge. I slammed on the brakes and put my hand over the stinging pain on my forehead. The hand came away bloody. I eyeballed the rear-view mirror, making sure Jerry wasn't there, as my fingers unbuckled the seatbelt to go check on the other driver.

Boom! Smash!

Again, the vehicle rammed my left bumper and tossed me hard into the steering wheel. My chest burned. The front end of my GMC slammed into the bridge rail at a right angle, crumpling the hood and buckling the driver's door. *Please, God, please.* The other car's driver kept moving forward into mine.

"No." Breathless, I gripped the wheel and yanked the emergency brake. I put it into reverse and for a moment I thought I'd be all right. But the movement continued. The bumpers scraped deeper into the wood, and splinters flew over the front window.

"Stop, stop!" My GMC inched forward despite my pleas. The driver's-side window blew, its shards pelting me. The headlights behind me blinded me, and a truck smashed into my passenger side door, crunching my last exit. Below me, water swirled in the rapids. I couldn't get enough air.

The truck backed up and pulled away.

Jerk!

A third jolt to the rear end of my truck pushed me again, this from another car trying to get out of there.

The wood gave way.

Everything stopped. The truck teetered toward the river. The car that had been slow-motion slammed into me was empty, its driver apparently having fled. No luck, no escape, yet instinct drove me against the seat, and another prayer escaped in a quick sentence. "Jesus, help!" Five minutes passed like five hours. Finally, I heard sirens and voices, and I tried not to hyperventilate. And I hoped.

Footsteps sounded behind me, in the bed of the truck. I didn't dare look. The GMC swayed, then rocked backward, and the back window exploded, showering me with more fragments of glass. "Nooo!" I cried out—my eyes shut tight, powerless to free my grip on the steering wheel.

A man's voice hushed me. "I'm here to help you. Cover your eyes." Low-pitched scraping pitched more glass forward. "Put this blanket around you. Let go of the steering wheel and keep your arms in the blanket." He cleared his throat and spoke slowly, as if talking to a small child. "You need to take your hands off the wheel."

"I can't ... seem to let go." He reached forward, pried my hands loose, then slid his arms under mine and swept me through the rear and off the truck. I clung to him, wailing in fear and relief.

"Shh, it's okay."

I let at least six months of locked-away tears overflow and then beheld my guardian angel's face. Rick Calhoun. Why, of course. Smallest town ever.

"Catherine? You okay? You're bleeding." He pushed my hair from my forehead.

I laid my head against his chest and wept again. Wonderful. The dirty cop saved my life. "I'm fine. I need to thrash the driver who tried to kill me."

"That I wanna see."

I hiccupped a few times from the sob session. "You didn't almost land in the river smushed to pieces."

"Everyone fled, including the truck that hit you. An F-250, someone said. Detective Tanaka's taking reports. Can you stand?"

The crowd of drivers that slowed and stopped worried me, and my fingers itched. Hairs lifted on my arms. The driver of the truck seemed intent on sending me down the river.

Steadied, I stepped around him, and he swiveled, inspecting my face. "What's wrong?"

I peered through his bent elbow. "Nothing."

He removed his jacket, then bunched his shirt against the gash on my forehead. He draped his coat around my shoulders.

Glittering jewels of blood spotted his arms and wrists. Calhoun led me to his vehicle to rest, ignoring my protestations.

Shaky, I needed support but continued to scan the crowd as we walked.

"Mike," he yelled over the din of horns, the rush of the river below, and my headache.

"Oh, please! My head—"

He mumbled an apology and thumbed his phone. "I called the towing company. They should be here soon."

Another officer jogged our way.

"Tanaka, call an ambulance."

I tried to push him away. "No, I'm fine. I need to see if my GMC is okay. I have to go home."

"Don't worry right now. I'll bring you a replacement until your rig is drivable."

The other officer checked my truck. He collected pictures and came back. "Doesn't appear to have any undercarriage damage. The tire's blown. Pretty well scraped up. You hurt? Did the airbag deploy?"

The flickering yellow lights of a tow truck caught my eye. "It has no airbag and was built to outlive me. The back window's shattered, thanks to Calhoun."

"You know this guy?"

I nodded.

"I'll be back to take your statement." He rushed back to other upset drivers.

I tugged at Rick's hand. "You can let go now."

He removed the shirt from my forehead, and I mouthed a complaint of pain.

"Big baby. It's just a scratch." He brushed a thumb across my cheek.

Jerk.

I looked at his arms. "You need to go to the hospital."

He plucked glass from my hair and pulled his jacket closer around me as I shivered, his eyes evaluating me. Something spooked me. Someone had orchestrated the accident. Maybe.

He asked, "What are you doing here?"

"Thought I'd see what going over the bridge was like, you know, my bucket list. I work for a living." I asked, "Is everyone here okay?

He motioned toward the cars. "Some folks got more ticked off than others, no one hurt, except for you. I need your phone number. Gonna call you later."

"Why? Can't you call the clinic and leave a message?"

He reached across me to rummage in the pocket of his jacket, finally pulling out a pad and pen. "Sure, for your office staff to hear."

Tense, I recited my cell number as he jotted it down.

The other officer returned and shouldered his way around Calhoun, clutching my hand. "I'm Detective Tanaka, but you can call me Mike. How do you know this guy?"

"This is Catherine Cade, she will be help—"

Mike interrupted him and straightened his tie. "Is she—I mean, is this Miss Cade, the civi? Gonna help on cold cases?"

"Yes, that's me. How did you find out?"

"Because Mr. Professional here doesn't have actual friends." He chortled.

Rick scowled.

"Dude, she's awesome," he whispered to Rick, then mouthing a "thank you" heavenward. He gripped my hand again and gave it a pump.

"You're rattling her teeth, and if she has a concussion, you're aggravating it." He elbowed Mike out of the way. "Do you mind?"

"I can drive you to the hospital—" He looked away when an annoyed stare came his way from Rick.

"No, thanks, I don't need to see any quack." The irony wasn't lost on me, but my gut quavered, and I didn't want anyone to take me to the hospital or home. "If my truck is okay to go, I have to leave. Baking bread tonight. Thanks for the offer."

"You're shaking. Sure you're okay? And the GMC is barely drivable," Calhoun said.

"Homemade bread?" Tanaka asked, eyes pleading.

"Yes. My forte. I'm fine, just shaken a bit. You need to have someone tend to your arms." I handed him his jacket.

The tow-truck mechanic sidled up and wiped grease from his hands. "Bodywork, that's about it. She's safe to drive home. I switched the tire with the spare. Should work fine until you get it replaced. Just don't drive too fast, okay?"

"Thanks." I pointed to Calhoun. "He's footing the bill."

Calhoun handed the tow-truck mechanic a card as I walked off toward my GMC. "Send the bill to this address." Then he yelled my way, "I'll call you in a few."

"It's a pleasure to meet you—Detective Tanaka, right?"

"Yep." He beamed.

"Answer your phone!"

"Whatever, Calhoun." I ignored him with a wave of my hand.

"Be careful," Calhoun yelled after me.

Right. Me, be careful.

"She doesn't like you much, does she?"

Calhoun, amused with Mike, eyed her as she drove away.

"Nope. I have to leave." He wrangled enough room to reach his truck. He scribbled a quick note about the pileup and pushed paperwork into Tanaka's hand. "Here's your list of manna from heaven. Ten cars in need of your tender loving care. Have to get my arms looked at."

Tanaka groaned. "No, you are not leaving me with these cars, these people, and all this paperwork. Not after I helped you. I refuse."

"Okay, Bambi. Tell the Chief." He jumped into his SUV, started the engine, and turned the wheel to navigate.

"You—you're going over there, aren't you? You're going to Cade's."

"You know," Calhoun said, "you should have taken her to the hospital. She may go into shock. And you let her drive. I think she needs x-rays."

"Hey," he yelled as he punched a fist in the air, Calhoun's direction. "She's my future wife, you toad."

"Yeah? Shoulda done your job, detective. What if she hurts herself baking bread?" He slapped the side of his SUV, saluted, and began to weave his way out of traffic.

CHAPTER 12

CATHERINE CADE
AFTER THE CRASH

I steadied my grip on my SIG, slid the key into the lock, turned the handle, and kicked the front door open.

After clearing the house, I flipped a switch, flooding the backyard with light. I checked the floor's loosened panel to make certain no one took off with my goods. Satisfied everything was safe, I holstered the gun and yanked the curtains closed. The mirror unfriended me, and I splashed water on my face to wash away the tear-stained visage and assess the wound on my forehead. My hands still shook from the aftermath and worry. Maybe it hadn't been Jerry, but taking chances was outside of my sphere.

I changed into jeans, tugged a clean T-shirt over my head, and headed for the kitchen, willing to calm myself into "ordinary."

Pot roast had simmered all day. The aroma of the meat, fresh-from-the-garden onions, carrots, sage, and lavender in a beef bouillon with a good amount of Worcestershire sauce welcomed me home. By rote, I peeled potatoes and added them to simmer.

A no-knead dough had spent the past twenty hours rising, and I placed the loaf on the baking stone inside a hot oven. Pain flashed across my forehead when, twenty minutes later, I bent over to check the bread through the glass of the stove.

I touched the spot and pondered the crash's aftermath. Mike Tanaka's flirtatious comment had not gone unnoticed. I drummed my fingers on the table. Perhaps someone dumped the vice detective recently. Why else treat me with such enthusiasm?

For now, thanks to the wreck, a hammer hitting me square in the middle of my noggin would be less painful. A bottle of pain reliever on a corner cupboard shelf shouted the obvious.

What a dreadful day. Everything went wrong. My desperate prayer had gone unanswered because there was no God to answer me. Now, agitated at that thought and aching, I stepped outside to calculate the damage to my truck. I yanked the driver's side door, and it groaned on opening and fought back when I tried to close it. Paint scraped from the passenger side, fender pressed in, jagged glass everywhere. No wonder Calhoun's arms had bled. I cringed.

I'd left the front door open and allowed the air from the cold snap to stream through, so I rushed inside and shut it as the rosemary and yeasty aroma of whole wheat bread filled the kitchen. I closed my eyes and breathed it in, and a wispy mental picture, a memory of a woman, beckoned me to help with a maternal tenderness.

Familiar. Comforting. *What was that all about?*

Was she my mother? I put a hand to my forehead to hold back the discomfort and realized I had never baked until fleeing Jerry's grip, hoping this was the last time he'd come after me. Did these memories come from her?

Warm water and soap slipped over my hands, and after, I worked my fingers through my hair, tucking stray strands behind my ears. I desperately wanted a good memory.

Not finding any more fragments of recollection, I focused on food. Nothing like comfort food to take my mind off the past, the one I knew, and now the one I'd hoped for—normal, if I ever figured out what defined normal.

Tonight's dinner would bring small satisfaction from today's disaster. I propped my elbows on the table and tried to place a name to the mystery memory woman's face.

A knock at the door brought me back to the present. I checked my pistol, clicked on the porch light, and groaned.

Calhoun—a different catastrophe. He'd blackmailed me. He also saved my life. Now, within a few days, he'd pried apart the emotional brick and mortar around me. How?

I opened the door a crack. He'd changed clothes.

"John Wayne. You didn't call."

He put a finger in the air, dug for his cell phone, and thumbed the keypad. My phone jingled. He rested an elbow against the clapboard, waiting.

"You're hilarious."

"Came to see if you were all right. I brought books ..." His voice trailed to a whisper after he inhaled and looked past me into the kitchen. "I'm interrupting your supper. I'll visit later."

"Thanks, I guess. I suppose you're hungry, too." I scowled as he stood there, stammering. "Oh, come in, you're goin' all puppy-dog eyes." I lugged him through the open door and led him to the kitchen. How pleasant to sit with a mate—dinner mate—for once. "I'm still waiting on the bread. Should be ready in another twenty minutes. Put the books on the table."

"What can I do to help? Here." He handed me a set of keys. "I'll take your truck in, so use the one in the driveway 'til the mechanic is done with yours."

"But I can drive it until it gets to the garage."

"You can't drive with the back window out, or I'll give you a ticket." He wiggled his fingers in the universal *hand it over* gesture. "You were shaking earlier. I think you should go to the hospital."

Of course, I should go to the hospital, but I didn't want my face on some computer database. I knew how those worked. I plopped my keys into his open palm.

"I'm in pain, but the ER can't help me. Might see if you can fan the flames in the woodstove and help me in the kitchen. First, come with me." I grasped his hand and tugged.

"Where are you taking me?"

"Follow me."

He pulled back. "Wait—"

"Quiet. I have a headache, and you're not arguing with me." I led him to the bathroom. "Sit. I take it you did this? Duct tape is not a bandage." Finding my kit, I cleaned and used butterfly tapes to pull the wounds together. I topped them with antibiotic ointment and wrapped them with gauze and self-adhesive pressure dressings. "This should do fine."

"Much obliged. Ow, hey—"

"Big baby. It's just a scratch." I mimicked his words as I removed my gloves, scrubbed, then returned to the kitchen sink, washed again, and readied for dinner.

I had a talent for milking a bad situation, and a wreck met that requirement. And I had a cop to do it for me. My slight pain proved my acting skills adequate.

"Can you help with some stuff? I need to get some wood."

"Point me in the right direction." Calhoun scouted one side of the living room to the open kitchen.

I faked an admirable shuffle to the woodstove. Coals in the old stove glowed with warmth, and I showed him the wood-pile out back. Decent work for a wounded cop. Even stacked enough wood to generate a fire for the rest of the week.

"Don't bust those wounds open."

"If I do, it's your fault."

The timer dinged. I limped, stumbled, and exaggerated my pain. "Bread." I pointed. He brought the round, crusty loaf out of the oven.

"Okay, turn it bottom-side up, so I can spank it."

"What?"

"It's a newborn. This is how I test it." I thumped a finger against the loaf. "It's ready when tapping on it makes a hollow sound."

"You say the most interesting things."

Then I gestured to a cupboard. "Platter and bowls."

"Yes, ma'am."

He followed directions well.

He brought the pot roast to the table and sat. "I don't think I've ever smelled food this good." He closed his eyes, and I almost asked him if he was okay. With head bowed, he mumbled something.

Ah. Got it.

His eyes opened. "What?"

"You bother God a lot?"

"All the time."

"I'm an atheist." *Agnostic.* "Didn't think cops prayed." I slouched in my chair.

His shoulders lifted in silent mirth. "You've never been in a foxhole."

I shook my head. "I prayed in the truck. You saved me, not God."

Calhoun pressed a fist to his mouth. "So you prayed to God, in whom you don't believe. And I showed."

"Coincidence. Don't attempt to convert and blackmail me. It'll be a cold day before I walk into a church. So what did you pray about?"

"Gave thanks for this dinner."

"Oh, well, you're welcome. Say it a little louder next time, and I can answer *de nada* since I cooked your meal, not God."

He smirked, tore off a chunk of bread, and dipped it into the pot roast juices in his bowl.

I grasped my reading glasses and beheld a tower of textbooks gracing my dinner table. "So I'm supposed to read and memorize these books."

"Before your volunteer work, you need training, and that includes testing."

"Can I have information on the Thompson case?"

Calhoun didn't answer. I took his silence as a no. He said something unintelligible and noticed me gawking. "What?"

I plopped my elbows on the table. "You stuffed your cheeks, and you'll choke before the night is through, and I refuse to save your life, considering your little blackmail scheme."

"Call the police. Be my guest. What, no CPR?"

Roguish. I could stare at him all day.

"You're skirting my questions. Heimlich," I said, correcting him. "In my unimaginable pain, it's debatable if I could do it." I bit my lip, reached across the table, and wiped his face. "If you're starving, you might as well plant your kisser in the bowl."

"Tempting." He attempted to talk around a mouthful of food. "Learned to eat fast in the military. I'm such a bad cook I live on junk food. You baked bread, too. I can't resist your cooking."

"You say it like you've been here."

"A passing dream, I guess." He held a thin crust of bread in his hand. "This isn't good."

"No?" I stopped chewing.

"It's outstanding. Nothing like fresh veggies and herbs. Like the basil in the bread, too." He drank some water.

"Rosemary, not basil," I said. "You're dodging the issue again. Did you figure out who removed the files from the evidence locker?"

"Not having this conversation with you."

"If you don't tell me, I'll dig on my own." I toyed with my fork.

"Yeah, right into a deep hole." He leaned, snatched the bread from my plate, dipped the crusty bread into his food, stuffed my food into his mouth. "I can arrest you. Put a stop to that."

"You—" I latched onto his bowl and pulled it close. "Don't you push me, Detective. I have a headache, a whiplash, and I am not taking no for an answer. You shook me for change like a bum, pushed a bogus death certificate on me, ransacked my house, and you expect me to volunteer to do your work, but not get in on Thompson's murder?"

His jaw tensed, and he pointed at the bowl. "I would appreciate my food back."

"What did you learn?" I returned it.

"Too dangerous."

"Dangerous? Who watches your—" I kept my cursing to a minimum, struggled for a word, and finally settled for "—behind?"

"Not you. You're on cold cases, Cade." He raised his eyes to mine. "Should I call you my favorite crook or my favorite cook? Did you enjoy living in Issaquah or Bellevue, Washington? Who did you rob, Bill Gates?"

What?

"You changed the subject!"

He continued to study me and stuffed more bread in his mouth. "I told you I know more about you than you think."

I was quiet, stunned. Somehow he had done some fast, thorough research somewhere and came up with information I thought no one could access.

"I need you to familiarize yourself with the police department. Starting tomorrow."

"Can't. I'm working at the pastry shop. The next day I can."

"Right, you're opening a bakery. When?"

"Almost ready, down to the sanding stage. How could you know? I don't even have a name for it."

"I have my sources." He wiped his mouth and helped himself to thirds. "A bakery. You any good?"

"No. That's why I'm opening it."

"Doughnuts?"

"Gee, I never thought to have a bakery with doughnuts."

"Cops like doughnuts."

"Thought cops and doughnuts were a joke."

"Try a stakeout on a cold night without doughnuts and hot coffee."

"Sounds exciting."

"You should try it sometime. Thought you medical folks made decent money. So why are you opening a bakery?"

I glided into my lie. "Making the rent is tough. Jonah Riley. Great doctor. Stingy businessman. I need two jobs."

"Sorry to hear that." He paused. "I won't ask where you gained the funding for your bakeshop."

"Don't have a clue what you're talking about. Speaking of funding, you left your credit card here the other day." I pushed a platinum credit card across the table.

Calhoun stopped eating, and his eyes became narrow slits. He grabbed the plastic, inspected it, and eyeballed me. "When did you ...? What did you buy with it?"

"Fourteen-hundred-dollar diamond necklace." I sputtered as his face turned red. "It fell out when you gave me your jacket."

"A con and a pickpocket. Never again, you hear?" He pointed his fork at me.

"Yeah, I know, I'll pay you in pain for that." I parroted Jerry's words without thinking.

Calhoun jerked his head up at my tone. He pushed himself away from the table and appeared disturbed. "Who said those words to you?"

"Never mind."

"No, tell me." He caught my gaze. "I'm guessing this is not the first time you've run. Is he the reason?"

I pretended to choke, thankful he let my comment slide. "Where's the bakery?"

"Sixth Street and G, across from the craft store."

"A block from the police department. How convenient."

Now I'd squeeze everything from the accident because he refused to give me details on the case. I rubbed my neck, and with a sad gaze, I gathered the bowls.

"Here, let me do the dishes." He stood, took the dinnerware from me, and went to the sink. "I don't see baseboard heaters. You heat only with wood?"

"Sharp eye. Rent is cheap when I chop the wood which lowers my electricity bill, too. The propane for cooking runs from the backyard to the kitchen."

"Propane. Doesn't sound safe back there. I should check for code violations."

"I'm living on the cheap. Don't kick me out of my home, please."

The corner of his mouth turned down, and he resumed the kitchen chores. With the dishes cleaned and put away, he caught my eye.

"Savvy little con, getting a cop to do your dishes," he said with a subtle wink.

"You gotta earn your keep."

"I'll keep that in mind."

I prepared a covered container with the remainder of the pot roast and a plateful of herb rolls for him to take home.

What a pleasant change, having him in my house, stoking the wood stove, doing dishes, and enjoying my food. But I conned him twice, once with the credit card, and again with the motor vehicle accident manipulation. He caught me in the act, and still, he went back and stacked more firewood, enough to keep the house warm for an extra week.

He returned and brushed my hair away, inspected the slight abrasion, and stepped back.

"I can't believe you picked my pocket. Why me, when you can rob someone wealthy? Maybe I'll find out. Maybe you'll tell me."

I rubbed my neck in feigned distress. "You've got the goods on me, Detective." There were plenty of crooked businessmen who wouldn't want the cops involved after I'd relieved them of their ill-gotten gains. Returning money to victims was icing on the cake. Calhoun would never find those burgles buried on the Deep Web.

His forehead wrinkled as I checked his bandages.

"You're my mystery to solve," he said.

My voice caught in my throat, uncertain if I wanted to be his mystery.

He held his hand out. "Let me have your smartphone."

I snort-laughed. "Sure. As in, I don't think so."

"Relax. All I want to do is put my number in there."

I grabbed the phone from my camo purse and handed it to him. "I'm watching you."

"Watch all you want." He glanced at me with a wry smile. "A camo purse? I'm in love." He bobbed his head.

My face burned in a furious blush. Despite the very small crush I seemed to be developing, I watched his every move. *Never trust a cop.*

Viewing him in the natural, wearing jeans with a navy tee shirt, I noted a peppering of gray throughout his hair and had to force myself to stop eyeing him as he fiddled with my smartphone.

"Need anything else?"

"Huh?" Torn from not-so-pure thoughts, I took a look-see at his face. He examined me, and when our eyes met, a familiar thorny prickling surrounded me, a feeling I couldn't—or wouldn't name. Time to wrap things up.

"I'm exceptional." My words spilled out as a tease, and horrified, I tore my gaze away. Subject change. "Thanks for your help, even if I did con you." I went to the table and retrieved the leftovers I had wrapped.

He pulled on his coat—an old Hard Rock Cafe bomber jacket. "Just earnin' my keep. Now don't go and set yourself ablaze."

"I'll try not to, but I see you're on speed dial just in case."

A crooked grin appeared. "By the way, you have flour on your nose."

I rubbed my face, self-conscious. "You could've said something."

"Yeah, I coulda. Miss Catherine, thank you for a fine supper. Have yourself a nice evening. Call me if you need anything at all." Calhoun's smile lit up my lifeless house as he doffed his Stetson, then settled it on his head and left.

"Dang it," I whispered, and alone in a vacuum, I wondered why I missed his presence. Why didn't he turn his back on me? Why did he enjoy being here? Worse, why did I want him to stay?

The door opened, and he popped his head through the opening. "What's for dinner tomorrow night?"

"Out."

He didn't belong in my life. I didn't belong in his. My hand rested on my chest when the door closed.

In the morning, I'd run my circuit, see the guy I called *Some Guy*, and forget all about the detective.

CHAPTER 13

I ran almost every morning at six a.m. Personal reasons. The gash across my head remained angry, but I refused to miss my course. From working at the clinic, I knew I probably had a case of whiplash. Even a fraud knows better than to jog the neck after an accident. So, I decided to not push it and opted to do a fast walk.

A path from my house, half a block to the next street over, then back to the store, and on for another five miles kept me on the same route as Some Guy in my neighborhood. I couldn't keep pace with his long legs when I was running and often wondered how many miles he ran once he disappeared up and around the hill. I tried it once and named it Killa Gorilla, then tackled it a bit further each day. With rock climbing, running, kickboxing, and Sundays at the range, I'd be ready for Jerry.

Once, I needed to be at the clinic at six a.m., so I left the house early. There he was, hauling his fine behind along the street. I craned my neck over my left shoulder, turned into a female Lookie Lou, and almost ran my truck into the ditch.

Not long after, running became my passion. With a great clinical assessment of his legs, I could appreciate them either way he ran. I contented myself with professional observation. I lived with constant paranoia and danger, and dating would be imprudent at best.

This morning I turned my thoughts to Calhoun. I planned on figuring out who he was, because he just didn't fit the cop profile. The texts on criminal justice had kept me up too late the previous night, and I was fatigued.

Some Guy passed me, running ahead. He always wore his ball cap low and concentrated on the lane. He wore earbuds sometimes, and sunglasses always. Never acknowledged me, but today just as he passed, he touched his cap and nodded as though he knew me.

What was that all about? I took my eyes off the course, caught my toe on my other shoe, and hit the asphalt hard. I rushed to upright myself just in time to see him glance back. *Oh, what perfect timing!*

I looked down, trying to ignore my embarrassment. After I brushed gravel from my legs and checked for skinned knees, I spotted Some Guy as he turned toward me. I held up a hand to wave at him, to indicate I was okay, when a strange whirring noise caught my attention. I fixed my eyes on the mom-and-pop market on the corner of my street, past him.

I scanned the parking lot. Kids on bikes, men with cigarettes, the everyday view. But today, a man with a remote stood there, and I strained my eyes to find the toy he controlled.

A blue Prius with a peace sign on the front bumper swerved around the corner and headed straight for me, and Some Guy was in the car's path. A surreal sense of fear descended, and nausea and panic overwhelmed me. How ironic. Death by Prius, with a peace sign.

I should've jumped into the ditch, but Some Guy didn't hear the quiet Prius's engine even as it revved. He was coming my way but not looking at me! I sprinted in his direction, and with his long strides toward me, the gap shortened. Then I tried waving my arms. *Fool!*

The car closed in as I yelled. My voice didn't get a response. He'd hear the whine of the engine, or at least the tire noise on the road, if his ears weren't plugged.

My thighs burned as I ran faster toward him.

Some Guy lifted his head, checked behind him, and raced toward me, as I pushed my way to him.

Jump into the ditch, you idiot! Instead, we almost clashed coming within inches of the car's front bumper. I flung myself airborne, fearful we'd be hit, I'd miss the mark, kiss asphalt, and we'd both die. I didn't think Saint Peter was ready to shake hands with me yet, and I was dubious which direction he'd point me.

He caught me midair, and we tumbled into the ditch.

Judging by the number of times we rolled, the Mariana trench would have been shallower. Every single bump and scrape as we tumbled through gravel and glass shards caused me to wince. He held my head to his chest, wrapped his legs around mine. Something sharp hit the back of my head, hard. My ribs crunched. Then everything fell dark.

I'd heard sternal rubs caused enough pain to bring back the dead. Now someone dragged their knuckles over my sternum.

"Ow, ow, stop—what the heck?" I grasped a hand in the darkness.

A voice far away told me I'd stopped breathing.

Right. What? Again, nothing.

Lips on mine caused me to raise my hands in defense, and my chest rose in response to CPR. Hand under my neck, my pulse checked, chin supported.

What happened? "Who are you?"

"I'm the man you saved. Guess I owe you one. The ambulance is coming."

His voice was a gruff whisper. Hadn't expected that. I said, "Oh. The runner. Well, back at ya." I opened my eyes and saw only darkness. At daybreak, winter or summer, things were never black. "What time is it?"

"It's morning. We were each on our run—"

"Morning?" A million thoughts had me freaked. "I can't see—oh, no. Please, God."

"You can't see me?"

"No," I cried out.

"Shh, it'll be okay." He wiped my tears away, tears I didn't know were falling. "It's me, Cal—"

"No, no—I can't, please help." I gripped his shirt.

"Here." He supported my head and carefully slipped his other arm around me. He whispered, "You'll be okay, but don't move."

He wove fingers through my hair, and dizzy, confused, and so afraid, I wept into his shirt.

To his credit, he was either the sweetest man on the earth or totally clueless how to react to a flood of tears. It mattered, and I thanked him. He had an accent reminiscent of Calhoun's, but his voice was raspy. But the face I'd imagined was his, and for those moments when things were quiet, I wished he was here, and changed panic to hope by picturing Calhoun holding me in a loving embrace.

CHAPTER 14

RICK CALHOUN

Calhoun kept an eye on the paramedics loading Catherine into the ambulance. He ignored Mike's stare and occupied himself wiping away gravel from his arms and legs.

Mike inched toward Calhoun. "You're hurt and bleeding. Maybe you need to go the ER, too. Did you rip open the wounds you got last night?"

He moved his arm from his side, swiping at dust again.

Mike asked, "So what transpired?"

"That car aimed at us. No driver turned up, and I couldn't find keys."

"I'll run plates and the VIN. It's possible we can locate the owner, and sweep for anything odd."

"Good."

"Lemme take your official statement here. How'd this go down?"

"I told you." His eyes followed the ambulance as it made its way onto the street. "On my morning run, I passed Cade. She must have seen the car coming before I did. The woman has a pair of lungs, 'cause she can screech. She flew through the air, and we took a tumble."

"I'll check the area, and hospital too, for a driver." Tanaka turned his pen in his hand. "So Cade didn't recognize you, and she tripped."

"Yeah. A minute before everything happened, she twisted my way and stumbled over her feet. I came back to help."

"Okay." Mike scribbled notes with a nod.

"She risked her neck for a perfect stranger." He paused. "I should have gone with her. She's scared."

"Yeah, you're a hero, she's a hero. And let's note, this is

the second time she almost died around you. Great romance you started."

"Not a romance."

Mike took his pencil and pointed. "So you headed one way, passed her, and turned around, right? But you didn't see her until she took a flying leap, so how did you realize that she tripped over her own feet a minute earlier?"

Speechless, Calhoun stood with mouth open and fixed his eyes on his partner. "I must have glanced back."

"And remind me, why did she need CPR?"

He pointed to the embankment. "It's a long fall. She hit her head, stopped breathing—"

Mike rocked forward. "Does Cade know you gave her CPR?"

"No, and don't tell her."

"Don't you think she'd be grateful?" Tanaka raised his chin when silence followed, and Calhoun glared at him. Mike tried to put his pen in his shirt pocket but missed. It struck asphalt and rolled away. "Well, kiss me, Kate. You made out with her."

"No, I didn't. She hit her head, that's all."

"No, you kissed her." Mike choked his words out. "What chivalry. If she stopped breathing, she wouldn't have kissed you during CPR. She passed out."

Rick said, "I gave her CPR, and there was no kissing. Her respirations were shallow. Hard to tell. Stop giggling like a little girl. Please tell me you have some class. She's lost her vision, and she's terrified, and she would misconstrue CPR as something else."

"Not a word. But, dude ... best blackmail material evah."

"Don't call me dude. You're an adult. There's nothing here to blackmail. What else can you get here? Do we need forensics?"

"Yeah." He sputtered.

Calhoun smacked a fist to Tanaka's rib cage.

Mike rubbed the painful spot. "Ow."

CATHERINE CADE

Arriving in the ER and still in total darkness, I hurt every-where. Hospital odors, the scent of bleach, and the reek of sweat assailed my nose. Footsteps shuffled in and out. Phones rang.

My chest tightened. Blind. No one to help. Not even here in the ER if someone slipped in to end my life. *Jerry*.

My thoughts ran amuck, and balling the blanket in my fist, I willed myself into no-panic mode. Slowed my breathing. Just because the electronic medical program digitized my picture forever didn't mean Jerry would find me. But in the ether, especially the deep web where sensitive documents were kept, anything was hackable.

A woman's voice startled me. It belonged to Jan, the ER doctor who spoke with me often regarding some of my patients who landed in the emergency room.

"Well, if it isn't our heroine of the day. How ya feel?" She stroked my arm.

"Like maybe I should skip heroine day." A wince was unavoidable.

"You have a gash across your forehead—"

"Had a car accident last night."

"All righty. You bumped your head. The CT scan is fine, but we need an MRI before they close for the day. Small towns and MRI schedules. *Tsk*," she said. "Then back to the MRI you go tomorrow, to find out if you have inflammation around your optic nerve. You remember what that does?"

"'My eyes! My eyes! They're doing it!'"

"Glad you remember a classic *Friends* line, Miss Sarcastic."

Jan ran me through an entire physical, asked my name, who was the president, and our location. Since I'd fabricated my life after the coma, I plopped a little distraction her way by reciting the Gettysburg Address.

She stopped me, gripping my hand. "Okay, okay."

"When does my eyesight come back?"

Jan owned several tells, unconscious physical giveaways to her psychological status, including some that showed when she was lying. She had one she didn't recognize—her inescapable scrape of fingernails across the earpiece of her stethoscope. "Probably tomorrow."

"You can't spring me today? I don't have insurance."

"Hello, you realize you have at least one, maybe two concussions? We'll look at what the MRI says. You can't see, we don't know why, and you're worried about insurance? Hon, I checked. You must have a sugar daddy because someone has arranged to pay your bill in full. There's a luxurious private room upstairs."

"What? By whom?"

"Girl, take that little miracle and thank whoever provided for you."

Someone was buying me off, or—? Another slice of panic slipped through a crack in my mind. A secluded room was a perfect spot for Jerry to slide in and commit a crime. Like murder. My own, in particular.

Jan said, "I'll give you something for those bruised ribs, but no narcotics. You have a few healed fractures and several scars on your back. Anything you want to share?"

"Not now." Misery, courtesy of Jerry, one of the many signs which shouted the outstandingly detestable life I'd lived.

"Something worth prying into later. Those abrasions will sting, but they should heal fine. You allergic to anything?"

"Falling into ditches and losing my sight, yeah. Pretty high on my list." I remembered Some Guy. "What happened to the man, is he okay?"

"Huh? No one else came through. He must have fared better than you. I'll check in with you in a while." She squeezed my arm.

Footfalls moved away. No more jokes, nobody to help. My eyes welled with tears when she left.

Jerry. I'd never see him coming.

THURSDAY AFTERNOON AFTER THE TUMBLE

I fell asleep not long after my tests and awoke in silence. Sight returned in inches. Incomplete, but coming back.

Nurses had positioned bars on the hospital bed, allowing

me to lug myself into a sitting position, but the process of sitting up caused pain. Those ribs burned. I turned my face toward a red fuzzy blob close by, and a chair nearby scraped the floor and made me jump and grasp my side.

"Who's there?"

"Me, Jules. Cade, how many fingers have I got?"

"Ten, last count." What hovered over the table intrigued me. "What's on the counter?"

"It's a rose. Came with a card. I read it in case you died or something, ha, ha. It says, '*To the best CPR instructor ever. If you need help, dial 9-1-1.*' Signed, *Anonymous.*"

I blew a raspberry in her direction. "That makes no sense."

Snippets rushed back as the flower fuzzed in and out. Heat swept across my cheeks. Oh, no, it was a dream. Right? Was it CPR, or did I kiss Some Guy? I remembered picturing myself kissing the pesky detective. If Jules thought I kissed a stranger like that, she'd send me to the psych ward.

"The nurses say you can have coffee. Want a cup of decaf?"

"Sure, thanks. Jules? Am I really in a private room?"

"Yep. I'll leave the door open. Be back soon."

Grateful for the quiet, I lowered my head against the pillow and put my hand over my eyes. "I'm so scared."

A knock on the door startled me.

"Hey, it's me."

"Calhoun."

"Don't be afraid," he whispered. "It's just me."

He'd heard every word I said. *How embarrassing.* "How did you find out I was here?"

He wiped away my tears. "Through the grapevine."

"Yeah, the whole mishap was weird. Thank you for coming to check on me."

"Of course. You okay?" He drew a gentle thumb across my cheek. "You don't sound like the cranky Catherine Cade I know."

"I now have two concussions. Could be a short-term personality change. Don't get used to it."

"Do you recall anything?"

Like I'd tell him I kissed a random stranger in a ditch. "You sound like a cop."

"Rumors. How do they get started? Hear tell you saved someone's life. Pretty heroic for a con. Catherine the Great has a heart after all. You're positive you don't remember anything?" He tickled my nose.

"It's a blank—hey, stop." I grasped his fingers and pressed them to my lips, then released them, mortified. *Oh, Calhoun—I have a heart, one wounded beyond repair. How do I tell you my trust tank is dry?*

He wrapped his rough hand around mine. This from a man who used his electricity bill as intimidation.

Rick said, "Tell me what you see."

"Light and colors. Think my vision is coming back but taking its time. Hey, can you do me a favor?" I dragged my hands from his.

"Sure."

He pulled a chair close. Oddly, the heart monitor wasn't working right. It beeped like crazy. Someone needed to tell the nurses to unplug the out-of-order machine.

I felt a fidget coming on, so I asked, "Are your sunglasses handy?"

"Yeah."

His weight shifted, and his scent came close, clean and personal. His hand brushed my cheek as he put his glasses on my face, and I closed my eyes, inhaling his touch like much-needed oxygen.

I tipped my chin. "Ready?"

"Always."

My head weaved from one side to the other as I sang my best Stevie Wonder impression. Caused me to giggle, and it hurt my side, but things needed to lighten up. A sightless future was a liability.

After a moment he said, "Very amusing. You know, though, the nurses should re-dress you."

"Am I bleeding?" I quickly checked my bandages for the moisture of blood.

"They put your gown on backward." He tugged at the garment.

If a bright light shone on me, I'd be tanning my tonsils. "You lech—I'm blind and helpless, and now you tell me my

86

gown is open." I grasped at it and found it was on just fine, and my face heated. "You're a horrible person."

"Payback for pinching my credit card. I recommend you keep your day job, 'cause Stevie Wonder would sue you for what you did to his song."

Day job. "How's the case coming?"

"What case?"

I put my hand out, found his shirt, and brought him close enough to bump noses. "Don't think I don't know what you're playing at."

"If you must know, I'm stuck doing your cold cases. Anything shared is between us, because, blind or not, one word and your behind's in jail."

Wonder what he'd say about my recounting everything to Jules. "So? Facts, please."

"Checking leads, interviews."

"Fruit of the poisonous tree. Careful there. You might find them inadmissible in court without having a proper warrant. Fourth Amendment."

"You applying for citizenship?"

"Reading the criminal justice books you expect me to learn. I was up 'til almost two a.m."

"That was quick. Heal up fast. I need you to work."

"Hey, someone paid my hospital bill, and that's weird. Can you find who?"

"I did. Like I said, you need to start working."

"I don't know what to say." *Who does that*? "Thank you, and as soon as they spring me, I'm all yours." A coughing fit overtook me, and grabbing my bruised-up side, I choked out, "Figuratively speaking."

Jules's scratchy voice caused me to turn my head. "Hey, you're Detective Calhoun, aren't you? I'm Jules Fergison."

"Nice to meet you. Cade here tell you about the accident?"

"The car and all, yeah."

I held my breath. She knew too much.

"Didn't bring enough coffee. Let me run and fetch another cup."

"I'm leaving, but thanks."

"No problem. I'm on my way." Jules's voice disappeared.

He shuffled from the bedside and grasped my fingers. "Going to work, but I'll see you later." He pressed his lips to my forehead and left.

Well. Holy chipotle.

Calhoun returned to the police station and at his computer, plugged in the thumb drive and retrieved his notes, viewed the pictures Cade snapped of Thompson's murder.

Thank you, Lord, for my little con artist. Even though she's not technically mine. Or anyone's. She was the complete opposite of Melanie. He chuckled at the thought. Calhoun viewed the corkboard she'd constructed, complete with her own surveillance. Impressive.

There were a lot of interviews to be done. He puffed a slow sigh.

She was perfect.

CHAPTER 15

Morning! I sat upright in bed. If not for my discomfort, I would have forgotten why I was there. The blur dissipated, and my sight had returned. Bit my lip. Everything in living color left me ecstatic and speechless.

Jan delivered the news after more imaging. Turned out my tests were perfect. Still no swelling on my brain since the first MRI. No residual visual fuzziness, and the hospitalist, clueless why I'd quit breathing, released me.

Jules drove me home while pontificating about my hurling myself in front of cars. I kept my mouth shut. She smoked like a chimney. I'd rather stick a needle in my eye on purpose than lecture her on her smoking. The view from the passenger side distracted me from her hectoring.

Having eyesight was outstanding, amazing, and not to be too repetitive, awesome. I turned my head to see the cascading waters of Whiskey River. I never claimed to be the outdoorsy type, but I'd kayaked part of this monster. It sparkled with placid diamonds in some areas, while mountains hugged its violent whitewater elsewhere. The highway ran parallel to the river's passage, a furious journey through the valley from its source in the icy blue of Crater Lake, winding through endless forests, pouring at last into the Pacific Ocean.

Not a short excursion, but worth every splash, as far as one could kayak. I lifted my eyes. Three towering ranges vied for the river's affections—the Cascades, the Sierras, and the Siskiyou Mountains.

They rounded the valley, an impressive span of snow-covered protection in each direction. Massive crags with thousands of pine trees, topped with the icing of snow, pushed against the purest blue sky imaginable. The townsfolk lived with capricious mountain weather. Rain, hail, and snow, occurring on the whim of the crags jagging the horizon. And killer heat in the summer. I should know.

Of all the worn-out cities I'd established as a short-term abode, Whiskey River in its God-given simplicity with its farms and ranches was heaven.

Jules dropped me off with a hug and a stern "take it easy."

"Thanks, Jules. You're the best." She really was, and as I waved her off, I figured soon I should tell her more about me. Maybe.

I pushed the door open and dropped the plastic baggie of hospital goodies, opened the windows, and made some limeade, and added sugar for a drink I called "cactus juice."

There was a knock on the door, and inspection through the window revealed a young blonde woman, a bit taller than me. I opened the door cautiously and asked, "How can I help you?"

The woman had a whimsical air about her and thrust her hand my way. "Hi, I'm Kim Pierson from, well, from the morgue."

"I knew I'd been in the hospital, but I'd no idea I was this bad off." I ushered her to my living room. "Sorry, I just came from the hospital. Minor car accident."

"Oh, I'm so sorry. You're okay?"

"Yes, I am, thank you." Interesting patient care follow-up.

"I know you're a forensic nurse practitioner, and I was wondering if you'd be interested in working in that capacity?"

I took a breath. "I'm not a sexual assault nurse examiner. I'm sorry, I work in a clinic."

The blonde, mop-headed woman shook her head. "It's a different type of program. A pilot program for a once-a-week volunteer in assisting with crime scenes and autopsies."

"Nice. Can I think about it, Kim?"

"There's a lot more information." She handed me a card with her number. "Maybe we can grab coffee and talk about it soon. It's an awesome place to work."

I wondered how many times she said, "I see dead people."

"I'd like that, Kim. Let me call you when I get a chance."

I must have looked like a disaster, but Kim was gracious enough to not say, or she was on a mission. Something I definitely would share with Calhoun.

But, behind a day on the bakery, needing to sand rough spots, I showered and scrubbed my face. Still in pain, I winced as I changed clothes. More than work, I wanted Calhoun to update me on Thompson's murder.

The GMC kicked out earth as I drove off, yet a small inner voice kept whispering an annoying but persistent premonition, forewarning me. *Go back! Things are going to fall apart.*

Every bump along the way made my pulse speed and my ribs ache more, but my bakeshop called. Calhoun's hassling worried me. Soon I'd leave Dr. Riley and the clinic, and the doughnut store I had only just started. If he interfered, my backup plan to run would come sooner.

The bakery, my next identity project, became my jumping-off point to hop out of town again. I couldn't count how many names I designed and résumés I built just in case I had to run. With meticulous dedication to each new skill, new character, I left nothing to chance, and I crafted each backstory with precision.

Alea iacta est. The die is cast. The fake PhD would melt away, and Catherine Cade would be a memory. My next personality and job would militantly end any joy I'd experienced here. I'd vanish to some ubiquitous, blank town to stay out of Jerry's sights. I knew I'd never forget Rick Calhoun. But with tightfisted confidence, I knew he'd forget me.

No matter, because I kept my IDs, passports, money, and plans tucked away. I mapped out my life, planned to the detail. Portland, my next stop, offered vast jobs for pastry chef positions. I never stayed in one town for long and changed my identity often. Except for Catherine Cade. Three years was forever wearing one moniker.

But lots of work awaited, and despite my slight sensitivity to coffee, I needed a real cup of Joe. I stopped at one of the hundreds of cafe kiosks in town and ordered a nine-eleven, six shots of espresso in one cup. Extra chocolate, please. I sucked the caffeinated jet fuel down before reaching the city limits. The probability of me being awake for days increased exponentially with each shot of high-octane java.

Did the wife do it? Calhoun's investigation led somewhere, and the old board game, *Clue*, came to mind. The coffee gave me a buzz. The gardener did it with the flowerpot in the kitchen.

I tempered my silliness because the equipment would be on its way. *Focus.* The bakery needed tender loving care, and scooping ample space to complete each stage meant working double-time.

A multitude of cars at the shop freaked me out. I jumped from the truck and found Jules. The espresso kicked in a hundred percent, and my eyes flew open. I talked faster than a country auctioneer. "What's going on, Jules? Are you okay? What are you doing? I don't understand. Who's scrubbing the floor? Who are those people? What are Calhoun and Mike doing? Who's she? How'd you—"

She gripped my elbow and dragged me to a chair. "Did you drink caffeine?"

"A little. A nine-eleven."

She clapped a hand to her head. "Have you lost your mind? Calhoun found my number and said you'd be behind schedule. He made a few calls and brought these folks from his church." She patted my cheek and whispered, "I'd give him a big old thank-you before you pass out."

Sweat trickled as I stood, sat, stood again, and paced.

Calhoun trudged my way. "Are you okay?" He turned to Jules. "Is she on something?"

"She drank a nine-eleven."

"A what?" he asked. Calhoun reached a hand out to check my eyes, and I batted it away.

Doesn't everyone know what a "nine-eleven" is around here?

"Six shots of espresso with a pound of sugar, I swear—for someone who can't tolerate caffeine," Jules huffed. "I can promise you, Detective, the outcome will, at the least, be interesting."

"What are you talking about? I have things to do. Calhoun, I have this—why do you keep pushin' me around? You're bossy. I can handle this without help. You have your head—"

Jules clapped a hand over my mouth.

Calhoun stood with jaw agape. "Cade, you're wound tighter than an eight-day clock."

Jules said, "I'm at a loss, Detective. Six shots of espresso can give a horse a heart attack. It'll wear off soon. I hope. Catherine is hypersensitive to everything—coffee, sugar, you name it. ... She can drink decaf. That's her limit. I promise, she doesn't mean what she's saying."

Jules kept a tight clamp over my mouth. My eyes didn't waver from Calhoun's, and I shook my head *no, it won't wear off*, and bobbed my head, as in, *yes, I meant every word I said.*

She checked my pulse and released me. "Your heart rate is fast. How did you think this would help?"

I dunno.

Calhoun supplied me with a scrub brush and a bottle of spray. "Should she go to the hospital?"

"No, but if I yell, I'll have changed my mind."

"Okay." He turned and toyed with my hair. "You. Stay."

Sweat on my forehead threatened to cloud my vision as I wiped it away. He pushed me to a corner and ordered me to sit, and I scrubbed the same circle at least seventeen million times. I lost count as time passed.

Rick came and knelt by me, placed his hands on mine to stop my incessant circles with the brush. "Anything I can do for you?"

"Hey, Detective. Did anyone ever tell you how cute you are?"

Crow's feet gathered at the corner of his eyes. "You're not so bad, yourself, Short Stack."

"Guess what? A young woman with very large ... a very large offer came to my door. Wants me to work forensics with her."

Rick coughed into his hand. "Really?"

I giggled.

"A little work in the morgue might not be a bad idea," he said.

I drew a finger along his cheek because his dimples were glorious, then leaned into him with a conspiratorial whisper. "Was it the gardener with the flowerpot?"

93

"Excuse me?"

"In the garden—you know, Thompson. Was it the gardener?"

"Cade, you sure you had coffee, not alcohol?"

What an adorable man.

The cappuccino wore off, and my fingers ran over my work as I slumped into the corner. I gathered my legs to my chest and rested my elbows on my knees. *I'm such an idiot.* Bad enough my left side ached and burned. Now my right arm came in a close second. The sugar dump pushed me over the caffeine cliff. My eyes fluttered closed. *How dumb. Thompson's gardener wouldn't knock him off.*

CHAPTER 16

A headache roused me, and a groan escaped my lips. I stumbled to the mirror, confirming my fears. I looked how I felt. Espresso overdose. Eyes bloodshot, with hair so catawampus, a brush could get lost finding its way through. Chickens fared better in a pickup truck at high speed than I did after six espresso shots.

I staggered through the living room straight to the window. No truck. "What'd I do, walk home?"

"Nope. I brought you back."

If it was physiologically possible to jump out of one's skin, I would have. Instead, I spun around, knocked over a plant along with its stand, and reached for my pistol. Gone.

"Calhoun—what the heck?"

"And you're welcome."

"But why you?" My favorite blackmailer relaxed on the couch with a magazine in his lap.

"You passed out. I brought you home."

"Where is it? I had been armed," I said, patting my side again. Did I miss it the first time?

"In your caffeine-induced crazy time, you didn't need a loaded gun. I have it."

I frowned. "Well, I want it back."

"No, you look like you want to shoot me."

He seemed too comfortable with his hands laced together behind his head, a smug grin crossing his face.

"You can't disarm me. Second Amendment, I'm sure you've heard of it. I'll just take it from you."

He lowered his cannons-for-arms. "You think?"

I squinted at him. I couldn't take him on, at least before java. He was too big. "I need real coffee. Lots and lots of coffee." I stopped on my way to the bathroom. "You stayed at my house all night?"

"Jules did. I went back and worked until—" He turned his wrist and checked the time. "An hour ago. Your truck is at the bakery, and I didn't want you to wake up with a heart attack since it's not here. I need you non-comatose, because some of us work for a living."

"Your whole church was at the bakery all night?"

He yawned and was too slow to cover his mouth. "No, just me. Most of the church folks left around ten p.m. Jules gave me instructions and keys."

Who does that? I said, "Huh. Christians might not be horrible people. Unless there's a catch. Like blackmail. But thank you. Let me shower." I yawned, circled toward my room, and listened to mumbled protestations. I grabbed clean clothes from the closet, ambled back to the bathroom, and let hot water flow over me.

Out of the shower, the mirror reflected an ample friends-with-the enemy grin. Calhoun. My expression dissipated. I willed my face into "uneasy" to stare back at me. He blackmailed me, didn't deny it, and dared me to take it to the police department. Saved my life, fixed my truck, helped me at the bakery, kissed my forehead—and attended church. I didn't know a soul like him. There had to be a catch.

My arm ached. What did I accomplish at the bakery? A big fat nothing while he worked at it all night.

With curls tamed and a smattering of makeup, I was presentable.

Once out of the bathroom, I caught the aroma of bacon. It coaxed me into the kitchen faster than the commercial for doggie treats. What an indulgence. Maplewood-smoked bacon hissed with a pop and spit in a frying pan.

Rick tended three pans on the stove, one with bacon, one with pancakes, and the last, with perfect, over-easy eggs. And something was baking in the oven.

Not wanting to help with this breakfast feat, I leaned against the entrance to the kitchen and talked.

"I thought you said you couldn't cook."

The toast popped up, and he caught both slices midair.

"In a nutshell, besides the military, I was a short-order cook. And roughneck, logger, and firefighter. My childhood dreams. Before the academy."

"Huh." I knew a practiced response when I heard one, and he'd handed me five on a verbal lazy Susan.

He flipped the pancakes in the air, caught them with the skillet, and slipped them onto a plate.

"Benihana, I'm impressed. Did you find out who took the evidence on Thompson's murder from the police department?"

"Not yet. Your work has been thorough and helpful. So hurry through training because I changed my mind. You'll be working with me on this murder."

I pushed from the doorjamb. "Really? When's the test?"

"As soon as you're done."

"I am so on it." I paused. "Look at you, a talented cook."

"I aim to please. Might want to hold the compliments 'til you try it." His eyes sparkled.

Across the kitchen, the coffee pot gurgled, spitting out a light, tea-colored brew. I ambled my way to the counter to suss out the problem. Only a tease of hot Joe wafted. "What is this?"

"Watered-down jet fuel. Enough to keep you from getting a migraine. You're not safe with caffeine. Who has a sensitivity to coffee?" He paused. "What's the gardener have to do with Thompson? You babbled like an idiot before you passed out."

"I don't remember." Liquid splashed in my cup. "Is this tea? What are you, British?"

"Do you see crumpets? Say thank you and enjoy your meal."

"Thank you." I sat at the table, made a face, and sipped *faux* café. I bowed my head in a quick "Thanks, God," not even sure why. In truth, I'd had a bellyful of the cosmos's emotional wood chipper.

The turmoil while he cooked calmed as we ate smoked bacon, eggs, toast, and pancakes. He stood when the oven timer dinged.

"I haven't had flapjacks, bacon, and eggs—"

After he piled homemade hash browns on my plate, he asked, "Want a biscuit and gravy?"

I felt my eyes open wide. "Oh, absolutely. I need an extra

twenty pounds. I've always wanted to see my house sawed in half while the Jaws of Life pried me from my chair."

A dimple appeared on his face with the smallest of grins. He poured country-style gravy over a biscuit. His eyes met mine.

"This is to-die-for good. You've added sage." Homemade sausage made with fennel seed, garlic, and nutmeg tantalized my taste buds, as well. In under twenty-four hours, he'd saved my bakery, brought me home safely, and cooked a breakfast fit for a princess. *So maybe this whole Christian thing wasn't an act.*

"Tell me about your coma."

And there it was.

The catch.

The fork fell from my hand, clattered on the plate, and bounced to the floor. One sadistic person—Jerry— understood my history, took advantage, and made me run for my life. Angry, and with fist curled, I pounded it on the table.

"How could you know about me? Was it you or Jerry who had someone try to run me down?"

Calhoun had my gun, my fork had fallen on the floor, and all I had was a slice of bacon with which to threaten him.

He stopped chewing. "That the name of your ex?"

Jerry's name brought sweat to my forehead. "Please don't talk about him. Saying his name might summon him. He makes the devil look like Saint Theresa."

"I'm sorry."

I crossed my legs and changed the subject. "How can you eat so much? How do you not gain weight?"

He raised a fork in the air. "That reminds me. The Chief wants me to get you trained, so you can defend yourself."

"From what, paper cuts? I run five miles a day. And I take kickboxing, you know."

"That's nice. You'll work on the cold cases in the bullpen in your spare time. I know you have two jobs, but you're not a free woman, not yet."

I hung my head. "I hate you."

"The bullpen is the office. Suspects aren't at the station because they're sweethearts. Since your tumble, we'll start with walking. Think you can manage?"

"No time to recuperate?" I asked.

"From a tumble? Suck it up, cupcake."

"I can run, thank you. You can keep your notes here, and I can go over them on my own."

"No." He jabbed a finger my way. "I don't want you anywhere near that investigation, not yet. You get cold cases, and not at home. Too dangerous for your own good."

"Pshaw. Danger is my middle name. I can handle myself."

"No, you can't."

"What makes you—?"

"You're a civilian. Plus, you're a crook."

"You keep throwing my past in my face."

Calhoun apologized, and we cleaned the breakfast mess. I made a few more comments on his coffee as he opened the door.

He stopped. "I forgot. Need your prints on file."

"Prints? What do you mean?" My voice caught in my throat.

"Fingerprints. Run them through identification classification. It's part of the background check."

A police department printing me would put my fingerprints through IAFIS, and Jerry would find me. The biggest mistake I'd made was getting a concealed carry permit in another state. Never having been printed before, I didn't think it would matter. I paid for that blunder because without knowing it, the FBI had a corrupt cop on their dole, and a warrant later, I was in Jerry's sick world again.

Calhoun's eyes locked onto mine.

My knees weakened. I had a plan. I always had a plan. My plans kept me alive. I knew I should have ditched Calhoun when I had the chance. But no, I didn't think beyond the handsome detective, and now look—I had walked right into a trap.

Rick seemed concerned, and his mouth parted. Why? Panicking was my job. Was this a panic attack? This wasn't like my usual relative calm panic.

I choked out words in whispers. "I can't—I can't. You can't fingerprint me."

Behind him through the open door, the wind churned, and I watched as a swirl of desiccated leaves swept into the wind as the whirligig spat them out. I struggled in his grip.

"Take a breath. Breathe. Deep breath." He closed the door and led me back to the couch.

"Please. Please." My hands pressed against him.

"Talk to me."

I'd promised myself to never cry in front of a man. Calhoun's gentleness and concern blew my rule. My tears gave way, and I melted into him. Rick held my head and ran his fingers through my hair.

"All I want is a normal life."

"Hey, it's okay. Let me in, Cade."

Never.

Breathless, I said, "I need to go."

"I'll help—"

"You don't understand. If you can find me, he can. If you print me, I'll be dead. I'll pack and go today."

He held me so I had to look straight at him. "No. You face it here, whatever happened, you face it here. Hear me? You have me, always."

As much as I wanted to believe in his always, it was impossible. Kindness wasn't natural. For certain, not forever.

On autopilot, I uttered familiar words. "A new car, new name, new town."

He captured my face again. "Hey—you will live a normal life, an extraordinary life, understand? I'll help you. I promise—" He fixed his eyes on me. "What?"

"You're squishing my face." My mouth puckered like a pufferfish, and the words became distorted, like *faysh*, not face.

He released me and kissed my forehead. "Now nod your head if you believe me. You will live a normal life."

No such thing existed. Not since—

The coma.

He hooked an arm around me and drew me into his lap, held me tight. Encircled by his arms, his confidence, and the quiet comfort he gave, I fell to pieces within his compassion.

At least he'd try to help. Funny, the desire to hate the man who blackmailed me disappeared. I didn't deserve his kindness. He rubbed my back, and I calmed.

I extricated myself and stepped into the bathroom while the miserable mirror revealed a Rudolph nose, puffy eyes, and swelling that would rival an allergic reaction worthy of an antihistamine. How pathetic. I sobbed into a man's shoulder for the second time in as many days.

We bundled into his car, and he drove me to the bakery, tapping his fingertips on the steering wheel, silent and pensive. A muscle tic in his jaw pulsed.

My stomach churned in the silence. He'd made a mistake. I was too much of a liability. He'd seen the real crazy, and who would want to deal with that?

CHAPTER 17

RICK CALHOUN

The police station doors swung open with a thwack as Calhoun slapped his palms on them. He breezed through and let them self-close.

Calhoun strode past Zoe and Mike and opened Chief Dumont's worn wooden office door without knocking. After he entered and closed the door, he leaned against it.

Dumont looked up and yanked off his glasses. "Someday, I'm going to have you recite my rules. Why do you always barge in without knocking? And you haven't changed your clothes. Looks like someone knocked you out, stuffed you into overalls, then ran over you with a tractor, son."

Calhoun grabbed a chair. "What's the book about?"

Dumont's forehead wrinkled. "What book?"

"*Sex Detective.* Is it a true story?"

"You bought it. You read it."

"No time, Greg, I'm serious. I need the recap."

Dumont drummed his fingers. "A female FBI agent back East stumbled onto human trafficking, drugs, and prostitution, murder for hire, you name it. Within another agent's circle of informants."

"What happened?"

"She wrote the book, and not long after its publication, she went missing. Why do you need to know this minute?"

Calhoun put a thumb and forefinger to his eyes. "I don't know yet."

"What's got you so wound up?"

"I'll tell you when I figure it out."

"I don't like surprises." Dumont gave him a long look. "Don't make it too late."

Rick closed Dumont's door, walked to his desk, and stewed. Catherine hid behind her Stevie Wonder impression, her insults, and her jokes. As clear as the sky was blue, she wanted no one to discover who she'd become, because she herself had no clue. He grasped the baseball from his desk and twirled it on his fingertips. He stopped as a thought struck him. *What if she had planned every crime after she escaped to save her skin from something worse?*

He sat before the computer screen, brooding. She had her act down like a slick preacher who ironed his Bible, trying to distract with her sarcasm and humor. The pretense should have been obvious. And he didn't want to see it. Then she'd plain unraveled on him. He sat back in his chair and rested a finger across his lip. Now he'd dig into her past with a renewed sense of urgency.

He trusted Amy, his partner of twelve years in a distinct and parallel career. Dodging bullets, avoiding plagues in Karachi, and giving her hand in marriage to Sam—all of this couldn't separate them from their work. Not since—not since Melanie.

With cellphone in hand, he stepped into the hall. He'd tell her what she'd need to track Cade's history. Ames would figure it out sooner or later.

"Amy, it's me. I found this woman—"

"Morning to you, too, Rick. Wait, did I hear you right? You found a woman? Hang on, gotta grab my calendar. Talk to me."

"She's a runner. Con artist. Her past has been tough. She's petrified of some man, maybe an ex, and won't—or can't—go to the police."

"This is a story I'll want to hear. What do you need from me?"

"I can't go through the usual channels. I need a back window, something no one can trace." He pinched the bridge of his nose.

"Tell me why, and I'll consider it. Talk."

Rick leaned against the hallway wall and told Amy the story. "When I mentioned fingerprinting, she came apart. I think her ex-partner is FBI, or at least someone who has access to IAFIS. Might even be somebody in our organization."

She whistled. "Not good. Have you contacted Olivia?"

"I haven't been able to reach her in the last month."

"She goes on silent mode when she's planning another job for us, and when she's in contact with her connections."

"I hope it's not another one. Repeated vacations get tough to explain."

"Agreed. Back to this woman. What else?"

"She goes by Catherine Cade." He listed three other aliases and her other Social Security numbers, all stolen. "I have the first name of her supposed ex, Jerry. With her fear of being printed, he may be a cop or in the military. Maybe even an agent or an informant."

"There's no way. Jerry might not even be his real name."

"I'll see if I can find out his full name from her. I assumed he's an ex, but there's no paper trail to prove it." Blessing in disguise. He pushed away from the wall and paced the hall. "She talks in her sleep—"

"Uh-huh."

He paused. "Cade was in a coma at some point in the past, but I don't know the details. Her friend stayed overnight with her and said she talked in her sleep, but nothing intelligible."

Amy asked, "Stats? Be the witness for me, Calhoun."

Calhoun rubbed his head and walked to the stoop where he first found her outside the police department. "Thirty-five, five-four, maybe one hundred twenty-five pounds. Long brown hair." Rick closed his eyes. "More like, chestnut-colored, waist-length hair, with a slight curl, high cheekbones, and full lips. Her nose is a bit crooked, and she has fine scars from well-healed plastic surgery. She's sarcastic. Trying to talk to her is like climbing over a barbed-wire fence in boxers."

"I see." Amy coughed. "Eye color?"

"Chocolate."

"Chocolate? Are we talking Turkish espresso with a splash of cream, milk chocolate, dark chocolate, or Belgian chocolate?"

"Shut up, Ames. Light brown with hazel when she's in the light. Darker, smoky when she gets mad, and don't even get me started about espresso." He turned and drifted back down toward his office door, one quiet step at a time. "Unforgettable dimples when she smiles. Her financials are hard to pinpoint. She works out at the YMCA, and I wasn't sure if she was meeting someone there. Since she's a suspect in an investigation, I followed and found her rock climbing and taking self-defense. Goes to the range on the weekends. She's in good shape."

"Um, do you have her measurements?"

"Amy!"

A muffled giggle could be heard. "Elemental, my dear. You would never hesitate to give me an estimate for stats. Your gallantry gives you away. You're in love."

"You know how I feel about love."

"Hmm, seems you can't wrap your noggin around romance."

"She's a con artist and a suspect in a homicide investigation. She may belong behind bars. Not much romance there."

"Not how I see it."

His hand curled into a fist. "Really, Amy? How do you see it?"

"You don't want me to go there."

"You mean Melanie." He paced.

"You're not afraid of this woman so much as you're afraid you'll fail her. If you didn't care, you wouldn't be on the phone with me." Amy paused. "You mentioned a coma. Does she have memories before the coma?"

"I don't think so." He paused for the span of a heartbeat. "Not sure I can do this."

"I know you. You're great at what you do, but sabotaging computers *and* relationships are your specialties."

"You and Sam setting me up on a surprise blind date wasn't a relationship, it was subterfuge. I didn't sabotage it, you blindsided me. Cade's a person of interest, no more." Calhoun paused again. "Can you find the information or not?"

After his phone call with Amy, Calhoun returned to the PD's office, closing the doors.

Zoe covered her mouth while regarding Rick, and he scowled. "Why are you giving me the fisheye?"

"No reason, sir." With her back turned to her desk, she shuffled paperwork, suddenly intent on police reports.

"And since when do you call me sir?"

"Since the day I made you get out of bed—" Zoe batted her lashes at Calhoun.

Mike Tanaka's head snapped up. "What?"

"What's wrong with your eyes?" Calhoun moved a hand toward Zoe's face.

"You remember, sir. I called you when Stephen Thompson died." She pushed Calhoun's hand away and smirked.

"Oh." Mike regained his composure.

"Calhoun, why do you still have sawdust all over you? And pardon me for calling it like it is, but you smell like bacon." Zoe glanced at Mike.

"You're a regular laugh track." Calhoun frowned in exasperation. "Don't you two have anything better to do than chinwag?"

Tanaka smiled at Zoe. "Whatever that is, I am sure the answer is no."

"Gossip, Mike." Her eyes flicked back to Calhoun. "Won't happen again, sir." She dropped her gaze as Calhoun appraised them, eyes narrowed.

"And to appease your appetite for gabble," Calhoun said, "I worked at the bakery until five this morning."

Mike's mouth spread into a grin. "Oh, no. There are absolutely no suggestive comments for that kind of dedication."

"Quiet." His old chair scraped along the floor as he dragged it to the worn desk and turned on his computer. Amy had sent the encrypted files to his email. What would she find on Cade?

His stomach roiled, livid with himself because he'd frightened her. All along, he'd treated her like a crook, and he knew better. He dropped his head into his hands. She hadn't been intimidated. She'd been traumatized.

It seemed late when he checked his watch—already seven p.m. The office was empty save him. He closed his work down and left..

Rick rubbed his fingers on the steering wheel, drove home and showered, then climbed back into the car. He passed Cade's house and saw her truck was gone.

Amy had pushed a salty finger into an old wound. He couldn't push Catherine away. He loved her.

CHAPTER 18

Catherine Cade
Saturday a.m.

Gray clouds congregated, shrouded by a misty drizzle. I scanned the street. Gusts of cold air chilled me as September winds poured into town, the same morning of Calhoun's impressive breakfast show—and my breakdown.

He pushed through my emotions like a paper wall. A cruel hunger for his presence accompanied an ache I'd never known and wounded my heart. Wasn't fair.

Thirty whole seconds passed since I'd last checked my watch. The overdue delivery truck left me in a peevish mood. Four minutes after nine a.m. Oh, c'mon, how late could they be? Too excited to stay indoors, I jumped up and down on the sidewalk to keep warm.

A utility truck honked and wheezed its way along Sixth Street with cockeyed headlights. Old funky truck. Must be for me.

I ushered the truck through the alleyway, out of sight of the street, close to the bakery. The men unloaded the ovens first, followed by pans, a commercial mixer, shelves, a large proofing box, and display cases.

Why Calhoun spent all night sanding and varnishing the floor was beyond my ability to grasp, especially when he had to work. I walked through the spotless bakery and pictured the detective singing baritone in church. He needed a huge "thank you" from me for both paying my hospital bill and for all the work on the bakery. Free doughnuts for life.

Somehow the floor survived the incessant scrubbing that had induced the pain of the morning. No more hardened froufrou coffee for me. Almost ruined my bakery. I spent an inordinate amount of time putting things away, rearranging fixtures and fittings and imagining the clatter of shoes, voices over the din, and the aroma of doughnuts. What would be a catchy name? A shallow sigh reminded me I'd leave without a goodbye, and the bittersweet moment lingered. I lost track of time while making a list of the bread, pastries, and other delectables to charm the masses.

Bam!

I jumped and looked at the window. Already dark out, and I hadn't affixed porch lights yet. Whatever had made the noise concealed itself in the darkness. With my SIG at my side, I asked, "Who is it?"

"Your best friend."

Did I want to entertain my blackmailer? Yes. Yes, I did. Like a kid offered a Happy Meal.

"Which one?" I asked.

Pause.

"I'm crushed."

I expected his answer and laughed into my hand.

Light from the bakery's interior spilled over Calhoun after I unlocked and opening the door. He held a pizza box in one hand and a bottle of soda in the other.

"Hey."

"Hey back. Thank you for your work. I didn't expect it."

"I owed you." He stepped in and inspected the finished bakery.

"For what?"

Calhoun scrutinized me as though I'd missed the obvious. "Supper. It looks ready for business. Nice job."

"It wouldn't have been possible without you and your friends. I can't thank you enough."

Calhoun beamed. "Carpentry is a hobby, so it was fun. I called, and you didn't answer. Couldn't find you at the clinic, so I brought food, figuring you'd be here." He lifted the lid to the box. "A giant."

"Guess I got distracted." I peered into the box and inhaled. The fennel seed in the sausage caused my taste buds to want in on this action. "Ooh, Italian sausage, onions, olives, extra cheese. Keep bringing me pizza, and people will think we're married." He parted his lips, and I swallowed air in a great big oops. "What? Did I say something wrong?"

"Maybe I'll be bringin' you pizza more often." The corners of his mouth slid upward as he put dinner on a wagon wheel table and ushered me to sit. "Better way to keep tabs on my volunteer."

Volunteer, my behind. "What do you mean?"

"Never mind."

"If you plan to hound me like this, the least you can do is read me in on what you've found," I said.

"Read you in? Where are you from?"

"That's the sixty-four-thousand-dollar question. Why?"

"Nothing. I can read you in because I need help with interviews."

I grinned and brought out plates, cups, and napkins. "What did you find?"

"Have news." There was an uptick to the corner of his lip.

"Don't tease me. You blackmail me, drag me into a case you refuse to tell me about, and you—"

"Thompson's widow."

"And?" I pulled the biggest slice, laid it on a plate, and set it in front of him. He eyed the slice of pizza as though it was evidence, stuffed half of it in his mouth, chewed with intensity, and licked tomato sauce from each finger with a neurosurgeon's concentration.

"What is wrong with you?" I said. "You're worse than a child."

"She has a ton of money. I'm chasing leads, who owned what and when, but with what she has now, buying this county and the next wouldn't be unfeasible."

"Excellent work, Detective. Motive and opportunity. I'd ask how you managed it, but I'm guessing there's a question of legality." I regarded the tomato sauce on a bite of pizza. "The mess the gun made says a .45 caliber did the job."

"Interesting." Calhoun rested his arm on the table, chin on the palm of his hand. "Because you're correct. The medical examiner found a spent casing at the crime scene. You familiar with the caliber?"

I swallowed. "Not sure. What about prints?"

"Still waiting."

"DNA on his clothes? Stray epithelials? Muddy shoes or particulates?"

He held up a hand. "Listen to you, Miss CSI. Nothing is in the data on prints. What prints the team retrieved, we ran through IAFIS and got no hits. There was a CCTV image of the person at the front door. Looked like someone who knew the place. Too grainy, though. Anything else, I can't tell you. Source is confidential."

Informant.

He stopped chewing as he watched me. "You tensed up fast."

The pizza no longer appealed.

"You afraid of me?" He frowned.

"No." My gaze lowered. Not as long as we kept things to simple blackmail.

"So talk."

I picked at the sausage. Why couldn't he leave me be? Where was my normal poker face? I didn't want to admit I cared about someone other than myself. How—no, why—would Rick Calhoun care for me, beyond blackmail?

Distracted by the tomato sauce on his chin, I stretched my hand to wipe his face with a napkin.

"Since you can't print me, you're stuck with your own cold cases. Sorry."

"You'll know, someday."

Let it go, Calhoun. "My identity? Perhaps we should forget it." With a quick glower, I grabbed my paper plate. I ran to the kitchen. I stopped at the cupboard and banged my forehead against it.

His voice boomed through the empty bakery. "You need to talk to someone."

I stood still, not clear how to slip out of this, and when I turned, he stood behind me.

"Calhoun—" My heart raced. He was both fast and silent.

"You need to trust someone."

I trusted someone before. How'd that turn out? I argued with myself. Would information help him or me?

He waited through my hesitation. Would he understand? Care? Believe me? I blew out a sigh and whispered, staring at the floor. "I'm not sure who I am." I pressed my fingers to my chin to stop its quivering, and his gentle hand touched mine.

"It's okay."

"No, it's not okay." I paused. "You need to know something, anyway. I remember he said there was a car accident. Jerry said he dug me out of our vehicle and brought me to the hospital. I was there in a coma for three weeks. When I came out of it, the doctors told me I'd been in a hit-and-run."

"Catherine," he whispered, giving my arm a gentle squeeze.

My voice quavered, and my eyes closed. "They called me the miracle child, but my current memory is the best the doctors could hope for. I don't even have a birthday."

"Nothing?"

"They call it retrograde amnesia. I only know life after the car accident." I kept my hand over my chin. "Jerry sat with me in the hospital every day. Said we were on a date. A truck sideswiped the car. It hit the passenger side door, crushing me. Jerry gave me a fake name. Said the accident blew our previous IDs. When we left, he promised to train me, and we'd be a team again.

"I've been on the run so long—six years, maybe longer, since the accident. I don't know how I've survived, because he always finds me when I stay too long in one town. He caught me once. Twice were near misses. I think he's sent someone to kill me here—" I teared up and forced the words. "I don't know what's real and what's not. He used me, and if I didn't do the job right—" I grabbed a tissue and blew my nose. "The forensics nurse practitioner job helps me outrun him, but you're right, the degree isn't real. Nothing has been real for years, and escaping him won't last. It never does. He's an informant for the FBI, but I don't know his agent handler's name." Without thinking, I whispered, "I'm a throwaway."

His voice cracked. "Oh, Catherine. Never."

Relief and regret came in a whoosh. "I wish I hadn't told you."

"Shh. C'mere." He embraced me as I fell apart. "We'll find out if he's coming after you. And someday, I'll be there to tell you your real name and birthday."

I was at my worst, with my weaknesses and fears. Holding me close within the safety of his arms, he promised to care.

He offered no empty words, judgment, or shame. I drew on his strength, sustenance to the starving. He cradled my head on his chest.

Aw, crap. I pressed my hands against him, snatched napkins, and dabbed them to my eyes.

"Wanna hear my plan?" His hands, so rough but gentle, rubbed the tears from my face with his thumbs.

"On?"

"Fingerprints."

I scoffed. "I don't have a death wish. If it's all the same to you, I beg you, release me."

"I told you I'd find a way around it." He leaned against the back counter.

"What's it entail?"

"You follow my instructions. Your decision. Let's hope this works."

"Hope? What if it doesn't?"

He lingered on the words. "I have it on good authority prison food sucks."

"Great plan. For you or me?"

"We'd be on the run."

I leaned against the counter. "I can't figure you. Sometimes you're Dudley Do-Right, chasing every lead, uncovering corruption, and other times you're committing felonies. What do you do, for real?"

A hint of mirth touched his face.

"When does this take place?" I asked.

"Monday, but we start on Sunday. The morgue has a Jane Doe about your age."

"Jane Doe? You plan to sub my prints for a Jane Doe? No planning on Friday or Saturday—have you got a screw loose? It takes at least two days to find a body to get viable prints which go nowhere. Find a fresh dead woman. Too long on ice in any morgue and IAFIS may find a match." My eyes widened. "Not that I have the faintest idea ..."

He stilled. "Some mighty interesting leanings you have."

"If you find out, please tell me."

"Fresh body? Viable prints? Sounds like a confession."

CHAPTER 19

Calhoun had told me to dress nicely for the pre-fingerprint-ing-caper rehearsal. I studied my watch and frowned. How did gussying up qualify for body-snatching practice?

I contented myself with a beige skirt, black camisole, and a black tunic draping my midriff. The leaves had turned early in September, but it was October and the nip in the air had made my teeth chatter.

"Dress nice, he says."

Cold Arctic winds tore into the west of the Cascade mountain range, and leaves skittered along the roadside, like red-curled dancers with brown and orange cloaks. We'd have snow if it turned colder. Black ice if our luck didn't last.

Calhoun's dark blue Dodge Charger turned into my drive-way, and exiting the car, he reached the entrance. He sported a tan suit, black tie, and spit-polished shoes.

He held my coat for me and escorted me out the door. Opening the sedan's passenger door, he supported my arm. A noble gesture, old-fashioned.

"Where are we headed?"

Calhoun flashed an unfinished grin. "You'll learn soon enough."

My foot thumped on the floorboard as my house disap-peared behind us.

"Did you ever interview Sarah Thompson?" I asked.

"Yup."

"When?"

"Before the mayor's office squashed the investigation. She never wavered from her story. I left you out until I decided you were harmless."

"Harmless? Go ahead, hurt my feelings." I watched passing cars. "Didn't Thompson's widow get her husband's seat on the board of commissioners?"

"With the help of the mayor. Evil is infiltrating the town, but I'm not done digging. I need to know why."

I changed subjects. "Why did you show up to my office with a hangover?"

His fingers played along the steering wheel. Finally he said, "I didn't."

Maybe I wasn't the only one with a secret.

"Not at all what it looked like to me." I turned my face toward the street again.

"Headache. Big difference." He still tapped the wheel.

Was he nonchalant about drinking? I shifted in the car seat. "Do you have a problem with alcohol?"

"Nope."

"You flirted with me."

"I insulted you."

I agreed with a tip of my head. "You did, and you flirted with *me* because *I* don't flirt. What happened?"

For a moment, his eyes met mine, and I saw sadness. He returned his focus to the road. "Here we are. Follow my lead."

"Spectacular save." I looked up. "Oh, no, you're kidding me. This has nothing to do with fingerprinting."

He opened the passenger door with a gleam of devilry. "Ready?"

I mouthed a *no*. Easier to fingerprint me. A fresh coat of paint gleamed on a white steeple. A hand-carved, deep-brown, myrtle-wood cross hung above the original old brick foundation walls. Black trim framed the white wood above the masonry. The dark brown of the cross against the white of the wood and brick building was stark but striking. Five stained-glass windows graced the length of the church, a stunning sight. I drove by this place every morning to work, but today the building's beauty took my breath away. Whiskey River Community Church.

"C'mon," Calhoun said with a sly yet appealing look.

"What is this, last rites? What happened to the trial run?"

"I said it would help with Monday's strategy." He put his

palm out, offering me gentlemanly help. "It's all part of my perfect plan."

It was a gesture I'd always longed for but had never observed beyond a DVD. A question, an invitation, no pressure. Anticipation in his eyes. My fingers slipped into his palm. His fingers curling around mine. Nervous, I clutched his hand, and was glad when he gave mine a squeeze.

"This is your plan? How does church work into the great print caper?"

"You'll see."

We ducked into the crowd and through the portico, and I looked about the big room. Calhoun must have sensed my confusion, and he whispered the name of each area we walked through, introducing me to the church. I remembered narthex, altar and sanctuary, blotting out the rest. The ceiling was arched, the walls a simple white, and no one had to tell me we were sitting in hand-carved pews.

When we were seated, the music began quietly, and I half-expected a Father Brown-type figure in full cassock but with a big pointy bishop's hat to stand before everyone and say, "Dominoes, fall down."

I was pleasantly surprised the pastor wore human clothes—slacks, shirt, and a tie. He grasped a guitar and welcomed everyone. I was thankful he didn't say, "So who's the heathen in the house?" That would have been awkward. The sermon would have been great if I understood Christianese, which sounded like part Greek and part geek. It all sounded too pat, too programmed.

When the service ended and everyone filed out, I said, "The hymns seem comforting. Even familiar. But the sermon was mumbo jumbo to me."

He leaned against the car. "Do you know if you'll go to heaven?"

I snickered. "Right. Me, a skeptical criminal." I kicked a pebble while he waited. "I assume, stop making wrong decisions. The good should overcome the evil, yada yada." I pushed pebbles around again because I had a record of a lot of bad choices.

"Try this. Suppose you plan a trip to Hawaii. But here's the snag—you have to swim there."

"Sure. Why not?"

"Imagine you and the Olympic swimmer Michael Phelps, along with a ninety-nine-pound weakling, are standing on the waterfront, all fixed to dive in for that twenty-five hundred miles. Who gets there first?"

"Michael Phelps."

"Not twenty-five-hundred miles."

"Yeah, that is a stretch. So we're all doomed."

"Without help, yes. Only God can give you heaven because it's not possible by human effort to get there with good deeds, just like none of you could ever swim to Hawaii, no matter how strong or good you were. We earned death. But he gave us heaven instead. It's called grace."

I squinched. That term was familiar in the religious sense, but it slipped my brain. I peeked up, requiring interpretation.

"We deserve death. Spiritual death, separation from God forever. The Bible says, 'the wages of sin is death.' Instead, he gives us grace—that which we don't deserve. Spiritual life, never separated from his love, for eternity."

"But what's with the cross? A bloody mess and suffering. Wouldn't it be easier to just wave the God-wand?"

"The cross fulfills everything in the Bible. The Old Testament is full of clues to what would happen on the cross—what's known as the prophecy of the Messiah. All you need do is believe that Jesus is Lord, that he was raised from the dead, and call on his name, and you will be freed from your sins. Without cost to you, but at great cost to him."

I shook my head. "See, that part makes no sense. What about children who've never heard of God? Why does he let so many folks die in crashes? Why does he let some people be rich, like really evil people, while good people suffer in poverty? Or what about the ones who are abused, murdered? The sick? The list is endless." Even though I argued, I wanted whatever peace and compassion Calhoun had. Wasn't about to tell him that. But I wanted answers.

He brushed hair from my face. "A lot of questions, there, Short Stack, but are you deflecting right now because I'm talking about you? Or is this the Saint Catherine who gives all to the poor and rescues everyone on her own?"

It was too simple. Nothing in life was free. I could peddle a boxful of jellyfish and call it a child-friendly ocean toy. Anyone who said Calhoun's version of heaven was free was hawking a Ponzi scheme with a facile grin and glad-handing everyone else's money. So what was he trying to sell me with Christianity? Turn me into a robotic Stepford woman?

No, thank you.

CHAPTER 20

Headlights bore twin holes in the morning Monday gloom as I sat in the GMC and waited. Calhoun parked, stepped out of his cruiser, and opened my truck door for me. With frayed nerves, I stood outside the double doors to the hospital, rubbed my arms, and awaited my fate.

Time to run over the agenda again.

"You look as nervous as a stick of butter in a roomful of frying pans."

I snapped, "Because I do this every day."

"You may have in the past, but your life has changed."

"You sucked me into your religious chaos theory. You're right. Being blackmailed by a cop is life-changing."

"*Detective*. So relax. Follow my lead. In there is the morgue, and the man who runs it is Jack McCloud, the medical examiner who is the exemplar of womanizing. If you go in there unattached, he will have you for lunch."

"Great."

We stepped away from the car and strode through the doors.

He seized my shoulders and turned me to face him. "We had a date. In fact, we are dating. Otherwise, Jack McCloud will swear he knows you, and if you're not careful, he'll charm you out of your scrubs before you can blink. He'll use you up and spit you out and won't care about the consequences. If we're a couple, he won't ..." He paused. "... go for the jugular. I hope. Consider church yesterday a date."

"A date? You took me to church for a date?"

"Means I'm not lying." He stuck his hands in his pockets. "It could've been a date. Either way, I'm glad you stayed."

I hugged my red hoodie close and gave him my best withering look. "Who calls going to church a date? You're not right in the head."

"Don't make small talk. We stick to the plan."

I smoothed my hair and walked through the metal double doors to a hallway resembling something from a horror film. Long rows of flickering fluorescent lights lined the corridor. Calhoun pushed open another entry, and I coughed, almost overcome, my nostrils assaulted by bleach. The acrid smells set off shaky memories.

McCloud, who was scrubbing an autopsy table, spotted us. Someone hung gleaming saws, blades, and pans with care on the walls. Readied gurneys, washed and shiny, waited to be bathed in blood.

Oh, Lord, help me.

The overhead fluorescent lights shone, with the surgical lights turned off. Creepy. Familiar, but creepy.

"McCloud, where's Kim?" Calhoun asked.

"She's out getting coffee."

"You have prints on the Jane Doe?"

"Yup." McCloud straightened. Tiny dimples highlighted his cheeks, and with framed perfect teeth, he turned an angled jaw. He was a lech, yet a steamy lech, and a "wow" escaped under my breath. Glad Calhoun had warned me. A hint of ribaldry mixed with debauchery shone from his eyes. I tugged my hoodie closer and stepped behind Calhoun. I resisted the urge to hold on to him.

Calhoun took my hand instead and spoke up. "Run Jane Doe's prints through IAFIS?"

"Yeah." Jack moved closer. "Who's hiding behind you?"

"What did you get?" Calhoun asked.

"No hits." He kept stepping our way. I felt Calhoun stiffen. McCloud was hot, but my gut said he was a malevolent hottie. I slid around Calhoun to hide.

"Who's your gal pal?"

"This is Catherine Cade. She's a nurse practitioner helping at the station. Cold cases."

"Cade." McCloud ignored him. "I know you. We've met somewhere. I didn't know nurse practitioners could work forensics."

"You'd be surprised what I can do." *Oh crap, oh crap.* I meant nothing by it, but even Calhoun gaped at me.

He slipped an arm around me, and Jack's observant eye took it in. "Let Kim know I stopped by," Calhoun said.

He shifted in the tension, and the heat of dislike grew between them until it was oh, so palpable. Jack bit his lip and turned a lecherous eye on me. Calhoun stiffened. "Prints, Jack. All I need."

"So, Catherine. You a cop jockey? Fresh meat for the lonesome detective? Do you get physical training?"

That's when the plan fell apart.

Calhoun's fist took McCloud by surprise. My hands flew to my face in shock, but then I got moving.

Away from the fight, near the refrigerated drawers, I ran my finger over the names and found "Jane Doe." The cold silver-gray table glided out with ease, and I found the print and inkpad paper, and went to work. I wiped sweat from my face, then rolled her dark and cold fingers from one side to another on the fingerprint paper. After wiping the ink away, I slid her steel death bed back to its cold, quiet sleep, with my new identification tucked under my shirt.

The melee over, Calhoun's eyes widened when he saw me.

I said, "Honey, let's get out of here."

"Honey." Jack stood and held a hand to his nose, then rubbed his jaw. His left eye already showed signs of swelling. And still a corner of Jack's mouth spread in a grin, then parted, baring a bloodied mouth.

Calhoun, unscathed, curled a fist. He glared at McCloud, and his expression worried me. *Why did he react with this level of violence?* The tension called for improvising.

I turned to Calhoun and did everything I could to communicate non-verbally, but without success. I stood on my toes, grabbed him, and drew him by the tie. His lips touched mine. He turned, lifting me in his arms, and whisked us out the doors while we kissed. In the periphery of my vision, I caught McCloud's eye as he gawked, drawing an arm across bloodied lips.

Walking out the door in a lip lock didn't belong in my comfort zone. But it didn't end there. Neither of us stopped, nor did we make an attempt to stop.

Oh, no.

"Let go." My voice shook.

"So much for my perfect plan."

My thumb traced his lips. It was *him*. He gave me CPR, and I'd craved that intimacy with the runner, yet with Calhoun in my imagination. He'd written the note and sent the flower. My breath hitched. Calhoun was the runner. But I'd been in a semi-lucid state, neither alert nor able to see. Calhoun, a cop and cognizant, implied responsibility for my well-being.

Fresh meat. McCloud's own words. Enraged, I shoved Calhoun with the palms of my hands.

I yelled, "Why didn't you tell me?"

"What?"

"Don't even—it was you in the ditch." I shoved him again, teeth clenched.

"Wait a sec—what are you talking about? What ditch?"

"When you came to the hospital, you could have told me." Bile surged with my anger, I shoved him again. "What happened to the honest Christian man?"

How could he be so surprised?

He backed away, with palms upward. "The ditch? ... I gave you CPR."

"Oh, as if." I raised a hand to my forehead. "Did you—did you touch me?"

"What the heck? Catherine, no."

"All we've shared are insults and blackmail, and yet, we—" I put my head in my hands. "I trusted you. I told you everything. Don't come near me. Leave me alone."

"Cade—I don't get it!"

"You're a drunk and a liar." Embarrassment, hurt, and anger coursed through me to my fingertips. "You beat the medical examiner to a pulp. You're no different from Jerry. You wonder why I run. You came to the hospital as he did, and you lied."

I threw the print paper with Jane Doe's prints at him. I ran outside, jumped into my truck, and checked my rearview window as he disappeared from view.

RICK CALHOUN

Calhoun sat at his desk, fiddled with his tie, and smoldered. He should have told Cade what happened in the ditch. *If only I'd gone with her in the ambulance, she would have known.* Long before the accidental make-out session while McCloud ogled them. Amy, too.

He'd never found decent dating advice for men his age on SeekIt, and now given Cade's anger, how could he ease her obvious pain without appearing patronizing?

He put his head in his hands and moaned.

"What's wrong? Got hit by a truck?"

"The cold cases, Zoe. Slogging through them is like canoeing in muck. I'd rather be fishing." He pushed back in his chair. Given his constant blundering, it was no wonder Cade hated him.

Mike loosened his tie and studied the crime map, tracking the different colored pins representing various gangs, or a cluster of thefts. He turned and faced Calhoun. "Where's your civi? Thought she'd be here by now. What's her name? You know, my future wife?"

"Catherine Cade."

"Yeah, I remember. Wanted to hear you say it."

Calhoun threw his pen onto the desk. "I'm not sure she wants to commit to working cold cases."

"Odd she changed her mind."

"It happens." Calhoun stood and left the bullpen.

In the hallway, he thumbed his phone.

Amy answered. "Hey, it's my favorite—am I talking to Calhoun?"

"I screwed up." He launched into his story, ended with what happened in the ditch, and Monday morning's fight.

Amy paused. "You're a nincompoop. Regardless of what transpired, she remembers the pain of her past and lies. You betrayed her trust. You lost your temper with one man, McCloud. It cost you Cade. Job well done."

"It's easier with you. Nothing there to mess with my head."

"Our job is hard enough. You were a wreck after Melanie. I guess things haven't changed much."

Calhoun rubbed his eyes. "Thanks for the reminder."

"Humble yourself, and let's find out her identity."

Amy didn't know. Neither did Sam. Even Cade was lost.

"Yeah, I will apologize. Tonight." He walked the length of the hall. *How will I accomplish an apology without also making another wreck of a simple 'I'm sorry'?*

"Not a bad idea. As long as she's not armed." Amy joked.

Cade. She was always armed.

CHAPTER 21

CATHERINE CADE
WEDNESDAY, TWO DAYS LATER

I spent two days avoiding Calhoun on my morning run by changing routes, and I worked off steam at the gym after the clinic closed. Graduated to the "expert" rock wall. The martial arts instructor told me to back off and made me use a punching bag instead of him. Apparently, he didn't appreciate full-contact Cade.

Calhoun called and left messages. I deleted them. Absorbed with final additions on the bakery, I still seethed. He'd withheld the truth. If he'd told me in the hospital, would my reaction have been the same? Truth was, I had suffered embarrassment because of an assumption. Mine.

He inched my history from me, yet all the while he gave me nothing. Oh, he wanted to help, all right. Maybe what he wanted was my criminal history. I put my hands to my head and groaned.

His attack on the medical examiner created a ripple effect in the darkest place of my heart—could he teach me to fight like he did?

I named the bakery the Who Donut. Not sure why. But it became my priority. I dropped hours at the clinic and decided to end them soon, because my plan included full attention to this new fling. I sighed and rounded the tables.

The tables. Now, these old souls had flaws, each with a profound personality. Glass topped the tables, covering rust-colored edging. The tabletops were like old gold miners, sourdoughs toughened with whiskey and weather. These old slabs were like people, each with imperfections and cynicism, each with a grand tale.

I should've left the day he walked into the clinic. The bakery became part of my favorite new identity, now bittersweet because Calhoun had crossed the line. The reason I stayed seemed clear. Thompson's murder investigation. I wanted to know who killed Thompson, where the corruption hailed from, and who'd squashed the truth. Sure, keep selling it to yourself, Cade. I scrubbed circles on the counter harder. *Rick Calhoun.*

The brain's limbic composition housed one's pleasure center—the amygdala—with its memories of both terror and desire. I couldn't deny it. The memory heated my cheeks.

He irritated me. He annoyed me. His explosive anger at the medical examiner frightened me. His gentleness terrified me, and his kiss was a collage of every heady emotion my dreams could conjure.

Why fool myself? Calhoun wouldn't want someone like me. How many times did Jerry's dreadful words dog me? Jerry used to beat me with whatever he found at hand, and painful words always followed. Now, memories of those old words tracked me, an image of disgust in my mirror.

My phone jingled. I checked the number and pressed SILENT. In time, I'd have to either confront him or grab my gear. I'd have to get gone before he came looking.

EVENING

A commercial kitchen specialist arrived at four-thirty in the afternoon to put in a cold room. Dusk fell while I stocked the new refrigerated room with restaurant-supplier foods. As I busied myself with work, sourdough bread bubbled and rose from the starter. I stuffed strawberries with sweetened cream cheese and swirled thin lines of chocolate around each and refrigerated them. In the morning, I'd turn them upside down, and top the stuffed strawberries with powdered sugar. I named them The Mount McLoughlin, replete with swirled chocolate "hiking trails."

Sweet dough for airy, melt-in-your-mouth doughnuts would rise all night. I whipped glaze to warm in the morning to drizzle over the treat. Last, I slipped filo dough into the refrigerator. In the morning there'd be sweet date, honey, and pistachio baklava. And for lunch, yet more filo dough stuffed with mouthwatering onions, spinach, dill, and parsley, and a touch of sauce and feta cheese in *spanakopita*. I surprised myself with how much I'd accomplished and hoped it was right. It wasn't out of the realm of possibility that I might put salt in the doughnuts and sugar in the *spanakopita*. Failure was not an option. But thoughts of Calhoun kept surfacing, and my concentration fled.

I readied to leave, turned off the lights, and climbed into the truck. Tired, I drove my GMC into the muddy driveway on brain-weary automatic. A note on my door distracted me. Tripping over the slick flagstones, I landed square on my tush, then hauled myself upright, snatched the paper from the door, and read the note.

I stacked wood because of the rain. Please call me.
What is an endocrinologist?
—Calhoun.

"SeekIt and ye shall find it." Steam from the cold air poured from my mouth like smoke. Inside, I stoked the fire and crumpled the note and tossed it into the flames.

I didn't want to talk to Calhoun. Later, I'd stand at the counter to search for my ex's whereabouts on my laptop. My PhD gave me near unfathomable access to government information. Inspired hacking opened almost every digital door. Almost.

For now, I wondered and raised my head. Should I? No. I refused to call him. I knew what he and his God would say about forgiveness.

Exhausted and shivering, I showered and changed into clean flannel PJ bottoms and a tee shirt. A robe kept the cold at bay.

I wandered into the living room, thinking about Calhoun.

Fine. Whatever. I'll leave a message. I dialed his phone number.

He picked up on the second ring.

"Hey," he said.

"Hey, back."

"I tried calling."

"Wasn't in the mood."

"Sorry. What is an endocrinologist?"

"It's a doctor who sticks a tube up your end to find your brain." The muffled coughing on the other end of the phone achieved my purpose. "What else?"

"Will you forgive me?"

"I haven't decided." While I shook the water from my hair with one hand, a knock on my entrance rattled my calm. "Someone's at the door. Stay on the phone with me, okay?" Nervous, I brought my SIG to the ready position.

"It's—"

"Quiet."

With the porch light switch flipped on, light flooded the entrance, and I peered through the glass part of the entry.

Calhoun waved.

I raised my phone to my ear. "You tricked me."

"You shushed me before I could tell you. Are you hungry?" He pointed at a bag.

I opened the door. Two days ago, he beat the medical examiner bloody. Now he wanted to play nice?

He came through the entry and headed for my burgeoning galley. "How risqué in PJs."

"Peeping Tom!"

"No, Wu Chen. Best Chinese food around."

"I'm not dressed for company."

"If you'll feel more comfortable, I can take off my shirt. Best offer. Me shirtless, you PJs, food Chinese."

"Really."

Calhoun rummaged through my kitchen cupboards and made a turnabout. "I'm sorry I didn't tell you everything in the hospital. Afraid you'd get the wrong idea. It was stupid."

I took a breath. "It's—"

"Worse, I jumped into that kiss on Monday. Mind you, it was unforgettable, but McCloud riled me when he insulted you. You witnessed my age-old anger with him and his disrespect. I made it worse. I apologize." He rummaged through my cupboards. "Forgive me?"

Unforgettable? Should I ask?

I hesitated a moment. Forgiveness wasn't a concept I understood, but apologies I could comprehend. "I accept your apology for the latter. But I overreacted and didn't believe you. To be honest, I wanted you there."

His face brightened. "You did?"

I leaned against the counter. "At least you know crazy me."

He touched my nose. "Well, crazy's a given."

What could we ever be? Nothing. So like the first day I met him, I stuck out my hand. "Friends?"

He hesitated, pretended to spit in his hand, and grasped mine with a grin. "Friends."

"Ew." I pulled my hand away. "What do you want?"

"Plates. So, I found out who the doctor was that Stephen Thompson saw. Checked online—"

Unsuccessful in holding back a laugh, I set the takeout carriers down.

"What?" he asked.

We walked back to the living room, sat on the couch, and set out the food on the coffee table. I handed him chopsticks.

"Nothing. I gather you found out, yet you still have reasonable cause to come here despite your find."

He shoved the fried rice between us. "I needed to apologize in person. Because, you're my ultimate source."

He grasped my palms and prayed out loud. I watched him, glossing over it as I focused on how my hands tingled, not caused by God or Calhoun. Just warmth from his light grip. Folks at a Chinese restaurant prepared this food and may have lit candles to Buddha or whatever, not God. And I bet they were nicer than Christians.

Afterward, I asked, "Apologies difficult? Orange sauce, please."

"No, women. I mean, different. That kind of difficult. I do everything backward. Can't even—dagnabbit, Cade, I can't talk to women." He pushed the sauce in my direction.

"I think I've been slighted. First, why can you talk to me?"

131

He pointed at me with a glare. "You will not make fun."

"Cross my heart." And I did.

"I may not be a chicken, but I still have some henhouse ways. If everyone's a suspect, or someone I work with, then I'm fine."

"What does that even mean, henhouse?"

He pointed to me, then to himself. "You hen, me rooster. I'm shy. That makes me skittish like a hen."

"I see. Which one am I, suspect or compadre?"

He grasped my free hand. "Cade. I wouldn't share anything with a suspect."

My neck heated. "Thank you for that. Figured I was your confidential informant for eternity."

"Well, that, too."

I shifted in my chair.

Rick said, "I found Stephen Thompson's doctor in Salem. He said some number remained normal. Something, something alpha numeric. A-one-something, maybe."

I crinkled my nose. "A-one-c?"

"Right. He said it measured five-point-two."

"Like you needed my help." I must've made a face because his crow's feet deepened. "His A1c is in the non-diabetic range. It explains why his labs never showed diabetes. He had it under control." I dredged Mar Far chicken in the orange sauce and shoved it into my mouth.

"Didn't you receive reports from his specialist?"

"They don't always send paperwork. Sometimes patients don't share information, and I get nothing. I've seen your notes, crime scene pictures. Those pictures showed—"

He raised a napkin to his mouth. "Thompson stood, but he was six-foot."

"Yeah, so?"

"I measured the phantom outline and the arc height on the wall, expecting about the same. You with me?"

"Yeah. It's when a killer's outline is seen in the pattern on the wall, floor, or wherever."

"Whoever shot him got splattered, leaving an empty outline of the shooter."

Not abnormal findings even for me to understand. "So what's not right?"

"I estimated his height standing at five-foot-five. The blood splatter should have been higher."

I stopped mid-bite. "You think someone helped him up, shot him, and he fell forward? The arterial spurt proved he was upright, more or less. Right? The phantom outline—"

He shook his head. "It's not always exact. At the autopsy, McCloud said the muzzle of the gun was at least seven inches away from Thompson's head."

I said, "Meaning, there was no way anyone was trying to get him to stand."

"He was surprised—"

I pointed at him. "And his reflexes were slow, but he was lucid enough to try to get up on his own."

"Exactly."

"The shooter was a woman."

"Or a short man, like Leo Smart."

"Who?"

"An ambulance chaser. Oh, never mind."

I pushed back in the chair. "And we have no way of proving this even if the case wasn't under wraps."

"Gag order. Not my first rodeo in law enforcement."

We both fell silent and fought over Moo Goo Gai Pan.

"Why does Chinese food always make you hungry again after a half-hour?" I let him have the rest while I brooded. "Who is after her money? Or sending a message? What if someone meant the bullet for her? A gunshot would wake the dead."

He frowned. "Stay on the topic. She denied hearing a shot."

"How do you not realize a gunshot has gone off in your own home?"

"Her soundproof earplugs checked out, meaning nothing."

"Think she witnessed the murder, and the killer is blackmailing her?"

He shook his head and avoided the question. "I hate this case."

"Then here's good news. I finished reading. Ready to put me to work?" My mouth was still full as I spoke.

He blinked. "That was fast. So in the two days you didn't talk to me you continued to study and finished? Huh. Ready for the written test?"

"Quiet. It was interesting. And yes, bring it on." I glanced at the remaining food. "With you here, it's hard to lose weight."

"Who said you needed to?"

"I'm not happy with pleasingly plump because we all know it's a euphemism for fat."

"Your curves are in the right places." His eyes met mine.

I looked at my plate. Chopsticks didn't make my food behave, and I chased the defiant rice around the unfolded Chinese oyster pail.

Calhoun stopped chewing. "Whoever put those kinds of thoughts into your head lied. I have to teach you how to fight dirty, anyway, so if you think you need to work it off, I'd be pleased as an upside-down possum to be of service."

I dropped a chopstick.

CHAPTER 22

Jules couldn't come by, but Kim Pierson did. As we chatted, and as my first customer, she ordered one of everything. She must have planned to feed the town.

Not long after, the bell over the door rang, and Calhoun came toward the counter giving me his signature lopsided smile. He tipped his forefinger in a salute to Kim.

"My second customer. What would you like?"

Calhoun raised his head and appeared thoughtful. "A day's rest from Whiskey River's warring mongrels, a senior nap around two p.m., and a dozen doughnuts. Can you deliver?"

"Senior nap?"

He produced a list.

I unfurled it and laughed. "You're serious? Tall order."

"Growing boy needs all he can get."

"Yeah, I've seen you eat. I'll be right back." I turned on my heel and prepared his order, bagging everything carefully. When I returned, I placed them on the counter and said, "No charge."

He made me ring them up anyway, and paid despite my protestations.

"Okay. Now, Miss Catherine, don't you eat none of those other doughnuts. I'll work you over twice as hard." He shot me a wink, and with three dozen doughnuts, éclairs, bread, and baklava in his grasp, he left.

Kim choked on her cream cheese-filled strawberry. "Did I hear him right?"

"No, you goof, he plans to work out with me. Gutter-brain."

"He has the hots for you. Can't you tell?"

I could dream. Instead, I shook my head.

We talked for an hour, while customers dribbled in. At noon, the door pushed open with a flowing mob, all civil servants, judging from their name tags.

"Kim, make butter. Instructions in the back." I panicked. "Slip the croissants in oven one, and more doughnuts in oven two. Everything is ready to go."

"On it."

Kim finished the chore I gave her. She left after we had a short chat, and I felt she was a kindred spirit. The end of the morning came after prepping for the next day, and I hauled myself to the clinic, but I'd made more money in the half-day at the bakery than in a week with Dr. Riley.

This was Calhoun's doing. I could have kissed him.

THE FOLLOWING MONDAY

In the police station's parking lot, my hands shook. Countless times doctors and cops had dismissed me in the past. How many times did some dirty cop call Jerry to pick me up from a police station, or a doctor phone him from the ER to come "fetch" me? Yet, here I was, at a police station.

With my gym bag in hand, I jumped into an irresistible puddle despite my unease. I splashed up the rain-slicked marble steps which shimmered in the lights overhead. With a groan, I heaved the door open and trudged through the courthouse to the police department.

A lanky woman stood at the counter and spoke on the phone. She raised a finger in the air and said, "Be right with you."

Four scratched-up desks butted against one another. Two stood empty, a third sat littered with paperwork, and the fourth table appeared neat. I peered at the tidy desk that belonged to Calhoun.

Mike Tanaka faced a board, intent on his task. With hands on hips, he evaluated his map. He pinned pictures and scribbled notes on it. My gaze lingered over Mike. Tanaka had a muscular build that appeared almost as impressive as Calhoun's.

"Catherine Cade, correct?" The woman rounded the counter and shook my hand. "I'm the dispatcher, Zoe Carter."

"I've been waiting to meet you. And yup, I'm Cade. Think I saw you at the bakery."

"Surprised you remember. Caffeine affects you?"

"Apparently."

"I'd hate to see you under the influence of alcohol."

"Never tested the theory."

Mike turned and met my eyes. "Hey, look. Cade, my future wife."

"Just ignore him," Zoe said. "Follow me."

Fluorescent lights flickered as we neared the locker room. She pointed. "This here is our little piece of sunshine. Keep in mind, no one stands on feminine delicacy." She strolled around the lockers and handed me a key. "No private spots, so good luck."

"Thanks for the warning."

We walked back through the doors. She jabbed her thumb. "Stairs go up to the gym. We call it the cage."

"You're late." Calhoun stood at the bottom of the steps, the corners of his mouth turned down.

"I just finished writing out prescriptions and making phone calls."

He narrowed his eyes. "First, you have a cold case. C'mon back here." Calhoun moved to an old desk pushed against his. He handed me a case file, cleared off the desk, and pointed me to it.

Faith Harrington. Talk about cold cases. Someone had encased this one in the Jurassic era. I blew dust from the file and leafed through each page. A woman died, a fatal gunshot wound to her head. No theft. Twenty years old, it had sat untouched, gathering dust. The death certificate noted "undetermined." I frowned. More information than Thompson's file. Most women overdosed rather than shoot themselves.

Harrington, a grandmother, died in her home and no real clues existed other than pictures and a rifling report. Engrossed in the file, I didn't hear a thing.

Calhoun lifted my chin and said, "Go change. Time for your workout."

"Sorry, didn't hear you." I went to the locker room, and when I emerged in my shorts and tee shirt, he pulled me by the hand up the stairs.

Punching bags, speed bags, and Filipino fighting sticks caught my eye, and I ran my hands over them. I recognized most of the items from the martial-arts training I'd taken up at the YMCA, almost a year ago.

"Have you ever used those?" Calhoun faced me.

I looked at them again, searching for something in my brain to grab. I glanced at his face. "We've never used them in the classes I've been taking. So, no, I don't think so. At least not that I recall."

"Follow me. Grab two later. Let's get started."

The workout was *torture*.

I tired after one hundred and fifty sit-ups and forty pushups. *Have mercy.* A big improvement since I'd started working out at the YMCA. Instead of the pull ups I'd learned with palms facing, gripping the bars, he instructed me to turn my palms around, holding on like one woud if pushed from a building and hung on the edge for dear life. I managed two. Rock climbing should have strengthened my arms, so what was up with that? Calhoun sputtered as my chin made it past the stupid bar ten more times with his help.

"Shut up."

"Okay, you ready?"

My breath halted. Something was wrong. "For what?"

"Workout." His eyes twinkled. "Limbered up, now?"

"What?" To my dismay, the agony was limbering up. "I need a break. Calhoun, stop making fun."

"Hey, you did fine for a beginner. I'll give you five minutes."

I glared at him, yet thankful that I'd been working out for a year, running and training in martial arts. That had to count for something.

He worked the speed bag and not long after, pointed to his watch.

Filipino fighting sticks came next. I'd seen these at the YMCA martial arts studio but never used them. Calhoun showed me an easy move. "Have fun with this."

"Sure." Instead, I backed into a corner for a moment and held both canes in one hand.

"Catherine Marie Cade, stop screwing around. Get your scrawny behind over here."

The bamboo sticks fell from my hands and hit the floor. In the past, somewhere in my memory, I heard clapping and woo-hoos in a school. Transported back, I executed an aerial cartwheel followed by two successive whip backs—that is, two back flips without touching the ground. I landed in front of Calhoun.

"Stop monkeying around."

"I didn't fall."

"So? I bet Sparky can do that."

Zoe and Detective Mike Tanaka had quietly climbed the stairs to watch, and Mike gave away their position when he yelled, "I heard that."

"Yeah, but I didn't have a clue I could." My socks slid along the gym mat, landing me in unintended splits. "Ow," I whispered.

"Need help?"

"Yeah, please."

He put his hands underneath my arms and hauled me into a standing position.

"I think I tore something vital, like my legs."

"We'll be done soon."

"Not done?" I wanted to go home and ice my thighs. Maybe throw myself into a vat of ice water.

"Not yet, cupcake. Let's work on boxing, and we'll call it quits. Karate gloves are more realistic than boxing gloves."

Boxing would be easy. I positioned the headgear and gloves. He moved fast, and I still landed on my face every time. Discouraged, I rolled onto my back. Boxing was different with a moving object that punched back.

Once again, his eyes invited while he extended his hand. "Graceful one minute, a klutz the next."

"Anyone ever tell you that you have no sense of humor?"

"I'm being a detective."

"Right." I harrumphed. "Right—right. The right side of the brain is creativity, arts, music. You're a genius. The left side is pure logic. Most gymnastics, dance, and music are choreographed."

"Dance? Music? That gives me an idea. What's your preference?"

How would I know?

Calhoun glanced toward the stairs. My cheerleaders were gone.

My cluelessness registered on his face, and he ran the stairs to the bullpen, yelling. "Zoe. You got your CDs?"

Rest. I sprawled out on the floor and hoped for a break. But, no. Moments later, he was on the landing of the stairs, not even winded.

Calhoun plugged in a CD player. "Let's see what we can unlock." He helped me stand and pushed a disk into the CD player. A waltz played.

An unknown woman's voice played in my head.

You are the art. Your partner is the frame.

I would swear the world created this waltz only for us. In his arms, the grace gave me newfound freedom, and I understood the old song: "I could have danced all night ..."

Dumbfounded, I stopped. The cheering section had returned. Despite my hideous shorts and my not-so-slender legs, they whistled.

He walked around me and assessed my legs. "Athlete's legs. Nice muscle mass in your glutes too."

The flush of heat crawled up my neck. My routine workouts helped the muscles but not the embarrassment.

He stepped away and tried another CD. "Professional observation. I'm not gawking."

Zoe yelled out, "Don't believe him, Catherine, he's so checking you out."

I ignored them and tried to remember as the music played, and hummed the melodies as he twirled me around.

"Who composed that?"

"Haydn," I replied without hesitation. "Where did I learn these things?"

"Private schools, heck, maybe even in public school. I learned Latin, played the trumpet in the marching band, and took part in baseball, football, and cross-country running. A year later, I was shooting and cleaning every gun handed me and learned to speak Dari." He caught my confused look. "Like Arabic or Farsi."

"Sounds familiar." An image stuck in my head. "But you took Latin? Like *Animal House*?"

"Funny."

"It's one thing to not know my identity, but now what?"

He changed the CD, and my face warmed again. Latin music. My repertoire included every dance including south of the border.

"I don't salsa or rhumba," he stuttered.

"I do." A lumbering voice came up the stairs, followed by McCloud. Before anyone objected, he'd curled his fingers around mine, and we danced the Brazilian tango. When the song ended, he dipped me backward, then to his chest, our faces close enough for our breath to mingle.

Oh, not good. Mystery and heat rose from Calhoun while steamy assertiveness came from McCloud. These two guys raised the temp to *muy caliente*. Now I appeared as immoral as McCloud.

Everyone clapped and cheered. Calhoun remained silent. Shamed, and convinced I'd receive at least a lecture, I kept my eyes to the floor. When Jerry disapproved, terrifying things had happened.

"Get out, McCloud. Now." Calhoun took a step forward.

There was a defiant tone in McCloud's voice. "Sure, when the lady tells me to go."

I looked up and forced a whisper. "Go. Please go."

"Sure thing, doll." He winked with a lascivious gaze and left.

"Who called him? Zoe? Mike?" Calhoun called out.

Zoe held papers in her hand. "No one. He brought results over and heard music playing."

He yelled at no one in particular, "Does anyone have an idea what he'd do to her? She's McCloud-naïve." His ire was palpable.

I swallowed. My eyes stayed focused on the floor.

Rick lifted my chin. "Hey, it's okay. McCloud can sell a pig to a rabbi."

I said, "Okay," sorry that McCloud had caught Calhoun's wrath, but happy he didn't direct his anger at me, and ashamed because of my relief. The cheering section disappeared. "I know how to dance." I rubbed my head. "Did I go to finishing school?"

"My guess, you attended a swanky private school." He reached for karate gloves. "You've been taking classes, so I want to see this. When a student learns effective defense techniques, it's like a dance. If you can change steps in a waltz, you can master martial arts and street fighting. Let's try some of that kick boxing you're learning."

We donned gloves and face gear. He reached for me, and I kicked. He caught my foot, and I headed back into another set of splits. Instead, he lifted me and threw me onto the ground, face into the mat. Fifteen minutes passed, and not once did I connect with feet or hands. So much for my tough *sensei*. Calhoun was the real thing.

Rick demonstrated a new move. I ran toward him intending to grab him. He turned away as my momentum propelled me forward. His arm crooked around my neck, and he pressed a hand against my forehead. He forced me off-balance and backward onto the mat with less effort than I believed possible.

"Surprise." His eyes gleamed. He taught me the same fluid motions and repeated several times as he showed me the body's weakest joints and the best maneuvers.

Exhilarated but breathless, I asked, "You think we can call it a night?" I put my hand to my head. "This differs from kick boxing."

"It's a combo."

I scratched my head. "But so familiar. You remember when you first came for dinner, after the accident?"

"Yeah."

"Before you came, I believe I saw a glimpse from my childhood. Now things I've never—dance and music—they're familiar to me. I recalled none of this. How are you doing this?"

"Me?" He shrugged. "I'm just trying to defend myself."

We stood, and I gazed at the blue gym mat. "All I've known was waitressing town to town, picking locks, and nabbing credit cards. I'm a thief, on the constant run, and I've stolen identities to escape." I wrapped my arms around myself.

He reached out and touched my nose. "Jerry lied. Forget what he said, everything he said. Have you heard of muscle memory?"

"Yes, it's the brain's ability to remember motor skills."

"And you've heard of neuro, neuro—"

"Neuroplasticity?"

"That's it. The brain's ability to rewire. Processing, repetition. It's why you're learning this fast. You're not learning, you're relearning."

I stood and shuffled a few feet away. "Why didn't I use them against Jerry?"

"I don't know."

"Retrograde amnesia." I swallowed. "Maybe I'll regain my memory. I don't know what to be more concerned about, Jerry coming after me again, or what I am. You're unlocking a Pandora's box."

"Treasure hunt."

"What if I put you in danger?"

"Because you can waltz? Do a few slick moves? Suck it up, cupcake. Each day will get more interesting. Can't wait to put you into real training. You name it, you'll be learning. No more of this pansy kick boxing." He grinned.

But I feared for him, not even sure why.

CHAPTER 23

Banging on my door continued.

"All right, all right, all right ... I'm coming. Oh, ow." My muscles screamed like a five-alarm fire as I inched to the edge of the bed and grasped the full extent of burning muscle pain. Calhoun's style of workout proved more taxing than mine.

With a wince, I lifted myself out of bed and hobbled toward the entrance and pulled it open. Still bent over in pain, I studied Calhoun's Nikes. *Kind of worn.*

"I gave at the office." I closed the door.

Two or three seconds passed, and the knocking resumed. I opened it again.

"Excuse me, but is your granddaughter home?"

I glared from my stooped position as he pressed a hand to his mouth. "You realize how much I hate you."

"I'm venturing a guess you don't want to run today."

"Go away, Miss Marple. I'm supposed to shower and go to work."

"The bakery?"

"Yeah, everything's done. It's a wasted day if I can't open."

"Let me call Jules. I'll ask if she can swing the day for you."

"What about the month? I think I'm damaged for life. I may have to apply for disability."

He held out his hand, put his other arm around me, and tried to help me straighten.

"Stop!" Pain stabbed at my back. "Okay, call Jules."

Calhoun pried my cellphone from my hand because calling 9-1-1 wasn't far from my mind. An ambulance, not the coffee special.

Jules's voice bubbled through the phone while Calhoun described what had happened. He hung up, approached me, and hands on knees, he put us face-to-face. "She's heading there now."

"Thank heavens she has keys. I need a hot bath."

"Can you stand?"

I clenched my teeth. "I am standing. This is your fault. That was the hardest workout ever."

He sputtered. "This from Miss I-Can-Kick-Your-Behind."

"Hush. I never said such a thing."

"Your eyes did."

I harrumphed. "How am I going to shower? Huh, smart guy? It's not a walk-in. It's an old-fashioned claw-foot tub. You think this is funny?"

"Yeah, kinda. Skip the bath today. To bed you go." He lifted me into his arms. "Bed or couch?"

A groan escaped my throat even with his gentleness. "Remote. Wheelchair. Drugs."

"Bed." He sat next to me and asked, "What next?"

"Would you put my hair up?"

He reached for the brush and sat next to me. I closed my eyes as he brushed my hair up and away from my neck.

"What is this?" He pulled on the back of my pajama neck, and I stiffened. "Scars?"

I hesitated. "Yes," I whispered. Painful reminders that had dogged me for years.

He pushed up my PJ top, ran his hand along the crisscross scars on my back, and his voice faltered. "When I find Jerry, it will take the hand of God to keep me from ripping off his face."

I lowered my head, mortified that Rick had seen Jerry's work, and more so that I'd cowered under Jerry's cruelty. Change of subject was in order. "You have information on me. Isn't it time I get a break, even a scoop on you? What about your parents, brothers, and sisters?"

"I guess that's fair." He slowed brushing my hair. "We lived in Georgia first, then Virginia. My dad died in a car accident five years ago."

"I'm so sorry ..."

"Dad was a military man. Gruff." Calhoun stopped a moment. "Mom remembered Dad before the war, but us kids, we only recalled him between deployments."

"Difficult to miss a parent even then, I bet." I reached a hand, touching his arm.

"It was our life. His death was tough on us but tougher on Mom. Family and friends made sure she ate, went to church, got to appointments, and socialized. I flew out almost every month to see her.

"Then one day, she packed to go to the airport. It came as a shock. She had been planning to move for months. She moved in with my aunt two years ago in North Carolina."

"That's a lot of hurt you've had."

"Well, my brother moved down there to keep an eye on her. She and my Aunt Maggie are big Agatha Christie fans, and you can only imagine what kind of trouble they make."

I laughed. "You have a brother?"

"Identical twin. He's also a cop."

My mouth fell open. "No. Identical Calhoun twins? I'm not sure the US could handle you on the same coast. Safer, though."

"I will take that as a compliment." Silence held the field.

Rick had a different life outside, but his family was real, and his voice genuine.

"Here I was sure something hatched you on a rock."

"Thanks."

"Have you told them about me?"

"Cade, why would I?"

Why would I ask? Who was I to his family? I blinked tears welling up for no reason. "Never mind."

"Of course I told them. Told them about the beautiful Catherine I know, the one who has a soul that can move mountains, even though she can't fathom it herself. Nothing else. Maybe you'll meet them someday."

Right, me meet the family. "Why did you move here?"

"Because."

"You could be more specific."

"I could."

As he finished with my hair, I shifted toward him. Time took a break, and I gazed into his eyes. I wanted to raise my hand to run along his jaw.

He pushed away. "I have to go. I can't—I can't—bad idea."

He rushed from the house, leaving me stupefied and judged. Yes, a bad idea. A sane person would feel the same. I lay in bed and cried.

RICK CALHOUN

Calhoun thumbed Sam's number while in the car, punching on the speaker. "Hey, Sam, how's Amy?"

"She's good—"

"Has Amy talked to you about what I'm dealing with?"

"Whoa, nice intro there. Amy tells me snippets. Here and there."

"I can't talk to her about this. I'm in over my head. This is not what I expected, and I'm at a loss."

"Yeah, I hear she's regaining a wiped-out memory. Keep going."

"Her skills freak her out because she fears she's something worse. She's been quick to recall her abilities. The situation is untenable."

"Untenable?" Sam sniggered. "Big word for a cop. I suppose you can't arrest her."

"Won't."

"Have you told her what you do, who you are?"

"I'm not crazy." Calhoun got out of the car and stood in the bleak parking lot. "Gave her the canned speech, military, logger, and so on. She'd run if I mentioned my other job was with Homeland Security. It would be like speaking her worst fear, the FBI."

"Hey, now. I take exception to that."

"Present company excluded. Would you trust me if you were already paranoid?"

"You kidding? I don't trust you now. What are your usual solutions?"

"Excuse me?"

"Say she could compromise you, put you in danger, or be your death? What about security issues, what happens then?

You have no idea what she is, other than a gifted con-artist."

"What are you insinuating?"

"What do cons do? They gain your complete trust. Is her backstory for you? For a cover up? You need to develop a plan and have your Springfield ready in case I'm right."

Calhoun parked, stepped out of the car, and turned in a circle. "You're worse than Amy. You're saying, take her out. This is why I called you. I'd stop anyone who tried to hurt her. By lethal means, if required."

An uncomfortable pause dangled. "What if your partner, Amy, found out Cade worked you for information and posed a threat to Amy's life? Who would you save? Cade, who you think you know, or Amy, your partner? My wife?"

Calhoun put a hand to his head. "It's complicated, more than either of you know."

"Right. Figure her out. Get her out of your system before she kills you or blows your cover. Don't get my wife killed because you're not thinking straight. If she checks out, follow your heart. You need a psychiatrist, I swear."

They said their goodbyes, and Calhoun mulled over Sam's words. He'd followed his heart once before. Losing Melanie almost destroyed him.

The walk to the bullpen seemed longer than usual. He sat at his desk, and the blank computer screen begged him. Introspection complete, he booted up the computer and re-evaluated his notes on the suspects. Except for Cade. He knew her by heart.

His list came together. This was more work than he wanted in interviews. Calhoun walked to Dumont's office and knocked.

"In."

He pushed the door open, closed it, and sat while Dumont blinked. "Who are you? Mercy, you knocked. What do you want?"

Rick tapped his fingers on the desk. "Greg, you've given me an impossible task. I cannot work cold cases, train Catherine, and work on the homicide under the radar. I have information to run with, but I can't do it alone."

Dumont tossed his pen onto a file. "What do you need?"

"I know we're mid-training with Cade, but I want her deputized."

CHAPTER 24

CATHERINE CADE
TUESDAY EVENING

My pain dissipated, and I rested, clicking the remote to discover means to relieve my morning's angst. A familiar tap on the door roused me, and it opened. The clock read five p.m.

"It's me, Calhoun. Don't shoot. I have something for you."

I hope it's my dignity, Detective. "What do you mean?"

He sat and swiped a wrinkle from the bedcover. "I have information, but it's time to get you deputized."

"Whaaa ...?" Didn't see that coming.

"You'll finish your requirements for the job, but Dumont will swear you in tomorrow. The gag order prevents anyone from interviewing Thompson's widow any further than I have, but I need help with other interviews and with tracking down information on Sarah Thompson. She owns a past, a disappearing past. Her phone calls are landline and all legit numbers, so if she has a cellphone, I can't find it."

"What do you mean, disappearing past?"

"Several years with an existence, then it slides away, as though she was never born. Sort of like Catherine Cade. It's making me nuts."

"Which one?"

"Both."

"Have you tested the cell towers near her, pinging and triangulating any phone on the block?"

"Where did you learn tracking?"

"TV, I suppose."

"Pinging cells in the area require an okay from the powers that be. However, I may ..." He trailed off. "I'll see what information is out there. I did get calls and texts from the editor's past. An enormous amount of money in his bank account. Five hundred fifty thousand, all in cash, over a year's time."

I whistled. "Did someone get bribed? Blackmailed?"

"It's tough tracking cash." He seized both my hands. "This morning—"

I withdrew my hands from his. "This morning reminded me of what's real and what's not."

"C'mon, Catherine, you made an assumption."

"I don't know what transpired this morning, but I know how you see me. Our worlds will never collide."

"Our worlds collided a long time ago." He stood. "I'll catch you tomorrow morning. Dress warm."

I had benefited from these tricks in my industry. He used deflection and deception, both simple for me to detect. A CD played a Beethoven duet for flutes in the background. I was about to be deputized, but my hands covered my face, hiding the rueful frown I bore. I wished I had never met him. It was a sting in the tail, another lousy joke in my story.

OCTOBER, WEDNESDAY

I pulled my hair into a braid and prepared for my five-mile run with Calhoun. I still puffed to keep up. Thanks to the daily Calhoun Death March, maintaining pace with his long strides, and losing weight made me lighter on my feet. Every time we ran, my legs took me faster than the day before.

Calhoun focused on the course, though he struck me as unsettled.

We were courteous, but that was all. I begged God, should I even care for Calhoun? As customary, I didn't get a reply. Why did I want to keep trying this God thing? I couldn't come up with a better answer than asking him.

We continued this day much like every other, and my breath puffed steam in the October rains with wind chill enough to cut through me.

I absolved him in my soul. Smoothed over the earlier pain, but I yet hadn't figured out his secrets. He was as enigmatic as I.

"Something on your mind, Cade?"

I scowled at him for seeming to know my thoughts. "Have you heard anything about the Thompsons?"

"He had an ex-wife, Camille Tate."

"Hey, you're withholding info." I swung my head at his uninviting countenance. "A spurned woman."

He said, "Another person of interest, at least."

I held one hand in front of me as we ran, ticking off points on my fingers. "He was already dying of insulin overdose, and rarely does anyone accidentally mix too much short-acting into the long-acting."

Calhoun turned his head. "You mean you've heard of it?"

"Sure. A little poor eyesight or mild dementia, or a combination of both," I said, raising both hands. "But Stephen Thompson was lucid and active. You have the prints wiped on both the bottles and the door handle. We know his wife had possession of the gun, but we don't know if she can shoot. Then she's on video running out of her house—not covered in blood—at the time of discovering the body. No gunpowder residue?"

"And that's where it falls apart, Catherine. The mayor squashed the investigation fast. The house was examined, negative for blood trace on a cursory exam, but it was shut down quickly enough that she wasn't tested for gunpowder residue, and she lawyered up. The interviews that I did later were under the radar."

"Lovely," I said. "Remember your conspiracy theory? How's that looking?"

"Not sure yet. I hit a wall with the widow. If we link corruption to murder, I must go to the FBI."

My feet took me in a one-eighty, back toward home.

"Cade—" Calhoun followed me. "You're not connected."

I stumbled and caught myself.

He held his hands out. "What do you want me to do? Not everybody is on the take."

"You're psychic? Can you point out the crook?"

"If they get involved, I'll get you someplace secure. You're out."

"Come on, let me help."

153

"Decide, half-pint."

"I'm in, okay, okay. Yeesh."

"Outstanding. Now, stop griping. Time to push, cupcake." He smirked, shifting his eyes back to the street. "Pick up the pace. I want to watch Fred Flintstone tackle the hill."

Dumont spent five minutes deputizing me after I passed the written exam. Next to come was evasive driving.

I was both excited and amused, being a con and working as a deputy. Could anything else be this ironic?

Because the investigation was hushed, Calhoun spent extra time at my home that evening. Pretty much for supper, I figured, but he brought in files and a list of Thompson's neighbors to interview. I had to find the time to interview, work the bakery, and handle the clinic, not to mention keep up my training. *Yay, me.*

CHAPTER 25

I might as well have crammed myself into a meat processor during hazing week with the rookies. Someone dubbed it the "crucible of Calhoun."

When Calhoun yelled, "move," which he did often, no one slacked, and we rookies stumbled over each other. I never speculated where he developed his tactics, but no one cut it, not according to our handler. Not one "survived" his muggings, attempted homicides, or his solid deceptive actions. We struggled to thump his moves. We laid wagers. None of us carried the medal of golden child.

I didn't stand a chance, and I whispered to Calhoun, "Why again do I need this intense discipline?" No one dragged a suspect into the bullpen requiring me to be this prepared. I pushed paper.

Aw, crap. His expression meant it was my time to be in the center of Hades.

He snatched the front of my sweatshirt and hoisted me to my tippy-toes. His eyes narrowed, and not quite nose-to-nose, he took his time with four somewhat intimidating words. "You questioning me ... rookie?"

Unintelligible consonants and vowels spilled from me in a jumble of words, none of which made sense. Moments later, a rational, formed word proceeded from my mouth, "No."

"Good." He released my jersey and thrust me backward. "Your turn." He angled toward the class and hollered, "Gather 'round. Cade here aims to show us how it's done. Aren't you?"

Without waiting for me to say "No, I'm not in the mood for getting my butt kicked," he'd already tossed me five feet across the mat. He came at me with gloved fists, and his leg swept at my feet. The second time, I stepped back but not away, and his next sweep felled me, landing me with a thud and oomph. In defeat from his fast choke hold, I slapped the mat.

"One down. Seize your gun or knife props. Whatever is handy."

"Yessir."

"Go ahead. Drop me."

Calhoun lugged on my arm. I planted my right foot behind his as he'd instructed me, but nothing happened as I pushed with leverage. He smirked at my bewilderment. It was like kicking concrete.

"You fell for the perp being helpful—and untrained. Nice try, the second one down."

He flipped me onto my back, I reached for my prop gun, faltered a nanosecond, and he levered it from my hand, shoving the prop close to my throat.

"Three down, and Cade's out. Some perps will be bigger, stronger, faster. You need to be better." He pointed at me for instructional purposes, no doubt. "If someone takes your weapon, it's a misconduct review and disciplinary action. If you're not dead."

FRIDAY EVENING

Friday, at dusk, my driveway loomed at last. Calhoun sat on my porch swing.

"How long have you been here?"

"Forever." He stood. "It's freezing and about time you came home."

"I made a few stops. Don't you have your phone? You make it sound like it's your place. I'm surprised you didn't break down the door."

"Funny. Isn't your specialty breaking and entering? You're late, and now I'm cold and hungry. What's for supper?"

"You waltz into my world, and all of a sudden, I'm your cook?"

"You always invite me for dinner." He held up a bottle.

"Because you stop by every night. I've created a beast. Help me put these groceries away." I didn't mention I knew the reason why he ate junk food. Other than breakfast, his cooking made even tree bark edible.

A pot of chili simmered. Calhoun wandered into the kitchen and hovered over the slow cooker. "Aw, and I had a hankerin' for chili. How'd you know?"

"You sent me an email." Fatalii peppers, cumin, Louisiana hot sauce, and red pepper flakes went into the pot for an added kick. "We have to wait on the cornbread. Patience. What's in the bottle?"

"Thought we could have wine." He poured a small amount for me but none for himself.

Sweet blackberry wine tingled my tongue. I upended a half of it in one gulp then shoved cornbread mix into the oven. He held my arm back.

"What?"

"Do you have experience with alcohol?"

"Sure." *In spades*. The unfortunate familiarity when Jerry drank a gallon of vodka followed by cocaine.

"Be careful." He searched my cupboards and found saltines. "Eat."

I ate two. "Hmm. Explain the grueling training." My crackers crunched, impeding speech.

"Baby steps. I don't want to harm you."

"Yeah, but I'd been kick boxing, running, and rock climbing."

"Uh-huh. How's that been working out?"

"Hush." I turned on the oven light to keep an eye on the cornbread. "The paper had an interesting article."

"You mean, 'Catherine Cade, found comatose after homicide detective cooked dinner for the famed local baker?'"

I tittered. "No, baby cakes, that's national news." I guffawed at his widened eyes at my words of endearment. "Sorry," I mumbled. "Public records from the tax assessor's office show Commissioner Sarah Thompson cast the deciding vote to rezone property at the north end of town. Beth Bray, the head of the department, reports to Darren Hughe. Developers welcome. Not to mention the extra revenue in taxes."

We sat on the floor. I squeezed my eyes shut and opened them. Blink. Blink.

Calhoun carried my thread. "Farmers are selling for big money. Beef is cheaper in Haiti and American ranchers find cut-rate land there."

"No, the current landowners in town settled for handsome prices for DG."

"DG?"

I held my glass high in the air. "Decomposed granite. Over time, it's crushed into loose pebbles. Those weeee pebbles are embedded into topsoil which is not at all safe to build on. One good solid rain soaks the topsoil, and DG acts like a conveyer belt, bringing the whooole hillside to the valley floor."

He offered to refill my glass.

"No, thanks. Someone cashed in. Who oversees land-use development?"

"I'll check Zoning."

I raised my glass and finished the wine. "Ha, ha. You don't have to. It's Darren Hughe. Remember him?"

"Thinks he's the definition of big time."

"Who oversees the committee and the mayor's office. The mayor's office oversees the board."

"Interesting."

Woozy, I held up the glass to my face.

"I'll get the food." He went to the kitchen and made a racket. He returned balancing bowls, cornbread, and milk, and sat down, then dug into his food.

"You didn't say grace."

"I prayed, but you're not a God-botherer, remember?"

"What if this time it's okay?" I grasped his hand and closed my eyes while he offered a short supplication. I even said amen.

When he finished, I continued. "What did Sarah Thompson gain from her husband's death besides his earthly goods? She's putting money on a dangerous game. Do you think it's just the land, or is there more? What if someone's playing marionette master? What if she's been bought and paid for?" I swept my arm around the room with theatrics. "Because I'm thinking that, too. You can draw a straight line from California through Oregon landing in Whiskey River. Then on to Washington State and Canada. The perfect spot for a nefarious business. Not enough man-hours to patrol. You think she's planning a well-funded terrorist cell?"

"Halt, woman. One question at a time." He dredged his spoon against the belly of the glass bowl. "What do you know about big or small town corruption?"

"Oh, I know corruption." I pushed my empty wineglass in his direction for emphasis. "I've seen how it can creep into the best people. Calhoun, why don't you have someone in your life? Is it hot in here?"

"Huh?"

I pressed my hand against my forehead. "Must be the peppers. What did I say?"

He crossed the room and stoked the wood stove. "Politics. Peppers. I have news also. Add this to your information. Stephen Thompson's daughter, was diagnosed with leukemia. She died about four months ago. He divorced Mom for Sarah Thompson years ago but didn't pay a dime for treatment."

"How sad. Why refuse lifesaving intervention for a child?"

"And motive for murder. His ex-wife, Camille Tate, received zilch after Thompson divorced her. And nothing after he married Sarah. No insurance for his child, no large cash withdrawals."

"Deadbeat dad. Revenge?"

Calhoun looked at me. "Widow Thompson had a bigger motive than to save a life."

That soured my stomach. "Call me what you want, but that's evil."

"I agree." He aimed his spoon my way. "Guess who was employed as their attorney years ago? Darren Hughe."

I almost toppled over. "Huh? So he has the ear of the mayor, knows the comings and goings of the board, and Tate. Does Sharahhhhaa Thompson have money to gain? Say, close enough even small calibers could mess him up. Further away, a .22 caliber will bounce around and create jelly. But a .45 caliber ..." I stopped. "Hey, you want dessert?"

He paused. "No, I'm good. Thanks, though."

I waved my glass in the air again. "*Nooo problemo*. It didn't matter if Thompson was sitting or standing, and perhaps the killer hoped the phantom outline would be part of the gag order. All the shooter had to do—" I made a finger gun, closed an eye, and said—"Peee-ew. Shoot, push the body over onto the floor, and place the gun in his hand."

"Why, you're as drunk as Cooter Brown."

"Well, Cooter Brown, I'll have you know, I'm skunker as a drunk, 'cause I don't drink, therefore, I'm not drunk. Where are you from?"

"I spent my formative years in Georgia. You had less than a glass of wine. Thought you said you had experience with alcohol."

"Sweet Georgia Brown, yessiree, I said I had experience with alcohol, the wrong end of the fist." I closed an eye and tried to fix a steady gaze on him. "Georgia Brown. Is she related to Cooter? One glass? Let's make it two and call it even. Get it?" My nose felt numb, and I snorted.

"I got it, and we'll be chatting about this tomorrow." He shook his head. "You're doing a great job. Once January comes around, we're going to Wisconsin, and afterward, you'll work with Jack McCloud exclusively for a month."

"What? The lech medical examiner?" I fumbled my glass onto the floor and crawled over to him. "Why? That's like Hotel California. No, that's an insult to Hotel California."

"I want you to gain more hands-on experience in forensics. Then back to cold cases."

"But I don't want my hands on McCloud. Have you seen the morgue? Do you know what he's like? Can't I just work with Kim? He scares me. Not you. Not one bit."

"You've got pluck, I'll give you that."

"What's in Wisconsin?"

"A small forensics training center, comparable to the body farm in Tennessee. We'll stay three days and fly back."

"Work on a body?" I'd already crawled into his lap. Funny how he looked at me.

"Yeah, dead body, Cade." He held me back.

"Darn. I had just the body in mind."

"Don't you dare kiss me, Catherine. This is not right, I haven't told you, you need to know—dagnabbit, Cade—"

He babbled on about something, so my lips teased the corner of his mouth.

"Woman, you're tormenting me."

I stopped teasing and pressed my lips to his. He clutched me against him, and his fingers wove through my hair.

Wow.

CHAPTER 26

Awakened by the doorbell, I sat. A headache ticked like a bomb ready to blow, taking over where my brains once lived. I eased into a robe and ached my way to the door.

I stood, withholding a groan.

A male voice called out, "Decent?"

I pulled open the door for Calhoun. "Of course, I'm decent. I'm always decent."

"Well, morning, cupcake. You look horrible." He held up two kiosk cups of coffee. "Decaf. Figured you might need this."

"Thanks. What happened last night? My head is exploding."

He sat across from me at the dining room table. "What was the last thing you remember?"

I wrinkled my forehead and wanted to cuss. "Ah ... the morgue. You want me to work with McCloud at the morgue after Wisconsin."

"And then what?"

"I said bye and got ready for bed." I refused to say anything else.

"Not exactly." He appeared satisfied and sipped his coffee in silence.

I pointed a finger and yelled, "No, you stop yanking my chain." I grasped my head. "Oh, what is this pain?"

"Hangover. I'd say drinking a glass of alcohol falls into Cade's stupid category. You can't handle a cup of coffee. What made you think you could handle wine?"

"You did this on purpose."

"Yup. And what do we think we've learned from this experience?"

I hid my face in my hands, then looked at him. "That I'm an idiot."

"Yes, but you're my idiot. I'm trained to find weaknesses, and last night, I found yours. You accepted a glass of alcohol, not knowing if I might have dropped a date-rape drug in it. Which I didn't, just to be clear. Always be in control of your surroundings. Alcohol helped you lose your inhibitions, forget your training, and could've ruined a budding faith in God. Be thankful I'm not the old me, because you were in the mood."

I groaned and grasped my head again.

Calhoun dragged me and my hangover to the shooting range. My dark glasses weren't dark enough.

"Quiz time," he said. "You think you've mastered these?"

My aching head. Couldn't he leave me alone today?

"Let's find out." My eyes swept over the table. I ran a finger over each gun, ones not from the PD's armory. "M-16, fully auto. AK forty-seven, 7.62 round." I inspected the AK for a bullet and replaced the magazine.

"Springfield Armory forty-five, service nine-millimeter, conceal-carry nine-millimeter, and a Glock nine-millimeter." I drew a finger along the rifle. "WinMag manual bolt-action, uses a WinMag 300. Has a range around fifteen hundred meters. This is an X-one-IR laser scope. Sniper rifle. These are different from what you've shown me. I didn't know the police department had these kinds of rifles."

"They're mine."

"You're a sniper?"

"Nope." He paused a beat. "Past tense."

On the defensive. Embedded in a kernel of truth hid a lie.

He pointed. "Range over there. You haven't worked the alley much. Let's get to that next."

"Grab a sandbag. No, grab two." I swept a confused gaze at Calhoun.

As easy as taking a breath now, I put one sandbag on top of the other and set up the short tripod and WinMag. We slipped on shooting glasses and ear protection. I turned my cap around and looked at Calhoun. He held a pair of binoculars.

Silent as death itself, cut off from communication, I readied to shoot. An odd thought nudged at the back of my brain, like a dog scratching at a door to be let in. Like a memory. I just couldn't reach it.

He gave me the thumbs-up, and lying on my belly, I vee-shaped my legs to keep centered and pointed my toes outward for full contact with the ground. Scoped the flag, adjusted for windage and trajectory for the point of impact. *Click, click, click*—until I made the final elevation adjustment.

These weapons were part of me. WinMag was short for Winchester Magnum, yet I didn't even know my real name.

I rested the side of my face on the adjustable cheek piece, took three slow breaths, looked through the scope, and pulled the trigger on the final exhale. The kickback was minimal as the bullet hit the target with a ping. I focused through the scope again. Satisfied, I ejected the cartridge and removed my ear protection.

Unintended, but familiar words tumbled past my lips. "I prefer the MSR." *Modular Sniper Rifle, Remington, Lapua, .338,* a voice echoed in my head.

"Excuse me?"

"Less recoil. Reduced IR signature. More options."

"You're below the sternum." His statement hung, suspended in air.

"Why waste two bullets when one bullet will do?" Those words didn't horrify me, but the fact they didn't, did.

"This isn't what I've been teaching you."

"Tell me about it."

I dug in my pocket for another round and kissed it before pushing it into the chamber. The *chi-chak* of the action snapped, and I slapped the magazine in place. Calhoun had trained me hard, and it paid off. I continued to hit right on throughout the ten-round magazine. He ran me through the range's fake city dubbed Calhoun's Alley, patterned after the one at Quantico. With both the M-16 and the pistol, the cardboard hostages lived, and I blew the bad guys away.

Calhoun clicked the stopwatch. "Each time we practice, you're faster. The MSR throws me. That's new."

"What am I?"

He removed his cap and scratched his head. "You've spent over a month training every day. That's it, nothing else, unless you've been in the military. The only way we'll know is if we fingerprint you."

"No prints. You know that." My migraine kicked into gear, and I pulled my visor around.

"And the MSR?"

"I've shot it before. I think." Half-ready for Calhoun to check me for an implant, I said, "What if I'm some sort of weird—?"

He held up a hand, palm facing me. "I refuse to feed into your Jason Bourne paranoia. Would you kill me?"

"Never. But what, then?" I sunk to my knees. "Am I a sniper? And if I am, who do I belong to?"

Calhoun knelt and put his arms around me. "You're a great shot, but you're not the Manchurian candidate. You make the best cheesecake I've ever eaten, but that doesn't mean you're Julia Child's granddaughter. Your skills have improved, and you've seen the MSR in a hunting magazine. Simple."

That wasn't true. "No." The breeze chilled my sweat and bit into my skin. "Learning this is worse than running from Jerry."

"How?"

I stared off toward the targets, feeling my heart twist in the newfound knowledge. "I've been trained to kill with one shot."

CHAPTER 27

Monday morning, Calhoun walked toward Dumont's office and rapped his knuckles on his open door.

"What now?" Dumont wore reading glasses. He thumbed *National Institute of Justice Journal* pages, feet propped comfortably on his desk.

"Chief, got a minute?"

"No, but here you are blocking any hope of escape. Talk."

Calhoun sat across from Dumont. "What's your assessment of me?"

"Huh?"

"I can handle myself, agreed?"

Dumont removed his legs from the tabletop. "If I could, I'd clone you in a heartbeat to wipe this town clean. What do you want now?"

Calhoun folded his hands. "I want Cade to carry when we're out on a call. In the city. In here."

Dumont leaned forward. "Why?"

"She may be a better shot than me. If you think I'm a weapons master, you should see her." He wiped his face. "She surpassed me on every score, on every weapon I've taught her."

Dumont leaned back in his chair. "Truth? You're a Marine sniper, and whatever else, you believe she's better?"

"On my life. If I need backup, and Mike couldn't help, she'd be there for me. On my own, I'm good. Put Cade alongside me, and people had better make room or make peace with their Maker."

"Well, then." He peered over his reading glasses. "And no military training."

"She's a fast learner." Calhoun ran a hand over his head.

"I remember your résumé, if you could call it that. Your past is still a mystery to me. How'd she handle Calhoun's Alley?"

"Better than anyone I've ever seen. I wanted to make her walk home."

"How's her street fighting?"

Calhoun stretched his legs out. "I'm still working on the kinks. She surprises me. For a half-pint, she's scrappy."

"Fine, she can carry. Doesn't bother me." He pushed up his glasses. "She's deputized, but if she shoots someone, it had better be justified. Don't make me regret this."

After a few more minutes of small talk, Calhoun left Dumont's office. He stepped into the hall and speed-dialed Amy.

"Hey. How's Miss Trainee?"

"Find anything?"

"Slim pickings," Amy said. "I think the Jerry she's referring to is Jerry Street. His name popped up, buried in an agency I can't pinpoint. I'll keep working, but it appears whatever agency he's with has been permanently redacted. However, his name appeared in the nurses' records in a third-rate hospital in Virginia. Court records showed he became her guardian, and he signed her out of the hospital. This fits the timeline. The coma victim's name was Sonia Newton. Street fell off the radar, and so did she. I found her aliases a few times in various hospitals. Listed as accidents, but looks more like domestic violence. Still can't find a marriage license. How's she handling things?"

Calhoun swore under his breath, wishing he'd found her long ago. He loosened his tie and fidgeted. "Let me mangle a quote. 'The women in Whiskey River are more dangerous than shotguns.' That's Cade."

"Take the cannoli."

"Yup. She's too small to take me on, but she's fast, thinks on her feet, picks up martial arts with no problem. No hesitation on weapons, including my WinMag."

Amy spoke, quiet. "Rick, I ran her through every network, and I can't find her. Hospital records on the internet have a trace on the deep web, where company information is shared.

Any links older than a few years, including photos, are gone. I can't explain that. Federal databases, Interpol, nothing. She may be somewhere my tech savvy can't go, and her car wreck and abuse doubtless wiped her memory. Best case scenario is she doesn't have any memories before the accident. Otherwise, she's playing you for something. Maybe about a job we had."

Calhoun curled his fist. Amy wouldn't find her, not without her real name, but she gave him what he needed.

"Be careful, Rick. Don't let her suck you into a romance you can't control. Can you handle her?"

"Make her my asset. I already started. She's terrified, but she trusts me."

He waited for Amy to speak.

"A reasonable place to start."

"I won't bring her in for interrogation." He squeezed his eyes shut, unable to imagine how a chemically induced serum could shatter her. Trust for which he'd worked so hard would be lost.

"Watch her, Rick. She may turn on you."

He paused, his stomach plummeting. "Yeah, death by half-pint."

"No joke, Calhoun. Push her, and I mean hard, not like rookies, so you're aware of her capabilities. Give her your real-world experience. Loosen her leash. Then pull her, make sure she trusts you."

"Hear ya."

"I need to see her. Bring her over on Christmas, and I'll get a feel for what she is."

Cade's not a what. He prayed Amy worried over nothing. Betray or be betrayed. He feared loss more than he feared a bullet, and Cade had held his heart longer than he wanted to admit.

This is a disaster. How would he fake a romance with an asset he was already in love with?

Cade was a landmine, and he was about to walk right into it.

CHAPTER 28

CATHERINE CADE
TUESDAY

There were very few neighbors on the list, so I made quick work of it with my shiny new laminated badge. First were Maude and Jelly Cullen, both elderly. Jelly was hard of hearing and fiddled with his hearing aids, speaking with a New Jersey accent. I figured his moniker was Jelly because of his weight.

Maude was his exact opposite. She waved her hands dismissively. I got nothing, other than she talked about hearing her neighbor scream.

The next nearest set of neighbors lived across the street from the Thompsons' house. June and George Potter. June and George were middle-aged, but George looked much younger than June, with his tousled blond hair. He was hurrying to leave for work, so I questioned him first—and fast. He had left early the morning Stephen Thompson was found dead, he saw nothing, and that was the sum of his information.

June, on the other hand, was willing to chat. She had one of those noses that reminded me of the *Wizard of Oz*'s Wicked Witch of the East. It was a long pointy schnoz, and along with her bright red hair, it gave her a somewhat frightening visage. I asked if she saw anything unusual with Stephen Thompson in general. A corner of her mouth raised.

"Ha! I didn't trust the news, and it wasn't a heart attack. I'll tell you what I heard. Something popped and woke me around five a.m. My husband wasn't home, but that's not unusual. He was working. Late." She turned toward the window.

I figured she knew her husband was having an affair. Easy enough for me to spot.

"Did you hear or see anything else?"

She lifted a cigarette to her mouth which bobbed with each word. "By that time, I was just about at the window. It was still dawn, like I said, around five a.m., but I saw someone leave the house, casually walking away. Someone wearing jeans and a baseball hat, just their back. He wore a green jacket which was weird, because it was the end of August. Oh, and what looked like white tennis shoes. But I didn't put anything together until later. I heard this crazy scream, and I jumped out of bed again, and out came Sarah Thompson. She fell to her knees."

I scratched information on a pad. "Thank you, you've been a great help." I handed her one of Rick's business cards. "If you think of anything else, please notify Detective Calhoun."

"Oh! Now I remember. Mrs. Thompson bolted from the front door like she thought she might be next."

I lifted my head. Odd, indeed, and detailed. "Thank you. I would appreciate your discretion in this matter. This still is an ongoing investigation."

She pulled an imaginary zipper across her lips.

I thanked her again and left just as my phone jingled. Rick. "Hey."

"Hey, back. How's it going?"

"Neighbors interviewed." I recounted the Cullens' information and June Potter's story.

"Huh. Interesting. Good job."

"What's wrong?"

"I'm exhausted. Got the interviews done, but got tied up in some interagency baloney. I managed to get some time with John Murray. Remember, he and Thompson quarreled a lot? He was engaged to a novelist, older than him, but he wouldn't tell me why they broke it off, so that's something I'll have to ask the lady about."

"What's her name?"

"Elsa Stephens. Writes crime fiction," he said.

"I know her name around town. She's quite influential and a good writer. I have a few of her books." I figured maybe I could hunt her down. "Anyone else?"

"Troy Abara. He's new on the committee, so I don't know much about this guy. Got an accent, and I asked about it. Said his folks were from Botswana." Rick sighed. "Andy Denmark, who we can place in the hospital at the time with a fractured femur. And last, Abdul Abbott, another newer member on the board. He has a family, and they recently converted to Islam. I guess my timing was wrong because he grabbed his prayer mat and ended the conversation. But supposedly he got on well with Thompson and the other members. Said they played tennis." He sighed. "I'm a wreck. I'm gonna sleep a week."

"Do you want me to fix you some dinner and drop it off?"

"Nah, I plan to fall into bed. I'll talk to you tomorrow."

I nodded as though he could see me. "Later, then." The call ended. Maybe I could pick up where he left off.

Perfect. I'd written the names of the board members on my pad and later I'd do a credit check.

I stopped at Elsa Stephens' lush home, surrounded by dogwoods, azaleas, and rhododendrons. An out-of-sorts rosemary bush was taking on a bonsai form near her front door. The Whiskey River's resident author and gadabout met me at the door, and as I mentioned John Murray, she rapid-fire spit a New York rant about him before I could even enter her home.

She was an angry smoker, blowing whirling clouds and rings, and thrusting her chin into the air as she talked. Billows of smoke came from her nose as she spewed hateful hope that John Murray's new wife would soon be fat.

I asked, "Did Mr. Murray associate with the rest of the board? Were they friendly?"

"Ha! If you can call him wanting people dead, friendly." She sighed. "I suppose they all did the same. They were all catty with one another. John was new to the political scene, if you can call it such in this burg. He didn't know what to make of the insults from Thompson, Abbott, or even Andy. Brian Jackson is a freak—thinking he's fooling anyone with his dreads. John didn't know the ropes, so after we hooked up, I took him to parties and the like. He dropped me not long after he met a little squeeze hanging on Brian Jackson's arm, not his wife."

"Did you ever meet Sarah Thompson?"

"Lovely woman. Kept to herself as much as possible. Not like the commissioners and spouses." She opened her mouth wide to laugh. "I think we all gave her a migraine. The poor thing lost her husband. Well, I am out of this little scene and moving and shaking with the Ashland artists, if you get my drift. More my style, which is why I am leaving Whiskey River's hamlet."

"You'll be missed," I said.

"I doubt it." She winked and closed the door.

It was a gem I tucked away. She never asked why I was at her door asking questions.

Afterward, I examined the notes I kept on my phone from Calhoun's original investigation. I wanted to talk to Sarah Thompson and the people that worked for her. There were gardeners, and one had disappeared shortly after Thompson's death. Santiago.

I didn't want to show up at Thompson's home as a deputy. I reached into my purse and grabbed a handful of laminated IDs and found one for "freelance reporter." With plan ready, I studied my watch, then shifted the truck into fourth gear.

Thompson's curved driveway, edged with Spanish-inspired tiles, led me to a large locked gate. Splashes of color hugged the drive, and Japanese maples had discarded red and golden leaves in an otherwise immaculate landscape. Crepe myrtles had long since dropped the last of their crimson blooms, replaced by dark green foliage, and the rosemary plants were beyond their violet flowers with the cooling weather.

"Miss!" A Hispanic man trotted toward me from behind a piece of lawn sculpture. He slowed as he came closer to the ironwork gate.

"Hi," I said. "Mr. Santiago?"

"I'm afraid this property is off-limits. I'm John Perez."

I caught myself. "It's okay, I'm not with the police. I'm a journalist. Can I speak with Mr. Santiago?"

"Rafael is no longer here." He didn't open the gate. "May I ask what's the reason for your visit?"

"I write freelance, and I'm working on a follow-up article on Commissioner Stephen Thompson's career, home, and his sad demise. You know, figured I could shut up those conspiracy nuts."

Perez studied me.

I showed my fake ID. "I'd hoped to speak with Santiago. Do you know where he moved?"

Perez waved a hand. "He took off after Thompson found out he didn't have a green card."

"Off the record, do you have a green card?" I pinched a sliver of hair.

"Lady ..." He shook his head. "Born in San Diego, my family, too. Served San Diego PD for seven years, then Border Patrol for ten. I realized I wanted to work outdoors where I wouldn't be shot at daily, so I came here. I told Thompson that Santiago didn't have a green card. You can check my story out if you want."

"No, I'm good, but thanks. Do you think Santiago might have had a motive to ruin Mr. Thompson, somehow?"

"An illegal immigrant tangling with the dude next to the mayor? What I know is Commissioner Thompson died from a heart attack. Lady, you talk like a cop." He gripped the bars. "If I was Santiago, I'd want out of town."

"My mistake. Anything else fascinating about Thompson's history that the public would enjoy?"

Perez scratched his head. "Paid us well. Mrs. Thompson brought us coffee in the morning and lemonade in the afternoon. She still does, and prepares lunch for the workers. What's your name?"

"Cade, Catherine Cade. Is Mrs. Thompson home?"

"No."

"Anyone else I can talk to about his life?"

"I'm the only one here today, sorry." He grasped a rake, clear he'd had enough of questions.

We shook hands.

"Thank you for your time, Mr. Perez, you've helped me a great deal."

He didn't let go of my hand. With a tight grip, he yanked me close to the gate. My face contorted. He looked side to side. "Watch yourself. It seems you're sticking your nose around, talking murder. People disappear for less."

A knot formed in my gut. He released his grip and left.

Stunned, I wobbled backward then walked past my pickup. I returned and twisted the key in the engine and sat. Murder. *Did I say murder*? I didn't think I'd said murder. Were his words a warning or a threat? He'd been a cop. Maybe he knew more than he wanted to say. Another background check in my future.

Taxi drivers, repairmen, workers in uniform, gardeners, and laborers, no one paid them any heed. Grifters blend in. I should know. So would an undercover cop—or killer.

But he was right. I was speculating, and I could become an endangered species even with innocent questions. Again, where was my game? And despite this, or because of this discussion, Perez didn't seem to know Sarah Thompson's whereabouts.

She stayed high on Calhoun's suspect list, and I drove to her office next. Took me a few minutes to stop shaking.

Thompson's assistant opened the door to the commissioner's lobby and bid me sit while she left to grab Thompson's desk calendar. I stood at the assistant's desk and read the papers upside down in a glimpse. Construction bids and floor plans for high dollar homes. She'd go for the lowest bidder with the least ethics. That was my guess.

The editor of the *Medallion*, another suspect on Calhoun's list, had invested in her land development and subdivision. I scanned the list and found several entries for the editor. It would be a question for Calhoun, because he'd find it interesting how the editor could smack enough dough into her disastrous real estate scam.

My eye caught writing on a small note—bakery. *No way*. I yelled an excuse and hustled out of the office before she returned.

Next came the mayor's office, before it closed. He'd pushed the false death certificate. Why?

Up the stairs, I slowed to consider the moneyed lobby. Plush furnishings and elegant paintings, works by Degas including *The Green Dancer* and *The Ballet Master*, were out of place in a public servant's office. Prints. I'd seen sublime forgeries in former days, but still, these seemed stunning.

An Edwardian mahogany desk rested between the pieces of framed artwork. No books, papers, or files. Nothing but opulence. Wealth off the tails of the voters.

Darren Hughe, a young attorney and the mayor's assistant, appeared immaculate with every hair in place. He gave me a politician's velvety handshake, a giveaway he'd never done an honest day's labor. His was a weak chin, lips stretched over perfect teeth, and he stood, unrelenting, holding my gaze.

I presented the real deputy's badge.

"Have a seat, Miss Cade. How can I help you?"

Pushed by Perez's warning—or threat, I went full cop role. "Stephen Thompson died under unusual circumstances, yet it's reported he died of natural or undetermined causes."

He tented his fingers together and stiffened. "He died months ago. He was irrelevant then, and he is irrelevant now."

"Excuse me?" Thompson was my patient, and Hughe's indifference and disrespect for the dead man turned my stomach.

"I seem to recall his healthcare provider was less than adequate. Surely you recall, despite your new role with the police department."

I maintained my composure, wanting to slap him while wondering how he knew or remembered. "He had neither disorders or chronic diseases. I can only assume the mayor's office tried to force a signature on the death certificate without a post mortem, which put me in an awkward position."

"Yes, I suppose it would. Did you sign it?"

"You know I was his provider, yet you don't remember?"

Hughe made circles on the desk with a long, slender finger, reminding me of the Grim Reaper's skeletal hand. "In your small mind, it would have to be suspicious causes because surely you wouldn't want to be known as the infamous provider who missed everything."

My face grew hot. "You're a liar, and you're doing a great job of that now."

His apology was almost incomprehensible. I jotted notes with a shaky hand. "Is the mayor in?"

"I'm afraid not, Miss Cade."

A clamor rose from the mayor's office, confirming his presence. My gut told me to keep my mouth shut.

He hovered a finger over the computer keyboard and proposed an appointment six months away.

I declined and figured the mayor was knee-deep in this mess. With Camille Tate, the board of commissioners, the editor, and Sarah Thompson, the mayor's involvement seemed clear in Stephen Thompson's death. Did he arrange for the murder, or did he help cover the gruesome act with prestidigitation and intimidation? What kind of sinister chess game came into play? What role did Hughe play?

Hughe's cold-steel glare didn't waver. He gave me a spine-chilling look of contempt. "Thompson's death was tragic, but it's ... over." He looked toward the ceiling. "Have you ever pondered those large floral arrangements in funeral homes?"

His head came back down, and his eyes daggered malevolent ice into mine. For the first time in Whiskey River, I feared for my life.

CHAPTER 29

Calhoun didn't show up for our five-a.m. run, and I wondered what time he made it to work. For me, threat or no, I figured I'd be safe at the clinic. For the day, I pitched in for Dr. Riley. I'd tell Calhoun about my interactions later.

Patients with lacerations, others carrying lists of questions, and kids with sniffles almost overwhelmed me. The drive home in the dark after work seemed longer than usual, and I returned home exhausted.

I longed for a face-plant into bed. I left a message for Calhoun that our workout was not happening. I forgot to mention the interviews and veiled threats, but they would wait until the morning. Instead, I stoked coals and heated a frozen dinner. I prepared bread dough, and for Rick, a sweet potato pie, and slipped them both into the fridge.

In my PJs, I checked notes for my private novel. Once I opened the laptop, my fatigue fled. Cold cases came in handy for my writing. A modern-day Miss Pinkerton hunted for her family's killer. It was a therapy that helped me deal with my constant anguish.

My fingers flew over the keys. I wanted a real-life bad guy—my cold cases helped build a believable villain. I wanted to make the antagonist as malicious as Jerry. But Jerry was a cardboard cutout of *Batman's* Killer Croc, with a taste for human flesh. Might as well add Croc twirling a mustache and laughing, *muuaahhhaa*. I tried. I really tried as I hammered out another two thousand words.

SLAIN
By Catherine Cade

SEVEN

Erica Slain fought the locks on the corner bakery door. Her hands worked a bolt, rattling the padlock while dark fell. She'd prepared the next day's ingredients for a morning rush.

She hid in his town, overrun with its share of drunk drivers. Robert "Einstein" Garrison lived, moved, and drove without regret for the lives he'd ruined.

Her brokenness and her memory. Her life defined by his name.

I stopped typing and breathed deep breaths, quieting my soul because writing this scene made me nauseous.

NYPD busied themselves in public relations and high priority murders. Hit-and-run deaths slipped further down their list. Five years passed in slow motion, and long past a cold case, she'd tracked him from one state to another, and closing in, she'd kill him without remorse.

My jaw tensed recalling another man and his sick glee as he made me suffer. So also, I'd kill Jerry. Just like my main character. I supposed it wasn't Christian, but Jerry reveled in his appetite for violence, and the world was a better place without him and others like him.

The last of the locks clicked. A loud swick escalated Erica's heartbeat, and she broke out into a sweat. Einstein once carried a police truncheon! Spun around, she reeled against a cold steel blade pressed against her neck.

"No." Her body shook.

"Slain." Einstein hissed. His foul breath spilled—

The phone's calypso ringtone startled me. "Hey."
"Hey, back," Rick answered.
"Did you get some rest?"

"Yup."

"It's late, what's up?"

He paused. "I planned to hit the rookies with a home invasion, including you."

"What? Why?"

"Bring a little world experience. But I won't do that to you."

I was touched and knew the reason. "Thank you."

"Catherine?" He halted. "I promise never to bring that kind of fear to your world, got that?"

Swallowing, I wanted to say so much more, and I teared up. "Yes, I do. Thanksgiving is tomorrow. Please join me, okay? I have a surprise."

Rick chuckled. "Like I'd miss Thanksgiving with you. I'll talk to you tomorrow, babe."

On that, he ended the call. *Did he just call me babe*? He had to be tired.

CHAPTER 30

I hired full-time employees, and the bakery produced more capital than Dr. Riley's clinic. Moving down to a half-shift at the clinic once or twice a week enabled me to work more hours for Whiskey River PD.

At the bullpen, my nose stayed stuck in paperwork. At five, I pored over crime-scene pictures, looking again at Faith Harrington, the first cold case Rick had handed me.

Death investigations had come to a near halt. A cutback in services at the PD left cold cases to sit like gnats stuck in honey. With the lack of case evidence and witness recollection, magnetized boots could drag along a steel floor easier.

Zoe fidgeted with paperwork, and I needed a break. I struck up a conversation. After professional questions, I asked more personal ones, and I leaned my elbow on the counter, and we laughed. A few more queries and answers, and I exclaimed, "Amazing coincidence. That's my mother's middle name."

A hand clapped on my back, and I felt fingers tighten on my collar. "Let's go, Cade. Leave Zoe alone."

"Hey, just making conversation."

He guided me across the bullpen and whispered, "Any more information and you'd have her bank account."

"I don't know what you mean." I outstretched my arms in a big shrug.

Calhoun clapped my back again, surprising me, and hooked a finger in my collar. He steered me toward the office's lunchroom, and we sat. "Dumont wanted me to tell you your work is outstanding. I think so, too."

"That's high praise from both of you."

"But it's volunteer, full-time if you can manage it. You're still the prototype for the program. He passed this on—don't make him regret this decision. Catherine, I have never regretted a moment with you, so I've no worries."

I looked down, feeling heat to my face. "You've a lot of trust in a con artist."

"No. I have a lot of trust in God working in you, and I trust you."

Kissing him was out of order, but I thanked him all the same with a church-style hug I'd learned.

Thanksgiving passed without incident, a lot of food, and one overstuffed Calhoun. I enjoyed myself far too much. He seemed far too happy to let me cook for him every evening.

The weekend was uneventful, and Monday arrived just in time to work off Thanksgiving calories. After our workout, I stood in the shower as hot beads of water gently buffeted my back.

Dumont must be nuts. Then again, he hadn't a clue about my colorful past.

I stood under the cascading water, frustrated. I had conned Zoe without thought. Scam artistry came with such ease. That moment had come, and I realized this ugliness followed me. I wondered, should I trust God? Would it hurt to ask again? I murmured a prayer. "If you're real, please help. I can't fix me."

I didn't feel much different after my shower. But I did remember that a recounting of my interview with Perez and Hughe's veiled threat required attention. Calhoun's, specifically. He'd be interested in the papers on Thompson's desk, too, and as I thought of it, he passed me on the way to the shower.

"Hey."

"Hey, back." He saluted.

I sat at his desk and twirled in the chair. I stopped, opened a drawer, and a wallet tempted, like always. It may have fallen open on its own. An old picture, unrecognizable, was tucked into a sleeve.

"Is this one of Calhoun's relatives?" I twirled the chair and held up the faded picture. She looked familiar, maybe Calhoun's niece. If so, she didn't have those rough qualities. An attractive young woman.

"Calhoun's wife—"

"Mike, you idiot." Zoe shook her head.

"Excuse me?"

Mike held his hands palms up. "Catherine, don't get upset."

Zoe put a hand to her head. "Shut up, Mike."

A lump formed in my throat and didn't want to comply with a hard swallow. I croaked, "He's married?"

Mike shot Zoe a look. "You never heard?"

Zoe groaned. "You're making it worse—"

Mike said, "I didn't get to finish my sentence."

"Catherine. There really is an explanation." She looked back at Mike. "We just never really got the scoop. I'm sure Calhoun has a reason why he hasn't said anything. Yet."

"I'm positive you're right." *Because it's a lot easier to cheat on a wife that way*. I placed the picture onto the desk and smiled. "I'll ask him. Let me get the information first-hand." They both nodded. I wasn't up for tears or drama. Meant nothing to me, anyway. Time to stuff my clothes in my bag and make a quick getaway. I walked the hallway. My mind raced, and drama or no, I wanted to scream. I wiped tears away.

Early planning helped me ease my anxiety. I'd hot-wire a car, grab the stash Calhoun didn't know about, and find a motel for the night. I had a name change, Social Security application, and money order at home readied to drop in the mail to a Portland P.O. box. No more Calhoun. My bag secured and strapped across my body, I stopped at the door.

I boiled with rage and planned to give him a dose of wrath.

In front of the shower, I yelled, "Nice picture."

He poked his head out of the shower curtain. "Something wrong?"

"You have everything on me and leave me wondering. Your *wife*. She's half your age, and you cheat on her?"

Great facial distortion. Like I surprised him.

He hollered after me.

Zoe and Mike received a polite goodnight from me. I'd see them tomorrow. *Right.* Mike tried to say something, but I didn't listen, and the doors closed behind me.

Hurrying along the steps, I steadied my nerves and hoped not to lose my lunch in the bushes. I'd take back roads, drive to Joseph, and find a cheap room. It would be safer inching my way west toward the Dalles, hotwire another, and then Portland.

"Cade." Calhoun followed me, shoeless. "You don't understand."

Palms raised, I shook my head. "Don't even speak. I don't want an excuse. Give me a few days."

My hands shook with anger and anticipation of a fast getaway. Calhoun married, and to someone so young? She couldn't be over twenty.

I pushed the speed limit. What happened? An honest job. A man I fell for and thought reciprocated. I got conned this time.

My truck lurched into the driveway, and with jaw clenched, I threw open the door, ran to the end table, pulled up the throw rug, and the loosened wood panel. I thrust my hand into my hidden space.

I had pinched a diamond for Jerry a long time ago, worth one hundred fifty thousand. On my own, I'd hacked corrupt businessmen along the way, increasing my ill-gotten gains. Jerry thought I had botched the jewel heist, and I told myself it was worth the beating. I fenced the diamond on my own. This made half my cache, two hundred and fifty thousand dollars in accessible assets.

How far did I push the bags back? I grunted, grappling for the stuffed bags.

Where were they? On my hands and knees, I pushed my arm further, then grabbed my flashlight, and dug further under the boards of the floor.

"Catherine—"

I slammed the cache shut and jumped to my feet.

Calhoun barged in, shirt unbuttoned, and strode to me with teeth clenched. He grasped my arms with force enough to lift me off the floor.

"What?" Fear laced my voice.

"Don't do this. You run now, and I can't help you."

I wrenched my arms from Calhoun's clutch, which proved more challenging than expected.

"Why didn't—?"

"I lost my wife. Years ago." He released me.

Well, shut my mouth.

"Her name was Melanie."

With eyes closed, an involuntary and sad "ouch" emanated from within me. "Oh, Rick."

"You couldn't count on me?"

"Well, that was my plan. Then there's her picture. There's this perfect show you've put on, leaving me to guess if there's anything else to Rick Calhoun."

"Not my intention, and I am far from perfect." His eyes cast downward. "There's much to tell, someday when it's right. But I don't inspect my belly button enough to learn how women think, much less how you think."

"That's an interesting view." I frowned and studied my fingernails. "Talk."

Calhoun fiddled with his shirt. "Melanie's picture reminds me how I fell so far, I almost didn't come back. I need someone to remind me to not tumble into rabbit holes."

"Oh, no." I ended my fingernail fascination, scanning his eyes. "I hope you don't believe I'm competent in that arena."

"No. It's my turn." He pointed to the loosened board, and I felt my stomach plummet. "I'm here every evening for supper. You must think I'm all kinds of stupid. Perhaps you wanted me to find it."

My mouth fell open.

"Yup," he said.

"Thief!"

"Reasonable cause. On my initial stop here, you assumed or hoped I didn't look at the throw rug. Besides watching you struggle to straighten it with your toes, I reckoned, now why would anybody put a piece of carpet under a table? I copied the front door key, found your stuff, didn't even leave a mess. It's in lockup, and all is well."

It was always the little things that could destroy a plan, like a five-dollar throw rug. I sank onto the couch. He'd seized my running cash, most of it painfully obtained. I divided my supplies, because leaving everything in one place could result in a calamity, just like this. It had been a considerable amount of cash—two hundred fifty thousand, from the jewel, and the "work" I kept secret from Jerry.

Pain behind my eyes formed a migraine. "You robbed me. You didn't have a warrant, nothing—"

"A warrant? You want me to call the judge? This is rock bottom, because there's no way to cover for you."

Why didn't he drag me to jail the day he found the money? *Okay, okay.* There was another stash secreted away.

"Don't be afraid of me."

"Right, you're right."

He squeezed my shoulders.

"Now what?" I paced, requiring time to plan. "Calhoun, I believed in you. And you stripped me of everything, and it's in the evidence locker of all places. I didn't steal the money. I earned it."

"Uh-huh. You had over two hundred and fifty thousand in non-sequential bills, and you want me to believe it's earned income. You think Jerry's after you for his money?"

"Trust me, blood and terror earned every dime. Do you need a reminder?" I jerked my shirt from my pants to show him my back.

He placed his hands on mine. "I remember. But Jerry forced you to steal for him, and that's still illegal."

I lowered my head. Yes, it was. But survival mattered, and what Jerry drilled into me, I used against him.

He shifted his gaze. "Okay, you want to hear my past?"

Deflection? Calhoun would give up a story to keep me from talking about the cash. I'd let him drone on while I formulated a plan. "Yes, Rick. I need to hear something more than 'suck it up, cupcake.'"

Laugh lines appeared, then dissolved. "Melanie was a young woman, married to a hot-tempered cop."

I lifted my head. I understood hot temper. Jerry's hot temper broke bones, a few of them mine. "What? You hit Melanie?"

"No, never. But, you remember the medical examiner, Jack McCloud?"

"Yes." Fighting or dancing?

Calhoun puffed his cheeks. "McCloud was the flight surgeon who saved my life. Catherine, look, you aren't the only one who has endured pain or loss. Life doesn't rotate around us."

I kicked at the carpet, and when I looked back up, caught him removing his shirt, revealing the well-honed abdominal muscles of a thirty-year-old.

"Hey, clothing-impaired not allowed."

"Come here." When he turned his back toward me, I gulped and ran my hand along a deep diagonal scar along his torso.

"How did this happen?"

"An accident." He pivoted. "Stop gawking. I'm not your average slab of meat. McCloud wasn't my buddy, but when we were in the hospital, he boasted about his ability to bed any woman. Later, Jack worked in the morgue in Los Angeles, and I worked the robbery and homicide division. Melanie told me Jack made an aggressive advance toward her."

"No wonder you hate him."

Rick held up a hand. "On my day off, I confronted him after Melanie left for work. Handed him her picture and asked if he'd ever seen *this woman*, like she was a victim. He didn't recognize her or her first name and figured it was a body that came into the morgue and said it was a shame she died. His exact words were ... 'She looked like a great piece of tail.'" Calhoun winced. "I may have broken his nose. I stopped at the precinct to let the chief know what I'd done, and on my way home had a bad feeling. Melanie wasn't home when I got there. Turned on the scanner and heard about a hit-and-run a few miles from where Melanie worked. When I arrived, it was too late. She was gone. I could've protected her. Instead, I pulverized McCloud." He rested his head in his palms.

Horrified by such a tragedy and my overreaction, I touched his arm. "I am so sorry. You couldn't have known. What man stands up as a protector for women anymore? She was fortunate. Blessed."

He pulled me into an unexpected hug, pressing his face into my neck. Unsure what to do, I awkwardly patted him on the back.

Calhoun straightened and wiped tears away. "Melanie is my past. I settled here. Didn't realize Jack lived in Whiskey River. Guess I'm slow in the forgiveness department, and it's up to God to chisel away this anger."

He made interesting statements, allowing God to do the new work in him or me. And Calhoun forgiving the medical examiner, something which seemed unforgivable. I wasn't one thousand percent sure what he meant. We both rested on the couch, and I laid my head on the backrest. "She told you the analogy about the swimmers and Hawaii, and why we need God to get to heaven."

He stammered. "How did you know?" His internal conflict showed.

"A hunch. But is she why you assaulted McCloud while we were in the morgue?"

"Did you just use cop jargon on me?"

"Maybe."

"I came apart because of you, not Melanie. Tell me how deep this relationship with Jerry goes."

Calhoun had become the man I envisioned, whose face invaded my every dream of intimacy, but I still was answering questions like a suspect.

"What I am is what you see. The money and scars on my back. I lifted money and jewels from Jerry."

His head bowed, and he turned it side to side. "That's it?"

"Yep." *Sorta*.

"There was no marriage license under your alias. He faked it, so he could deny knowing you if the cops hauled you to jail."

My breathing halted. *Blown away* didn't describe my shock and relief. It was the first "Thank you, Jesus" moment I'd had.

"Until I decide what to do with you, I'm in charge of your cash and your truck."

"Why?" My voice cracked. "You wanted the truth so you could help me. How does taking my truck help?"

"What did I walk into? The door's open, the truck's engine running? You don't trust me or anyone else. If you have a vehicle, you'll run, and if you run, you'll find another car. You have more cash, and you'll start over. A truck or car goes missing in Southern Oregon, and I won't have to guess who has it because freaking out about the truck kinda clinches it."

And there went my freedom.

"You're leaving me no safety net."

He rubbed his head. "I'm your safety net now. Trust in me. Trust in God."

This was how God helped? "Thanks, I feel much better now. I have nothing. How do I work at the bakery? What do I tell Dr. Riley?"

He placed an arm around my waist, pulling me close. "The bakery has taken off. You'll be a wealthy woman with all that dough, pardon my pun. You no longer need to work at the clinic, considering you have a fake license."

"No clinic?"

He tugged on my hair. "Nope. With all those doughnuts, you'll have no problem affording anything. And you'll have plenty of company, seven days a week. Soon you'll have cold cases and homicide in your dreams."

More like murder would be on my mind. I asked with jaw clenched, "What do you mean, seven days a week?"

"Glad you asked. Zoe, Mike, and I will keep you close. We'll take shifts."

My voice faltered. "You told everyone?"

"Jerry's hunting you. You're not to be alone. They don't need to know you'd run. Not unless you give me a reason to tell them, along with the Oregon State Police and the FBI." He rubbed the stubble on his chin. "With all those passports, Interpol may become involved. When I told you I'd make an honest woman of you, I wasn't joking. Besides, we have a murder to solve. Oh, put those bug eyes back in your head."

Conciliatory words came from my mouth, and I tugged at my sweater collar. My escape plan had jelled. "When does this babysitting start?"

"Tonight. Grab blankets."

With arms crossed, I asked, "Why?"

"Zoe will need them." He thumbed his phone. "Zoe? Come on over and bring the cot. Cade's ready."

He fixed the couch for me to sleep on and nailed the windows shut. We waited for Zoe after he nailed the doors tight, dashing any hope I had of flight.

He wanted me to trust him and babysitting made it obvious I was untrustworthy. Made me antsy. If I didn't know everyone in the crew, taking off might be tricky, but I'd be in Portland before anyone figured I'd given them the slip. Portland, here I come. With or without the money.

A con's gotta run, and that's what I do.

CHAPTER 31

Rick Calhoun

Zoe settled in with Cade, and Calhoun snatched his ball cap, drove toward Salem, and found a reasonable hotel. He wove his way into the parking lot.

Once the door opened, he dropped his bags and flopped onto the bed. No blinking lights, no sirens wailing in the distance. Still, sleep escaped him. Almost like Cade.

Would he go after her if she ran?

She complicates my life. Didn't matter. He knew her history. Soon, he needed to explain everything to her.

He lay in bed, and ten excruciating minutes ticked by as he counted the ceiling's dots. He clicked on the lamp and sat on the bed's edge. Calhoun glanced in the mirror and rubbed the way-past-five-o'clock shadow on his face.

Here he sat, a forty-year-old loner, his temples graying. Around his hangdog eyes, the corners etched with crow's feet told of a hard, cynical life.

How would he reconcile his desire for Cade, a knockout with a penchant for running from the law, more specifically him? She had a warrior's soul and a servant's heart. How long would it be before they either self-destructed or found peace?

Jerry abused Cade, and she owned the scars to prove it. Rick figured he'd never be able to keep watch on her twenty-four-seven. *I'll train her harder.*

She was like a splinter, impossible to work out, cantankerous, sarcastic, and hotter than a stolen tamale. A little lollipop triple-dipped in psycho. Go figure. He loved her, a height-challenged con artist, and nothing could stop his heart from wanting to marry her.

Stop this or forget Camille Tate's morning interview.

How had Camille Tate interacted with Thompson, the dead commissioner, and the father of their daughter, Lily? He would press Tate to tears if necessary. Strong emotion, something to prick the heart, could bring her to confess either her profound grief or murder. How had she managed finances after her daughter's chemo and funeral? Should be interesting.

Calhoun had plenty of questions for her, and a side trip to Portland to discover more answers, not with the Thompson case, but with Cade. He pinched a sliver of paper from the bedside table, held it to the window as moonlight shone on it. Then he turned a storage-unit key between his fingers.

What will I find this time?

At last he fell asleep with his Springfield tucked nearby.

TUESDAY

He woke to the shrill ring of the automated wake up call. He grabbed the handset and slammed it back into the cradle. Grousing his way out of bed with a yawn, he rubbed his face and ambled to the bathroom.

Coffee brewed, far better than the station's, but not like Catherine's. He dressed and readied for the interview with Tate. *Cade.* Her crazy antics may have changed their lives. Soon, he'd ask her for a real date.

If he didn't hyperventilate first.

Cleaned up and coffee'd out, he found his way to Tate's home for a *tête-à-tête*. A short green hedge, neatly sheared, rounded part of the home. An archway covered with bare grapevines greeted him, and he pushed the gate open and ambled through. The two-story Craftsman home boasted a mid-sized A-frame, white paint with blue trim. Ferns curled in the near-freezing cold while bare red and orange leaves on the lawn spread like a blanket around wintering Japanese maples. Showy winter cabbages took over, while creeping thyme was surviving the cold air just dandy.

Armed with a fake name and badge, and with a bogus warrant stamped OFFICIAL, he rapped his knuckles on the arched but simple wooden blue door.

"Yes?" A redheaded woman, about fifty years old, opened the door. "How can I help you?"

Calhoun presented the ID and paperwork. "Mrs. Camille Tate?"

"Yes, that's me."

"Good morning. I'm Detective Jacob Schultz, with Salem PD. I have a few questions about your ex-husband, Stephen Thompson."

Confusion crossed her face. "But he died months ago."

"Yes, ma'am. Just dotting i's and crossing t's."

"I'm not sure I understand. He had a heart attack, I heard. Come in, have a seat. Care for a cup of coffee?"

After stepping through the doorway, he eyed the living room. "Thank you, no. When did you last see Mr. Thompson?"

She twisted her hands. "A year ago? I can't recall."

"Was there a specific reason for your meeting him?"

Her words came in a whisper. "Yes, I wanted financial support for our daughter. He refused. Why?"

"Standard questions. Do you remember his state of mind?"

"Yes. He appeared depressed. I suspected his wife said no to monetary help."

"Did he have health issues?"

She paused. "He had diabetes, didn't control it well. Is that how he really died?"

Calhoun looked her in the eye. "Routine follow-up, that's all." He launched into his next question. "When did you divorce, if I may ask?"

"I–I ..." she stuttered "... four years ago, December."

"Thank you." He turned toward the door, then made a circle, raising a finger. "Oh, ma'am, before I go, I have a warrant to search the home for items that could prove evidential in his death. I understand you have a pistol. I need to collect it. Routine. I'll return it."

"Then there's more, isn't there? She killed him! She shot him, that witch."

"She, who?"

"His widow." She shook her head. "I hope he left her as high and dry as he did me. Homewrecker."

He bagged the gun, thanked her for her time, and left.

Calhoun made his way through Portland's spaghetti-noodle freeway to the labyrinth of storage units that wound a circuitous route. Near his parking space, he found Cade's small room locked. He hesitated.

Rick turned the key, removed the padlock, and raised the door. With hands on hips, he said, "You gotta be kiddin' me."

CATHERINE CADE

Around-the-clock protection still stuck close. Calhoun's supervision kept me trapped. I hated being confined. There were more reasons to leave Whiskey River. I was convinced Jerry had found me, and the ominous events were messages from him.

Calhoun wanted too much from me. Or maybe I wanted something I couldn't have. If he wanted God to change me, the Man Upstairs was sure taking his time. And, despite the trust Calhoun had put in me, we still circled one another like wolves.

Time to leave. And like a punch to the gut, the foreverness hit hardest that last night. In the morning, I had to excuse myself to the bathroom just before Zoe and I left, under the pretext of allergies. I spent time alone in the bathroom and wept, then fixed my makeup.

I bid Zoe goodbye after her night shift. Mike whisked me to the Who Donut, and his job meant sticking as close to me as a thin spread of mayo on wheat bread. I mulled over my plot and pulled my emotions together.

Another scam. I liked Mike, but again, things weren't much different from many other marks I'd once conned.

I'd begun serving espresso in the bakery after number-crunching showed I'd be selling black gold. It didn't need a rocket scientist to make the frothy goodness, nor a tough old gold miner to appreciate a double whammy of chocolate in a cup of coffee, strong enough to raise a mammoth. Mike's favorite was double-chocolate-double-espresso, and extra whipping cream, topped off with scones, Devonshire clotted cream and jam, and Mike wouldn't be able to run if forced.

He droned on regarding work, dealing with the underbelly of crime. Identity thieves, prostitutes, and drug dealers kept him busy. Mike Tanaka was quite adorable. Smart, charming, and fun, he'd soon find himself among many vice detectives who'd tried but never caught me.

I pressed my hand on his, and the time came to close Operation Run. Mike had almost slathered over me when we first met. The perfect mark.

"You have a mustache." With a finger against his lips, I wiped the frothy cream away and licked my finger.

Like fireworks on a moonless night, his eyes widened. It always worked.

I pulled off the whipped cream, flattery, and bedroom eyes flawlessly. A vice detective required everything in my repertoire.

I dropped my gaze and measured a beat before I raised my eyes to his face. Mike stared. I played demure and delicate.

Today, I'd run.

We sat for another half hour, and I caressed his arm occasionally. Superglue couldn't have made his grin more permanent.

"So, this is a high-sugar lunch for me. Want to work off these calories?"

"I–I–"

"Mike, let's go for a run around Whiskey River Park, what do you think?"

"Uh." He swallowed.

"Yeah." I licked the whipping cream off the Swizzler. "Can't though, Calhoun being my boss, since he's in charge." I paused. "Besides, we'd be sweaty after workout."

"Well, it's not like I'm incapable. I can police myself."

"You're funny, but I'm going stir crazy. I can run while you keep an eye on me." Timing was crucial, and I chewed my lip and lowered my eyes. Then I rose from the table and stretched.

"No, you're right, I'd have to shower."

A camera would have captured precious moments. Like when Mike dropped his scone and sprayed coffee from his mouth.

CHAPTER 32

I ushered Mike to a bench with a clear view of my path, so he could track my every move, almost. Several trees gave me a twenty-second lead.

I'd zip across the street, hot-wire a car, and be on my way.

"Okay, this is a two-mile run. Two laps?"

"No problem." He pointed. "Don't disappear."

"You have eyes on me." I kissed him on the cheek, and he blushed. I tapped his binoculars, started a slow jog, and chuckled.

About five minutes into my run, I stopped out of Mike's view and headed left onto a side street toward an empty car with a window down. A van slowed next to me and blocked my view of the park. The voice stopped me cold.

"Sonia."

Jerry.

A wire of terror tightened around my neck at his voice, and I spun and clenched my fists. My breath came in small gasps.

"Hi, sweet cheeks." He beamed as he jumped from the van. I'd seen this look before. Despite his boyish and charming appeal, his blondish hair still in a mullet, my world was about to end.

Bile rose in my gut. My hand swept away the sweat from my face. I was frantic and unable to see Mike.

"How did you find me?"

He grasped my arms. "We have a job. Remember? We go home richer than Midas. How did you like my reminder?"

"The ditch?"

"The bridge." A maniacal, guttural jeer escaped his throat. Like when he snorted cocaine. "How could you forget?"

"What job? What home? This is your fantasy, not mine."

"You're my wife, and you are here because you're supposed to be working, checking schematics, ingratiating yourself. Instead, I find you working in a doughnut shop, hanging around cops. Not smart." He tightened his grip on me. "And you took what doesn't belong to you. It's time you do a little sharing."

My voice quavered, and I twisted my arm free. "Leave."

"What did your cop boyfriend think, you being a con? Here's the perfect job, our retirement, and you've swerved from the plan with lover boy. Yeah, I know all about Calhoun." He ran a finger across my cheek, then slapped it. "He ain't here." Squeezed my face with one hand as my gut wrenched. "You changed course over a cop. Never think with your low IQ."

"What did you do to Rick?"

"First name basis?" He pulled my arms. "I wouldn't worry about him. Waste of a good bullet."

"Leave!" A handful of people turned heads my way but kept walking.

"Sonia, you've never screamed at me before. How I've missed the groveling." Jerry grinned, lifting my chin. "You have plenty of time to start again."

Sonia Newton, the identity he'd given me, had died. Catherine Cade took over. "I want you out of my life and my state."

Jerry reeked of alcohol. His eyes widened, and he spewed angry cuss words. Now, with any public view shielded by his vehicle, he grabbed my hair, and rammed my face against the van. "Angel, it's time you pick up the slack. You will help finish this job."

I came close to fainting from fear. I'd played Mike. Rick might be dead. This was my reward.

He hissed in my ear, "Who's the one who came to take you home and keep you safe from the world? We finish what we started and go home."

"Safe? You wouldn't know the difference between good and evil if it hit you on the head. All you've ever done is use me." My sweat and tears mingled as I trembled.

He'd shattered me, ruined my life, and the abuse would start all over again.

"Used you?" His breath and stench, hot against my face, gagged me. "Honey, I ain't even started to use you. If you don't finish the job and come home with me, I will end your worthless life."

Jerry's breath, heavy with cheap beer and stale cigarettes, hung in the air. If I cried and begged him to stop, it wouldn't end there. If ever I could use God's help, this would be the time.

He opened the van door. The vehicle reeked of tobacco, rotgut liquor, and sour sweat. A splinter of light shone on a filthy mattress. His reunions entailed a focused peak, fueled by cocaine tempered with alcohol. *No, this can't be.* The hairs on my neck pricked in dread.

A broken mirror and straw lay next to the mattress in the van. My knees gave way. He grasped my hair, and his icy fingers found my throat from behind.

I said, "You–you–can't do this."

He pressed his mouth to my ear in a whisper. "Oh, she quakes. You see, prostitutes cost money, and they don't scare. You do what I tell you and tremble because you respect me."

No one would know. He'd force me to steal again and hand him whatever he wanted.

My plot included escape. It didn't include Jerry. No. No! Anger replaced fear. I'd had a plan for him for a long time.

I found my determination and shoved my hips back, braced my hands against the van, and turned on him. Didn't even bother with my gun because a bullet wouldn't bring the satisfaction I wanted. With a turn of my hip, I slammed the heel of my hand against the cheekbone beneath his eye. He reeled backward, but I lunged forward and slammed my hand into his face again, his nose cracking beneath my palm. He howled in pain. I repeated a slam to his other eye.

Jerry couldn't see me. My right hand curled into a fist, and with the strength coming from my hips, I shoved my fist into his bared neck. He crumpled like paper, falling to his knees under the strike. He grasped his throat, gasping for air.

I fell backward as he clutched my leg. I kicked his face with the other. He tumbled onto his back and cried for mercy. I clenched my teeth, stood, and stomped on him. Lost count of my kicks.

You will never hurt me again.

I yanked my pistol from my holster and chambered a round.

"No, no, please," he begged, with blood and tears criss-crossing his mangled face. He held his hands up. "We can work things out."

"Really? Okay, let's work it out." I dropped the magazine and put it in my pocket, gripped the barrel of the pistol, and dropped a knee to his mid-section. "This is for killing Rick and destroying my life." With the butt of the gun raised, I readied to finish the job.

A hand jerked my arm behind me, pulling the pistol from my grip. I yelped in surprise. Before I could turn, someone yanked me back. I pivoted and shoved him. Dropped a side kick to his hand, and he dropped the pistol. Then I threw a left kick to his groin. Thought he'd hit the ground, but he buckled instead, pitched forward, and he rolled me facedown into the dirt.

A knee pressed into my back and I cried out. He pulled my hands behind my back in a sharp move and zip tied my wrists. When he flipped me over, I could taste blood in my mouth. I couldn't see for the dirt in my eyes.

"Let me go!"

Click. "Ambulance to Whiskey River Park Road."

"Get off me!"

The man said, "Quiet, now—"

I spat at his face.

"Okay, if that's the way you're gonna play it." He flipped me back to my stomach and tightened the zip ties on my wrists.

"Send a cruiser to Whiskey River Park Road. Suspect is apprehended."

I cried.

"Catherine!" Another voice yelled.

I jerked against the ties, screamed, and whacked my head on the ground.

My chest shuddered with ragged breaths. My body ached, but the shaking subsided. Sirens wailed.

Rick and Mike. Calhoun talked as he raised me to my feet. His eyes were on Mike, his jaw muscle twitching. "Why did you let her go off on her own?"

"I—"

"Go deal with Jerry. Ambulance is on its way."

Everything hurt, and my hands trembled, but I calmed as he cut the ties. With his jacket, he wiped my face, then helped me around the van.

I placed my hands on his chest, needing assurance he was real. "He told me he killed you."

"I'm pretty indestructible." He glanced around. "Put your hood up and face me. A crowd's gathering, and you're bleeding."

I flipped the hoodie up and rubbed my wrists. "It's not my blood."

"What happened?"

"Jerry found me."

"You played Mike."

"I wanted to go for a run." My teeth chattered.

"Right." Calhoun led me to the cruiser while the emergency medical technician rolled the gurney past with Jerry, a pile of hamburger with a pulse.

"Check the van."

He looked into the vehicle and swallowed. "Catherine—"

I kicked errant leaves on the sidewalk and pointed at the van. "Jerry's mobile house of horror. You saved me again."

A line creased across his forehead—his thoughts easy to read.

I said, "Jerry's violent and fixated on me. You taught me to survive."

"Not like this."

My hands throbbed, and I checked for fractures. "If you didn't, who did?"

He didn't answer. "I'll have Mike take him over to Booking. I'll charge him with drunk and disorderly, aggravated assault with a deadly weapon, attempted kidnapping, and attempted murder. Kidnapping is a federal offense."

"He didn't—what weapon are you talking about?"

Calhoun motioned to the vehicle. "His van. He slammed you into its side." He glanced toward the media and gently moved me away from them. "I'll get you out of here, get him processed through the hospital, and we'll book him. He's going away. You'll give a statement downtown. Will you be able to testify?"

"Yeah, I can."

At last Jerry resembled the monster he'd always been. Now he had a monster's face.

CHAPTER 33

After the ER checked me over, we returned to Rick's. I showered, turning the hot water on and scraping my nails through my scalp and hair to get rid of the blood. I clenched my teeth at the water's nearly unbearable heat. Finished, I stood before the mirror, tears still streaking my face as I scrubbed my fingernails, embedded with blood.

Calhoun knocked. "You okay? It's been an hour."

"Out in a minute." My hand ran over the sweats Calhoun gave me, and I dressed and went out to the living room.

Calhoun came to me. His fingers tugged my collar, and he checked the back of my neck, then my hands.

"I can't get them clean."

"You near about burned yourself, and there's nothing in your fingernails. Is this about Jerry or guilt?" He strode to his refrigerator and handed me a frozen steak.

I gaped. "Why would you say such a thing?"

He turned, his voice bordering on harsh. "You could have put a bullet in him. No, you could have emptied an entire magazine into him, and it would have been ruled justifiable homicide. What you did—"

"What I did brought a hallelujah to the lips of every woman ever abused." I thrust my chin in the air.

"You sank to his level. There's no hallelujah in that."

"You've never been in my shoes."

I handed him the steak and he returned it to the freezer. He walked to the living room and switched on the TV.

"Late breaking news tonight." A TV anchor spoke, a young man with well-groomed blond hair. "An unidentified woman survived a savage assault at Whiskey River Park. A witness caught this video on a cell phone."

The upper corner of the TV screen showed a man slamming me into the side of the van.

Calhoun said, "Zoe found a mug shot of Jerry from the California Department of Corrections and faxed it to the newsroom, by the way." A menacing picture of Jerry replaced the video.

They edited the part where I rearranged Jerry's face.

The anchor continued. "Reports state he has a history of kidnapping and aggravated assault. The DA's office declines further comment."

Calhoun paced. "You played Mike, but instead, your ex-partner grabbed you. You figured you'd outsmarted him, and he still caught you unprepared."

"No. I could've killed him."

He snapped his neck my way when he returned the steak to the freezer. "You could've killed him? I'm not okay with that. You were in a zone I'd never seen, and it wasn't you."

"If not for you going RoboCop on me every day, I'd be another Jane Doe on McCloud's slab. Each day you train me harder than the day before. Jerry taught me how to endure life on the streets, but you taught me how to survive Jerry. What I did was in self-defense." I crossed my arms.

"I didn't recognize this—this *you*." He sat on the couch, clicked the remote, and the screen flickered to black. "I know out-of-control when I see it, and this wasn't rage or righteous anger. You weren't in the black zone. You'd planned for a long time to murder him." He held up a hand. "I get it, he tortured you. But you can't make up the law."

My voice raised. "And you can? Calhoun, you said you'd rip his face off, and you didn't."

"Because you did it for me, didn't you? And now we'll never know."

"I thought he'd killed you. After that, I didn't care if I was tossed into a prison or dead. I just didn't care."

A few moments passed. He put his arms around me and sighed.

Pressing Calhoun's head against me, pensive, my fingers traced the lines of his forehead. "I want a heart of stone."

Calhoun pushed from me, holding me at arms' length. "It

took a long time for God to soften my heart. You want to be a stone? Empty?"

I examined my hands, painful, scuffed, and swollen. "But I feel strong—knowing I can be a stone."

"Tell me, Catherine, what happens when that's all that's left? I won't train you, not if you want to kill without conscience."

I flicked my view away.

"From what I saw, you controlled what Jerry received. But you didn't opt for justice. No, no, not Catherine Cade. She's above the law. Whether it's Mike's job, Jerry's life, yours, or mine. You attacked me. Once you swore you'd never harm me. If I hadn't taken your gun, I'd be on the slab next to Jerry. It says in the Bible that God will take vengeance. Here, by the law, and in the afterlife. I believed I knew your heart. Guess I still don't."

What he said stung. I'd been living a sociopathic life, like Jerry, and I was in control enough, so I could still see my calculated moves. Even though he ended in mush, I hadn't seen him coming.

Worse, Calhoun's words pained me. *I believed I knew your heart. Guess I still don't.*

The full weight of the attack sacked my emotions. I'd wandered from what I thought was right into what was certainly wrong.

I sat next to Calhoun and buried my head in his chest and wept. He hesitated, and then wrapped his arms around me.

But he hesitated.

MONDAY

Things normalized between us. Calhoun's chill toward me thawed, and we fell into our old routine. Alone in the police department at lunchtime, he eased his way toward my plate of spaghetti. If I didn't keep vigilant, noodles disappeared onto his fork and into his mouth.

"It's apparent you're not getting enough food. There's more in the fridge." I tugged the plate from him.

"I'm so hungry I could eat a horse and chase the rider. Can you heat a plate for me?" He tried to sneak more noodles from my dish.

"I can't believe you're guilting me into microwaving your lunch."

He rubbed his hands together. "I don't want to eat so fast that I'm finished before I get started. What's for dinner?"

I located the spaghetti and peered at him over the fridge door. "What am I, your servant?"

"Yup."

I focused a drill-bit evil eye at him which he missed. I thought back to something that continued to vex me. "Remember the Prius the day I tackled you?"

He nodded. "Yup."

"On my run, I saw a man at the store fiddling with a remote control."

"You didn't mention this before."

I pulled a face and shrugged.

He scanned my empty plate and seemed forlorn.

"Can I go to where it's kept in evidence?" I took oven mitts, brought the breadsticks from the microwave, and placed them on the table.

"Nope."

"The way I see it, bumping you off would end this case."

"Should I be worried?"

"Keep testing me." I brought him more spaghetti.

His face brightened, and he dug in. "Mike found the vehicle identification number. A car dealer leased it to a man in California. He fell behind making his payments and when the car disappeared, he believed they'd repossessed it. His alibi checked out."

He chewed and reflected a moment. "Whoever took the Prius would have hacked into the car's computer system to allow remote control. That kind of specialized knowledge is way above most hackers' pay grade."

"You heard about the board member who died the same month as Thompson? A woman—I don't recollect her name."

A noodle hung from his mouth as he considered. Then he sucked it up, and said, "Nicki Griffith. Car crash."

"Convenient. The last voice against land development."

Calhoun ditched his fork and scooped a few noodles with his fingers. He upturned his chin and slurped, grabbing the last breadstick and slopping up sauce.

My expression much have given me away, because Calhoun asked, "What?"

I got a napkin and wiped sauce from his chin. "I can't take you anywhere. When was Camille Tate's daughter diagnosed with leukemia?"

"Age fourteen, six months before she died."

"Still puts Lily's mother as a person of interest."

He chewed on a breadstick. "Which is why I interviewed her."

"When?"

"When your babysitting started."

I belched out my interviews with total recall. "Well, I interviewed the mayor's dandy, Darren Hughe, and John Perez, the Thompsons' gardener. I also found out an illegal immigrant once worked maintenance on the property. Rafael Santiago."

He choked on his food. "You what?"

I smoothed my slacks and studied the pattern on the linoleum floor.

"When did you plan on telling me?" he said. "I didn't want you interviewing anyone else."

"You couldn't question them."

"What if you interviewed a killer? Those were the people I didn't want to question."

His words unnerved me. I swallowed.

"Now they have your name."

"I—I didn't think—"

"No, you didn't." Calhoun swiped an arm across his face. "Okay, spill it."

I told him about what Perez said, about Darren Hughe's veiled threat, and at Sarah Thompson's office, the note with one word written on it—*bakery*. And last, the editor's investment on the low-bid development. Then I told him about Elsa Stephens, the ex-fiancée of John Murray. "Turns out he used her considerable social connections to get the votes to put him on the committee. He dropped her right after he was elected."

Calhoun growled disapproval. He took my plate and shoveled more spaghetti into his mouth. "Camille Tate and Stephen Thompson shared the same caliber gun."

He'd promised to take me along. "We have to find the—"

"Rifling report is on your thumb drive. We need to compare weapons."

"When?"

He caught my eye and looked away, busying himself with his spaghetti. *Convenient.* "Jerry Street turned out to be an FBI informant. He may have killed a woman before he grabbed you. He linked up with the agency, and they gave him a deal." Calhoun quieted. "People I care for. It's unconscionable."

Like a putrid mass of emotional compost, he dumped the information into my lap, and misery tainted my meal. The FBI cut a deal, no surprise. I was unaware of another of Jerry's victims. When the nausea passed, I forged on, angry.

"You can't stop slopping through my past, can you?"

"Do you want to keep running? Don't you want to know who you are? I told you we'd face this together, good or bad, and I meant it."

I twisted away, wiping tears from my face. Of course, I wanted to know my identity. Of course, I wanted to stop running. If Jerry had spread his torturous misery and murdered another woman as the FBI looked away, they might as well have given him their blessing.

Calhoun put both hands on the table. "The contact I have. I haven't told you who, but this person found information, and it may have fallen into the wrong hands. The final blame falls on me. I promised to protect you."

"It wasn't your fault." I composed myself. "Jerry said this was our retirement job. That's how I found Whiskey River." I pointed to my head. "That factoid is here. Locked away."

"Now he's locked away, and there is no job."

What kind of heist would require me to move to a rural town for three years? What had I forgotten?

CHAPTER 34

CHRISTMAS

Christmas came, and Calhoun dragged me to his friends' house, more like a palace. Guests filled a foyer the size of my home. Sam and Amy introduced themselves, and Calhoun abandoned me while Amy hooked her arm in mine. She asked interesting questions which I deflected as best as possible. Lovely Christmas or convincing setup?

I spotted McCloud with Kim on his arm.

"Amy, how long has Kim been dating McCloud?"

She whispered. "Off and on. Convenient for both. He's the medical examiner, she's his lab tech. She's a crazy blonde, but she's fun to be around."

Hmm. Morgue Day was around the corner. Later, I caught up with her and told her where Calhoun and I were going in preparation for my forensics stint. Working with Kim in the Dead Room, I decided, would be fun.

JANUARY 2ND

I called Jules and wished her a belated Merry Christmas and updated her on my new status as a Christian. She laughed and called me a Jesus freak. I protested the freak part.

Calhoun brought me to a home study with other people once a week for food and Bible stuff. Life-changing. *Yawn.* The transformation department must have a waiting list. My attention waned within minutes over difficult passages. It was like reading Tolstoy to a three-year-old.

Fears changed in other ways. Calhoun shoved aside the cynic in me, and I was a true believer in a happily-ever-after. I never remembered being in love, but my heart told me Calhoun was the one.

I packed for the forensics conference in Wisconsin, where I'd lose myself in a crowd for a few days. Two thousand miles from Whiskey River, I could forget memories of Jerry, which alone made the trip worthwhile.

We drove to Medford, and at five a.m., boarded the plane.

I pressed my nose against the plane's window after we settled in our seats. The sun peeped over the distant Siskiyou Mountains as the plane taxied.

I turned to Calhoun who gritted his teeth. Note to self—*Calhoun, terrified.*

"This is the best part. The rush to be airborne." I buckled my seat belt. "Thanks for the window seat." The whine and screech of the engines, the groan of the flaps brought me excited anticipation.

The jet rushed forward, pushing passengers back in their seats. I leaned, taking in the excitement as the plane sped along the runway, lifting airborne, past trees and buildings. The wheels hissed as the hydraulics raised them into their wells with a final clunk.

We flew over Upper and Lower Table Rock as the plane climbed. I'd hiked Lower Table Rock but had never flown over either plateau. The plane inched over the mountains, and I played with my ponytail as the pilot made sure people in both aisles could appreciate the sight, dipping the wings one way and another.

I loved to fly. And here, a more magnificent sight could not be found. "Rick, have you ever seen this from the air? It's amazing."

"Takin' your word for it."

"Where's your childlike enthusiasm?"

He didn't answer.

I watched the disappearing view of Upper and Lower Table Rock. I wondered in awe how the Whiskey River had channeled its way through until these two statuesque sentinels stood guard over the valley floor. They were trekkers' heaven in spring when the blooms burst, covering the dry mounts with wildflowers.

I turned back to scrutinize the detective.

"It's supposed to be foggy in Portland," I said, trying to elicit a response as I rubbed my hands together. "Makes for interesting landings."

"Thanks."

I studied his stiff, stoic posture. He faced forward with eyes closed. A soldier scared stiff at thirty-thousand feet in the air cruising around five hundred miles per hour brought the thought—how fast can a planeload of people straitjacket a panicked soldier?

We were to connect for another flight to Wisconsin. He'd need plenty of alcohol to manage the next journey.

"I have an extra barf bag if you need it. One might not be enough." I pressed a hand on his arm. "It's a plane, not a nuclear bomb."

"Says the woman who can shoot to kill but jumps in my arms when she thinks she sees a bug."

"Once. It was huge, like a tarantula."

"It was a fishing lure."

"Hmm." The plane climbed, easing past the clouds, and Calhoun's knuckles were white. "So what happened?"

He opened his eyes and turned his head my way after a lengthy silence. "Marine. Long before Whiskey River." He stared at the seat he faced.

This tidbit was familiar. I allowed him thirty seconds, then asked, "Which gave you the fear of airplanes."

"Am I going to get out of this?"

"You don't have to explain."

"Good."

I exaggerated a sigh and peered at him. The Marine remained unmoved. Five minutes passed, and I coughed. Pretended to sneeze. Cleared my throat.

His head twisted back and searched my face. "I knew you wouldn't let this go."

I frowned.

"Twenty-fourth MEU."

"Huh?"

"Iraq, 1999. Ancient history."

"Okay." I lowered the window shade. I didn't want to unravel more, asking what MEU stood for, not on the plane.

Once in Wisconsin, I'd tap into my favorite search engine. The quest would wait. I unpeeled his fingers from the armrest and held his hand.

The commuter plane dipped and shuddered. Taken by surprise, Calhoun let loose swear words I'd never heard him utter, while at the same time crushing my fingers. *Ow.* My attempt to suppress a wince failed.

The pilot came over the intercom. "This is your pilot. We're in for a little turbulence, folks. A regular E-ticket at Disneyland."

"You okay?" I chewed the inside of my cheek. "What's an E-ticket?"

"My worst nightmare."

"Want to pray?"

Calhoun was wide-eyed. "For real?"

"For real."

He curled his fingers around mine. "Just to let you in on a secret, I've been praying for you ever since I met you."

I didn't ask why. No need. I knew why.

He straightened in his seat and apologized for his earlier reaction. His lips brushed my hand. I scrutinized this action.

"Kissing your boo-boo. Get over yourself." He closed his eyes. "Now shut up, I want to sleep."

But for the rest of the flight he intertwined his fingers with mine.

CHAPTER 35

We made it to Wisconsin without the need to feed Calhoun alcohol. He dropped me off to nab the keys at the Crowne Plaza desk. I wandered the wide hallways and admired the hotel's circular impression, then thumped the card against my fingers while waiting for the lift's familiar ding.

The doors opened, and unprepared for an elevator mate, I stepped forward and looked at a handsome young man with an infectious grin, impossible not to return. He sported a scruffy beard and ponytail. My hands full, I asked him to press floor number five.

"Sure." He stretched across me and pushed my floor number. Then he checked me out, craned his neck, and took a gander at my key card. I played my key to the vest like a poker card and pulled away. *Yech.*

He murmured an apology with a smirk.

I pushed the door to my room open. "Wow." The clean white walls and bedspread contrasted with the dark cherry armoire near the double bed. My bags dropped from my hands, and I placed my computer on the burnished table.

I set my thumb drive's coin purse by the laptop and rushed to put my clothes away in the armoire. I sprawled on the bed and collapsed in comfort. *Ahhhhh.* My eyes popped open when I remembered, by a whisker, the mission to find MEU. I fired up the laptop and clicked on the search engine.

Twenty-fourth MEU. Marine Expeditionary Unit. A footnote said it was a "mission of mercy." The names of two survivors from the faltering helicopter caused me to sit back—Rick Calhoun and Jack McCloud. Calhoun's scar. That's how the injury happened. *How did he survive a percussion impact from a blade slicing through the air?* It defied belief, the laws of physics, and anatomy. I'd evade plane transit, too. We'd drive back, even if I made a lame excuse.

When Rick rapped on the adjoining door, I stopped, closed the browser, and turned off the computer. I went to the door and pulled it open. "Who are you looking for?"

He glanced up, then lifted his head and squinted. "Keep the door open a crack."

"Why?"

"Because I know you." He showed off his crow's feet around his eyes with an upturn to his lips. "Be grateful I don't take your computer hostage."

"Do not touch my computer, understand?" I waggled a finger at him. "On pain of death."

He held a palm in the air. "No worries. I don't read romance novels."

We'd ordered takeout pizza, and it rumbled in my gut at 1 a.m. I stared at the clock after tossing and turning, and decided to do something productive. I polished the first chapters of my novel and hit SAVE.

The front desk clerk on the phone informed me the pool was open. Within a few minutes, I was in my swimsuit, and towel in hand, I headed for a swim. The same man I'd seen in the elevator hours before sat in a chair at the end of the swimming pool.

The hair on my arms rose. "Hi."

He gave me a wave. "Hello. I'm Sal, the lifeguard."

"You've been here all night?"

"No. I get a call from the desk when someone goes for a swim."

I acknowledged him, slipped into the pool, and counted laps. A splash caused me to turn. I halfway expected Calhoun.

No one occupied the lifeguard chair. A man's arms cut through the water in the next lane. He moved into my space, closing fast. His hand brushed my ankle. I panicked and dove to the bottom, then propelled myself up onto the cement that surrounded the pool and ran.

The tile beyond the cement lip was wet, and I slipped. I snatched my towel and glanced back to see Sal coming in my direction, leering. I caught my balance and sprinted to the locker room. I skittered and slid around the corner, crashing my way through the shower room, certain his footfalls splashed in puddles behind me.

Calhoun woke to a door closing. He yanked on his jeans and pushed the connecting-room door open, flashlight in hand. The light shone across the bed, which was empty. He twisted the knob on the light, illuminating the room.

He knocked, then pushed against the bathroom door. "Catherine?" Flipped the switch. Nothing.

Red splatters on the bedcovers stopped Calhoun dead. His chest tightened. He examined the bedspread, snagged a tissue, dabbed at a crimson splotch, and waved it under his nose. He bowed his head. "Thank you, Lord."

Pizza sauce. *Miss Manners has her moments.*

The desk clerk told him she'd called regarding pool hours. Relieved, Calhoun heaved a sigh. It was unreasonable to escort her everywhere, and Jerry was in prison. He checked his watch. Ten minutes. She might run, but never without her computer. He grasped the doorknob and halted.

The computer.

The laptop hummed, with the thumb drive in the USB port. Her novel. He glimpsed back at the computer and extended his hand toward it. What was the harm? He squeezed his eyes shut. No, it wouldn't be right.

At their first face-off in her home, she'd climbed over him to close her work. Could it be an autobiography? Crime fiction? A romance?

This needed a thorough evaluation. He sat on the couch, raised the screen to the laptop, and unexpected words in French tumbled across the screen. When he hit ENTER, the screen went blue.

Tapping keys without success, he whispered, "No, no, no!"

I sprinted the length of the hall and slammed my hand against Calhoun's door. Frantic, I looked over my shoulder, weirded out. I was certain Sal would appear any moment.

"Calhoun, open the door!" My heart pounded, and nauseated, I ran to my door and fumbled for the key card. Breathless, I kept calling his name. My door flew open, and Calhoun ran into me. Frantic, I pressed against him, suppressing tears.

"What—" He snapped his head toward the hall. "What happened? You're shaking." His arm drew me closer. "You okay?"

There was no one in the hall, no pounding footsteps approaching. "I—nothing. Paranoid." Calhoun calmed me without realizing he did so, and I pushed my hair out of the way. "A Jerry moment, I guess. I'm fine." The creepy pool guy wasn't chasing me—he'd gone for a swim. Accidental lane change in the pool. How could I be such an idiot?

I pulled the towel around me tight. "Calhoun, why do you have my computer?"

He held my laptop in one hand and stuttered, another side of him I'd never seen.

"Rick?"

We sat at my desk, and I studied him as his eyes bored into mine. Beads of sweat formed on his face.

"I ... I killed your laptop." He put the computer on the table and pointed. "I'm praying there's something wrong with it, 'cause I don't want to be the reason it crashed."

"What did you do?"

"It was fine. Then I touched it."

"Thought you weren't interested in what I wrote."

"Well, um, I was prying, and then the screen died." He thrust his hands into his pockets. "I'm sorry for both looking without your consent and murdering your computer."

I raised the laptop's screen. It remained blue until I entered a password onto the blank page. Words tumbled upward, and the page erupted into a quivering mass of French. "It's a screen saver." I forced a smile, because my heart still fluttered from unfounded fears.

He straightened. "Okay. I guess I'll go on to bed now. See you before the conference."

"Yeah." I followed him to the adjacent door between our rooms and stopped him. "Hey, can you keep the door open all the way?"

His hands rested on his hips. "Want me to sit in your room?"

"Yes. No, I mean, can I take a shower in your bathroom?"

"Why?"

"Nothing." Goosebumps crawled along my arms.

"Sure, I'll wait in your room."

"No. Sit right there." I pointed to his desk.

I closed the door and showered, still shaken. Accustomed to Calhoun's expressions, I recognized the worry on his face.

Unable to sleep after my encounter with the lifeguard, I turned on the computer to search out information on interviewees Calhoun had discussed. I did a deep search and found interesting information on Tony Abara's background. His lie intrigued me. Why would he fudge the information about where he was from?

I passed out around four a.m. and woke to the clock's alarm. I jumped out of bed and dressed. We met up in the hallway, and I was thankful to see him.

Calhoun wore brown slacks with a matching jacket, pale blue shirt, and dark tie, complementing his blue eyes. I wore an above-the-knee black skirt with a side zip and a pink sweater. My usual attire consisted of jeans or simple slacks, and I found myself pleased with Calhoun's lingering gaze.

I said, "You clean up nice."

He faced forward. "Thanks, so do you."

A roomy breakfast bar offered strong coffee, but I stuck to decaf. Calhoun scanned the cafeteria.

I did the same and searched for the pool guy while I munched on toast. Overactive imagination. The seminar brochure attracted my attention. "I can get fifteen CMEs."

"Okay." Calhoun shifted in his chair.

My mouth full, I gestured with toast in hand. "Continuing medical education units. I have to renew my certificate and give proof of one hundred fifty CMEs for the last two years."

"Aren't they supposed to be relevant?" He scouted the cafeteria again.

"Are you kidding me? Skeletal remains, blood spatter, DNA testing, fingerprinting, mitochondrial DNA? How is that not relevant?"

"You must enjoy school."

"I loved the training." My statement halted all other thoughts. I set down the toast. "Rick. Maybe I went to college."

"Indeed." He reached his hand across the table and gave mine a squeeze. "You look kinda shook. Maybe you should relax and work on your novel. I got this."

How could he suggest such a thing? I pushed back in my chair after a minute. "I am not playing. My life story can wait. Who knows when we'll be back? Blood, guts ... we're talkin' forensics, and you want me to chill?"

CHAPTER 36

Calhoun sat next to me. With legs kicked out in front of him and arms crossed, I suspected he napped. I nudged his foot, and he opened an eye. *Tsk.* Yet the few times I went to raise my hand, Calhoun tugged my hand and shook his head.

I tossed an indignant scowl his way. A few brave souls wrote in their notebooks. Calhoun snatched mine and scrawled *ask me later.*

Evening
I perused the hotel menu. "Room service is above my pay grade. Chinese takeout?"

"Sounds good."

We walked along the sidewalk, talked forensics, and ambled to the nearest Chinese restaurant. While we chatted, he scanned the perimeter.

"I find it odd Thompson would hire an undocumented worker, what with his conservative values," I said.

Calhoun snorted. "You're an undocumented worker."

"Requisition specialist. Big difference."

"Uh-huh. Like Cade is your real name."

"It could be."

"For Thompson, what's worse—hiring an illegal alien or denying his daughter the money for treatment? He should've kept her on his insurance. Deadbeat dad. Wonder why Camille didn't drag his butt to court?" He mumbled. "He ran on a ticket supporting conservative values."

"Perhaps the newer model of Mrs. Thompson made sure the money stayed where she wanted it. Maybe she didn't want the embarrassment. Perhaps she didn't want court attention on her."

He let out a grunt. "You're making excuses for him. He needed to man up. If she wore the pants in their relationship, and considering his daughter's health, then there is one sad story. Tate believed his daughter's death depressed him. His wife did not. I believe Tate."

"Really? I'm not convinced. Yet."

"Ooh, hoo ... look who's the big-time detective?"

"You wanted me deputized."

"For cold cases."

We returned to the hotel, bags of food in hand, and ate dinner in Calhoun's room. A man crooned on a TV music channel in the background.

"You never told me about Stephen Thompson's money," I said.

"You never asked. He was a businessman who kept his ear to the ground. He knew the market, what stocks to buy and when to dump them—"

"Insider trading?"

"Nope. He made a lot of money in the late nineties and bailed before the balloon burst. He's the one who purchased the land north of town."

I held my chopsticks in the air, surprised. "I get the idea that Camille, the ex, has a bigger stake in this. Revenge."

"What about Sarah Thompson? She inherited money, but also the land he purchased. She could afford to find sleazy contractors who'd put up homes on the land the board opened for development. I've been looking for shell companies, because it would be a political conflict of interest and a motive for murder."

"The money-lust-power axiom you've been pounding in my head." I sipped my water. "With that line of thought, she does emit a certain odor. Oh, I checked on your Abdul Abbott, and I couldn't find any connection to extremists. Troy Abara, now, he's got some 'splaining to do. You said his parents were from Botswana?"

"That's what he told me," Rick said.

"They're not even remotely from South Africa. His surname is Nigerian, so I did a little digging, and his family tends toward extremist political leanings, though they came from England. He's never been on anyone's radar."

"You did all that? I'm giving you a raise."

"Lemme do the math. Nothing plus nothing equals ... oh, right. Nothing. I think something bigger is at work—perhaps your conspiracy theory."

We sat silent for a few moments, and Calhoun leaned across the table. He nabbed my notebook.

He shuffled through my paperwork. "Well, what did you think of the lecture? You looked like a second-grader raising your hand."

"Most of it is basic. A refresher isn't a bad idea. However, he ought to teach correct concepts."

"How so?"

"Well for one, he ignored the basic rules of forensic procedure. Second, his understanding of alternative light sources for finding body fluids was inaccurate. If he teaches it, he should at least be correct."

Calhoun sat back. "I suggest if you want to come back, you nod real polite-like, and later you can teach me the finer points of forensics."

I puffed, disgruntled. "Maybe Whiskey River should spring for the University of Tennessee's forensic training. The FBI trains there."

"Huh, you been there? You seem to have an awful lot of experience."

"Not like I would remember," I mumbled, and stood, tugging on his hand to change the subject. "Let's dance."

"I—"

"No excuses."

We slow-danced. He rested his hand at the small of my back and drew me close. I laid my head on his chest, smiling as I listened to his heartbeat. He rested his cheek against my hair, and the heat increased as we swayed together.

With his breath against my neck, I wanted CPR. No. More like intimacy. Frustrated, I wished we were married. Awkward.

Reluctant, I dragged myself away and twisted around, so he wouldn't see me blush. "Well, it'll be morning soon, so it's time for shuteye. Goodnight. Thanks for the Chinese. Where did you learn to dance? You're quite good."

"I'm a man of many talents."

Yeah, he was. I returned to my room and left the door open a crack.

"Oh, I see how it is. Leave me with the dishes," he yelled.

I held a hand to my mouth, then sat on the bed, fell backward onto the mattress, and screamed into my pillow. CPR my butt. The open door offered no safety because the straight shot into his room made me nuts. *This is so not fair.* I jabbed my finger toward Calhoun's room, arguing with God.

"Ahem."

Lifting the pillow, I sat up. "How long have you been standing there?"

"Since I heard you yell." He pushed himself from the doorjamb and began a slow walk my way. "Are you angry with me?"

"You heard me talk into the pillow?"

He continued coming. "It was louder than talk, but, yeah."

I put my hand out. "Stop."

"What?"

"Nothing." I coughed.

"Whatever you were arguing with God about included me. You can't scream at him and not tell me."

"I wasn't screaming at God."

"Yes, you were."

I thanked my inner self for saying nothing more incriminating out loud before. "No, ah, crisis of conscience."

"What about?"

"I–I–

"You want dessert?" He beamed.

My expression must have been priceless because his eyes smiled.

He brought out a fortune cookie. "Dessert."

"No, no thanks, I'm good."

He sat on the chair next to my bed and my heart twitter-pated as the cookie cracked under his fingers. He read the fortune out loud. "'Don't despair. Your soulmate shall return to you.' How do they conjure up this stuff?"

"I don't know. It's late. We need to go to bed." I pretended a yawn.

"Really, now?"

"I mean for classes," I said, flustered. "Not what you're proposing."

"Excuse me? What kinda notion do you think I have going through my mind? *Tsk*. I'm a man of honor."

I fell back on my bed and covered my face.

He lifted the edge of my pillow. "Am I safe with the door open?"

CHAPTER 37

Vivid dreams caused me to bolt upright in bed when I awakened. Drenched in sweat, I fell against the pillow. *Holy cow.* Calhoun did not belong in my dreams.

He met me in the hallway. "How did you sleep?"

My face heated. "Fine." My dreams had worn me out, and the quavering settled in my stomach as we entered the elevator.

I needed a swift kick in the butt and a cup of decaf to focus on forensics. Oh, how awful. I had no control over my dreams. Was there a church nearby? Today I needed one. Did people still spill their guts in confession? We didn't. What if I prayed right now? Something simple. *Hi, God. It's me, Cade. Can you help me if you're there? I'm messed up, and I need a hand.* It was going to be a long day.

After breakfast, we broke into groups, suited, and braved the freezing outdoors. The instructor walked us through a secured gate. I put my hand over my nose, the stench overwhelming, familiar but still disgusting. What would it smell like in summer? Calhoun, in another group, gave me the once-over with mischief.

Twit.

Patterned after the Body Farm in Tennessee, this farm had bodies scattered over the property.

Another déjà vu moment. I strained my brain cells trying to recall.

EVENING

We picked up menus and reading glasses. I blinked.

"Trade," we said in concert, swapping glasses. We agreed on junk food and brought bags back to his room.

"If Darren Hughe was Tate's attorney," I said, "he might have thrown her to the wolves, with an eye on the future. If he believed or knew that Sarah Thompson was coming into the picture, perhaps part of the mayor's or Hughe's plans included more than we thought."

He answered with a mouthful of a loaded cheeseburger. "Now you're catching on. What about Thompson or Tate? You seemed pretty set on those two yesterday."

"I know Tate didn't get money for chemo, but did she land any property or have long-forgotten boxes of cash hidden away?"

"Nothing. After his death, everything went to Sarah to be mixed with her own ill-gotten gains. Like you."

"You're giving me a complex."

"Good. You need one. Sarah Thompson had amassed a large sum of money with the means to go anywhere. Yet she chose Stephen Thompson. Why him? Callousness?" Calhoun crossed his arms.

I tucked stray hairs behind my ear. "From my standpoint, not all thieves are heartless mercenaries. You know my story. I ran, yes. I knew nothing else until I met you."

"Yet, you still want to run."

His steely blues bored into me. Why? I propped my chin on the heel of my hand. "It becomes instinct. Fight or flight. When the game is up, or something stirs the pot, a con has to flee."

"Game." His jaw set. "You say that with such ease."

"I didn't mean—"

"Maybe you're saying what I want to hear. You don't have to take off." He lifted my chin with his forefinger. "You'd bolt if you could."

Shaking the urge to take off never leaves. It just sits dormant. I said, "Troy Abara has to explain why he lied. Did Thompson figure out Troy lied about his past? It wouldn't just affect his part in politics, it could affect him and his family's immigration status. Murder, maybe."

He ticked points off with his fingers. "Someone stood close enough to shoot him and leave a shadow arc on the wall. If Sarah's life came to light, that's a motive. No one else has access to the home, and you said it yourself, the neighbor saw the same coat. And the alarm didn't go off when the front door opened."

"You make a good point."

"Tell me, would you murder anyone? Is that a shark's calling card?"

I examined the pictures on the wall. I'd always considered myself a grifter. Such a benign word with a pleasant ring to it. Like, *yes, dahling, here's my card, Grifter Extraordinaire, at your service.* "I don't know. I guess if I needed to protect myself—"

"Not my question. Could you, or a con like you, murder someone?"

I scratched my forehead, shaking off the offense. "No. I don't think so. But we still don't know what I did with a modified sniper rifle, do we?"

He cackled. "Yeah. I'm still kinda hatin' on you for that."

"What?"

He gave me the evil eye. "Suck it up, cupcake. We will forever be in competition."

"You're afraid I'm better than you." I put a finger over my lips to still a smirk.

"Moving on. When I interviewed Thompson, she cried, saying she'd forgotten to tell him she loved him the night before. Means nothing, but it sounded genuine. But if she was a plant ..."

"Terrorism? Something would have blown to bits."

Calhoun yawned. "Not yet."

"Huh. What does everyone have in common? From the editor to the mayor's office to Stephen Thompson? Money." I snapped my fingers. "Darren Hughe. Something about his whole demeanor. Like he's in charge, but I don't see him as the triggerman. Someone is the go-between. But who?"

Calhoun rested his chin on his hand, searching my face. "Maybe."

The silence sucked the air from the room. My eyes glued to his, and his to mine. I snapped to and checked my watch. Past midnight. "We fly back after the big finish, and this cupcake has to go to bed."

He stretched and agreed. We said our goodnights. I retreated to my room, readied for bed, and tugged on my bedcovers. On an impulse, I got up and tiptoed back to the barely-open connecting door.

This time, I stood there, listened, and sighed.

He opened the door wide. "Something wrong?"

I fumbled for words, surprised. "I'm, uh, making sure you're safe."

"From anyone in particular?" His gaze shifted while a half-smile appeared.

"Not so much. G'night." I turned, and he tugged my hand. We shared a hug, and he said he appreciated my concern for his well-being. His eyes twinkled.

Lady killer.

CHAPTER 38

My dreams were vivid again, but when the strong arms gripped mine, I popped wide awake. The squalid odor of stale alcohol and cigarettes and the rough, scruffy beard identified my attacker—the lifeguard, Sal. I got out a yelp before his hand clapped my mouth shut.

"Shh, Catherine," he whispered. "I have one job to do, and if you keep quiet, I'll kill you quick. Otherwise, I promise you'll beg. Do you understand?"

I wondered how he knew my name but managed a muffled "Yes" through his hand.

He stroked my face, and I closed my eyes while tears slid down my cheeks. A point of cold steel pressed against my neck. He slapped duct tape over my mouth. "Get up. Make it quiet."

I bit my tongue and tasted blood. My heart pounded as I tried to form a plan. Lying on my side, facing the window, I started to raise myself to a sitting position.

The lifeguard shouted, and I felt his hands lose their grip. The light snapped on. Someone had grabbed him. I turned to see Calhoun as I ripped the duct tape from my mouth. I seized the phone and called 9-1-1.

His hand still gripping the knife, Sal freed one arm and swung the blade toward Calhoun's neck. Rick dodged and in one swift move slammed Sal against the wall, snapping his arm in the process.

Sal howled through clenched teeth. Calhoun's fist sculpted my attacker a new face. Sal twisted, now slick with his own blood, and broke from Rick's grasp. He jumped over Calhoun and disappeared out the hotel room door. I sobbed in shock, fear, and relief—then confusion. *Where did he go?*

"You okay?"

I nodded.

Calhoun ran after him but returned, shaking his head.

Security arrived with the police. Their boots thumped along the floor like elephants.

The usual questions followed. Calhoun stood by the door, covered in blood. My teeth chattered as I clutched a blanket.

The police checked the rooms surrounding mine and the lock on the door. A female officer came toward us and spoke to Calhoun.

"The lock had been tampered with. Do you know this man?"

"No."

"Yes, I do, sort of." I shifted, still shaky.

Calhoun asked, "Are you sure?"

The officer spoke. "Go on."

I explained from the first day I saw him to the swimming pool incident.

"Well," one officer spoke, "we suspect from your story that this guy fixated on your girlfriend—"

Calhoun interrupted him. "Ya think? And you address her as Miss Cade."

The officer tapped his notes, looked at me, and continued. "Right. He went to great lengths. We'll check everything for his prints and DNA."

Great, the FBI.

Detectives interviewed us in separate rooms at the police department. Standard operating procedure. After my statement, a sketch artist busied a computer program. He swiveled the screen, and cold creeps nipped my flesh. The face was Sal's. The sharp blade at my neck was a raw memory I'd be happy to lose.

To calm my jittering nerves, I paced as the detectives talked to Calhoun. What was he saying? I ran out of nails to chew. Five minutes more passed. I heard a sigh as he rounded the corner with his incredible calm, dressed in too short sweat pants and a tee shirt. Officers ushered us toward the back door, and a detective drove us to the hotel.

The rest of the day and the night awaited us.

"What took you so long?"

"Your attacker left DNA all over me, so I had to turn over my clothes for processing."

"No one tall enough there for your size?"

"Their tall detectives only work the day shift. They wanted minor details, like how I heard you, and found my timing unconvincing." He rubbed his face.

"What did you say?"

"I said you scream like a banshee."

"Thanks."

We packed, climbed into a rental car, and left, while Calhoun kept an eye on the road in the rearview mirror. Thirty minutes later, we arrived at a different hotel, not nearly as swanky, but we still managed to get two suites.

"He planned to kill me."

"Had he succeeded, we'd be off track for days. Aren't you glad we kept the door open? I am going to Velcro you to my hip. You okay?"

"Sort of." His words were not comforting, but he didn't only protect his investment, he protected me. "Scared. Would you hold me?"

"I'm all yours, to protect and serve." We sat on the couch, and his arms surrounded me. He held me as though we would never come undone.

My mind raced. He'd saved me so often he deserved the truth. I told him everything about my life—the life I'd known since the coma. Every con I'd ever committed. So guilt-ridden, I came close to confessing to be Jack the Ripper. This time, I stuck to my criminal past. But I withheld a few things. "Cade isn't my real name."

"Is that right?" He sprawled out against the back of the couch. "I know your aliases, but I'm fond of Catherine Marie Cade."

"How did you find—?"

"I'm a detective. It'd be tough to run anymore. Not without money or your stash in Portland."

I propped myself on my elbow against the sofa back in surprise. Not even a decent swindler's front would have helped me.

His eyes twinkled again. "It's in lockup."

"When?"

"I made a side trip after interviewing Camille Tate. Drove to Portland. Among your belongings in Whiskey River, I found a key with a name and number under one of your aliases." He played with a wisp of my hair. "Gathered money, IDs, and several interesting items." He stopped. "Is that a real Monet I bagged?"

"*The Waterloo Bridge*? No, don't be preposterous, it's a forgery. The real one has never shown up." I goggled. "Don't look at me. I can't paint."

He poked me in the arm. "You planned to sell a sham."

"Oh, Calhoun. You think so little of me. That would be like fencing a dime-store wine glass as the Holy Grail." I chuckled.

"Then explain why you keep a fake?"

"There's a Vermeer underneath it." I snugged my head against him.

"A what?"

"*The Concert*. By Johannes Vermeer. Jerry told me his parents nabbed it."

He facepalmed. "Art theft, a gentleman's work."

"He didn't take over their legacy. He sold most of the paintings to get in on a cocaine ring. When the Bureau caught him, he turned informant. But I know where it belongs and how much the finder's fee is on it."

"Payment for the requisitions specialist."

"Oh, no. This is the Acquisitions and Divestments Department. Jerry once told me his parents stole three paintings worth three hundred million dollars. They'd never get the amount they wanted on the market because the paintings were hot. They planned to copy the originals, sell them on the black market, and collect the reward money on the original.

"The Vermeer is over a million in haul. I mean, reward fee. The museum seems stingy, a million-five for a Vermeer. I mean—" I raised my head. "I planned to take it to Boston where it belongs, collect the reward money, and search for my memory. Then you came along. Ruined all my plans."

"Do you remember the book you were reading, *Sex Detective*? Do you think you were the missing detective? What if you worked for an agency?"

I considered his words. "About the cocaine bust and human trafficking? The FBI detective believed dead?" The tragic end of a brave woman's life gave me pause. "I'd have a bullet hole in my chest. A mother and wife, gone. Sad story."

"Maybe I should have a gander. It's possible you have a tattoo covering a scarred-over bullet hole."

"What?" I did have a tattoo. Just kept it under wraps. "You looked! You are not getting a gander."

He crossed his arms. "I was doing my job, giving CPR."

"Pervert."

"Hey, now, that's just plain rude."

"Well, I have seen all of you," I lied. "And nothing to write home about."

He hit me upside the head with a pillow, and I failed in suppressing a giggle when he said, "Brat!"

We fell quiet. I didn't want to be alone, but he would soon have to return to his room.

I voiced my private plan from the airplane. "When we leave Wisconsin, can we drive back? If you can you deal with my antics?"

"Easy. And cross my heart, I'll stick to you like glue. Tighter than two coats of paint."

My heart lost its grin. We were total opposites. How could he live in peace with a scam artist? How would I live in peace, not knowing who he'd been prior to the man who now dogged my every move?

"Did you or Mike ever get anything from the car crash scene?" I whispered.

"Yeah. It was remote controlled."

"How do they even—?"

"Technical stuff, half-pint. Get your search engine fired up."

"Fine. Why didn't you tell me?"

"Part of the investigation," he said, sleepy. "I didn't want you to worry."

Here we were. A kiss would end me right here. I struggled with what I wanted versus what was right. As his eyes fluttered closed, I brought my lips close to his, then backed away.

Certain he'd fallen asleep, I whispered, "Never thought I'd fall for a cop."

"Detective."

I steered him to the bed, removed his shoes, and covered him with the blanket. Then I went to his room since he now occupied mine.

I settled in with the door open between us and turned over in bed. No return of the same sentiment from him, and now embarrassed, I tried to will the heat from my face.

But a disconcerting thought kept me awake. With my past over, how did another evil slip into my life and almost end it? And why?

CHAPTER 39

RICK CALHOUN
MONDAY

Calhoun didn't bother to knock on Dumont's office door. He closed it behind him, dragged a chair toward the desk, and plopped into it.

He explained what had happened as Dumont peered over his glasses, listening. "The attack wasn't a coincidence, Greg."

"Explain."

"Jerry Street could have orchestrated it from prison." Calhoun scratched his head. "But how did he know where she'd be staying? If he wanted revenge, he'd have to have hired someone, and it's not likely he has access to information or money. It was a well-planned execution attempt. Something is way off, and it seems like too many people are involved."

Dumont nodded. "Someone might have contacted him, someone who knew where you were going." He sighed. "He must have terrified Cade. Yet Sal Ventura slipped away."

"In the literal meaning. He was too slippery after I relieved him of some blood and broke his arm." Calhoun mopped his face. "She's my responsibility. This cannot happen."

"Maybe it's time to stop the volunteer deputy project." Dumont reclined in his chair. "Is she a responsibility or an entanglement?"

"You're reading into something which doesn't exist. And she's safer with me."

"With you?" Dumont plucked a Who Donut éclair from a doughnut box. "Everyone knows how you feel about Catherine. Haven't you received the memo? The Marines issued you a wife, and you'd best get on it."

"No wedding bells. Not yet." He stood, pushed the chair back, and headed for Dumont's door.

"Not yet?"

He left Dumont's office, threw a case file on his desk, and rubbed his temples. He had to handle her like an asset and was having a bad time of it. Didn't help when she professed her heart in her own way. She wasn't ready. Worse, he hated he couldn't tell her what he most wanted her to know.

He changed, made his way up the stairs, and waited for their workout.

CATHERINE CADE

The trip over and the worry over my attack gone, I knew my chest ached for something with Calhoun that didn't exist.

I needed to keep things professional. Check my business.

A familiar cracked sidewalk led me to the Who Donut, which on outward appearances had fared well without me. After gallivanting through a field of dead bodies, my body might have been there. Now it was time for a reality check.

Time to face the doughnuts.

Chief Dumont's birthday was tomorrow. His wife had called me before my trip to Wisconsin and asked for a surprise, one that brought an arch to even my brow. The new recipe required perfection. Who Donut's staff made a batch during my Wisconsin trip.

"How'd it go over?"

Victoria beamed. "You came, you cooked, you conquered. Nothing left after lunch. Good thing we had plenty of milk."

"Excellent. I'll be back noon tomorrow for a batch."

She saluted. "Yes, boss."

"I'll need a dozen éclairs, too."

I returned to the police department, noting Calhoun was nowhere in sight. Zoe didn't say hello, and Mike focused on paperwork. Not like them.

Time again to call Kim for coffee and a shopping spree to avoid this new pain. Best not to run into Calhoun.

I hadn't said a real *I love you* to Calhoun. But he'd heard me, how I fell for him. Now crushed, I didn't want to face him anymore.

The trip back from Wisconsin had been a miserable drive. There was no opportunity to express my emotion except to cry quietly in my bathroom at night.

Now a case file—the first one I'd received—left me in a jumble. The pictures and notes on the twenty-year-old murder of a grandmother kept pulling me back to Stephen Thompson's killing. Both diabetic, both shot with the same caliber gun, both showing excess insulin in the vitreous humor of their eyes, and neither crime scene showing any evidence of theft. Similar autopsy findings again.

Calhoun always talked about trusting his instincts. Three things tied them together, not including my gut. But the years and their different social strata became a rift not even I could jump. That meant I needed to talk with that man, Calhoun.

I left the locker room and hurried up the stairs toward the cage. Calhoun stretched on the mat.

"You're late," he said.

So matter-of-fact.

I said, "Things to do. Let's get to it."

"You think we should talk?"

"About what?"

"A connection between Jerry Street and Sal Ventura?"

"How would I know?" My failed sideways cartwheel caused a fall. I was unable to roll out of his way fast enough, and his full weight dropped onto me. It knocked the wind out of me, and he moved away, apologetic.

"Catherine! You okay?"

I wheezed, "Fine." Taking a deep breath, I said, "Jerry's about money. He planned to wield his coke and sadism to use me in a heist. What did he plan to steal? I can't imagine anything worth stealing in Whiskey River."

He held out a hand. "I can."

I pushed him away, angry with myself for telling him my feelings, embarrassed he heard me, and sad he'd said nothing in return. And that statement was a flirt, one even I recognized. "Back to that cold case. My gut tells me something relates the Faith Harrington case to Thompson."

Calhoun stopped me. "Gut? Show me the evidence. If it's related, you need to share."

I twisted my arm away. "Then pay attention."

"What's eating at you?"

Yeah, lemme think, what's eating at me. "Nothing." After scramming down the stairs, I stared at Harrington's cold case file until my eyes watered.

CHAPTER 40

The next morning, we went for a silent run. I cleaned up, drove to the Who Donut, and spoke with Victoria. She greeted me with a hearty hello, a pot of chili with a touch of Carolina Reaper pepper, and a loaf of spicy jalapeño bread.

I hefted the pot and crossed the street as a man snapped pictures. He turned and walked in the opposite direction. Someone taking pictures of me after having been attacked twice? No such thing as a coincidence.

The guy seemed familiar. A green SUV hugged a nearby curb. I'd seen it before. Something to talk to Calhoun about after Dumont's surprise. I strode into the bullpen, empty except for Calhoun. I presumed Chief Dumont hid behind his desk in his office, his nose in a *National Institute of Justice Journal*.

"Where is everyone?"

"Zoe's dealing with the divorce papers. Mike's out on a call."

"Divorce? Zoe and Zach?"

"Don't ask me. Handling you keeps me busy." He frowned. "Hey, slow down. What's in the crockpot?"

"Handle me? What are you, CIA? I have nothing for you." With my head high, I knocked on Dumont's door.

"Enter."

I backed through the door. Dumont fired questions my way, but Mrs. Dumont had given clear instructions. I put the chili pot on the desk, walked straight to the Chief, leaned him back in his chair, and planted a big sloppy one right on his kisser.

Dumont, never speechless, widened his eyes. Out of the corner of mine, I glimpsed Calhoun leaning back in his chair staring, jaw unhinged. I closed the door with my foot and snapped a picture of Dumont's priceless expression, then took a selfie of us. Then I pressed SEND.

He found his voice and pointed at me. "You, you listen here, girl, I'm a married man—happy, too. What do I tell my wife? I've never kissed a white woman before." He grabbed his antacids and popped four. "Explain yourself."

Entertained, I gave him a note. "Happy birthday, sir, and with all due respect, I didn't kiss you. Your wife did. She couldn't be here, so she sent the messenger."

"What?" He unfolded the note and slipped on his reading glasses. "That woman. Says, 'don't shoot the messenger.' A piece of advice for you? Never marry a Cajun unless you're ready for these kinds of pranks." His eyes met mine. "She really put you up to this?"

"At Christmas. She called about a special birthday dinner she wanted me to make—chili, Cajun-style—and gave me strict instructions."

He jumped from the chair, and too late, my warning went unheard as he took a bite. This dish would set a crowded sweat lodge on fire. He almost went into orbit with the heat, and I clamped a hand over his mouth.

"Don't open your mouth. The air will make it worse. Milk will stop the capsaicin's effects." I popped my head out of Dumont's office with the Chief in tow and my hand over his mouth. "Calhoun, got milk?"

He glared at me.

"I said, move, soldier, medical emergency," I yelled. Dumont would not die, but Calhoun grabbed the milk.

TUESDAY

At his desk, Calhoun remained quiet.

"Something up?" I asked.

"Nope."

I raised my head with a smirk as Dumont strode from his office to the coffeepot and back to his office, whistling. Calhoun narrowed his eyes at me in a cold glare.

I ignored him. Sitting at the desk abutted to Calhoun's, I perused Lily Tate's date of death in May. Commissioner Stephen Thompson died in August. The connection seemed thin, but revenge can beget violence. I should know.

"Rick, this case is like a song on repeat. Faith Harrington's grandson, Kevin Wood, ran heroin and got busted over the county line. Joshua Noble, the cop who grabbed Wood, found over a hundred pounds of heroin hidden in the nooks and crannies of the car. Without a narcotics dog, how could Noble know to check?"

"That case has been stuck in your craw ever since I handed it to you. You're talking about the case about the infamous beat cop who confiscated heroin from Kevin Wood. Drugs went missing from Jackson County's evidence locker, and the cop became a congressman a few years later. Imprisoned for trafficking."

"Joshua Noble. What about a money trail?"

"Not our jurisdiction."

I curled a fist. Once again, he wasn't listening. "Rick, Kevin Wood ran drugs, and Noble arrested him in Jackson County. Faith Harrington, Kevin Wood's grandmother, died in this county. A diabetic, too much insulin in her vitreous humor, then shot. And the bullet was a .45. No coincidences, you've said. Put a hit on Grandma to keep Kevin Wood quiet—and he still went to prison."

"You wanna reopen Faith Harrington's case. Why?"

"I think it's related to the Thompson murder."

"How?"

I chewed the end of my pencil. "Twenty years of politicking, maybe murder. Stephen Thompson is dead, and I want to know if someone ordered him dead. Thompson and Noble ran in the same circles before he married Sarah." I held my hands out in a half-shrug. "Is it possible something like that could happen?"

"A swindler might launder money through a prominent member of society, maybe through his political campaigns. Maybe Sarah Thompson found Noble's scheme and made an anonymous call to the police."

I asked, "You think she's someone's confidential informant and the reason for her husband's murder? And she's next if she screws up?"

Calhoun lifted his shoulders. "Right now, your guess is as good as any."

"A con as a CI plays both ends. A smart con avoids drug dealers and cops. The confidence artist looks to the future, the next take or stake, keeping their profile clean and invisible. Noble's heroin dealing could've been the end of her career, right?"

"Correct."

"Isn't that too close for scrutiny? My thought is keep the gig going or risk leaving a red flag without the goods. I would have done the same thing—if that's what she did."

He paused. "I'll check his campaign finance transactions. Records go way back. The congressman died in jail. Hung himself."

"How coincidental."

"I need to make a call."

"To who?" I touched the pencil's eraser as he turned to beat feet.

"Be right back." He grabbed his phone and stepped into the hall.

I studied the eraser. I wanted to know Calhoun's informant's name *Definitely need a new pencil.*

When he returned, I asked, "What if the guy with the remote on the Prius is the same guy as Sal-whatever-his-name-is who attacked me in Wisconsin? You digging into the Thompson case started this whole thing. I wasn't a target until I worked with you. Someone's trying to shut the case permanently."

Calhoun removed his reading glasses. "I thought the same thing. Here's something. Mrs. Thompson's credit card account showed a few interesting details. There were regular gas station stops between here and Salem since August. Nothing since."

"She's a politician, and Salem—"

"Is over an hour from the state's capitol."

SUNDAY

I was now the proud owner of a Bible, and it took everything I had to stop Calhoun from inscribing, "To Swindler

Catherine Cade from Detective Rick Calhoun." That's how I landed in church every week holding the sacred text and muddling through its pages since the entire book was divided into, The Book of ..., and worse, The Letter to ...

Today, he seemed subdued. No bellowing of hymns, though we still headed toward the after-church-heart-attack specialty restaurant.

The Gold Nugget held the air of a casino, even though the restaurant had no gambling, unless cholesterol-laden meals counted as Russian roulette. Original pictures of the main street, circa 1880s, studded the walls. There were pictures of farmers, railroad workers, gold miners, and ranchers. Antique phones hung on the walls, and artifacts and arrowheads rested in shadow boxes. Tables were rough, chairs were old, the patrons gritty, and the waitresses armed.

We wound our way past the tables and found a booth. The servers came and took our orders.

When the food arrived, Calhoun put out his hands toward mine and held them in a near-death grip, saying grace while I grimaced in pain.

I caught habits from Calhoun like a bad cold and talked with my mouth full. "Your source find information?"

"Not yet."

"Nothing?"

"Nope."

I asked, "What's with you today? You've been weird all morning."

"Explain Dumont."

"Oh, yeah, that."

"Oh, yeah, that." He mimicked. "He's a married man. I can't believe you, you—"

"Kissed him with passionate fury?"

He stopped chewing.

I chortled. "His wife called me about his birthday. She wanted to pull a prank."

"What?"

"She set it up. I snapped a picture on my camera."

"He's not a young man anymore. What if you'd stopped his heart?"

I tried to make a serious face. "You're no spring chicken yourself, but kissing me in front of McCloud didn't stop yours."

Calhoun's expression stiffened as I leaned over the table and brushed my lips to his ear.

"You didn't hear a thing in church today, did you? Don't go unbuckling that Bible belt, because I think you need to recite the verse about 'judge not, lest ye be judged' a few times. Don't you dare criticize me." I grazed my mouth across his neck to the corner of his mouth. "Hear me?"

I sat and sipped at my coffee and pretended to peruse for dessert.

Calhoun raised a hand for the waitress. "Glass of water?"

MONDAY

The day came to present my case on the Harrington murder to Dumont. I followed Calhoun into Dumont's office. I was flying solo, and my nerves were on edge.

"Go on." Calhoun nudged me.

I grabbed a chair and placed a folder on Dumont's desk.

"We'd like to invite Kevin Wood to talk with us to help find his grandmother's murderer. Victim's name, Faith Harrington. Calhoun ran plates on the car she owned."

"Uh-huh."

"She was blind, and Wood helped her with her needs. He bought her groceries, drove her to her ophthalmologist appointments. Eye doctor, sir."

"I know what an ophthalmologist is, Cade."

"Except he involved himself—" I launched into my spiel, and Dumont interrupted, thrusting a hand in the air.

He rested a finger over his lip and eyed Calhoun, then me. He held his hand in the air. "Boil it down, Cade."

"But—"

He sighed and spoke to Calhoun. "Will this ever stop?"

There was a subtle shake to Rick's head.

Aghast, I leaned forward. "Sir, you want all the facts, don't—"

Calhoun interrupted me. "Long story short. We have info on the car. Wood packed heroin in it. Caught by Grandma and the police. We think Wood or an accomplice shot Grandma. We did some digging. Joshua Noble, the upstanding cop he was, had hinky finance campaign records. Noble went to prison and died, and Wood's doing time. There's a connection from Faith Harrington to Joshua Noble through Kevin Wood. An interview would help."

"Fine by me."

We left the office, and my fists clenched. "What was that?"

"Chief wants the bottom line. You lost him at eye doctor."

I pressed his back to the wall, so he wouldn't walk away, and spat words in a near-whisper.

"You condescending jerk." I yanked away from him. *Done.* "Mr. Holier-Than-Thou, you accused me without facts about Dumont's birthday. Then you didn't warn me about the bottom-line report, and last, you didn't let me finish my sentence. Like you'd treat a screaming three-year-old. I'm done with you."

I walked away, wondering why he seemed confused. Nothing, nothing, nothing. I directed my frustration toward Calhoun. He was like a bad rash. But if you change a bacteria's environment, it won't stick around. I hoped distancing myself would work a similar medicinal cure for unrequited love.

What had I been thinking? We'd have a white picket fence and a bushel of kids?

I jumped into the GMC and wiped my eyes.

"So much for happily-ever-after." The gearshift didn't cooperate, and it ground and slipped into first gear with a shove. Horns honked and shook me out of my funk. I drove into traffic and moved along.

I'd lost myself in him, wanted him in every way, and if he asked me for more, I couldn't have said no. But he felt nothing for me.

It was over. Really over.

CHAPTER 41

My interview with Kevin Wood passed without event. I left without speaking to anyone.

Both detectives observed my interview with Kevin. They watched behind tinted glass while I pitched gentle and non-intimidating questions to establish Kevin's normal behavior. A digital video rolled. When I finished, I circled my finger in the air, giving the "all clear" sign.

I wrote Calhoun a brief note and left it on his desk. "Calhoun, you're a pretentious prig."

Winds picked up, and the tops of pine trees bowed in submission on my drive home. I needed to wash salty tears away. After rinsing my face, I called Kim's number while I climbed into my truck.

She answered her cellphone. "Catherine, I so need a coffee date. You read my mind."

"I have another idea. I'll come to the morgue today. What do you think?"

"Serious? I can't wait. Calhoun says you're tops with cold cases."

"Oh?"

"Through the grapevine. You must be awesome if Chief Dumont gave you pilot project status, a deputy no less."

"Maybe because I work for free."

"Well, come on, BFF. Dr. McCloud is due back from Medford. I'll give you a tour of my favorite place on earth. I want to get the scoop—"

"On my way. Gotta go." I pressed END. She wanted to hear the latest on Calhoun. Did I care if leaving early upset Calhoun? Not so much. I'd spun a fantasy about him, he sent mixed signals, and then he kicked me to the curb, the same thing he said McCloud would do.

How could McCloud be worse?

"Catherine, I didn't know you were back." Kim, McCloud's blonde, mop-headed assistant greeted me. "It's been over a week."

"I know. It's good to see you, too."

"How was your trip to Wisconsin with Detective Calhoun? Did sparks fly?"

The last time here, Calhoun busied himself beating the living crap out of McCloud for insulting me. "None. I guess I was wrong."

"Don't give up hope. If he turns my best friend down, it's his loss."

"I like how you think. Oh, I didn't tell you. Some crazy stalker dude attacked me at the hotel."

Her face paled. "Oh, no. What happened?"

"He broke into my hotel room and attacked me in bed. If not for Calhoun, I'd be six feet under."

Her mouth hung open. "Calhoun broke the guy's neck ... I hope." She slipped a finger around her necklace chain.

"No, this guy, Sal Ventura, slithered away. In worse shape for stalking me." Although that phrase he used, "I have one job to do ..." niggled at my brain.

"You know his name? Wow. I'm just glad you're okay." She hugged me, and she gave a shudder. "I want to know why you think Detective Calhoun dropped you. For now, we're touring Dr. McCloud's infamous Dead Room." She pulled herself together and began her visitation to every item like a gothic horror museum.

Bleak tables, empty drains, low scales that hung like macabre chandeliers, and buckets for drippings seemed to cry out, *Run!* My eye glanced at bowls for organs, morbid as the Dead Room itself. The acrid odor of formaldehyde and chlorine almost overwhelmed me. I sputtered and covered my mouth and nose. Another flashback of a different morgue caused me to reach out and steady myself.

Nearby instruments stacked or hung on walls reeked of death. Tree pruners for snipping through ribcages. Saws and garden clippers. Just another morgue. Like Wisconsin but without puking attorneys, numerous investigators, and Calhoun.

The aloneness of this place made it dark and frightening.

Whether from the chill or the creepiness, I rubbed my arms. Kim droned on about her special place here, most of which I spaced.

I knew, somehow, I'd spent time in morgues, but never with a libidinous medical examiner like McCloud. Once, his eyes grazed over me, and I'd cringed and hid behind Calhoun. Now I'd be front and center.

Calhoun and McCloud. The door, not twenty feet away, tempted me to run. Those men generated enough heat to put me into a hormonal tailspin.

Rick. Dark thoughts steamed my cheeks, until Kim interrupted my intimate musings.

"Isn't this the best?" Kim, enthralled, twirled, like Maria in *The Sound of Music*. I could see her singing, "The morgue is alive …" She continued. "A warning—Dr. McCloud is a charmer."

"Okay."

"He hates outsiders." She squeezed an eye shut. "I heard he danced with you. Impressive."

"I don't know about that."

"Doc's not a big talker. It's not personal. He grunts instead."

"He what? You mean, like a pig?"

"No." She guffawed. "Learn what he means. He has the good, the bad, the indifferent, the lecherous, and the angry. It took a while, but he broke me in."

I blinked for lack of words.

She bit her lip and giggled. "You've been hanging around Mike Tanaka too long. That man can turn the most innocent comment into a sexual innuendo."

I jumped when the doors flew open as Jack McCloud, my supervisor for the next month, came through in scrubs and moved through the maze of tables. We made a wide swath for him as he grabbed a lab coat.

"Dr. McCloud, Catherine Cade is here."

He looked back. "Get her into scrubs and bring out Jane Doe."

Not so charming now.

Her scrubs were large—but they stayed put. I tucked them in, tightened everything as best I could, and returned from the locker room.

The autopsy table awaited. McCloud prepped Jane Doe, and moved to a Mayo stand with instruments. "Kim dashed off, had to run an errand, make a call, or something." He pointed. "The body's washed."

"Okay." As I stared at the slab and the body, my past unfolded in bundles. This one made me dizzy.

I gripped the counter, and the wave of dizziness passed.

"Hey, you okay?"

His *hey* came out in a grunt, and gathering my wits, I straightened. "I'm fine. It's working in front of a mentor. Hope Kim didn't get some bad news." I desperately wanted her here. I slipped on gloves and slow-walked examining Jane Doe.

"She seems flaky," McCloud said, "but don't let that fool you. She's sharp, not just as a CSI tech and assistant, but a great shot. She's been taking me to the range." He chuckled. "Guess her target practice at the gravel pit is paying off." He flashed those pearly teeth. "Okay, to business. You're a volunteer, but you're to tell me what I'm doing and what I've found. If you have potential, I'll supervise you on John Doe. Legal issues require an eagle eye by a medical examiner." McCloud raised a clipboard and read Jane Doe's stats.

As we continued, I gave him instructions until the autopsy was complete. I washed the table after we slid Jane Doe into her cold bed and John Doe onto a clean table. Where was Kim? Was she doing this on purpose?

"Outstanding. Your turn." He sipped coffee and stood back. "Step up."

"Who have we here?"

"Unknown Hispanic male, found in the homeless camp off Parkway. No ID, no tattoos."

"He's clean-cut. Did you scrub under his nails?"

"Nope."

"His crew cut and nails don't scream homeless."

"His clothes were filthy, torn up." McCloud crossed his arms.

I checked his hands and clipped his nails for evaluation. "That's not conclusive. Callouses on his hands with arthritic changes are consistent with manual labor. Musculature to upper and lower extremities well-developed. Any trace evidence? Dirt or grass from a different area?"

"Kim is going over the clothing and particulates. We got samples to compare."

"X-rays? Did you get prints sent to IAFIS, swab for DNA?"

"Done." McCloud pointed to the x-ray boxes.

I evaluated the films. "He's had good dental work. Here's a nasal bone fracture with tissue swelling suggesting a fall or altercation." I stepped to another light box. "Vertebrae show cervical fracture, thoracic and lumbar fractures. What's this?" I examined an image of his leg. "Spiral fracture."

"Good."

"Not for this poor guy. Turn on the mic when I tell you. Lower the table, if you please."

"Comin' down." He did so and winked.

Gonna be a long autopsy.

"You sleeping with Calhoun?"

I gasped. "You know, I can walk out. What if you had the mic on? Calhoun and I never dated, not that it's any of your business."

He brightened. "Mic's off. Do I have a shot? What about that kiss I saw?"

"A kiss is just a kiss, right?" I straightened, catching him making an effort to glance down my scrub top. "Move back." I waited until he moved.

I said, "I'm here to learn. You're drinking coffee in the autopsy room, hitting on me, making comments like ..." I held a hand up. "You need to apologize for starters, and a refresher course on professionalism." In truth, I wanted to run screaming like my hair was on fire because then I could file for hazard pay.

His mouth hung half-open, and I would have bet I was the first person to put him into his place. "Ah, um," he said, shifting, "you're right. Guess I've been on the job a little too long."

With palm raised, I turned to face my current patient. "Talk to me, John Doe. Tell me why you died." I clasped my hands and began a walk around the table. "Please turn the microphone on, Doctor. This is an adult, well-nourished Hispanic male, approximately mid-thirties. External exam shows multiple bruising over right posterior to right anterior neck. Abrasions to right lower leg. X-ray indicates spiral fracture. Mic off. How am I doing so far?"

"Great. You found an unusual leg fracture and bruising around the neck—"

"Hard to miss that."

I clicked more pictures.

"What?" McCloud asked.

"I've seen this before. The leg fracture and abrasion pattern. I could be wrong, but I think he caught his leg in a chair or ladder and fell, causing a spiral fracture to his leg and fractures to his back and neck."

"You saw this at school?"

I didn't attend grad school and couldn't answer that question. "Sometime back. Facial films show a fractured nose and the surrounding tissue is engorged with blood, visible even on plain film. The fracture to the cervical vertebrae is different. Any wood, plant particulates I want collected."

"Thoughts?"

"Mic on." Silent, except for recording the procedure, I made an incision from one side of John Doe's head behind the ear, extending over and across his skull, gently pulling skin and muscle away to within one centimeter above his eyebrows. Then I exposed the back of his head. With a vibrating bone saw, I cut across the center of the forehead to the base of either ear. Further cuts and notches allowed me to remove the top of the skull, examine, and lift out the brain for closer inspection.

"No antemortem injury noted to the skull, despite fracture to cervical vertebrae three and four. The lack of bleeding in the brain and interstitial tissues is inconsistent with a fall. Bruising to neck, both sides, and the upper back muscles—mic off."

"Well?"

"Need music to drown out your voice."

"Boss lady is snippy."

I didn't look at him. "Oh, gee, I wonder how many times I've heard that one. Mic on."

Easiest was the Y-incision from collarbone left to right, down to the pelvis. "Snip the sternum and grab the enterome scissors above you. Hand them over when I ask."

I snapped my gloved fingers, held my hand out, and weighed each organ after snipping them open. "Obtained samples for biopsy of mouth, esophagus, stomach, colon, prostate, liver, trachea, lungs, heart, bladder, spleen. Mic off." I handed each to McCloud after I weighed the organs, and he put samples in fixative solution to be sent to Histology.

I asked, "What did Calhoun think happened to John Doe?"

"He waits for me to tell him."

"Forgot. He's just homicide. What did you think?"

"Undetermined. Scuffle got out of hand, maybe."

"Microphone on. John Doe's liver normal. No sign of cirrhosis, no enlargement." I added what McCloud told me. "Alcohol negative, awaiting other toxicology. Mic off."

"So far, correct."

"Mic on. Postmortem fracture base of skull. Bruising on his neck, pre-mortem. Blunt force trauma noted postmortem, no signs of bleeding. Mic off. Why? Okay, I'm spit-balling here. Maybe he was in a choke hold—"

"You're channeling Calhoun."

"I was right. He did speculate. It's possible John Doe fell from a ladder and caught his leg, or someone helped him fall. Someone busted his nose and held him in a choke hold until he died. Then the killer fractured his neck after death. There's no blood associated with that trauma." I hesitated. "Despite evidence, my gut says someone murdered this man."

"You think the killer knew John Doe?"

I tented my gloved fingers. "Impossible to say. His fractured neck isn't conclusive." I shivered and thought what Calhoun and I had worked out. John Doe appeared to be a laborer. What if John Doe turned out to be Thompson's missing gardener, Santiago?

"We'll toss it back to Homicide. So, tell me, Catherine, is it true? You're a church mouse?" McCloud scrutinized me.

"Who told you I go to church?" I asked.

"Who do you think? Your pal, Calhoun."

"He's not my concern."

"Interesting." He straightened.

I tossed my gloves into the hazardous waste trash and found the showers.

McCloud showered and waited for me. I found him leaning against the wall in the corridor, with one ankle crossing the other. "You're a pro in there. Where did you study?"

"Oregon Health and Sciences U." Another mumbled lie.

"You came a week earlier than we predicted. Calhoun the reason?"

My eye twitched. "Maybe."

"That kiss? You were into him. Listen, I'm a straightforward guy. I'm available for a good time. That means dancing and whatever."

With arms crossed, I challenged him. "Then a question. Did you try to get Melanie to sleep with you? Did Calhoun confront you?"

He waited, then spoke in a hush. "Yes. And yeah, he confronted me." A pensive look crossed his face. "There are things I wish I'd never learned in med school."

"What does that mean?

"Matters of the heart." He shook his head. "Not up to talking about my life, if you get my drift. Let me just say that Melanie was just another face I'd forgotten. Calhoun has every right to lose his temper and there are days I egg him into a good beating. I know the monster I've become. When it's too much, there's the therapist."

"You see a therapist?"

"Yeah. Dr. Jim Beam."

"I don't know what to say."

We wandered into the parking lot, and he booted a pebble and shoved his fists in his pockets. "Tell me you are not seeing Calhoun."

"Nope. He wasn't interested."

"What a sucker. Maybe it's time for real company. How about we go dancing tonight? What do you say?"

"Thanks, but no." I may have still been glum, but McCloud was on my side. There was a story behind his own pain he wasn't sharing. I got that.

He stooped to meet my eyes. "You're so short, how do you not get a headache looking up all day long?" Playful, he gave my shoulder muscles a light squeeze.

Okay. I could deal with this.

CHAPTER 42

"Ow." Lost in darker thoughts, my lack of concentration landed me flat on my back.

"You never miss that move," Calhoun said.

"I've got stuff on my mind. Why didn't you tell me the medical examiner was so creepy?" Mouth guard and dodging mitts impeded clear speech.

"He works with dead bodies. What did you expect?" Calhoun dodged a kick, grabbed my ankle, and pushed my face into the mat. "We need to talk."

He dropped with an elbow, missing my gut by a bare inch. "No explanation needed."

"Catherine, what is going on with you?"

Golly, I dunno. "There is nothing going on."

He went for another slam. With knees bent and tight thigh muscles, my feet propelled him backward. I grabbed my prop gun, told him to roll over, and yowled as he twisted it from my hand.

"You're not getting off easy," he growled, tossing me like a pillow. Calhoun seized me, took my head in a choke hold, and pinned my arms against my sides with his. He wrapped his legs around mine. Immobilized and crushed as usual, I found enough room to slap the mat. He turned me over and cuffed me. "How do you like McCloud and the infamous Dead Room?"

Frustrated, I let go a swear word. The wager among the meager office crew had grown to a hundred bucks. The winner who could take down Calhoun won cash and respect. Wasn't going to be me.

"That good, eh?" He grabbed me by the shirt and sweats, shoved my face into the vertical mat against the wall, and removed the cuffs.

"Well, besides being weird and devilishly handsome, he reminds me of you."

He stopped. "What do you mean?"

"All business, but creepier." My karate gloves and headgear were off, and I removed my mouth guard.

"Creepy? You called me creepy."

"Creepier than you."

He crossed his arms.

"Creepy, as in, you withhold secrets and give mixed signals. At least McCloud speaks his mind." I headed toward the stairs.

"Hey, wait up." He grasped my arm. "Don't go out with him."

"Listen to yourself." I jerked away. "You don't run my life, and I'm going dancing tonight."

He followed me into the locker room. I tore my shirt over my head, and he shoved it back at me. "You know his history." Calhoun jabbed his finger at me. "How have I not been clear? He'll try to take advantage of you."

"I did two autopsies yesterday and three today. Jack and I are going out because I'm fried."

"Please ..."

"Stop. Is this case-related?"

His words were soft. "Think before you go. Be careful what you say and do. Don't drink." He put his head in the palms of his hands. "What a disaster. I spent too much time trying to ... and didn't tell you, part of it I couldn't tell you. And McCloud—"

"What?"

"He thinks we're exclusive." He held his breath.

"Exclusive, how?"

Beads of sweat formed on his forehead. He wiped them away with the back of his hand. Pressed his lips. How interesting. He looked just like he did in Wisconsin, guilty, like when he had my computer in his hands, stuttering his confession that he'd tried to read my novel.

"I intimated we were dating. He knows we go to church."

"He called me a church mouse. Wait, you told him we were—?" I pointed at my chest and his. "Guess what? He said he goads you because he can't reconcile what he did, so he pushes your buttons."

He searched my eyes. "Who's pushing whose buttons now?" He left the locker room.

Shocked, I squeezed my eyes and shook my head vigorously.

After my shower, stopping at the desk, I motioned to Mike and Zoe. "I'm taking off for the day."

"Luxurious shower?" Mike asked with a grin.

"What did you do, time me?"

"Oh, no, that would be tawdry. We timed both of you."

"Then we giggled," Zoe said.

FRIDAY AFTERNOON

It was dusk at the station. I found Calhoun and gave him a curt nod. "Hey."

"Hey, back."

"Gotta tell you something."

"Me first."

"This is more important." In a moderately low-cut red dress, I sat on the corner of his desk. He stopped tapping his pen.

"You seem to have a wandering eye, Detective Calhoun."

Mike coughed himself into a fit.

Calhoun glowered and opened his mouth.

I said, "There's this boxy green SUV following me. I forgot to tell you. The first time was on Chief Dumont's birthday. Remember?"

"Somehow that image is burned into my memory."

"Well, someone's following me and taking pictures. It's getting spookier every day."

"Plates? Model?"

"Starts with an A. Oregon plates. Don't know the make. I see it late at night."

He scribbled. "Ever see it at your house?"

"No. I pass New Hope, make a turn when I get into Murphy. The trees give enough cover to cut the lights and pull behind the store. Then I shoot over past the fish hatchery, pass your place, stop, and wait to see if anyone drives by. If not, I go home."

Mike scoffed. "Good grief. You're as paranoid as Calhoun."

Calhoun studied me. "My house?"

"Yeah."

"I'll follow you home."

I drew my finger along the rim of his desk. "No, thanks."

"Hey, you didn't give me a chance to talk. Don't walk out."

I sashayed my way out, and overheard Mike say to Zoe, "Mom and Dad are fighting again."

My date was waiting, and I drove to the Whiskey River Bar and Grill to meet him. It was a few minutes before Jack parked his Crown Victoria. He slipped an arm around me and escorted me into the bar.

RICK CALHOUN

Calhoun followed her and the green Nissan Cube to Whiskey River Bar and Grill and parked in the darkened alley. He choked on his coffee as McCloud put his arm around Catherine. Her stalker, the paparazzi, parked along the curb in his expensive new Cube.

"Aw, man." Calhoun shook the hot liquid from his fingers while raising his camera. Leo Smart must have made money reporting on Thompson.

Calhoun waited. Took pictures of the vehicle parked a half-block away. Nervous, he rubbed clammy palms and whistled a song. Drank coffee and called for takeout pizza. He prayed she wasn't drinking. He reckoned McCloud to be a jerk, but he never figured she would go out with him.

Calhoun punched the radio on and listened to country music. How depressing. He jabbed the button to turn off Brad Paisley's *Whiskey Lullaby*. There was no way he was going to cry again. In his cruiser.

Should he confront them? Truth spiked her note. *Pretentious prig*. He should have moved forward with her. Interrupting her while conferencing with Dumont had been idiotic, and he could only be angry with himself.

Pushed her into McCloud's sights. Not again.

The temptation to call Mike or Zoe to come was close to overwhelming. He stopped brooding, zoomed in on the green SUV's tags, then snapped more photos and ran the plates to be certain.

"Now why is Leo Smart following Cade?"

CATHERINE CADE

The interior overflowed with music. Waiters wove between packed tables with platters of food and libations. Waiting patrons consumed peanuts and ale at the bar.

My gaze swept the bar and grill. "I've never been here."

"Want to dance first, talk later?"

"Let's. What's your favorite dance?"

He touched my elbow. "Latin music one night, line dancing the next, ballroom another night. I like them all."

"You know this place well."

"I enjoy dancing."

"I see. Do you find your dates here?"

McCloud flashed his eyes at me. "No. This is a hobby, it's fun, and I bargain for a great night of drinking and dancing."

I said, "Listen, Argentine tango. My favorite."

McCloud led me to the floor. My dress was loose enough to spin and tight enough to wrap around me. He encircled my waist, eyes drilling into mine. The dance called for quick footwork, twisting, turning, and twirling. I pushed him away, and a gasp caught in my throat as he drew me to his chest with his lips near. When the song finished, we found a booth. A waiter came and took our order.

"Unaged rye for me, and a Tom Collins for the lady."

The waiter thanked us and left.

"I don't drink."

"Do you avoid alcohol for religious reasons?"

"No. Calhoun told me don't drink."

"Seriously?" An uptick to his mouth appeared. "You do everything he tells you?"

"No." I fiddled with a napkin.

"Consider Tom Collins as code for a Seven-Up with a special hint of flavor."

The waiter returned, and the drink's tang surprised me. "This is different." I downed half before he raised Calhoun's name.

"Calhoun's an idiot for not—" He held a hand in the air. "He didn't even give you a shot."

"I want to shake his puritanical world a bit." Where did that come from? I rested my chin in my palm and took another sip of soda. McCloud was disarming. His words soothed. Yet thoughts of Calhoun still set me ablaze, and I fought against my feelings for him. "So, how about one night?"

What did I just say? The glass required a long stare.

He blinked. A corner of his mouth raised. "Been a while?"

I gasped and hid my face with my hand. "I don't know why I said that. I'm not the kind of girl who would—"

McCloud slid his hand across the table and clutched mine. "You're hurting. Trust me, I know."

Unable to finish my drink, I pushed the glass away. "I think dancing wore me out. Gotta better idea. We go to his church. That'll ruffle his feathers."

"You want revenge at church. Did you lose your mind? Best thing to do is pretend we're getting it on. Or do so. Sure, I'll help."

"Church, or it's a no," I said with a thick tongue, "go."

"Are you okay?"

"Something's wrong. Can you call me a cab? I need to go home."

McCloud threaded a hand through his hair. "You okay on your feet?"

I stood and wobbled. "Of course." Bad idea. "Not so much. Gimme a hand."

"Catherine, you don't look right." He swallowed hard. "I confess, the Tom Collins has a little alcohol, and I think you're wasted."

"What? What did you do?"

"Sit. I'll drive you home," he said. I tried to keep an eye on my watch, but it fuzzed in and out. We walked out of the Whiskey River Bar and Grill, and McCloud held me close, steadying me.

"Catherine, I didn't know you couldn't hold your liquor. I'm sorry, I should have told you, and I swear, it's not supposed to do this. Just to loosen that tension."

"Calhoun? What happened?"

His voice was garbled. "I should have guessed. You can't stand Calhoun, yet who do you call?"

"Huh?"

Halfway to the car, the world spun, and the asphalt came hurtling my way.

CHAPTER 43

RICK CALHOUN

Calhoun jumped from the cruiser. He sprinted toward McCloud. "What did you do to her?"

McCloud snapped his head toward Calhoun. "What are you doing, spying on us? Look, I didn't know she had a sensitivity to alcohol. She's not allergic, is she?"

Calhoun took her from him. "She's sensitive to everything. I told her not to order a drink."

"Skin's not flushed. Pulse normal. She didn't vomit. She didn't mention a problem. I didn't know. She wasn't just blindly following your orders. You found out she was sensitive."

"Ya think? Take a cab home before I arrest you for attempted assault. I'll drive her home. I can't believe you. Things never change, do they?"

"Hey, I planned to take her home. I'd never molest an unconscious woman."

"No, you planned to seduce her while she was drunk."

"Look who's talking. You rejected her, pushed her away. Don't you take advantage? Because I wonder, how do you know about her alcohol sensitivity?"

"You don't know the facts." He walked away, her head bobbing with each step.

Calhoun buckled her into the front passenger seat, rifled a gaze at McCloud, and drove out of the parking lot.

He swore under his breath, angry at McCloud, livid with himself—how he'd missed multiple opportunities to tell her everything. He curled a fist, navigated the cruiser into her driveway, and carried her into her room.

He put Cade on her bed, removed her shoes and covered her with a blanket.

She stirred. "Rick?"

"I'm here, baby, everything's okay."

"Hospital," she slurred.

"Why?" he asked, alarmed.

"Heart's broke, can't fix it. I wished, wished we were real." She raised a hand to his face and traced a finger along his jawline.

Her hand fell, and he caught it. Lights out. "It was always real, Catherine."

She quieted, and her eyes closed. He pressed his lips to her fingers, then rolled her onto her side and put a pillow behind her back. She was a constant problem. Stubborn woman.

Reluctant, he left her house but figured he'd use nighttime to roll around town and discover Sarah Thompson's activities. He dropped off the cruiser at his house, dressed in jeans and jacket, and climbed into his truck, heading back to the PD. He planned to place a GPS tracker under Leo Smart's SUV. At the bullpen, he rummaged through his desk, checked his notes, grabbed the records on Thompson, and collected his gear. Last, he found a menu from Wu Chen's.

Wu Chen's Chinese restaurant was quick with his order, and Rick paid for his takeout. He climbed into the black Ford that didn't scream cop-on-a-stakeout. Before sunrise, he'd stop at Catherine's place, but for now, he found two spots he could park where he'd be able to see Thompson's house without being seen.

Glass windows surrounded most of her home, and not every curtain was closed.

No sign of her. He tore the paper off a pair of cheap pull-apart chopsticks and held them in his teeth while he set up the old telescoping antenna. Fiddled with the staticky stationary transmitter he'd brought from the station. He snatched the night vision goggles to read the paper.

"Ugh. 'Local elections passed, and City Commissioner Sarah Thompson won by a landslide.'" Sure, because Leo Smart painted her as the single-handed heroine of Whiskey River.

The paper landed on the floor of the truck. "You'd think she won the Nobel Peace Prize," he mumbled.

He stuck chopsticks into the box filled with Wu Chen's sweet sesame-dotted orange chicken and scooped the last of the food into his mouth. It didn't take long for his favorite Chinese dish to promise a devastating night of heartburn. Rummaging around, he found a half-empty bottle of antacid.

With binoculars trained back on the Thompson mansion, Calhoun noted a woman of her height and build strolling through the third story. She disappeared behind a wall and emerged into another room. She fussed with her hair as a man crept up behind her. Calhoun, alarmed, prepared to intervene.

Instead, the man scooped her into his arms. Calhoun took pictures, incriminating enough to show Sarah Thompson's love life, but not much else. He struggled to get a picture but caught them in nothing more than a kiss.

The place went dark. Done. He turned the key, started the engine, and drove toward Leo Smart's apartment.

The rundown apartments in the poorer part of town were stuck in time—rent cheap, the stucco and brown-roof complexes run down, and crime high. The *Medallion* hack's domicile. Calhoun remembered his only other homicide in Whiskey River was at these apartments. An unarmed woman against a bat-wielding boyfriend.

Calhoun parked at the curb and set up his listening device. He wasn't expecting much, but hoped for a striking piece of information. He walked to Leo's Cube. Locked. He placed the GPS device under the wheel well.

Headlights turned into the parking lot. Calhoun moved to the opposite side of Smart's SUV.

He squinted. Sarah Thompson. The editorial connection came as no big surprise, but this clandestine meeting between polar opposites—the rich and classy versus the working hack and creep—might be an exposé of its own. Calhoun waited until she ducked around the apartment building's corner, and he sprinted to his truck to get Smart's apartment into view. He slipped his fingers into a shirt pocket, popped a piece of gum into his mouth, and put on earphones.

Leo Smart's short silhouette appeared at the door.

Calhoun grabbed his camera and snapped photos of Thompson disappearing into Leo's apartment.

He wrote the glamour pieces on Thompson, and he followed Cade. But what was his connection with Thompson? He snatched the listening device and pointed the parabolic dish receiver toward Smart's window, cursing the old equipment.

"Commissioner Thompson."

"Leo, please call me Sarah."

Silence. Calhoun flicked the dish receiver twice, hearing his finger thwap through the earphones.

"Uh, please, come in. I haven't cleaned. Hope you don't mind."

"Nonsense."

Voices competing from other small apartments interfered, and he adjusted his gear.

"I wanted to meet you, Leo. Thanks to you, I won the commissioner's seat for a second term. You headed the campaign. It has not gone unnoticed."

Calhoun said, "I bet."

Silence. Did the reception go out? He knocked the receiver again.

Leo said, "My pleasure, Commissioner—Sarah."

"I have a proposition. Do you have a five or ten-year plan?"

Another pause. "No agenda for me. Idealism. I'd hoped for the Pulitzer someday. Something beyond small-town news."

Calhoun scratched notes.

"I never planned to marry Stephen, and when his daughter died from cancer, I could help no one, not Lily, her mother, or Lily's father. I wandered without a plan too, but I decided if this was the path intended for me, I needed a strategy."

"What, may I ask, is your strategy?"

"I'm a commissioner. I want to work my way up. My goal? Governor, but I can't do it alone."

Calhoun's gum fell from his mouth. Not the bombshell he expected.

"Not meaning any offense, but why share this with me?"

"You've been nothing but supportive of me. I need a PR journalist. I want you to work for me."

"I–I'm sure there is someone far more qualified."

"Please tell me you're not turning down the job of a lifetime. I've read your bio. You landed here by accident, but I see impeccable credentials."

"I'm stunned, Commissioner Thompson. I'm honored and humbled at your offer. But, you truly believe I am up to the job? Small potatoes here. I just have—"

"Leo." A pause. "If you would like to think about it, that is fine. But I believe you have the talent to head my campaign in your status as PR."

Another pause.

"Commissioner, consider me on your team."

"Wonderful. I'm curious, though. Why are you following a baker in town?"

Calhoun's ears pricked, pen readied.

"Fascinating story, however, I'm certain you're aware I must protect my client's privacy."

"Good to hear, Leo. Means you'll protect mine, as well."

"We all have secrets."

Another silence followed. Then, "Don't we, though."

CHAPTER 44

I woke with a headache, scrounged for aspirin, and prepared a pot of coffee, reliving my encounter with Calhoun long ago. What had happened last night?

Was this a hangover? Again?

I lifted my palms to my face when I read the internet's definition of a Tom Collins. One and a half ounces of gin, seltzer, but not a drop of Seven-Up.

A scroll of cuss words ticker taped through my brain. My vision darkened.

In a rural town with fewer than twenty thousand, going public terrified me. I pressed my cellphone to my skull. Calhoun, should I call him? I'd shoot McCloud if he'd touched me.

Any assault kit evidence would pass through McCloud's grip, which he'd bury.

Fragments of our conversation emerged. Last night, for a moment with alcohol on board, I considered a one-night stand with him. Then the parking lot. The last thought was tunnel vision. I dropped my head into my hands with tears. What an appalling lapse of judgment. Please Lord, tell me he didn't harm me.

With a half-empty coffee cup in one hand, I clasped a pillow to my chest. Small town, big talk. Me, in a bar with a respected member of Whiskey River. I had said to him, "I don't drink." He didn't listen.

A knock on the door startled me, and my lukewarm coffee splashed as I twisted, grabbing my gun. I looked through the window to see Calhoun and McCloud. Figured best to lay my pistol on the table. I strode to the door and jerked it wide.

Calhoun held a scraped-up McCloud by the back of his shirt.

I slapped the medical examiner across the face, then squeezed a hand over my mouth.

Calhoun spoke. "No one hurt you, and I brought you home. You drank alcohol and passed out. Dr. McCloud wants to say something, right?" He pushed McCloud into the siding of the house, and his head thumped.

Jack pressed fingers of one hand to his reddened face and the palm of his other hand toward me. "Catherine, I'd no idea. You suggested a one-night thing. I figured you'd relax with a lightweight drink."

"I said church. I changed my mind within thirty seconds, remember?"

He raised a hand and rubbed his face. "Tell Calhoun what you told me. Tell him."

I regarded Calhoun. "You hurt me. Your mixed signals threw me into an emotional den of lions, then to Jack." I turned back to the doctor. "And you. I'd rather be heartbroken by Calhoun than deceived by you."

Calhoun stood still, his mouth clamped shut, but his eyes never wavered from mine. He handed keys to McCloud. "Go."

The medical examiner mumbled another apology as he walked to his vehicle, backed out onto the street, and left.

We faced each other.

"I was sure I'd been—" Swamped in a wash of anger, fear, relief, I stopped.

He entered, wrapped himself around me, and let me cry.

"Nothing happened. I was right there."

"Thank you."

"I'm always here for you. Tell me how to make this right. I'll do anything."

A lump formed in my throat like a chunk of gristle, and I struggled to swallow. "I believed we had a connection. Look, I'm a grownup, and if you're not interested, it's okay. It may hurt but at least I'd know."

He closed his eyes. "What have I done? I'd been grieving and alone for so long, I'd given up. There's—"

"You mean Melanie. I'm not her."

"Shh." He stared at his feet then lifted his eyes to mine. "You're a unique treasure, different from Melanie, and there's no excuse for my behavior."

I snagged two cups of coffee and ushered him to the couch. "You're apologizing?"

He sighed. "Again, yes. You'd had enough of the bad, and you, well, I planned—"

I raised my hand. "Hang on there, big fella. You just said, 'alone for so long.' There's been no one since Melanie?"

"Nope."

"You've never moved on."

"Yes, I have. But you. Why choose McCloud?"

"You came off as judgmental and controlling."

He placed his coffee on the table. "I was wrong. Forgive me?"

"Always." I rubbed a tingling thumb and forefinger.

"But I have to ask. You went to a bar with McCloud."

"I wanted someone to talk to."

He snorted. "You wanted something altogether different."

"Hey, the thought crossed my mind for maybe thirty seconds because of the alcohol."

"It took a full thirty seconds to change your mind?"

"Hush."

"Tell me, what did you learn?"

I made eye contact with him, but I couldn't maintain it. I stared at a spot on the table. "That I can't do everything on my own. That I need help. I think I've been playing around the edges of this being a Christian thing. I get it, you know, the swimming to Hawaii thing. I want what you have, but I've no clue what's next."

He raised his face toward the ceiling, then back down, settling his gaze on me. "One more story. This one true. When Jesus was being crucified, on his right and left were two criminals, both also crucified and dying. One man was a thief. After the other felon laughed at Jesus, the thief begged Jesus to remember him when Jesus came into his kingdom. Jesus said to him, 'Today, you will be with me in paradise."

I blinked back tears. Yeah, I'd heard it before, but it hadn't registered. "Why does it seem so simple?"

"Because it is. 'If you speak with your mouth that Jesus is Lord and believe in your heart that He was raised from the dead, you will be saved.' It means you are sorry for your past and you want Jesus to live in your heart as the risen Christ."

I swallowed hard as he took my hands in his, and we prayed. I'd done terrible things, yet pouring out a request asking for God's forgiveness lightened my soul. Calhoun held me as I wept again.

Jesus cared about the thief. He cared about someone like me. In spite of everything, he cared. And a voice, softer than yesterday's dreams, breathed through my heart. *And he still cares, even now. For you.*

My weeping turned to joy in that split second. Calhoun smiled as I chattered on and on how things looked different. I dashed outdoors and stood, shocked.

"What's wrong?"

"Everything seems ... different. Brighter." I turned my head toward the sky. "Look!" I pointed. "That's ... a blue I've never seen. Why can I see the blades of grass? Why?"

He grinned and picked me up. "Cool, isn't it?"

"Beyond cool."

Later, after I calmed my smiles and tears, I changed the subject, still reflecting. "Any word on the green vehicle?"

He said, "Ran the plates. Turns out a reporter, Leo Smart, is following you. Need to find out why." He drained the last of his coffee mug.

Alarm rose in my chest as it did my voice. "What about the who? Who is Leo working for?"

"I have an idea."

"I knew I smelled smoke."

He tickled my neck. "I found a surprise at his place. Sarah Thompson showed up. Asked him to be on her public relations team. But he didn't tell her why he followed you. He probably answers to someone above her pay grade."

"It's not Thompson. The mayor's office?"

"I'm not sure, but I do know Sarah Thompson has a lover. Got pictures and everything."

"I'll take your word on it."

Calhoun wandered to the kitchen. "Not those kinds of pictures." Cupboards opened and closed, and the coffee blender whirred. I followed as he opened the refrigerator. He fumbled for food and found an apple.

I fiddled with my cup. "More coffee. We'll be up all night."

A lengthy silence caused me to glance up at his face.

"Uh, I've never—" He stopped and turned the apple in his hand, staring at me. "You and me, well, I haven't—"

"You haven't what?"

He wiped his face. "This is different, not saving your butt. That didn't come out right. What I'm trying to say is, well, ask, is ..." He gestured with his hands and uttered a small "hey."

"Spit it out, what's wrong?"

"Geez, I feel like a cat in a dog pound. You're doing this on purpose. I'm trying to ask you on a date. Dinner, you know, and a movie."

"For Pete's sake, I thought you were having a stroke."

"Yeah, well, it came close."

"I don't get it. We've gone bowling. Fishing—"

He cleared his throat. "Who dropped the bowling ball and broke Mike's toe? Who did I drag kicking and screaming to go fishing, and who caught a tree limb with her line during that outing, landing me in the drink?"

"Okay, okay. Point taken. Why is it hard to ask after almost a year?"

"Been a stretch." He examined the floor.

"Bad timing, after my experience with McCloud, don't you think?"

He rubbed the nape of his neck and groaned. "I'm just as sharp as mashed potatoes today." He raised his chin, held his hand out, and I took it. He drew me into his arms as the space between us disappeared. He dropped the apple, and his hand hugged my head.

Our lips met, and he matched my hunger in a kiss.

Longer than expected, shorter than I'd hoped for, my lips already begged for more.

He swept a light kiss across my hand, bringing tingles along my arm. "I've another confession."

"Ready."

"Amy."

Huh? "What? As in Chandler?"

"She's my teammate, never a romance."

"Wait, you're not still in the service?"

"We're a unique unit."

"Can you tell me?"

"No. But before I met her, my partner was Melanie. Our duties were similar."

Words about honesty were on my lips, but if they were partners and he a sniper, this story might be one no one should be privy to except a trusted part of his life. I reflected on the day we first met. He knew what Dengue fever was, and I'd wondered how he knew, and what he understood of the infection. The US always denied wet work. He was entrusting me with a lot.

"You're a government hit man. I knew you weren't a cop," I whispered. He and his wife were snipers. Where and what sort of risky adventures had they participated in, globetrotting, taking out bad guys? I wanted to hear stories but knew I couldn't.

"No." His voice faltered enough for me to hear.

Liar.

We sat on the couch in silence and sipped more morning brew.

"What are you doing today?" I wasn't sure how I felt about falling for a Christian assassin. I had no frame of reference.

"Hanging out with you." He gave me a look that said more than a Sunday morning preacher.

"But are you here to babysit me?"

"Not unless you plan to run again. Can you say it? 'I will never run again.'"

My tongue stuck to the roof of my mouth. "I will, won't— never will ... oh, for crying out loud."

"Yup, I'm babysitting. Someday you'll call this place home."

"What is wrong with me? I can't even lie."

"Sincerity becomes you. Kinda cute watching a flim-flam, flop. Lying was your experience, and not being able to fake it is growth."

We turned passion into a quiet game of Texas Hold'em, since that was his favorite, and I let him deal. "I read the Book of Solomon," I said, studying my fingernails.

He shot me a brief look over his cards. "Unsupervised. How scandalous. What did you think?"

"I didn't understand it. Sounded kinda weird."

There was an uptick to his mouth. "It's a love story between King Solomon and his bride-to-be. The king saw a lovely vineyard maid and asked her to be queen. They waited for their wedding despite their longing."

"Wait. The Song of Solomon is a romance novel? In the Bible?" I sputtered and choked for air. "And you gave me grief."

"It's about timing." He shifted a card's position then grasped my hand. "Waiting on God according to his will can be difficult."

"Explain waiting on God."

"His timing is always perfect. We rush our plans because it's easy to choose the path of least resistance. It gets tougher being a Christian."

I gaped at him while my cards fluttered to the floor. "It gets harder? Shouldn't you have shared that with me earlier? Why doesn't the Surgeon General post it on church doors?"

He chuckled. "Trust me, God will tap you on the shoulder when you're wandering off."

"Great." On the floor, I crossed my legs and changed subjects. "I read about two people in prison who've affirmed the whereabouts of the Vermeer, and if the news gets to Jerry, it's game over."

"He'll send someone after you," he said. "I'll make a call or tip Mike, which would swell his Japanese heart."

I snorted in laughter. "He's like what, fourth-generation Japanese American?"

He nodded. "Making him very confused about his cultural heritage."

We played cards for an hour until he wearied of losing money, so we switched to gin rummy.

Half an hour later, he huffed and threw a hand of cards onto the table. "I'm out of greenbacks. You cheat."

I relinquished his cash and grinned. "Pick a card, any card."

"Figures. We need to work on the case and have you get into Leo Smart's computer, scan his emails and maybe find out why he's following you. I put a GPS tracker under his SUV, but I want to crack into his financials. He may have information on you and Sarah Thompson. He's her new PR, there to scrub her past pretty." He tapped his fingers. "And who's her new guy?"

"Wait. That's illegal."

"Technicalities."

I shook my head and sighed. "You want me to pry for you."

"Of course. I can make a phone call if you'd rather—"

"I can neither confirm nor deny I have the ability to hack, but what do you want?"

His mouth opened in silence.

"Cakewalk. Close your mouth. I don't want you drooling on my floor."

As computer hacking goes, things change overnight, even without firewalls, fail-safes, passwords, and virus protection. I figured they were all scams. I never attained or surpassed a Dark Dante type, but I could hold my own. An important aspect of my past criminal life.

"Let's drive to Medford. There are great internet cafés there."

"Why Medford?"

I nodded. "Good point. It's too close. We could go north to Portland or south to Redding. Excellent idea, putting us out of range. We craft a new profile and gain access to an out-of-state IP address and ISP. You're good."

"Wait, what's an ISP address?"

"It's the business you use to hook up to the internet, like a phone company. The IP number is a unique number that the corporation assigns. It's a geographical address. There's more, but that's it for you, Mr. Computer-Illiterate. We could stay here and bounce the signal all around to Russia and back, but a knowing eye will find my IP address, Whiskey River. If we use yours at the police station, someone will know we're trying to slip through the basement window."

He frowned. "What if you get blocked?"

"Me? Well, what about your friend? I say twenty bucks there's a three-letter agency backing him or her, and you can bet those letters aren't *F*, *B*, or *I*. Portland, here we come."

He put on his jacket. "What about California? Why not hit Yreka?"

"Not enough espresso shops and a small population. Someone would remember." I handed him the keys. "Besides, in Portland, we stand a better chance of tasting coffees, and you can buy me a new computer."

He grumbled. "Why not go to San Francisco?"

"Brilliant! Tons of opportunities."

"Next time, I'm keeping my mouth shut. Do I need to bring stuff for overnight?"

"You have a decent mind, for a cop." Excited to put my computer skills to work again, I rushed to my room, grabbed my travel bag and my password-breaker thumb drive, and returned to the living room.

Calhoun said, "Well? Ready for a short trip?"

"A six-hour drive? You call that short?"

"We'll be back in time for church tomorrow." He pulled the door open. "The five p.m. service, that is."

CHAPTER 45

CATHERINE CADE
MONDAY

The Who Donut needed evaluation. My visit wouldn't take much time. In Dumont's office, a stoic Calhoun crossed his arms in refusal. It wasn't difficult to persuade the chief to overturn his decision. The chief needed a doughnut, and I needed a break from the murder case. And a doughnut would come in handy. Still, he protested in Dumont's office.

I yelled back. "A Kevlar vest? A chaperone? No. I'll be right back."

"You're not listening—"

"You know, someday I'll snap, and you'll be sorry." I turned and headed out as Dumont ribbed him.

The visual sweep of my shop passed inspection, with sparkling counters and customers clustered around tables. I watched as their eyes closed with each bite, and backed out of the glass doors with two doughnuts in hand. I was content, and in love.

I began a slow stroll along the sidewalk, and my smartphone rang. Calhoun keeping track of me? He'd given me five minutes to check the Who Donut's quality assurance. Figured I'd find a GPS tracker under my truck next.

Jules's name popped up on the phone's screen. She'd been gone a month, and our talks were short, but I had a cheesy bulletin for her. The man I used to dislike had won my heart. She gave me a sad update instead.

"What do you mean, you're staying in Salem?" A tinge of panic in my voice. "You will come to visit, right?" A mouthful of doughnut muffled my words.

"You—a—better." Static.

One chocolate éclair and one light puffy, melt-in-your-mouth doughnut with sweet frosting impaired my ability to keep a tight hold on to the phone. I pivoted to check for a better signal.

That's when I heard the noise, a sharp bang, like a fire-cracker's pop.

Something slammed into me, knocked me back, and spun me around. I staggered. My phone fell from my hand, pain erupted from my chest, and people on the sidewalk screamed and scattered. My knees gave way.

What just happened? My insides quaked. I rested back on my wobbling thighs, unable to yell as air squeezed from me with each out-breath, leaving me in sizzling pain. Blood soaked into my clothes.

I cringed, inching closer to the phone on the concrete. Half-crawling on my knees, I made my way to the phone and finally grasped it. Stupid, stupid, stupid, not listening to Rick. I wrestled between pain and panic. My vision blurred.

Calhoun.

The cellphone slipped onto the ground again, out of reach. I could no more stop the falling tears than stop the blood from flowing. My chest throbbed.

The hole in my chest needed to be covered, but nothing lay nearby to use. Trembling, using the only thing I had, I clapped a hand over the wound and cried out with pain.

Someone yelled, "Get an ambulance!"

My thoughts encompassed the world of people I'd conned. I sent a universal "I'm sorry, please forgive me" into the icy blue sky.

God! Please send Calhoun!

Things weren't going well. My hand weakened and slipped, and I watched the sky fade from blue to ultramarine, then down to dead gray.

RICK CALHOUN

A distant but sharp pop echoed in the department. Calhoun was running almost before he was out of his chair. He yelled for an ambulance as his feet hit the pavement outside the department. He ran the block, fear hammering at him, until he reached the bakery and saw her bloody form on the sidewalk.

She knelt, left arm hanging at her side. "What ... took you ...?"

"Oh, Catherine."

She rasped, "I hate it when you're right."

"Here, let me help." Calhoun sat behind her, pressed his hands to both wounds, applying pressure. Her body shook.

She closed her eyes. Her teeth chattered. "I'm freezing."

He kissed her neck. "Shh, the ambulance is on its way."

She slumped against him.

"Hey—don't pass out on me. Don't you dare die. Don't die on me, not now."

"S-scared, Rick."

Terrified, he pressed his forehead to her neck and blinked back tears. "Big baby. It's only a scratch."

Her words were quiet, slow, breathy. "I–I want you to know ..."

Mike's cruiser scraped the curb as he drove up. The screech of the ambulance closed on the scene. He ran toward Calhoun after a quick scan.

"I'll cordon off the area and obtain statements."

Calhoun held a failing Cade in his arms as the EMTs jumped from the ambulance with a backboard and loaded her into the vehicle without a wasted move. One EMT checked her pulse and called to the other. "Her blood pressure is dropping, and she's in tachycardia. Pulse is thready."

"I'm going with you—" His mouth opened, his eyes darted from her to the EMT as he climbed into the emergency van. "What does tachy-whatever mean?"

"Rapid heartbeat and weak pulse." One of the EMTs cut her shirt away to attach monitor leads.

Calhoun grasped her hand. "Is she going to be okay?"

"We don't know yet. Her wound caused the lung to collapse. Beyond this, I don't know." Dan, the first EMT, cleaned the wounds and placed a HALO dressing over the chest wound.

Another EMT flipped a switch to record the event and called the emergency room as he drove.

Dan checked her pulse and blood pressure, and he wiped sweat from his forehead as he followed the instructions from the emergency room doctor over the radio.

"Pressure's dropping, seventy over forty." He opened the IV wide, allowing more IV fluid to rush into her.

"Explain."

"It means move out of the way. She's losing blood and her blood pressure is dangerously low. This is a thirty-minute drive, pushing it."

Calhoun looked at the woman he loved and prepared for the longest ride of his life.

It was nightfall when the doors opened and the surgeon came out.

"How is she?" Calhoun asked.

"A lucky woman. She lost a considerable amount of blood, but the bullet did minimal damage, because it was a through-and-through gunshot. She's one lucky woman. She'll be in critical care for at least twelve hours."

"Is she awake?"

"She's in post-op and still groggy." He looked toward Mike. "There was no bullet recovered. It appears the bullet struck her from the front and exited from the back of her shoulder."

Calhoun frowned. "Mike, did they find a bullet at the scene?"

"Don't know. I'll go back and double-check. The team should still be there." He nodded toward the doctor, then turned back to Calhoun. "I'm heading back. Take care of her."

"I will." He watched Mike leave, then spoke to the surgeon. "I need a cot."

"I'll let the super know."

"And I need to control who comes and goes."

The surgeon raised a finger, walked out of earshot, pulled out his cell, and returned a few moments later. "I gave the supervising nurse the info." He stopped. "We did a CT scan on her and found multiple areas of bone damage, aside from that caused by the bullet. Most are small, consistent with extreme athletes and dancers. A few fractures healed, a previous car accident, perhaps. She's had minor facial reconstruction." He hesitated a moment, as though awaiting an answer.

Calhoun leaned forward. "What?"

"There are scars. Reportable scars. You understand?"

"Yes. Yes, I do. I'll look into it."

The surgeon nodded, then turned and left.

Calhoun buckled into the chair and wept, knowing she could have died in his arms. He'd seen those scars on her back. He prayed and paced, waiting for her to come out of post-op, then called Jules and explained what had happened. "I need your expertise to gather a group of people to keep watch, so drive down."

Jules cried and choked on words. "Okay, I'll be there in a few hours. Detective Calhoun, she wanted me to find out who followed her."

"The green vehicle?"

"No, a different car. She thought nothing of it until a few weeks ago, so once or twice I followed it."

"What? Why didn't she tell me?"

"I don't think she wanted you to worry. She figured someone from the police department was making sure she'd get home okay. Once it stopped at the police department."

"What kind of car? Plates?"

"Muddy plates. White four-door sedan. A Ford."

He punched a fist into the air. "Get here now. I need your help." Calhoun thumbed off his phone. Sarah Thompson. Something bugged him. Did she figure in these attacks?

What did Cade know that kept her life in such constant danger?

CHAPTER 46

CATHERINE CADE
Fluorescent lights glared overhead as my eyes fluttered open. Three people in scrubs surrounded me. A rough hand held mine.

Calhoun.

"Hey." I forced words through my cotton mouth.

"Hey, back."

"What's happening?" My voice slurred.

"What's the last thing you remember?"

My recollection fell short, but I'd needed Calhoun. "Don't know. You were there. I prayed, and you were there."

"And I'm not leaving you."

Visions of pain, blood, and trouble breathing returned in a flood. "Who shot me? Did Jerry get out of prison?"

"He's still there. Sleep, babe. I'm here."

"Missed center mass."

The gurney turned, the lights changed direction, and I almost retched. Then nothing.

An anesthetic fog surrounded me when I woke again, this time in the dark. A sliver of light slipped under the door. Muffled voices exchanged words, and an electrocardiogram beeped.

Snippets of memories returned. Someone had shot me outside the Who Donut. Calhoun had held my hand as he ran beside my gurney after surgery.

Burning pain shot through my chest as I tried to turn. "Oh, ow."

"You okay?" Calhoun took my hand through the bed rails.

"You scared me. Hurts. Have you been here the entire night?"

Our fingers interlaced.

His voice was gruff. "Yeah. I was afraid I'd lost you."

"I kind of entertained those thoughts myself. Can I shoot whoever shot me? Tit for tat."

"You're a deputy, but I've got a bigger badge." Calhoun sat at the side of his cot and rubbed his eyes.

The stubble on his face drew my finger to his jaw. He touched a kiss to my fingers. His five o'clock shadow brought out his rugged features, more so as he gave me a fatigued half-smile.

"Stick-in-the-mud. You need a shave. You're a handsome devil." Truth spilled out under the effects of mind-altering drugs. Anesthesia lasts, and people can say interesting things when they're fuzzy.

"Funny. My mother always said I was an angel from heaven."

I believed that.

He stood. "You can get shot, and you're still the most beautiful woman I have ever laid eyes on, but no more running for doughnuts without a bulletproof vest." He cupped a hand under my jaw. "There are too many people after you. You must know something."

"As soon as I remember, you'll be the first I'll tell."

"I'll get it out of you. Someone told me I'm good at what I do."

I tugged on his shirt and he leaned down. "Bet you are." I stroked his face, and he kissed me despite my wooly teeth and morning breath. "This is an interesting first date."

"Not even close."

"I don't remember ever being on a date."

"You will, soon." He squeezed my hand. "Everything leads back to Thompson, and you're connected. Someone came for me once, but now you're someone's target. Do you think Thompson was part of your history?"

"Not that I recall." I was silent for a moment, and scoured internal theories with my one working brain cell in the post-anesthesia fog. "I take it you think at least Tate is off the hook."

"Not enough hard evidence."

"Did you figure out who hired Leo Smart?"

"Wasn't Thompson or the mayor. My money's on Darren Hughe."

"Hmm."

"You didn't tell me there was a different car following you."

"Figured you had someone follow me, since I'd forbidden it."

Calhoun pushed the small cot further back to sit comfortably. He rested his forehead against one of the hospital bed railings. "I'm waiting on information. What would the mayor's office want with Leo Smart? I'm slogging through the emails you found. Not much there, but he has a side job, and it's you."

"Can we pray?"

He looked surprised at my request. "I haven't stopped, but you bet. Thank you, Lord, for divine protection. We pray for quick and pain-free healing. In Jesus's name, amen."

"I don't know how to pray."

"You just talk to God. You're not weaving a sermon, just having a conversation."

A conversation. Again, it seemed too simple. My head went fuzzy again, and I felt my breaths deepen. My eyelids fluttered. "I want McCloud's job."

His eyes narrowed. "Why?"

Sleepy, my lids closed. "Because I can do an autopsy with my eyes shut."

"What do you mean? You mean McCloud is incompetent?"

"No. Said what? Can't remember now." The yawns overtook me.

"How many autopsies have you done?"

"Shh. Wanna sleep."

RICK CALHOUN

He fixed his eyes on Cade's face, holding her hand to his cheek until she fell asleep. He hoped this piece of the jigsaw puzzle had fallen into place for her. That she'd remember. How and why she'd learned her skills. Now he needed to prove it to her. Her identity.

He dialed Mike. "Hey. I need a favor."

A half-hour later Mike sauntered into the room and handed Calhoun a small packet. "What's going on?"

"Still hitting on nurses?"

"Hope springs eternal, so they say."

"Good. Distract the nurse at the counter. Five minutes, max."

"Do I get an explanation?"

"Later."

After Mike left, Rick collected Catherine's prints. He tucked the print paper and ink back into the envelope, into his pocket. Calhoun leaned over the railing. "And you thought you were the thief. This time I stole your heart," he whispered as she slept. His lips brushed hers.

"Hi, Detective."

He straightened, surprised at Jules's stealth. "Jules. When did you get here?"

"A few minutes ago." She pushed away from the doorjamb with wry smile.

"What?"

"Nothing. Just that you fingerprinted Catherine and confessed your undying love."

He gave her a hard-edged glance. "This is just between us. I've given the nurses the names of the people allowed in here." He handed her a list. "Check each medication. This is a list of staff assigned because she's not out of trouble yet, and neither are you for withholding information."

"Detective, you can't fingerprint a patient without verbal permission, and most detectives don't profess their love to a shooting victim in a hospital bed. Unless there's something more. You give either of us crap about withholding information, and the police department will hear before she hears it from you."

"We've told each other." Calhoun said. *More or less.*

"Why did you print her?"

Calhoun ushered Jules to a chair in the corner and closed the door. He explained what he could, but he couldn't keep all of her criminal history a secret.

Jules swung her gaze back toward the hospital bed with its white sheets, white bedspread, and its occupant. "What? I should have ..." She choked out confused and angry words with her tears. "She lied. How could she? Why wouldn't she tell me? She was so alone, and I, well, we became best friends, I thought. Why would she do this to me?"

"I can't say, not yet. But I need you to be her friend."

Jules stiffened. "I don't lie to my friends, by commission or omission. Three years, she conned me. *Three years.* She betrayed me." She cried again.

"Lying to you, me, and even to herself was self-preservation. What if the truth destroys her? Don't shatter her fragile hold on what little confidence she's found. Patience here is key."

Jules clenched her teeth. "She's toxic, and you're in love with her. Her type makes a living off people like us. What happens when the truth destroys you?"

CHAPTER 47

Catherine Cade

Hallway chatter woke me, suggesting I'd slept a good while into swing shift.

Jules sat in a corner, reading.

"Hey, Jules."

She came over and touched my arm. No grin to cheer a flagging mood. The corners of her mouth were turned down.

"What's wrong, no jokes?"

With a blank expression, emphasizing each word, she said, "Someone shot you. Ever since you met Calhoun, your life has been in danger, and you've inched closer to death each time." She kissed me on my forehead. "There aren't jokes about being shot, Catherine. You've been my friend, on your terms, but I won't watch you self-destruct with your lies. You conned me into being your friend. I'm going back north, and I won't be back. Tread with caution. Someone else on Calhoun's list is coming to keep watch."

"Wait a minute—" My mouth hung open in surprise and hurt. How did she find out? She left the room. Oh, no. Stupid me, not truthful from the start. Now our friendship had died on the vine because my deception starved its growth. My friendship wasn't a con, was it? She was my friend. I called out to her, but she was gone.

Jules, come back.

Tears rolled down my face, and my chest burned. Lying was a fault I had to own. Now I saw firsthand the hurt my survival skills had wrought in Jules.

After my tears turned into a dribble and the hiccups started, I buzzed the desk, and a nurse came with pain medication. She pushed it into an IV port, and reminded me to call her if needed.

The medication kicked in fast. My angst fell away, and my thoughts cleared. I'd win Jules's friendship back. I'd earn it. Also, I'd never accessed the mayor's office. It would be easy to slip in and pop a thumb drive into his computer. The building was older than Methuselah, and there had to be holes in security.

I feel awesome ...

Cognizant but a bit floaty, I decided it was time to put my plot into motion. The county clerk's office housed blueprints and entry points. I could bypass the access codes, though that could be tricky. Corrupt politicians always kept double books, whether buried in computer files or in safety deposit boxes. I chewed on a fingernail, thinking a call to Calhoun might be in order. Nope. He was working. I wouldn't bug him.

I swung my legs over the bed, and there was no pain. Was that a miracle? My head swam with ideas and dizziness. Didn't matter. Where were my ropes and full-body harness? What had I done with my glass cutter? I stood and grabbed for my clothes.

My vision darkened, and the floor rushed up to meet me. How odd.

When my eyes opened, I was in McCloud's arms. Two nurses prattled nearby, and an IV stand lay on the floor. One righted the stand while the other bandaged my arm where the needle had jerked out. What happened?

McCloud asked, "Where were you going? You almost got 'skull fracture' added to your diagnosis list."

He put me back into my bed as I swallowed and said, "Not sure."

Both nurses chattered a lecture and walked me to the bathroom. Who knew pain medication could make a person giddy? Once I was back in bed, they restarted the IV, still clucking about my fall.

After they left, I steeled my eyes on McCloud. "You. Why?"

"Evening shift, genius. Jules called. She couldn't stay."

Still fuzzy from the pain medication, I said, "How did you get onto my protective detail?"

His hand raised. "The specifics of my visit include an apology, and since Kim was coming in, I thought you'd be more comfortable if I spoke to you while she was here."

Kim appeared from the chair tucked in the corner and took my hand. "Hey, we'll miss our shopping, gossip, and coffee date, Miss Trouble Magnet."

I could feel a smile on my face. "That's not fair. Planning to find trouble never crossed my mind. Now you owe me my decaf."

"Deal. Dr. McCloud, I can sit with Catherine. You're busy."

"No, Kim." He squeezed her hand. "I plan to hang out with both of you ladies. Cade, your idea to go to church stuck, so I dove in, head first."

"Huh?" Pain was at fifty percent and climbing, and I winced finding a comfortable position.

He grabbed a tissue from a box on the table and fiddled with it. "I had a lot of time to think about how I treated you both. And Kim, I want to apologize for not being man enough to see the wonderful woman in front of me. Got a lot to talk about, don't we?"

Kim's lips parted. Nothing like that had happened since she showed me the morgue. We'd be dishing about this until a wedding happened.

"So, I've been to church, twice," Jack said. "The first time was on my own."

"Then, with me," Kim said.

McCloud aimed a look at Kim, then at me. "We wanted you to know."

My mouth hung open. "And did you like it? Either of you?"

NIGHT SHIFT

My personal guards chit-chatted away outside the door. The clock ticked another minute. I decided to give them thirty more seconds before buzzing the nurse and demanding she drag Rick in.

I counted back from five under my breath, ready to hit the buzzer when he walked through the door.

"Geez, get the *Cliff's Notes* already. Sounded like you were dictating a novel out there."

"My, aren't we demanding?" He came alongside the bed. "Do you need pain medicine?"

"Gossips." Something smelled good, like something-to-eat-good. "I've been waiting for you all day. Have I got stuff to tell you."

The uptick to his mouth gave his amusement away. "Is it gossip?" He tossed a sack onto his cot, revealing a pizza carton in his hand. Rick lifted the lid, and I decided he was a godsend as he waved the pizza under my nose.

My eyes closed in a passionate *mmm,* after grabbing a slice and sinking my teeth into a slice of heaven. I tasted spicy Italian sausage, extra garlic, onions, and peppers. "So much better than gelatin."

"McCloud and Kim distracted the nurses so I could sneak this in. Turns out you're sprung as of tomorrow."

"Sweet," I said, my mouth stuffed. "Are you ready? Here it is. McCloud and Kim became Christians."

"I know, I—"

"But there's more. When the pain medicine kicked in, I stumbled onto something, and without pain."

"Kinda how it's supposed to work."

"Quiet. Help me with this." I explained how I'd made a mental list, things not even Jerry knew.

"Huh."

"When you took the Vermeer in Portland, the painting, did you find climbing gear? Ropes? Diamond glass cutters?"

"Nope."

"How do I know these things? Each part of the plan just fell into place. Simple rock climbing at the local Y doesn't explain everything I told you."

"Just breaking into the evidence room."

"Stop. But I know how … go ahead, name a knot. Better yet, bring me a rope, and I'll show you every knot. Name a security figuration—"

"You think you're a cat burglar, too."

A pause thickened the air. "I don't know."

"In the Marines, we learned knots, rappelling. But rock climbing as a teen was a natural progression for an adrenaline junkie. You must be enjoying these conspiracy theories."

I considered a moment while I chewed. "More like paranoid theories. Should I be this scared?"

"We're on this journey together." He sat on the cot and leaned back against the wall. "I stopped at your place and grabbed what you'd need because you'll be staying with Amy and Sam Chandler."

A disquieting reality seeped into me. My home wasn't safe, and I was unable to protect it on my own. Weakness in my left arm, an ache in my chest, numbness in my fingers, and someone wanted me dead.

"You okay?" He grasped my face and peered into my eyes.

"Yeah." *Not so much.* I'd made a plan to break into a government building. Memories were returning, but a better outcome was not materializing. The need for reassuring words overcame me. "Rick, tell me it will be okay."

"I can't, but God can."

"Oh. And here I wanted to hear something comforting, not judgmental."

"Well, then listen. 'God says, For I know what I am doing. I have it all planned out. Plans to take care of you, not abandon you, plans to give you the future you hope for.' Paraphrased, but that's his truth."

I yawned. "I like that." Those hallowed words made a quiet rumble of courage somewhere deep inside my heart.

CHAPTER 48

"Gotta call someone. Be right back," Rick said.

"What do you—" The unwieldy wheelchair and the orderly behind it prevented me from turning around. "Men. Present company excluded."

Gotta call someone. Whenever those words spilled from his mouth, and he sought isolation, my suspicious finger pointed toward his snitch.

If Calhoun thought his informant slipped confidential evidence to Jerry's gang of goons, either by accident or on purpose, why would he call?

Doors opened, and the orderly rolled me out into cool spring air melting the chill of winter. Calhoun pulled up to the walkway in his black pickup. It had been mine for a short while when Calhoun loaned it to me after that bridge accident long ago.

"Thanks, I'll take it from here." He lifted me from the wheelchair into the truck and buckled my seat belt.

Free at last. Hallelujah.

He rubbed his thumb against my cheek. "You ready for a stop at my place? Sure you are."

Rick's inner sanctum. His house, more than his living room.

Calhoun, always on alert, checked his rear-view mirror several times.

I played with the hospital ID wrist tag. "How about we vacation at Tennessee's Body Farm?"

"A holiday?" He scanned my face. "No. Someone tried to volunteer you to the Body Farm. I aim to find out who."

"Any new information on Thompson's case? And Jerry?"

"Jerry's at Eastern Oregon Correctional. The man you did the autopsy on died differently than Thompson. It's murder, but I don't have enough to link those together."

"Yet," I said.

He swung his truck into the driveway, clicked his garage's remote, and idled forward. Giving me instructions to stay, he hopped out and walked around the truck to my side. For such a big, tough guy, he did "gentle" great. He carried me over the threshold of his door and set me carefully on my feet.

"Don't mind the mess. I haven't cleaned for a while. You steady on your own?"

"If you're suggesting there's pain medicine in my system, you're wrong."

He laughed and disappeared through a door.

Calhoun's house. Austere. Fuzz trying to find a home would become clinically depressed.

Neat.

I wandered the room. There was no clue that there was lint, much less a mess.

Freak.

Crime journals, hunting, and fishing magazines were on his hand-carved coffee table. Big surprise there. My finger trailed along a bookshelf and stopped at *Crime and Punishment*.

Record player? I opened the lid and saw a record on the turntable. Lifting the needle with care, I played a random song. A sublime, mournful melody emanated, one not in character with the gruff man I adored.

Calhoun appeared at the door, face crestfallen, and he spoke five haunted words. "I know you by heart."

Confused, I straightened. "What?"

"A song by Eva Cassidy. I don't need that reminder. If you could turn it off, thanks."

My heart stopped. "I'm so sorry."

"No need to apologize. You didn't know." He turned. "Wait here."

I swallowed, knowing this song was killing him, I even knew why. But his "wait here" didn't work for me, and feeling relieved, I padded behind him in silence through the kitchen and living room. He stepped into his bedroom and pressed a hand to a section of the wall. A panel opened, revealing a digital pad. He pressed numbers, a door opened, and he disappeared.

Not to be outdone, outwitted, or outsmarted, I moved closer for a peek.

"You didn't."

Surprised, he faced me. "Oh, yes, I did."

"Hey," I said. "No judging here, but apparently there really is no honor amongst thieves." Everything I'd once stashed between Whiskey River and Portland was now stacked in his personal armory.

"You know the old saying, the 'pot calling the kettle black'? Told you in Wisconsin, everything you squirreled away in Portland is mine. Well, at least safer here than anywhere else. Grab your SIG and whatever else you might want when you go to the Chandlers'."

I harrumphed, thankful he'd lost the sad puppy look, and yanked at a bag. "Fine."

"Money? Put those bags back. Which weapons do you want?"

The spacious armament, crammed full, required a full walk-around. Another door opened, revealing a studio-sized apartment. "Zombie apocalypse preparation?"

"Go ahead, make fun. It's a safe room."

I scoffed and turned back to the guns. "WinMag would be nice, but I don't see shooting up their home. However, gimme the Springfields and my SIG. Hold the mayo."

"Springfield, short, two to go. Lettuce?

"No lettuce. But I want both service Springfields."

He handed them to me. "Let's roll, cupcake."

"I need ammo and a belt."

"You are so high-maintenance."

I blew a raspberry. "What about a magazine loader?"

"Might be easier for you to load a BB gun."

"You're hilarious."

He rummaged around and found one I liked.

"Looks like someone else needs a mag loader." I snatched the UpLula from his hand.

"Hush, woman." He held out four seventeen-round magazines and a bag full of ammo.

With magazines tucked into my pockets, my next task included gingerly grasping the sack full of nine millimeters in my working hand. With my left, I rubbed tingling fingers together, unable to tell if the sting meant the feeling was coming back, or an itch, cautioning me.

In the truck, he carefully snugged his palm beneath mine.

We found our way to that palatial mansion out of a fairy tale. I'd been here once in their grand room where we celebrated Christmas. Mike had bobbed his mistletoe headband over me, grabbed me around the waist, and had given me a kiss with enough chardonnay to make my tongue tingle. Calhoun had grasped my hand to twirl me into his arms as he shot Mike an evil eye.

Now, Amy greeted us at the door.

The marble flooring sparkled as we stepped in, and we walked under the chandelier that hung from the vaulted ceiling. Their foyer spanned into a grand circle, leading into a marble ballroom in one direction, and in another, a formal sitting room. A spiral staircase rose two flights off to the right of the reception area. I turned a full three-sixty trying to take in the view.

Fingerling hallways led wagon-wheel style to who knew where. I hadn't believed the rumor of a large gym in the basement, but with the size of this home, the story rang true. Great for physical therapy.

Calhoun rubbed my arm. "Gotta go. Work, work, work."

"So soon?" I asked.

"I'll swing by later. Amy, excuse us, we need a moment."

"No problem." She winked at Calhoun.

He put his arms around me. "You gonna be okay?"

"It's a little overwhelming. I'm alone in this place."

"You're not alone. Find a movie and a restaurant you haven't tried." He kissed me, and with his scruffy beard and to-die-for smile, he left the house.

Don't leave.

I swore under my breath and chastised myself because getting that swearing habit under control wasn't a simple trick. But I could no more control my reactions when it came to Rick than I could halt my breathing.

CHAPTER 49

The rich marble reception area surrounded me. Amy returned, and her dimples highlighted crow's feet gathered along with her welcome. "Amy, it's magnificent. So different from when we last stopped here at Christmas."

She took my pack. "We jam our halls on holidays." A ballroom faced me. "Remember the tables, chairs, and food piled high?"

"Best Christmas of my life." That I remembered ... and the party was impressive. Kim and I had a raucous time until she disappeared to explore on her own, I assumed.

Amy slipped her arm through mine, and we climbed stairs where we dropped our shoes and walked on plush cream-colored Berber carpet. A hallway overlooked an expansive floor below, leading past a large picture window with a window seat. I halted.

A breathtaking cottage garden lay below, leading my eye out to the meadow beyond. Manzanita saplings spread across the acreage with stout madrone trees behind them. Distant pine trees pointed my gaze toward the Siskiyou Mountains, while misty fingers crept over the foothills into the valley.

Spring. And what better view of its glory than right here.

Amy pushed open a door. "Here's your room. If it's not satisfactory, we have a few others."

"Are you kidding? I think my entire house would fit in here. This is spectacular!"

"I have Cinderella's attic if you prefer. Want a tour of the house?"

"Think I need a nap first. It's amazing how getting shot can wear on a person."

Her smile revealed a small overlapping tooth. "I'll wake you in forty-five minutes. Sound good?"

"Perfect."

She closed the door, and I walked and scanned each piece of furniture and knickknack, even a vase with perfumed lilacs from her garden below, lavishing this chamber without flaw.

After exploring my room, I placed my gun on a bedside table and lay on the bed. What a wonderful place to spend time. No more shooting, nix my pain, and kick back. My eyes fluttered shut. *How did Calhoun's friends get so wealthy?*

A staccato of gunfire woke me. At first, I wondered, had someone shot me again? Searing pain brought me conscious. An ache passed through my left arm and chest as I pushed myself upright with the wounded arm.

Gunfire continued, and I grabbed my SIG.

I held my SIG at the ready, and with my left hand quietly opened my door. A painful fire coursed through my limb, and I dragged the door inward.

I ran along the hall, low. I was barefoot. I was silent. I was ready.

RICK CALHOUN

Calhoun walked out of Who Donut, set his coffee cup on top of his cruiser, opened the door, and slid into the seat. Distracted with thoughts of Catherine and the confounding cases surrounding her, he backed his vehicle out. A moment later, the cup descended in a cascade of his favorite coffee showering his front windshield.

"Aw, man." He stopped and snatched a now empty cup. Catherine had spoiled him, and now he didn't look forward to the over-boiled, burnt brew awaiting him. He hiked the steps to the courthouse and pulled open an entry to the bullpen to find utter silence.

Why a less than an enthusiastic "good morning" from Zoe and Mike? Nothing, not them, not splashed coffee, or even crashing his computer could blow this day. He turned on his archaic tower and unwrapped his treat. Today, his future changed. The box with the ring slept for now in his pocket.

He bit into his pastry. A crisp opening snap of a newspaper to his side caught Calhoun by surprise while he snacked on the bear claw.

"What?" With his mouth full, he lifted his head to see Dumont.

Greg plopped the paper on Calhoun's desk. "Whaddya know about this Leo Smart? Can you explain this?" He pointed to a picture.

Calhoun swallowed and licked icing off his thumb and fingers. He yanked his reading glasses from his suit jacket, moved closer to the paper, and evaluated a picture of Cade passed out in his arms. "Cade told me about a car following her. Turned out to be Leo Smart."

"Sleaze ball. But it doesn't explain how he got this picture. Have you any idea how this makes the PD appear?"

Mike said, "Sir, I'm sure he didn't get her—"

"Am I talking to you?" Dumont snapped. The Chief pointed Calhoun toward his office. "*Now.*"

Dumont jutted his chin out. "How'd she get liquored up and in your arms?"

"Jack McCloud gave her an alcoholic beverage. She passed out in the parking lot, but I caught her before she hit the asphalt. I was there for the fallout."

Dumont's eyes turned to slits. "Did he hurt her?"

"No. I made him apologize. She is incapable of holding a glass of wine in her hand without passing out."

"You have a special way with women, Calhoun."

"Don't I know it."

Dumont jabbed a finger at the paper. "This is bad PR, not what I want shone on the department."

"It doesn't look good. I know that, Greg. *If* she's called as a witness in the Harrington case, the photo may surface in court. But I know now how Leo just happened to snap that picture, and who hired him to do it."

"Read it." Dumont popped three TUMS and shoved Calhoun, paper in hand, out of his office.

He read an inflammatory article on page one. A caption accompanied the large picture reading, "Your tax dollars hard at work: Catherine Cade, owner of Who Donut, offers so much more to Whiskey River Police Department." The rest of the article was nauseating.

On page two, a full-page picture of Sarah Thompson splashed on it and a full-page article printed on the next page. She stood with one hand on her husband's gravestone and the other to her mouth. He didn't bother reading the article. He frowned. Sarah Thompson was a shameless, impudent trollop gallivanting around with her public relations specialist during the day and her Latin lover at night.

He rubbed his head. If someone couldn't put Catherine into the ground, they'd bury her reputation.

Zoe and Mike stood elbow to elbow blocking Calhoun's way. They scowled with arms crossed against their chests. Zoe gripped a file.

"Nope," Calhoun pushed through them.

Mike had a copy of the paper. "What *is* this? Doesn't look good at all. And you had an airtight case against Kevin Wood until now. How did this happen?"

"You believe this hack? He took this before someone shot her. It's resolved, and I'm not taking a fall for something that never happened. If you want to know what happened, ask Dumont." He was glad Cade left his WinMag at home and pushed past them. "I need to go."

Time to take a trip to Eastern Oregon Correctional and question tight-lipped Kevin Wood.

Kim appeared, dropping paperwork on Mike's desk. "Detective, you look mad."

"Ain't happy." Calhoun grabbed his keys and strode toward the door. "Zoe, I'm heading out, gonna talk to Kevin Wood."

"Got it."

He was at his car when he realized his phone was still in the bullpen. He strode back through the door to see Kim stabbing numbers into the phone.

"Detective Calhoun—your phone!" She wiggled the phone at him.

"Who were you trying to call?"

She laughed. "The funny thing is, I was going to text you."

Calhoun shook his head. "Goofy. Thanks for grabbing it, Kim."

Once on the road, he pointed his cruiser toward Eastern Oregon Correctional. It was likely either Wood or Jerry Street knew who wanted Catherine dead.

She'd go into orbit if she read this article and glanced at the news. Should he warn her now or comfort her later?

CHAPTER 50

A guard at Eastern Oregon Correctional Facility buzzed the gate open and placed Calhoun's phone, wallet, badge, and watch into a basket, then swept him with a metal detector.

The guard said, "You can claim these on your way out. Purpose of visit?"

Calhoun nodded. "I need to see one of your inmates. Kevin Wood. I called earlier."

The guard went silent for a long moment. "Let me, uh, I need to call my supervisor."

Calhoun's muscles tensed as guards scurried like ants talking rapid fire into radios. He had a bad feeling.

The guard's supervisor with a bulldog face motioned to Calhoun to meet him in the office. The supervisor shuffled through a stack of papers and finally said, "Kevin Wood is dead."

"When?"

"Two days ago. A fight broke out after chow, and someone shanked Wood. After that melee, two guards were found dead in the parking lot on their breaks. We had OSP here all day while we scrambled for a replacement." He turned his head side to side. "A shame, too. Both great guys."

Calhoun rubbed the hair prickling his neck. "Who were the guards?"

"Dead boy was Chuck Moser. Nice kid. Murray Simms was a month from retirement."

"Can I see their pictures?"

He pointed to pictures on a wall. One, an older man Calhoun didn't recognize, and the other, Sal Ventura, cleaned and shaved. The lifeguard who almost killed Cade in Wisconsin. "What about Jerry Street?"

"Let me find out." He phoned a guard and spoke a few moments. "Nothing in particular."

"Your warden available?"

Escorted by a guard, Calhoun met with the heavily mustachioed warden. The two shook hands and sat.

"Warden Jenks, I need Jerry Street in solitary confinement."

Jenks, tented his fingers. "Why?"

"His life is at risk, or he is part of a murder plot. I'll be back to talk to him later, but for now, keep him safe. And I need his personal effects photographed before they're whisked away by OSP. Please send them as an attachment." He scribbled down his email. "I sure would appreciate it."

Calhoun tried Catherine's phone from Jenks' desk. No answer. She wasn't out of danger yet. Isolation may have improved Street's safety and the likelihood of getting answers from him, but with Ventura murdered, Calhoun needed to warn Catherine. His worry meter climbed, and he picked up his items at the gate.

Kevin Wood and Sal Ventura dead, and no witnesses to either murder. Wood, Ventura, Stephen Thompson, and an attempt on Cade's life. Information whirled in his head, but nothing yet made sense. Evidence he might have obtained from Wood in a pointed interrogation at the prison vanished, and shaking down Ventura for information on an assassination attempt disappeared. Someone with deep pockets and a lot to lose played chess master. The mayor, Darren Hughe, Sarah Thompson. A game where pawns kept falling while someone grasped for power in Whiskey River.

"Of course. Why didn't I see it?" The jewel he once tried to tell Catherine about, a military secret, a small piece of manufacturing worth billions and Whiskey River's claim to fame, had been under wraps since Shock and Awe. But with a conservative, pro-military Thompson out of the way, a politician with sticky fingers could enliven the town, or line their pockets with gold, not caring about national security.

That was Cade's intended job.

Calhoun pushed the pedal to the floor, turned on the lights, and raced the empty roads. Through the tunnel to Whiskey River, he raised his phone, ready to call Cade and warn her, but he couldn't get a signal through.

Once through the dark concrete, he slowed and parked on the side of the road. He left the car and jogged west. "You jokin' me?" He raised the cellphone in the air, turning the phone left and right.

At last, a cell tower.

He thumbed the phone to ON.

Kaboom!

His car exploded behind him, rising above asphalt into the air. Calhoun, thrown and pitched backward, scrambled away from blinding hot metal hurtling toward him from across the road.

CATHERINE CADE

I should have listened to that nagging voice wondering how these two managed this wealth.

My gun trained back and forth between Amy and Sam. Every fight-or-flight emotion seized my heart in fear.

They stood before me, mouths agape, flabbergasted.

"Drop your guns, kick them toward me, and get on your bellies," I yelled.

"What?"

"Now."

Amy tried to speak.

"Shut up," I hollered. "You're Calhoun's informant, aren't you?"

"Catherine, what's going on with you?" she asked.

"Are you or are you not Calhoun's alphabet soup informant?"

She fumbled for words. "I was a CIA analyst with connections. We go way back, and sometimes he asks me for data unavailable through normal channels."

I blinked. In any other situation, her CIA remark would have been over-the-top and worthy of a giggle-a-thon. If her words were true, it meant Calhoun worked for them, too.

"Sam, what about you?"

"Retired FBI. No connections. Other than my wife."

"FBI?" I cried out, now with sights trained on his head.

"Retired!"

"I want proof."

He asked, "You think we carry old badges around the house?"

"No, but you're carrying semi-automatics, and I heard gunfire. Get up, slow." I yanked their weapons toward me. "Jerry Street tried to kidnap me, I've been attacked with a knife, and I've been shot. Calhoun said his source may have leaked information by accident or design, and here you are with guns. You might understand if I'm having trust issues right now."

Sam grunted. "If we wanted you dead, do you think we'd shoot holes in our house, so you could get the drop on us?"

I holstered my gun and slung their weapons over my good arm. "Be careful. One step too quick and I might not worry which one of you sees God first."

"There's a shooting range in the basement. I told you I'd wake you in forty-five minutes. Practice after your nap. Remember?"

I lifted the SIG out of my holster again and shifted the pistol in my hand. "Show me proof."

I stood in Sam's office as both Sam and Amy brought out dated ID badges. I ran my fingers over paperwork. Then touched Sam's old FBI badge and Amy's laminated ID from the Central Intelligence Agency. I could falsify something similar with time and resources, but if they wanted me dead, I would have been *muerta* without the ruse.

"Do you think Rick would have brought you here if he didn't trust us?"

"Walk. I need to think."

"Where to, now?"

"Kitchen." We sat at a dining room table. "Explain."

"I bet I left your intercom on in your room."

Great. My sanity was sliding. Somewhat assured of my safety, I slipped my pistol into its holster and ran a hand through my mussed-up bed hair. No one spoke.

Amy stood and brought a pot of coffee and came toward me. My hand went to my SIG as she poured a cup for us. I grabbed Sam's mug and drank a few sips from the cup of steaming black Joe. Too late, I realized she poured caffeinated java. Could be problematic.

"You are paranoid." He drank from my mug.

"I'm sorry." My voice, quiet and tremulous, sounded like a child's.

Amy said, "When you live a certain lifestyle, it's hard to let go. It's easier to do what you know to keep you and everyone you care for safe. It's called hypervigilance."

"Survival. Anyone could be—"

"A murderer," she said.

"Yes."

She led me by the elbow. "Follow me to the basement." Stairs greeted us, and we wound our way down. Amy continued talking while descending each step. "Sam and I met in battle. I wasn't always a political specialist, and he wasn't FBI. I became ill, and my superiors felt me important enough to send a Special Forces team to bring me out. The area crawled with terrorists, but Sam put his vest and helmet on me, carried me and took a bullet in the back for me. Still, he ran with yours truly in his arms. Brought me home."

"Oh, how romantic," I said in a soft, wistful tone.

She chuckled. "Well, it didn't feel romantic, but he hovered over me. He annoyed me to no end, but the president refused to sanction Sam to be summarily shot since he saved my life. So, I married him."

"You were ill? Dengue fever?"

She snapped her head my way. "How did you know?"

"First time I met Calhoun, we didn't get along so well. He bugged me. I suggested he go to the nearest emergency room to be evaluated for Dengue fever. He knew what it was, but it's rare in the US, and I was flummoxed at first. My money is on Karachi. Did you meet Calhoun when he was in the MEU?"

"You'd be a great analyst." She blinked.

Sometimes reading people sucked, because Amy was lying. As far as I could tell, the MEU had not quarried for Taliban hideouts in Pakistan. Not openly. I'd need quality time alone to toss their house for incriminating information. Calhoun, the sniper. And Amy ... I wondered what she really did? She was no bean counter analyst.

Sam came barreling through the door, breathless. "There's a problem. We need to go now. Cade, you stay here, and we'll be back as soon as possible."

"What's wrong?" I asked. "If it's Rick, I'm coming."

He waved an arm. "Fine, let's go."

I was right behind him.

CHAPTER 51

RICK CALHOUN

Calhoun never thought the whine of sirens could sound so sweet. Fire trucks, an ambulance, and Oregon State Police cars scattered about the scene, along with a large white response vehicle he recognized as an Alcohol, Tobacco, and Firearms Incident Command Center. Surreal against the backdrop of pine trees and the white of the river below, yellow crime-scene tape fluttered in the wind near the destruction.

The ringing in Calhoun's ears from the explosion made it difficult to make out what the agents and EMT said, but the routine was familiar. He provided his phone to the ATF and sat on the edge of an ambulance with the bay doors open. The EMT checked for burns, shock, and abrasions, and moved around to clean the wounds. Calhoun opened his mouth and stuck a finger in his ear to stop the ringing.

He lifted his head as a streak of lightning came his way. Cade.

CATHERINE CADE

The crime scene cordoning tape didn't deter me. Spurred on by caffeine and adrenaline, I ditched Sam and pushed the tape up. Then I ran, holding my arm.

Unable to stop me, Sam yelled, "Don't shoot her! Don't shoot!"

Calhoun's shouting cemented Sam's orders.

An officer put his hands in the air to slow me down, and I jammed my elbow into his gut, knocking the wind out of him.

I yelled, "Make a hole, move it, make a hole. Catherine Cade, NPI—move, move—"

A hole opened, and I barreled through, as Sam and Rick continued waving their hands. "Don't shoot her."

I pushed the EMT out of the way and began checking Calhoun's wounds. "Is he okay? What happened? Rick, are you hurt?"

He sat with his legs dangling over the edge and tugged my shirt. "We have to stop meeting like this."

Cradling his face with my hands, I kissed him, while he wiped tears from my face.

"Ma'am, you shouldn't be on the scene," a man's voice behind me said.

"I'm a first responder. I work for his doctor."

An ATF investigator stepped close and grasped my arm.

"Stand down." I jerked my arm away. "I'm Catherine Cade, NPI. What happened here? What's your name?"

The ATF investigator produced a badge. "Agent Ted Halloway. NPI? Do you have identification?"

"I was in the gym, so I rushed here without my ID." Hoped he wouldn't see through that little charade.

"Okay. Per Detective Calhoun, he had to exit the car to get a signal from a cell tower. When he activated the phone, his car exploded."

Rick whispered as the investigating agent stepped back. "Listen to you, all in charge. I like your first aid better than the EMT's."

"Okeydokey," the EMT said. "I wasn't trained in the hugging, crying, and kissing portions of being a first responder. Must be in the new classes."

I checked Rick's wounds again. "Superficial abrasions and road burn. He needs a full exam in the ER for internal injuries. I'll want to talk to the ER doc."

"Yes, ma'am."

I questioned the ATF investigator. "The question is, who rigged his phone and when?"

He said, "Well, we can't comment yet since we don't have all the facts, and the investigation is still in progress—"

"Rick, did you try calling me or anyone before the explosion?"

"Yup. From the Correctional Facility's phone. They put all cellphones in a box, keys and such, like the TSA."

Ted Halloway took a stab at a theory. "It sounds like someone had quite a plan."

"Whoever it was just conveniently happened to be in the parking lot after I entered the prison."

I said, "Someone tampered with Calhoun's phone after getting access to it and gave information to a guard here. This assumes he was close. He was on a fifteen-minute break, and he had to make time for a cigarette, likely not where he set up a bomb."

"How do you know he was a smoker?" Halloway asked.

"A guess. He'd have to be out here to plant a bomb. Wouldn't it be suspicious if he wasn't smoking? Who can find out what the state has from Woods's T-shirt? Ventura probably paid a prisoner. Two, Rick, where were you that phone wasn't?"

"It stays with me. It had to go through the prison's routine and stayed there until I left."

"Halloway, check on that. CCTV isn't everywhere."

Sam jogged to the ambulance. "Cade, who lit a firecracker under you?"

Calhoun touched my nose with his finger. "What's the NPI?"

"I couldn't think of anything else. It's the National Provider Identification number." I looked at my feet. "So, Detective, does this constitute our first date?"

"Nope."

Sam rubbed his forehead. "At least you didn't impersonate law enforcement, Cade."

Agent Halloway spoke into his radio, an angry glance thrown my way. "Miss, you aren't supposed to be here. I could charge you with obstructing a federal investigation."

"Agent Halloway, she works with the PD and is our best detective." Calhoun wrapped his arms around me and kissed me. "Try not to upset the Feds, Cade. They had every right to shoot you."

"Is she always like this?" Halloway asked.

"I'm right here." I pressed my forehead against Calhoun's.

Sam spoke. "She's stubborn and loyal, yeah, and you don't

want to get in her way. I know from personal experience."

Rick caressed my back, holding me close.

Sam leaned toward us. "Okay, you two. Catherine, you now have evidence on you."

I didn't move, and Calhoun hadn't let loose his hold.

"I'm not kidding."

Calhoun ignored Sam and ran his finger along my jaw. "You'd be a terrible hostage negotiator."

"I don't negotiate. I'm a little more lethal than simple negotiations." And I was serious.

"A warrior woman, and the one who makes my heart quicken."

I glanced at my feet, blushing, not sure why.

The ATF investigator grasped me by the elbow.

Sam stopped him and presented his badge. "Special Agent Sam Chandler, FBI. Catherine, what do you suggest next?"

"I'll ride in the ambulance with Calhoun. You're active FBI?"

"Yeah, well, I didn't want to get shot."

I hopped into the ambulance with Calhoun and said, "Sam, you and I will have a little heart-to-heart about honesty."

"Oh, goody."

The EMT closed the bay doors, and Calhoun and I were on our way to the hospital.

I asked, "What did you find out from Kevin Wood?"

"Kevin Wood is dead, too. It's back to work. But Camille Tate is off the list."

CHAPTER 52

Why did every federal agency smash their acronyms into three letters? I figured they couldn't count higher than three. With Calhoun's spectacular explosion, everyone with a badge would descend on the scene and police station.

Within a week, the ATF came first. It wouldn't have surprised me if next would be the FBI, the NSA, CIA, DHS, DOD, National Park Service, the IRS, and the Better Business Bureau showing up in town.

My life of larceny could alert an official to my presence, so keeping scarce at the Chandlers' was my best bet. Rick stayed away from me for similar reasons. How I missed him.

Sam put my phone in a box and sent it to New York City from the post office. "Let whoever's attempting to harm you track that." He handed me a new burner phone. "You can call Calhoun's new number, but no one else."

After two weeks of physical therapy, and to keep out of trouble, Amy and I practiced mild martial arts in their gym. I spilled my life story between breaths—of what I knew.

"I know."

"Everything?"

"They didn't call me an analyst for nothing. Calhoun did the heavy lifting, but I helped. He's a ditz around computers."

"That he is."

We circled the mat. Confident in my abilities, I didn't grasp how fast her foot could meet my face gear. Gravity and the mat greeted my back without warning.

Stunned, I guffawed. "I wouldn't want to meet you in a dark alley."

Gracious, she gave me time to stand and adjust to her moves. "Let's hope you won't."

I sidestepped her jab and adjusted to her height and abilities, neither of which improved my odds. The grin on her face said she was intent on beating the crap out of me, which she did rather well.

I fell on my backside in a remarkable display of grace and conceded defeat with a groan. "I'm done, I'm done. That was not an easy workout."

"Come on, Catherine," she bobbed. "Physical therapy."

"Hey, someone shot me."

"Shot? That was two weeks ago. You can't use that worn-out excuse anymore." She took off her gear. We slapped hands back, forth, and bumped knuckles.

Whatever happened when we slapped hands made me giggle. "Man, this reminds me of—" I didn't finish my sentence. Words got stuck and refused to pass because whatever it was had disappeared.

"What? Reminds you of what?"

"I almost remembered something, but it's gone." Absentminded, I tugged at the tie holding my hair, which tumbled from the tight weave of my bun. "Amy, thanks for kicking my behind and granting me another measure of humility. You'll excuse me while I go shower and weep bitter tears of defeat."

"No problem. Cookies later will help."

After my shower, I rifled through clues to the case.

Who had strong motives to kill Thompson in such a gruesome manner? My dry marker eeeeeked across the board, while I listed names, victims, and motives.

Money, sex, and power, things I knew and learned. With money came power and corruption that was so oft-quoted to be its partner. Sarah Thompson had money. She had power, a lover, and plenty of cash. Did she have a twisted hatred toward her husband? I gnawed my knuckle, flopped on the bed, raised my hands, and begged questions heavenward.

"C'mon. I'm a con, not a murderer. How am I supposed to do this?"

"Need help?"

I raised my head. "I'm trying to put puzzle pieces together, but there are mainframes I can't hack without tools."

Amy leaned against the doorjamb and stuffed her hands in her pockets. "I have tools."

"Invitation?"

"You bet. This should be fun."

I agreed. Get Amy's room schematics in my head and later toss the room. I gathered up my papers.

Amy's computer hummed. I sat on her bed trying to make sense of the explosion, shooting, and murders.

An ID on the first John Doe I autopsied would help. The Hispanic man McCloud was sure was homeless, but I'd thought was Rafael Santiago. Had that autopsy tainted my opinion?

I scratched the names of Sarah Thompson, the board members, Mayor Guy Mahn, and his assistant Darren Hughe across my board and stood back. John Murray's name I scribbled as an interesting prospect. His sole motivation to date a socialite was to find his way onto the board, and he managed to swing it his way. Using her well-known name, Murray managed to get the votes. Then he dumped her. Why press so hard to get onto the board? Evaluation of his pocketbook showed why. He was a poor guy getting anonymous donations or gifts in cash. Added the names Camille Tate and Marcus Stewart, editor. Then I scratched out several names. Voting affected change, so why murder the commissioner?

What about crimes of power, passion, revenge, and fear? And while we were at it, why not throw in the occasional psychopath?

So many reasons to murder.

Plausible motive. A large land purchase on decomposed granite? The circle widened; secrets revealed. Too neat. I bumped the capped end of the marker against my nose. "Rick removed Camille Tate from his suspect list because of the explosion, unless he could prove she was a bomb-making, cookie-baking mom. Revenge?"

"Why?"

"I don't know." A frustrated breath escaped my lips, and my arms dropped to my sides. "I'm too close. I tried to murder Jerry because he killed my past." I turned my head side to side. "It seemed promising."

"I don't want to destroy your confidence, but Rick does have years on you in the business. Sorry, kiddo."

"I know, and he's also a fantastic teacher." I didn't add *and a fantastic kisser*, but ... "Okay, so Thompson has money and power. Now, everything is Sarah's, and there's a mystery man wooing Widow Thompson. Money, love, or lust?"

"That's interesting."

"Yes, and I bet he's the missing Rafael Santiago. I'd heard he was an illegal immigrant working at Thompson's home, and I think he returned or maybe never left. Sarah Thompson's position takes her all over the state, yet Sarah Thompson's credit card shows trips straight to Camille Tate's town and back. Coincidence? If she were a house representative, I'd consider it, but not as a commissioner. Did she give him the car? Is he running around? I can't imagine why he'd go to Tate's. The only thing I can imagine is to wreck her."

"Or put her in prison for murder and money."

"That's a strong possibility, if Tate blackmailed Thompson to ruin her with the truth about her daughter's suffering—or, she's paying Tate off. I want Tate's financials."

"Got it, but slow down, let me plug this information in, so I can find the money trail."

"But if this isn't true ... plug this in—Sarah Thompson is a con but not a black widow. She planned to shake the political scene in Oregon with Leo Smart, the hack. Something is way off because grifters work the game with panache. They generally don't get involved, and they leave with booty. In, out, and onto the next mark. Something went wrong."

"Stop—you're going too fast." The tapping of computer keys sounded. "These are gas stations between here and Salem. CCTV comes in handy. I'm running facial recognition software now."

"Was she in love with her husband?" I wrote across the board—mob-style hit? "What mob would be interested in Whiskey River?"

"Gangs from El Salvador and north are moving into the county, while Russians are here, but most of the time, they work the coastline from small-time organized snatch-and-grabs to trafficking anything—or anyone."

I paced. "Disgusting. The still-living victims include Calhoun and me. Over twenty years, these are among the dead—an innocent Faith Harrington, a drug-busting cop-turned-congressman Noble, Stephen Thompson, and Kevin Wood, who was the original drug runner. Let's not forget Sal Ventura, my would-be assassin. And an unusual death regarding a woman on the board of commissioners. How very convenient of her to die in a car fatality weeks after Stephen Thompson died."

"Death is going around."

"Worse than the Spanish flu, because they spanned years, and they're ramping up in speed." My neck ached. I gulped water and rolled my neck side to side. "Add John Doe. I don't know if he is part of it or not. Perez told me to be careful because asking questions suggesting murder could bring about my disappearance. Words to that effect." A shudder passed through me. "As you said, death is going around. Whiskey River is a dangerous town. Who knew?"

Jerry Street. He found Whiskey River with ease. Granted, he didn't appreciate the training Calhoun gave me, but where did he fit? Who were his connections? How did I get planted in town and have no memory? What was his last planned job? I needed to understand these questions. "Did you find pictures on those gas stations?"

Amy clicked the key until the face turned into unrecognizable pixels. "No, too blurry, but I think I can get a partial plate. This could take time."

"You work the CCTV, and I'm gonna fiddle with more theories in my room. When I'm done, I'll knock." I yawned, closing her door. "Naptime, too." I ambled the length of the hall and shut the entry to my room. The tall mountains east of here were spectacular, topped with snow, and I pressed my nose against the glass.

A breeze warmed my face as I opened the window. Rosebuds and lavender mixed with the eye candy of feverfew's white and yellow flowers bobbled in a breeze. As an interloper in this fairyland-like castle and almost overwhelmed, I inhaled the sweet lavender and roses.

Sam was downstairs. Amy would be busy for at least four hours. I'd be back in three.

CHAPTER 53

Three stories down and odds stacked against me—no rope, gear, or car, and with one weak arm.

My tennis shoes dropped first out the window. Then, hiking myself into position, I put one leg over its ledge, twisting, turning, squeezing through the bars. Just a normal day.

To my right, there were more barred windows. With fair handholds on the rocks, it was time to go, because a short side trip was in order. Precarious as it was, over-thinking it could stop my plan. Three stories were far enough to cause damage where thorny roses wouldn't break my fall. As long as I only used my left arm for stability, I'd be good.

Go.

Four holds—rock, rock, reach. Grabbed a window bar on my right. Three holds, grab, stabilize, find another hold. Four solid holds, place right foot on next rock, test. Strong. Solid.

Descending was slow going.

Three holds, grab. Careful with that arm. *Whew.* I felt shaky and stopped to breathe.

Two of three holds crumbled, and I dropped faster than reasonable. I flung my weight to the right. Grasped for rocks, missed, and caught air. Grabbed onto the window's bar below while one foot found a rock, then the next. Pure luck, because my left wing wouldn't have supported me.

Everything counted on solidity, and measuring distance in a new survey showed me a *gemütlich*, one comfortable, idiot-proof descent.

Three automatic sprinklers came on, drenching me. Rock climbing required skills that didn't include an onslaught of water.

I pushed away as soon as water hit the rocks, clearing rose bushes, but I crushed lavender, feverfew, and rolled into the mud with a silent howl of pain.

Great.

That accomplished, I hopped into my shoes and dashed down the driveway.

I kept low, ran to Amy's SUV, and rummaged for the remote, opening the gate. If Amy studied the computer, she might stumble onto something. If she glanced my way, she'd view her SUV gliding through the gateway after I found the keys and slid it into neutral.

A uniform would come in handy, but the closest thing was a pantsuit with a blazer, so parking the car a block from my house, I slipped through the back and packed a day bag. A pair of cream pumps and I'd be the woman in charge.

Now, for a shiny badge, because my deputy lanyard wouldn't pass.

With everything tucked and folded into a backpack, I crept through the backyards. My questions begged real answers, but the image of Jerry's face made me sick.

With no one outside to watch me, I hustled to Amy's SUV and parked in Calhoun's driveway.

The locks to the back door were easy to pick. *Tsk*, Calhoun. Even a silent alarm would take the cops thirty minutes to respond.

Perfect. A mudroom where he cleaned up, hung caps, and one waiting for me to grab, Whiskey River Homicide Division. Where would he keep a badge? Whiskey River PD used the plastic IDs with lanyards, but I bet he stashed an old-fashioned badge somewhere. I smiled. Still quiet, I tore his place apart, rifled through drawers, gleeful in flinging out boxers, pants, shirts, and *voila!* An old-style badge.

The mirror caught my eye. I was full of mud and grass. No, this wouldn't do. I dropped my muddy clothes, jumped into the shower, and toweled dry. Dressed, with the ID clipped to the blazer, the outfit was complete. But would it stand scrutiny? My fingers worked to braid my hair.

Calhoun's bed. I sat. Soft, and running my hand over the bedspread, it invited me to rest. Should I call him? Pray? I chewed on a knuckle. No time. Besides, I'd be back in three hours, and my plan was solid.

I checked my outfit in front of the mirror and preened a moment. It was time to tuck the braid inside itself and adjust the cap. A red dot shone from the wall, blinking as I pivoted.

Spiffy. Caught on camera.

I hustled through the door and secured his house.

RICK CALHOUN

Calhoun's phone beeped, and he thumbed it, his eyes drifting over the screen. The home alarm.

Catherine.

He left the bullpen and examined the phone's video. If they weren't in deep kimchi before, they were now. He winced as a flash of metal shone while she examined the badge and stroked her thumb along its surface.

Rick whispered, "Please don't. You left the old life behind."

When she finished, she turned and stared right into the camera. Brazen woman. She was on the run and with a badge. He returned to the bullpen, observed as the two remaining FBI agents combed through records. He strode to the Chief's office, ready to face Dumont.

"Zoe, make sure the agents have what they need."

"Sure. Agents Grey and Watts, need coffee or assistance?"

"Sir, I need to talk to you." He closed Dumont's door.

"About?"

"Surprises. I know how you feel about them." Calhoun strode from one side of Dumont's office to the other. "I wasn't forthcoming about Catherine, and certain things about her are now coming to light."

Dumont's voice dropped to baritone. "Such as?"

"She's a con artist."

His tone a hiss, he asked, "What?"

"A con running from an informant. Jerry Street."

"The man from the park?"

"Yes. She's had long-term amnesia, apparently from a car wreck years back. Street found the advantage, forced her into his life, and used her to steal." Rick wanted to add Street had brutalized her, but Catherine's story wasn't his to tell.

Dumont stood with face reddened and forced a whisper. "You brought a criminal here, and you knew?"

"You wanted me to investigate. That's what I was doing in the evidence room. I caught her on video going through the locker, taking pictures of Stephen Thompson's case file, and I understand why she took those photos."

"Pray tell." Dumont folded his arms across his chest.

"She wouldn't sign the death certificate on Stephen Thompson and broke into the evidence locker. I made a visit to her house. She'd taken pictures, not to steal evidence, but to bring Thompson's murder to light. It was a big risk for her. Our only evidence comes from her B and E. I take full responsibility, sir. If you want my badge—"

He stood, his face redder than Calhoun imagined possible and whispered again, "You'll take responsibility? Yeah, you will. You stepped so far out of bounds, I can't tell if firing you could be enough. But who's in charge of you? Me." He jabbed a thumb to his chest. "The courts could toss everything regarding this case. You've created a nightmare and dropped it on me. Now she's a deputy, and you don't know what she's doing, do you?"

Calhoun swallowed. "No, sir."

Dumont stood. "Later, you and I will discuss this further and decide what action I should take. Where's she headed?"

"Sir, I can't be sure."

"Consider yourself on unpaid suspension. Gun and badge, now. I don't want FBI's Thing One and Thing Two to hear this. I need a game plan. Go home, Calhoun. You've done enough damage. Out."

Calhoun massaged a temple. He arrived home, and surveying the mess Cade left, mumbled to himself. He opened the safe room, unlocked a small closet past the armory. One she didn't know about. Rick grabbed another Springfield. His hand ran along a dozen badges and diverse licenses he'd laminated long ago, and he stuffed one of each in his wallet. With the others put away, he walked to the cruiser.

Calhoun tried her cellphone and got voicemail. "Cade. Answer your phone. You're on camera again. Call me when you get this."

His phone rang, and he grabbed it. "Cade? Where are you?"

"Hey, this is Amy. Catherine took my car, and I don't know why."

"Which car?"

"The Ford."

"Tap into the GPS for me. Can you ping her cell? It's off."

"Done and done. East. Toward the correctional facility." Amy's tone changed. "I'm worried. She's a loose cannon. I didn't see this coming."

"She's a con. She fooled me, too."

CHAPTER 54

CATHERINE CADE

My palms sweating, and second-guessing myself, I slowed. Rick and Amy could have helped. Why did I escape? Things had changed, hadn't they? Was I running? No. I planned to pry information from Jerry and return, but who might see my intentions as such? I wouldn't, and I was the ex-grifter.

Oh, no.

Calhoun believed in me, and abusing his trust was how I repaid him. He protected me from prison and tried to keep me safe even when I spun out of control. An apology wasn't enough.

I wanted to trust him but this was the ultimate betrayal to the man who'd given everything for me. The man I'd fallen in love with, but what a way to show him, with duplicity. Tears stung my eyes.

My plan fell apart, and I slowed the SUV to a stop.

Paranoid freakazoid.

I once stuttered, not able to promise Calhoun I'd stay, and I struggled with faith. My decisions and choices remained awful. I didn't ask Calhoun. If God was trying to make me a new person, I'd stonewalled him.

I'd abandoned those who cared for me to get answers from the man who didn't. An old Paul Newman movie summed it up: *What we have here is a failure to communicate.* I'd almost grasped love and a life worth something bigger than me.

If I drove through this tunnel across the county line, I'd have to end life in Whiskey River. How could Sam and Amy understand? *Calhoun.* How would he forgive me when my past brought me to deceive even myself?

I extricated myself from the vehicle. With forestlands beyond me and snowy massifs as the idyllic backdrop, I sat on the side of the isolated road in the dirt near a culvert. Oh, yeah, what a real thinker. Cooking in the penetrating sun, my brain betrayed me with delusions.

My neighbor Mrs. Calloway's high-pitched voice rang on the imaginary newsreel in my head. *Yes, Catherine Cade, always so quiet and helpful. And my, how she danced with the nice detective altogether like Audrey Hepburn and Cary Grant. Hard to believe she's a criminal.*

"Aargh," I yelled. The likelihood of anyone finding me was a million to one in the boondocks of Oregon.

My self-centeredness could destroy Calhoun. No more. He deserved someone worthy of his love, someone to rely on, trust in, and not a work in progress. How many times had I wanted to run from him but stayed? Now, I had to leave. Funny, trickery had been my tool of the trade. Get a mark's trust. The thought repulsed me because I used deception and destruction wherever I lived.

There were two options, both terrible. Run again or face prison.

"Why?" I sobbed.

Before I made you in your mother's womb, I had you in mind; before you were born, I set before you a task.

Those were not my words. I remembered reading them, but who said this? What did it mean?

Great, let's add insanity to the list.

The squelch of a police cruiser and flashing lights caused me to look. My weeping didn't stop because my mind went south and repartee with voices had commenced. Add evading an officer of the law, and why not throw in a psych hold, a fifty-one-fifty? Yessiree, officer, please haul me off to the nearest nut job ward.

I recognized the cruiser. Calhoun, the person I hurt the most. He stepped from the car and slammed the car door. He strode toward me, his eyes narrowed, his face hard.

"I trusted you." Calhoun stood over me, arms crossed.

My heart shattered as pain bled from his words.

"Why did you stop? Why not keep going?"

With mouth shut, I handed him his badge.

He spoke harsh words spiked with devastation. "You broke into my house, conned me, and humiliated me. You can't stop, can you? I fell in love with you, Catherine, a concept you don't get. People don't run off when they're in love. They count on each other. I've tried to help you retrieve your memories, and I've had your back through everything. I thought you loved me, too."

He grasped the back of my shirt, yanked me upright, and led me to the cruiser. He cuffed my hands behind my back. "Catherine Cade, you are being arrested on charges of breaking and entering, forgery, impersonating an officer of the law, identity theft, and in general, pissing me off. You have the right to remain silent."

The rest of his words I glossed over.

"Do you understand your rights as I've explained them to you?"

"Yes."

"Watch your head." Calhoun pressed me into the back of the cruiser, climbed into the driver's seat, and turned the vehicle back toward Whiskey River.

He thumbed his phone. "Found your car. Yup, found her, too. I'll bring you back later to get the Ford. I'm tossing her into jail. Bye."

"I wanted to talk to Jerry."

His eyes met mine in the rearview mirror, his anger palpable. I had victimized and betrayed him, and subjecting him to lame excuses was over.

"Sure. You know, get your stories straight, maybe break him out. After all, you're good at breaking and entering. Talk about how you missed your S and M sessions."

"No." My eyes closed.

"I wish I'd never found you."

My eyelids fluttered open in shock. "You know I fell for you. Why do you love me, a con? Why even bother?"

"You used me." His voice churned in a growl. He didn't look back, and I didn't blame him.

We passed several mileposts of forestland in silence before I spoke. "Can you answer a question for me? What does this mean?" I recited the verse and hoped Calhoun wouldn't call me an idiot.

"It's paraphrased from the book of Jeremiah, Chapter One, verse five." He stopped at the side of the road and twisted around, staring at my tear-stained eyes. "It means God created you for a reason."

"No," the word choked out, and I cried. "Why? Rick, why would he put me here to hurt people? Why would he put you in my path, only to have me betray you? How does my wrongness fit into God's plan?"

"I don't have those answers, Catherine, but I know he didn't make you wrong."

"Who does?" I shouted, throwing myself into the wire partition. "I'm a curse to everyone who has the misfortune of meeting me. Why couldn't you find someone who loves you like a normal person?"

"Stop it, you'll hurt yourself. How do I know you're not trying to con your way now?"

A moment passed. "You don't."

We sat in silence, minutes passing. I was angry with God for making me a deformed sociopath, and I hated him for it.

"Why did you stop?" he asked.

"Because … because God wants better for me, and this isn't it."

Calhoun turned off the engine. He stepped from the cruiser, opened the door to the prisoner transfer seat, and reached for me. "Am I going to regret letting you out of your cuffs?"

"Don't—" I crawled to the opposite door. "Turn me in, please."

Calhoun's eyes didn't waver from mine. He snatched his phone and pressed numbers. "Zoe, I am going to Eastern Oregon Correctional Facility to interview an inmate. Let Dumont know."

"Hold on, he wants to talk to you."

Rick put it on speakerphone. Dumont's voice was quiet and forced. "Where in the blue blazes are you? I said suspended."

"Understood, sir. I'm near the penitentiary, and I want to question Jerry Street before you fire me."

"No, your suspension is over, and you're out. I am not telling the FBI yet. Do I have to call the prison or are you coming back?"

"No, sir, I will be back."

"Good." Dumont ended the call.

"Why?" I cried again. "You didn't break the law—"

"Yes, yes, I did. I brought you into the station under false pretenses, didn't tell the truth, fudged your prints, kept your name from the Feds, and got the office involved keeping you safe. List goes on a bit."

I'd ruined his life. "What now?"

He grabbed the front of my shirt and dragged me from the cruiser. "I've got cash. When you find a hotel, I'll wire more. Your money and the Vermeer oil painting, too." The hard lines of his face softened. "If you want me, I'll come with you. We can get the cash and Vermeer from my house."

I felt my face twist in confusion. "No. Listen to yourself."

"You still don't get it, do you?" He slipped the skeleton key into the lock of the cuff and spun me to face him.

"What does that mean? I will turn myself in, but please don't do something you'll regret."

He slammed the car door closed. His mouth in a tight line. "Oh, would you just … shut … up." He pushed me against the cruiser, grasped my hair, and pressed his lips to mine in a fierce and hungry kiss.

Oh, wow. If we kept this up, I'd go to prison with a smile on my face.

He stopped and held my face in his hands. "If you want me, even a little, nothing will separate us. Not ever again."

I broke out in waterworks again. "Forever?"

"Forever." Entangled, he kissed my nose, my eyes, my lips, and teased my tongue. The cellphone rang, and he stopped long enough to locate it and answered as he worked magic along my neck. He put it on speakerphone.

"Mm-hmm?"

"Calhoun, it's Amy. I'm in Catherine's room. There's damage to the flowers and prints in mud everywhere. She climbed down three stories to the garden. I wonder why she didn't use the front door?"

"Mm-kay."

"Calhoun, are you okay?"

"Mm-hmm."

"Cade's work is paying off."

He stopped. "What do you mean?"

"She's got solid clues and theories on Thompson's murder. Quite a twisted little plot, and despite everything, she deserves kudos on her work. It's not done, but she's got it nailed."

"Amy, I'm on the road, can you piece it together when we get back?"

"Sure."

Calhoun thumbed off the phone. "Now I understand why you want to squeeze Jerry for information. You're too close. Go back to Sam and Amy's." We drove the short miles back to Amy's truck, our fingers interlaced. Rick said, "Promise me you'll be there. I have something for you."

"Promise." I climbed into Amy's SUV and turned the key.

Holding a hand up, he came to the driver's side window. "Drive safe, Miss Catherine. Keep your phone on." He winked. "I intend to call on you later."

"You tracking me?"

"Oh, yeah." He yanked the SUV's door open and kissed me. "Someday, I hope Whiskey River will be our home. Together."

I bit my lip. "Let me inform you, Detective, Whiskey River is home. Our home."

His forefinger traced my jaw. "I know."

CHAPTER 55

RICK CALHOUN

Seated in the not-so palatial Eastern Oregon Correctional Facility's interrogation room, Calhoun waited as the prisoner across the table sat like a bum. Jerry Street. Calhoun had shrugged his jacket off, hung it over the chair, and waggled his phone in front of Jerry to let him know the session was going to be recorded.

"Anytime, Jerry, anytime." He leaned back. "How did you meet Catherine Cade?"

Jerry sat, cuffed in an orange jumpsuit, his face still bearing scars from Cade's blows. "We met at a bar. Love at first sight." He rolled an unlit cigarette between his fingers. "Your girlfriend's juicy, ain't she?"

Calhoun surveyed the red plastic table and imagined how he'd take this guy apart. "She gave you a whole new look. Suits you. Here's the deal. Someone's sweeping away the trash."

Jerry mumbled a feeble comeback of disdain. "And she's it, waste of human flesh."

Calhoun leaned forward. "No, Jerry, you're the trash. Count the bodies. Solitary confinement was for your protection."

"Don't see the relevance, Detective."

"Huh." Calhoun popped a piece of gum in his mouth. "You didn't kill Kevin Wood."

Jerry paused. "He was my cellmate."

Calhoun scoffed.

He thrust his jaw in the air. "I didn't kill Stephen Thompson, either."

"I know."

Jerry dragged jagged nails over his hand. "I wanna make a deal."

Calhoun rolled his sleeves past his elbows and cracked his knuckles. "A deal? Let's try again. Someone sent you to do a job with Catherine. Problem was, you'd beaten the memory out of her. Intimidation and physical violence didn't work, now that she can fend off killers like you. Someone hired Sal Ventura, who failed to kill her, twice. Now he's dead."

"She's a vicious animal. The best-case scenario is she'll betray you and leave you alive." Jerry wiped sweat from his brow. "What do you mean, twice?"

"Someone shot her after she took care of business with you in Whiskey River."

"Somebody else's loose end." He cleared his throat. "Got nothing to do with me."

Calhoun walked around the table, made a finger gun, and pointed it at Jerry, with a wink. "For a presumed ringleader, you're not very bright. Don't you call it the get? The big one, the job to end all jobs. And you want protection. I can't help you if you don't talk. You'll be dead in days." Calhoun sat and crossed his arms. "She remembers everything, even the job."

"The useless woman spilled it." He shook his head. "Yeah, the heist was the big payoff. I'd never have to work again."

"But your ex-girlfriend put you into your current state. Shame. Who's the buyer? Who gets the money now?"

Jerry picked at his fingers. "No one told me the buyer's name. Whoever can get into the building gets the money. I placed Sonia here to work there, Catherine, whatever you call her."

"How did you find her to start?"

"In a car wreck."

Calhoun paused the recording. "Care to see your ex-partner for a new match?"

"You know that won't happen."

"I can sign you out, where you meet the woman you tortured, and we'll see how it goes." He closed and opened his eyes lazily. "She's a weapon. I didn't fashion her, just adjusted the sights. I saved your butt. Show some gratitude."

Calhoun resumed the recording.

Jerry's leg twitched while Calhoun waited for an answer. "I had orders to follow her, find out what she'd seen, and then kill her."

"Why?"

His eyes settled on the wall past Calhoun. "She nosed around, taking pictures. If they found I didn't kill her ... I had to get her trained, or ..."

"Who gave you the kill order?"

Jerry rubbed a greasy hand on his cheek. "We never met. It was always by phone."

"Tell me how it happened." Calhoun put his feet on the table. "Hang on, the longer we wait, your bosses will come to the logical conclusion you talked. Without protection, you're a dead man."

Jerry crossed his arms. "She was crossing the street. I rammed through the intersection. It was a solid kill. Someone must have called 911. When the news came on, I panicked, planned to finish the job." He bumped a cigarette, nervous. "I need a light."

"What stopped you?"

Jerry didn't move. "ICU was too small to slip in and finish her. When she came out of her coma, she thought I was her doctor. I improvised and returned every day." Jerry smirked. "Told her she was my fiancée, and she bought it. They released her, and the best part, she agreed to marry me. I got a fake preacher and a fake wife. I needed amusement." He raised his eyes and stopped speaking for a moment. "Kept her pretty well locked up, so no one would know she was alive."

Calhoun pushed a finger on the phone to stop the recording. He pulled another piece of gum from a wrap, folded it, and put it in his mouth. He curled a fist. "You didn't save her out of compassion. It was fear of your boss. Not because you loved her, but because you needed to cut someone. So, you trained her to steal."

"If she hadn't come with me, she'd be dead. I did her a favor, so yeah, trained her, disciplined her like an animal. But she was a spirited little sh—"

Calhoun leaped from his chair and slammed Jerry against the concrete wall, a hand gripping his neck. "Well, don't that make you a hero," he hissed into Jerry's ear. "Who runs you?" He tossed Jerry back into his chair, sat, and began the recording.

Jerry rubbed his throat and coughed. "Someone in DC. Ties to groups, terrorists, people with big money."

"Names."

He clomped his feet onto the interrogation table until Calhoun shoved his boots. "Wayne's Gems. So, what do I get for cooperating?"

Bingo. And that was the end of the recording. Only verbal information would be given to Olivia, his "real" boss.

"I said, names."

Jerry scratched his armpit. "Ibrahim Youssef, an Arab national who's been here for twenty years, making a name for himself. Enforcer, assassin, whatever. He's looking for big money."

Calhoun stopped chewing his gum. "He kill Faith Harrington twenty years ago?"

"Rumor. A semi-botched job to get Kevin Wood's heroin into the cop's hands, Joshua Noble. Enough money to get him into office."

"Where is this Youssef now?"

"Heard he stuck around Whiskey River, taking odd jobs, learned Spanish."

That kindled Calhoun's interest. "How long did he work for Thompson?"

"I don't know, long enough to get Thompson's routine memorized." He spat on the floor, wiping spittle from his chin with his shirtsleeve.

Calhoun mused through Jerry's silence. Someone wanted a way into Wayne's Gems. That meant someone greased palms to give Cade access.

Jerry continued. "Had she stuck to the plan, she would have downloaded the schematics."

Calhoun waited. And with Thompson out of the way, Youssef became Santiago. He seduced the widow to do what they needed to obtain blueprints. *Must have been worth an easy twenty billion on the black market.*

Jerry smirked. "With him and Youssef's woman still on the loose, your girlfriend is dead."

"Woman? Who's his woman?"

"Rashida."

"Description."

"Never saw her. Now when do you get me protection?" Jerry spit on the concrete floor again.

"For helping me fulfill a promise I made a long time ago, I brought you something. Here." Rick pressed a pocket-sized New Testament into Jerry's hand. "There is something important that you'll want to read. Check the bookmark. Important information."

Jerry sneered but pulled the bookmark. He turned it over. "What's this, heaven on one side, hell on the other?"

"Keep an eye on the passage. For your protection. The guards share all info with the feds."

Jerry tossed it and the bookmark onto the table, then a violaceous blotch began to spread from his fingers up his hand. "What is this?"

Calhoun leaned. "That's a nasty rash. I'd call the padre."

"You mean, doctor." He turned his hand, squinting at the growing spot. "Hives. Never had 'em."

"Call the padre now. Looks like a nasty bug bite. Look, you touched your face, and another spot there. Hmm." Calhoun squinted. "And kinda taking the flesh ... pretty soon, you won't have a face."

Jerry's voice trembled as realization dawned, "Oh, man."

"Wow, that's fast-moving. Your rash is worse." He pointed to the deepening blotch.

Jerry grabbed his wrist, raising it for his closer inspection. "But why?"

"Once I promised Cade I'd rip your face off. This is the closest thing possible. You can't undo what you've inflicted on her."

"Where's the padre? Can you get him?"

"Sure." He lifted the garbage can and pointed. "Toss the paper in here." Jerry complied, as his arm quickly turned purple. He couldn't save his life, but if Jerry was truly remorseful, he'd meet God under better circumstances. He put a hand on Jerry's shoulder. "Well, then."

Calhoun summoned the minister and left. He thumbed the phone.

"C'mon, pick up, Cade."

CHAPTER 56

CATHERINE CADE

Both Sam and Amy were waiting for me. Amy crossed her arms, and Sam had thrust his hands into his pockets.

Oh, boy.

Amy scowled. "Catherine."

Sam stood by his wife's side. "You're not alone in this."

"I wasn't thinking."

Her hand grasped mine. "No, you weren't, young lady. We have leads to follow, a case to solve, and cookies to finish."

She hauled me through the kitchen and handed me a glass of lemonade. We moved around furniture and stopped long enough to whisk a plate of cookies from the counter.

I'd been in her room, but not her office. This was a whole other ballgame. There were no decorations. Two large plasma screens attached to opposite walls were on, while a vast library and cabinets surrounded the large room. A stack of folders lay on her desk. She moved the files to a drawer and locked it with a click.

A personal war room like NORAD. *Trés* cool. Too bad I was on the wrong side of the law.

"Is Sam following up on our bonanza of data?"

"Yes." She pressed a button to turn on a different flat screen monitor. "Hey, Sam."

Sam swiveled in his chair, from wherever he disappeared to, while screens behind him ran algorithms and pictures out of focus.

"Hello, ladies."

"What did you find on Sarah Thompson?"

"Here's the lowdown. Catherine, you're right. Thompson is not just any grifter, she's an international player who wiggled her toes in the wrong sandbox and conned Russian diplomats. The heavily armed and angry type."

My face must have puckered. Every other anatomical part on me shriveled because conning a Russian politician was a career-ender. In the most severe way. "What?"

"Rumor has it she found her way to a Faberge egg."

Part of a cookie fell from my mouth.

Sam said, "You're green with envy, Catherine. Seems she fell for Thompson, because, like you said, since when do grifters stay around? Or the Russians didn't let go, and her penance meant building a charm school in our little village. They used her to turn the tide of politics, my guess. When Stephen died, she isolated herself, or tried to, until the last woman on the board of commissioners had her fatal accident. Sarah Thompson became commissioner, and if things weren't going her way, or whoever ran her, there was a hefty price to pay."

"I sense a 'but.' Am I right?"

"You are." Sam turned in his chair. "She had a gardener working for her, Rafael Santiago. Her name is on the plates." A few taps later, CCTV images flickered onto the screen from a gas station. "Receipts for gas from Thompson's place to Camille Tate's. Check this."

The CCTV's remote control brought another car into view. "ID?" I asked.

"That's the answer to a question not yet asked," Amy said.

"That's right, Amy. It's grainy, though. Look at the date, Catherine." Sam pointed.

I sat forward. "Well, holy fish sticks. We need rifling reports."

"We confiscated both guns." Amy tucked stray hairs behind her ear.

I felt my eyes widen. "Do I want to know how? You're still active."

"Active? Oh, no, dear, I'm just low-level clearance, retired really." Amy pushed the plate my direction. "Cookie?"

Nice distraction, but I knew the truth. Not one to miss another homemade cookie, I accepted. "What did the report tell you?"

"We have her. Thompson's gun matched the bullet."

I was quiet. It was perfect. Clean. Too clean. "The commissioner's insulin levels were high enough to do the job. So, why the horse's head message? Simple, easy. Unless it was a message to his widow."

"Then why the excess insulin?" Sam asked.

I chewed on a nail. "I got nothing. Gotta call Calhoun." I thumbed speed dial, waited, and swallowed. "It went straight to voicemail."

RICK CALHOUN

Rick, frustrated, stopped trying to phone Cade, Sam, or Amy, and parked his Dodge. He dashed through the doors to the PD.

Zoe twisted around and whispered. "Calhoun, I heard."

"Yup. I need to talk to the boss." He moved past the desks, knocked on the Chief's door, and opened it. "Chief—"

Dumont jabbed a finger his way. "I wanna know how she wound her way into your life."

"Greg—"

"Don't you Greg me," he said. "You call me Chief, or sir, or Dumont. She ruined my best detective."

"Excuse me?"

"Until that woman conned her way into your life, things were fine. I was happy to have you as a selective mute. I thought I fired you. What do you want?"

"Cade's in trouble, and I can't get hold of her—"

"Well, sweet mamma's apple pie, there you go. You're a Marine, and look at you, you're all," he wiggled his fingers in the air, "touchy-feely."

"Again, Cade's in trouble. And I need to clarify her status. She's on the run, and her identity theft was for self-preservation." He held up a hand. "I know, that doesn't make it right, but I found out from my sources that she had good reason to fear the police and the FBI. Greg, whoever is behind the corruption thinks she's the last one left with information on the Thompson murder."

"Your sources. I know about your sources." He cleared his throat. "What do you need?"

"Shooters, spotters—meaning you, Zoe, and Mike. Those two agents." Calhoun turned.

"You want Special Agents Thing One and Thing Two on this?"

"Grey and Watts, yeah. We don't have enough manpower. I'll make a call to the sheriff's department en route. There's no answer at the Chandlers'. Greg, this has to do with Wayne's Gems."

"What does a crafter's fake gem business have to do with Cade?"

"This is national security. It's not jewelry. It's the Guardian Missile System. Wayne's Gems is a shell business for the research and development for the missile system. Jerry Street planned to use Cade to download the schematics. His bosses in DC likely killed Stephen Thompson and blackmailed his wife with the Russians. With Sarah Thompson forced to work with the mayor, his assistant kept quiet while she sold unstable property. The money in the development was a distraction or a business transaction. Who knows, Sarah Thompson may not have even been aware the tests from the property were doctored. But Jerry Street's bosses would sell the missile guidance blueprints to the highest bidder. Youssef Ibrahim is an assassin, and I think he's here for Cade."

"What's her take on it?"

"She doesn't know. I need McCloud, too."

"You plan to shoot him?"

"Tempting. I hear he's become quite the shot. I'll grab the gear, meet you at the car."

Zoe buzzed Dumont's office phone. "What do you want? We're on our way out—what?" He handed the phone to Calhoun. "For you." Dumont strode out of the room.

"This is Detective Calhoun. Yeah, I sent the prints." He closed Dumont's office door. "Olivia? I've been trying to reach you for months." He gripped the phone. "Find someone else for a few days, a week, maybe. Olivia, brace yourself. I found her. She's not safe. Can you FAX me the info on our secure line now? This is what I need."

He grabbed the paper as it spit from the FAX machine, tucked it into his pocket, and left the office.

"Who was on the phone?" Dumont asked.

"Got Cade's information. And this." He handed him a box. "You wouldn't believe me if I told you. National security, meaning you're under my orders as my backup, Sergeant Dumont."

"Your orders? Well, this changes things." He turned the box in his hand. "What have we here?"

Calhoun bumped Dumont's arm. "My surprise. Keep this safe for me."

Dumont oohed. "Well, all righty then. Let's go rescue our damsel in distress."

CHAPTER 57

Catherine Cade

Sam walked into Amy's office and palmed a cookie as he coughed into his free hand. "My office is downstairs. Felt left out."

"I see." My mouth closed in mirth.

Static overtook the computers, and the screens went black.

"Sam, what did you do now? You're as bad as Calhoun." Amy swiveled in her chair.

"Honey, I didn't touch anything."

Dusk had passed. The indoor lights flickered and went out.

"What happened, other than the obvious?" I whispered, and we dropped low. Drawers opened and shut. Amy shoved a flashlight into my hand.

Sam whispered, "The doors locked?"

"Always."

"Break-in?" My flashlight flicked on, pointed to the ground.

Amy peeked out the window. "Someone smashed the lights around the house, but the neighborhood is fine."

I grasped Sam's arm. "You're compromised. Do you have night vision?"

Amy yanked open a drawer and thrust NV goggles into my hand.

"We have two vests." He snatched both and pushed them our way. "Here."

"Got a backup generator?"

"In the basement, past the gym," Sam whispered.

"Sam, Amy, let me run to the generator room, and once it's running, you two take out the threat, yes?"

Sam and Amy exchanged glances. "Who are you?" Sam snorted.

"No questions, not now."

"Wait a second," Amy huffed. "We may be semi-retired, but we know the house well, thank you, and we have a panic room for you. Someone's tried to kill you at least twice, so you are not on point."

I motioned to the door. "Let's check the landing, first. Logistics. Explain the house's layout."

"Five doors to the outside." Sam pointed in each direction. "House is in a spoke-wheel fashion. The east side garden's door is vulnerable if someone figures how to get to it, and leads to the generator, but it's well concealed and protected." He stopped. "And on electric."

Amy said, "I told you we should have gotten rid of the behemoth generator. We should have switched to a wireless system."

"I wasn't—"

"Not the time to argue, guys." I jiggled my phone. "My phone isn't working."

"Mine either. Sam?"

"Nothing." Sam checked the nearby landline. "Out, too.

"Jammed." We each shook the batteries from our phones to disable any tracking. Someone knew where we were, maybe even knew the house's layout. "Sam, you cover me while I run to the generator room. Have Amy cover you."

"You're our responsibility not the other way around. No giving orders." Amy pushed the vests into Sam's hands and headed for the stairs.

I cursed at her in a whisper and turned. "Sam, let's go."

I clacked a magazine into the M-16 and strapped the weapon over my back, bringing the rifle to my chest with a wince. I grabbed a Springfield and my SIG and prayed for protection.

RICK CALHOUN

Across the street from the house, Calhoun and company knelt in the ditch as he trained his binoculars on the Chandlers' home. Jack, Zoe, and Kim, packed into one car, parked a block away, and spread out. The FBI agents who'd investigated his car explosion were also there and in position. Then they joined Calhoun and Dumont. "I'm on point," Calhoun whispered to Dumont.

Dumont grasped his NVG and nodded.

Calhoun silently directed Mike and Zoe to the left of the house, Dumont to the right. "I'll take the back entrance."

Calhoun hustled low to the backyard. The hidden entrance's ivy and camouflage was ripped open and revealed where a thermal breaching tool had burned an opening through the door, large enough for an adult to squeeze inside. Calhoun's flashlight shone across the damage.

"Oh, no."

A body on the floor inside lay in a pool of blood.

CATHERINE CADE

Pop!

I heard what sounded like a gunshot, off somewhere near the gym. Amy, the furthest away, may have taken a shot. I prayed for her while I advanced to clear the foyer and the kitchen with the Springfield. The SIG, tucked into my pants holster, bit into my hip. The night vision goggles itched like crazy. I braced myself, set my jaw, and pushed ahead.

More gunfire. Sam had gone to cover Amy with his M-16. My steps faltered as I started into the foyer and spotted a figure crumpled on the foyer's floor. "Sam, Sam—" I whispered.

I bent to check his pulse. Strong. Grazed at the temple, he bled, but not in abundance. For now he'd have to survive on his own. I passed another bay window on my way through the foyer and watched seven figures fanning out in various paths to the house.

Five magazines, seventeen rounds each. Plenty.

I cleared my approach to the generator room. Two figures, one down. *Amy?* It had to be. I moved silently until I recognized the figure who cradled her. I lowered my gun just as he whirled and trained his pistol on me.

"Calhoun, it's me."

He lowered his weapon. "Praise God, you're okay. Can you get the generator going? We have two FBI agents with us. Stay sharp and stay with Amy."

"Okay. Who else is with you? I saw people coming from every direction."

"We brought everyone we could find, including the FBI agents, Grey and Watts. They've been trying to find who blew my car to smithereens."

Great. The FBI.

"The Oregon State Police should turn up soon."

"Rick, I—"

"I know. Me too. Be careful."

"See you on the other side."

I ran to the room where the generator hulked against the wall. Sweat dripped from my hairline. My hands shook. Sick to my stomach, I prayed under my breath for Amy. I fumbled and jerked at the stubborn ON switch, fighting to pull it down. The generator made a hard, ominous *whomp*, and the lights flickered on. I jerked off the night vision goggles before the flare of light blinded me.

Then I returned to the front of the gym to Amy. She lay quiet and still, too still. I was helpless, but I prayed God would bring her back to Sam safe.

The door swung open as I pressed against it, and I juked to the left of the foyer. I hoped that what I'd just heard was Calhoun clearing another hallway.

Movement. I raised the Springfield. Several figures wound around the corner, military fashion. One of them was Zoe, moving along the hall without a shiver of fear in her movements.

Back to the foyer. Clear. Sam's office came next. I stepped into the room. A figure loomed. We raised our weapons.

"Mike!"

He lowered his gun. "Clear."

"Have you seen Calhoun?"

"No."

I vee'd two fingers toward my eyes and pointed toward the stairs, then jabbed a finger toward him. He tipped his chin and disappeared.

I began to fret. No communication. Amy and Sam down. Killer—or killers—in the house, location unknown.

The foyer and halls were covered, so I headed downstairs to the gym. A large group of trained officers may have run our quarry to ground. Perhaps the assassin had fled.

Before I reached the stairs, Calhoun's voice boomed.

"Cade! Behind you!"

I pivoted. *Perez.* The man I'd interviewed at Thompson's.

I raised the pistol and pumped two rounds into his chest as he pumped two into mine. I dropped and lost my grip on my gun. Unfazed by my shots, he swiftly holstered his gun and drew a large blade from the strap across his back.

I rolled to my left at the same instant he plunged with the blade. It struck the marble and deflected out of his hand. With a curse he grabbed it and wrapped his fist in my hair, wrenching my head back and baring my throat.

A gunshot rent the air nearby, knocking Perez off-balance and tossing the blade out of his reach. He screeched in anger and pulled his gun. Another gunshot cracked, savage and sharp.

Calhoun.

Perez straddled me, and baring his teeth in a killing frenzy, he pressed the barrel of his gun flush to my forehead.

The sting, heat, and pain under my vest kept me from lying still. I looked for evidence of a soul in his eyes. None. I swallowed, knowing I was about to die, and that he'd be coming with me.

"Okay, okay, Perez. Tell me why."

He sneered. "Santiago. Perez is dead, and I'm not here to take you alive."

His momentary gloating over my death gave me a split second to pull the SIG and fire point-blank into his face and throat. The shot jerked his head backward, but then he slumped forward, his dead weight pinning me to the floor.

"Youssef!" A woman's cry, a high, wailing voice, called out his name. As soon as I heard it, I knew who she was.

The others reached the foyer.

"Kim," Jack McCloud yelled. "What are you doing ?" She jeered at him and shot him in the knee. He collapsed with an agonizing scream.

Panic rose in my chest. Santiago had fallen on top of me, pinning me down. Dead, he'd rendered me immobile, defenseless.

Kim strode toward me, and I could do nothing with my arms restrained by Santiago's body. Her voice was colder than an open grave.

"You killed Ibrahim. You should have never poked your nose in the cold cases, especially not this one."

Another shot whined past me, and Kim fell and gasped for air as I turned my head. Calhoun held his pistol in his left hand, his right arm hanging limp at his side. He pulled the trigger again, hitting her a second time as she raised her arm and shot him in the chest. He fell backwards, his left hand against his heart.

The FBI agents rushed in, holding their weapons over her.

Zoe pulled the dead man off me. I slid on my knees to Calhoun, yanked my vest off, and held him. He leaned hard against me as I put pressure to his chest.

"It'll be okay." I prayed.

He raised a hand to my face. "You're alive."

"And you'll be fine, I swear."

Zoe orchestrated the ambulances, directed them to Amy and Sam first. Sam held his wife's hand. "Come on, baby, you can do this. You're strong. Come on."

They left in the same ambulance.

I bit my lip hard to keep from crying. Amy wasn't going to make it. Her motionless hand showed no color. The doors closed, the sirens screamed, and the ambulance rushed toward the hospital.

Two more ambulances arrived for Calhoun, Kim, and McCloud. I gave the EMT information he asked for and listened as he flipped the ambulance's internal switch to RECORD. I patted Kim down for weapons before they loaded the two into the ambulance.

"Kim," I choked my words out. "We were friends."

"You didn't follow orders. You should be dead."

"What?"

"I was to pay your failure in death."

McCloud's voice lost his usual growl. "Kim, what are you saying?"

Despite her wounds, she snorted. "The missile system, you fool."

"Terrorist group?"

"Does it matter?"

"Why Cade?"

Kim closed her eyes. "I failed."

"What part did you play?"

"She'd be dead if you'd left the hospital that day. Youssef," she halted, "he trained me. I almost had her."

It all fell into place. The dead man in the woods, my first John Doe autopsy, was Perez, and Youssef had killed him. Youssef then became both men—Santiago to Thompson, and Perez to me. A chill stabbed at me. The white car that had followed me for several nights had been Kim's.

Kim was the common thread in all of this. She was the shooter who'd caught me outside the bakery that day. If McCloud hadn't stayed in the hospital room when they visited, she would have finished what she'd started.

She could have contaminated the evidence from Stephen Thompson's case. Kim may have been the evidence locker thief. And she'd shared McCloud's bed. She could have slit his throat any night they were together.

CHAPTER 58

I paced in the hospital lobby. Trauma teams rushed through the triage doors.

McCloud swore for pain medication or gin—whichever was handy. "And if it's gin, plug it into an IV port. Straight to my liver. It already knows how to handle alcohol." He griped at the nurses prepping him for surgery as they ran.

After riding in the ambulance with Calhoun and watching the EMTs work, thankful he was alive, experience told me this would be a long, worrisome wait. Kim's shot had been lucky, somehow bypassing his vest.

On the way to the hospital, he wouldn't shut up. We swapped stories, and he elaborated who did what, where, and when, including Youssef/Santiago/Perez. We held hands while an EMT started an IV and put pressure on his chest wound. Calhoun, morphined up, kissed my fingers with a goofy grin. "What's all the fuss? Just another day in boring Whiskey River. There's so much I want to say. First, kiss me, you silly wench."

Happy to oblige. Our lips met several times.

At the hospital, Amy and Sam disappeared into surgical suites. Pressure inside Sam's skull from bleeding on his brain made him a surgical emergency. Kim, stabilized, languished in a guarded hospital room. Before nurses whisked Calhoun away to prep him for surgery, I kissed him one last time.

His voice had weakened. "Love you."

Before words squeaked from me, nurses turned the gurney into the open pre-op doors. I raised my hand and resisted throwing him a cheesy air kiss. Then I prayed because he looked so vulnerable.

I turned and wandered to a chair while fuming about Kim.

Kim had deceived me into a fabricated friendship. She used everyone around in her little terrorist world. I rolled my thumbs over each other, supposing all my cons hadn't been too far from what Kim did. Well, minus the whole become-a-terrorist-because-he-said-to death cult concept.

A familiar face appeared. Tristan Phillips, the rookie who, according to Rick, had thrown up in the bushes at Stephen Thompson's crime scene, was barely recognizable with his golden whiskers all grown out. He'd left for Chicago after I started as a volunteer. Still a cherub in uniform, he managed a furrowed brow and huge grin when he saw me.

"Tristan." We hugged. I said, "Can't stop, gotta get a report from the G-men, but promise me you'll stick around to give me the Chicago scoop."

"You bet."

Armed with the rifling report, a partial thumbprint from a bullet, and information from Sam, I contacted the sheriff's department. I called a taxi, and once home, grabbed a bag, took the GMC. The crunch of gravel under the tires interfered with my thoughts as I jumped from the truck at Rick's house and walked up to the door. Darned if I didn't have to break into Calhoun's again. He'd be under anesthesia, I hoped, because if not, his cellphone's security would play havoc with my plans. I needed a few minutes to grab my things in his armory.

Once inside the house, I stood before the security panel. It was a simple trick to open the panel, but remembering the sequence of numbers would be sticky. When I first saw this room, the security panel's tones were the last thing on my mind. With eyes closed, my senses traveled back to the day his arsenal opened wide. Seven numbers.

Think.

I replayed the musical tone in my head and punched in the numbers. The door to the gunroom opened. After grabbing a few things, I locked up and opened my bag. I bit my lip. What if I needed to ditch Whiskey River after I talked to the FBI? I stuffed everything I might need into a sack. Money, passports, licenses, birth certificates. I stopped at the bookshelf.

Who keeps three Bibles? I grabbed one and added it to my sack.

I slipped into a sleek black outfit, meant more for stealth at night than a midnight tryst.

My truck glided through the open gate after I switched off the headlights. Through the large glass windows, I spied Sarah Thompson seated on a couch, plus two familiar figures. I'd told Tristan Phillips I'd find the FBI agents, but I had no idea they'd be here.

With the engine off, I slipped from the driver's seat and grabbed two loaded and chambered Glocks liberated from Calhoun's closet. With one holstered on each hip, I crouched in between Thompson's and the FBI agents' vehicles, and recorded the video with my smartphone.

These FBI agents were at the police station after Calhoun's car exploded, or so Rick had said, and at the Chandlers'. Were they meant to flush me out?

Gabriella Watts balled a fist and hit Sarah across her jaw, knocking the widow back.

Oh, I don't think so. Bile rose in my throat as I remembered Jerry's violence. I stuck my phone back into my pocket, checked my holsters, and burst through the unlocked door. I pulled the Glocks in one smooth motion.

"My, my, my. What have we here? You two making a bust?"

The agents fumbled for their guns. Feds. So slow.

"Ah-ah, you think that's a good idea?" I moved a half-circle around them.

The woman rushed me, slamming one Glock from my hand. Her teeth bared, she backhanded me, and I stumbled against the wall. She twisted my wrist, turning the other pistol toward my face. I kneed her in the gut, then kicked. She lurched backward. I side-kicked her twice, one to the face, the second to the chest. She dropped, and I shot her in the foot. Watts shrieked.

The male agent, Grey, had Sarah in a choke hold, his Beretta to her head. "One move."

"Have at it." I waved my hand dismissively. "Never met the woman."

"I will shoot—"

My hand steady, I acquired my target—him—in my front sight. "Shut up and do it. I'll shoot you and your lady pal and call it a day. It will look obvious, and I'll disappear."

Thompson yelled, "You're going to let him pull the trigger?"

Instead, Grey shoved Sarah to knock me off balance, but I pushed her to the floor as he dove and grabbed for my feet. I fell onto my back. With one leg loose, I kicked him in the face with my heel. Why do people always try to move faster than bullets? I put one in his leg. He grasped it and howled.

"You idiot," Gabriella screamed. "Shoot her."

He raised his gun. I raised mine. *Deja vu. Again.*

"I'm going to kill you," he hissed. "Why are you smiling?"

"Batter up."

"What?"

"Behind you, John," Gabriella shouted.

Sarah smashed him in the head with a high-dollar maple baseball bat. I hoped she hadn't killed him outright.

I twisted in time as Gabriella attempted to pluck her gun from the floor. I kicked her mid-gut and knocked her pistol out of her reach.

I made sure both agents had been temporarily rendered harmless, then looked up at Sarah. "Where did you learn *that*?"

Sarah beamed. "Women's softball. I could hit four homers a game."

"Excellent. Glad you didn't kill him, though."

"Yeah, that would have been awkward."

Glad she connected before a bullet took flight. I'd expected a facedown with her, not a shootout with the FBI, and I'd left my bulletproof vest at home.

We began the tedious job of tethering two crooked agents. John Grey and Gabriella Watts were worse off than either Sarah or me, and when Grey came to, I piped up. "Pretty slick, holding your guns on Kim, taking her into custody. I'll bet you were supposed to deliver the guidance design to the Russians, or Sarah if she didn't have them already."

We cuffed the agents as if we packed for a picnic, wrapped their wounds, and stuffed them into the back of the agents' car. I took Sarah aside, out of the FBI's earshot. Didn't want to talk about my deputy status. "I'm not a cop. I'm a grifter. Was a grifter. Catherine." I stuck my hand out.

She grasped my hand as a small gasp escaped her lips. "You're a con?"

"Past tense. You may be going to prison. Rafael Santiago's real name was Ibrahim Youssef, and he was an assassin. He played you, and I believe he played Camille Tate. I found evidence that supports the theory that he mixed your husband's insulin to make a lethal dose. Camille didn't know Youssef had already dealt the fatal blow, and she drove here and shot Mr. Thompson." I didn't mention I'd notified the sheriff in Salem.

"You sound like a cop."

"Not even close."

Quiet a moment, her eyes brimmed, and tears spilled down her cheeks. "Why Stephen? He was a mark, and I fell for him."

"It'll be on national news soon enough. Messy business, putting your hand in the Russians' cookie jar. They found you. Did they sell your skills to the highest bidder, like al Qaeda, to turn the town? Forced penance?"

"Something like that," she said, tears still pouring. "They scripted everything."

I touched her arm, and we moved toward the government SUV. "Special Agents Watts and Grey were part of the plan."

Grey yelled from the open window. "No one will ever find you. We will take care of you. Burying evidence is our specialty."

"Shut up, John," Watts said. "They have nothing. There's no way to prove what she's saying. It's the FBI's word against criminals. No one will believe their story."

I dissolved into anger. "Which is what? Grab the missile guidance blueprints and bribe Darren Hughe? The mayor didn't even know, did he? You guys made Jerry a deal, planned to sell national security to our worst enemies, leaving bodies in your wake. Homeland Security will love this."

"So what?" Grey sneered. "The Russians, al Qaeda, it doesn't matter who gets it. You're no different. You're in it for the money."

"In what, the murder-for-hire business, or the sell-out-your-country business? Neither, because I don't murder people or betray my country." I turned back to Sarah and yanked a smartphone from my shirt pocket. I played the conversation back, hit SAVE, and pressed SEND to Calhoun's phone. He'd enjoy the show later.

CHAPTER 59

Sarah wept for what seemed like forever, reliving her favorite memories of her husband, angry that in her loneliness she'd allowed terrorists to infiltrate her life and kill her man. Defeated that she'd been beaten at her own game, and people died because of it.

We moved away from the car again and sat on the stoop. I said, "I didn't see it at first. But someone didn't give me what I deserved, namely judgment and prison. He gave me mercy instead. My friend taught me that God gives us grace, too, a gift we don't deserve. Me accepting His forgiveness took away all my wrongs. I did a lot of stupid during the thinking-it-over process."

She scoffed. "Isn't it a simple way to justify being judgmental about everyone else?"

I took a deep breath. "Not real Christianity. But I had to face my past and understand I was against God. Then admit this and ask forgiveness. Trust me, I was just like you, I didn't believe. But Jesus is Lord. When I figured out that Jesus wasn't turning me into a robot, but making me more *me*, only better, I gave my heart to him. That's the Gospel. Clean slate. Then do what's right."

Sarah asked plenty of questions, and what usually came next could often be difficult. She proved me wrong, and grasped my hands in prayer.

She asked, "What now?"

I raised my eyes. "Calling the police would be right. But you'll read a verse I marked out for you. I'm paraphrasing, 'Which one of you has never committed a crime? If one of you is accusing her, then let him be the first to punish her.' And it ends with, 'Jesus spoke to the woman, your wrongs have been wiped away. Go your way and do what's right by God's word.'"

"You're not turning me in?"

"And turn myself in, as well? Someone who should have turned me in didn't. He, too, let me go. Like you." I led her to my GMC and shoved my hand into the bag from Calhoun's, the bag I packed when I wasn't sure if I would run or stay and do the right thing. "I may be swell in God's eyes, but I'm not so sure the law would see it His way. Here, this is your manual on how to live. It's a Bible. Find a church wherever you land. Are your parents alive?"

"Yes, and my sister."

"Maybe it's time to reconnect. But if you can't, here are birth certificates, passports, and Social Security numbers."

Sarah rubbed a thumb over three new identities. "Thank you."

"Hang on." I produced the bagful of money I brought and hesitated. "This is a hundred thousand. You'll be living on the cheap. If you spend it in one place, someone will notice. It's enough to start over while you find real work."

"Wait." She rubbed away tears on her face. "Part of your heist?"

"It's complicated ..."

"Boost a new car, a new town, find a job—"

"Sounds familiar. No more hot-wiring, stealing, or scamming. Get out of town, buy a cheap car for cash, and head east."

She smoothed her hair and glanced at the FBI agents in the back of the car. "I don't know where to start."

"Start small and be content. Use what you know to catch the bad guys and become a private detective." I scribbled my phone number on a piece of paper. "Call me. Never know when I'll need a PI."

Her voice choked. "I don't understand why you're doing this for me. I owe you."

"Because someone did the same for me. Showed me kindness, waited patiently, and stuck by me at my worst. I'm counting on you to do what's right, not what's easy."

We parted. She drove off in my GMC after we hugged.

Not the last of my stash, but a darn good wad of cash.

I prayed, hoping I'd made the right decision. I'd hate to see a countess pop up in Europe.

Now I had to face Calhoun.

I took the FBI agents to the station and locked them up. I called Mike and drove back to the hospital to make the rounds.

The rest of us waited on Calhoun, who had not yet come out of surgery. The pressure to Sam's head wound required surgical release, but he'd be fine. He'd sustained a shot to his neck, missing an artery, with a concussive injury to his head.

Amy didn't make it.

I found a chair and cried. Needing comfort, I was anxious to find Calhoun even if he was in post-op. After waiting for what felt like hours, I wandered, checking on everyone.

I stopped to see Jack McCloud.

He slurred. "Heeeyyyy, doll. I think they gave me gin. Wanna join me?"

"Thanks, but no. I'm making sure everyone is doing okay. How are you? Kim and all?"

"Yeah. Her." His smile vanished. "Think I'll go to church again. Spend quality time there."

"Not a bad idea."

He closed his eyes, and I left him to his pleasant post-anesthesia dreams.

Sam would awake without his wife. I stood at his door clutching my chest. I wandered toward the lobby and found Dumont while Zoe dabbed a tissue at her eyes.

While we waited for news on Calhoun, I took Dumont aside. "What did Calhoun tell you about Thompson's murder?"

"Calhoun gave me a bit of information. He said you'd know more."

We wandered to a seat near the window. "Thompson's widow didn't kill him," I said. "She was strong-armed into working for some shadowy group in DC with Russian and al Qaeda ties. Darren Hughe appeared to be the mediator to change the politics here, hired to murder Stephen Thompson, to get him out of the way. Bribed by foreign big bucks. Didn't work out as he planned."

"Calhoun told me Jerry forced you to steal."

"Yeah." I didn't elaborate. "Camille Tate murdered Thompson in revenge for their daughter's death. Someone had hired Youssef, who masqueraded as Santiago to get close enough to Thompson to kill him. He switched the insulin bottles to make it look like natural causes. Camille wasn't aware Youssef had overdosed Thompson, so she walked in, used Thompson's gun, and shot him. I called Salem, and the PD picked her up. No doubt she's lawyering up by now."

"Why did Youssef stick around?"

"It would have been too obvious if he left. Amy and Sam—" I looked at my hands to compose myself. "Amy and Sam found the connection. Youssef had to take credit or risk no pay. He identified as Santiago for years, admitted he killed Perez and took his identity. McCloud found the insulin dosages. Somewhere along the line, Kim became involved with Youssef. She's the one who shot me from the car while I was at the doughnut shop. The Russians bribed Hughe, blackmailed Sarah Thompson, and Camille Tate just pulled the trigger and muddied the waters."

"I can't believe everyone went behind my back." He gave a *tsk*.

I hid a smile, knowing he had sent the note attached to Thompson's death certificate. "Everyone wanted the truth. I suspect McCloud wasn't happy with his name on the DC. Calhoun didn't want you framed for a cover-up."

"Sarah Thompson, the grieving widow, became involved with Youssef?"

I nodded. "Unaware of who he was, while Tate, not knowing anything but her anger, came to Whiskey River. Youssef made regular trips there with Thompson's car to Salem, playing both Sarah Thompson and Tate. After Thompson was shot, he needed to grab the gun and establish her guilt."

"Where is the elusive Sarah Thompson now?"

I coughed. "Don't know. After I sent the videos to Calhoun, I brought the agents to the station. I shot them."

"You what?"

I grimaced. "One in the foot. One in the leg. Watts and Grey ran this whole circle."

"Figures, Thing One and Thing Two probing the office."

We sat together with Zoe, commiserating over the loss of Amy, when Mike walked through the door.

"Calhoun's still in surgery." I grasped his hand. "We lost Amy."

His head bowed, and we wept. How would we tell Sam?

The doors to the surgical suites opened, and the surgeon stepped out as the doors whooshed.

"How is Calhoun doing?" I asked.

He mopped his face. "We did everything possible."

"What?"

"There were complications. The bullet passed through the underside of his shoulder, where there is no protection with a bulletproof vest. It entered his chest and the wound damaged a large artery, causing too much blood loss, and the bullet to his shoulder wasn't a priority. We gave him eleven units of blood, and ... we simply couldn't replace his blood volume fast enough to repair the damage. It's never easy to say this, but I'm sorry for your loss."

"What do you mean, loss?" I turned to Zoe. "Zoe, what does he mean?"

"Oh, honey—" Zoe put a hand over her mouth.

I felt a total disconnect from reality. *No ...*

Mike stepped forward. "Calhoun's gone?"

I trembled, grasped Mike's arm, and looked at the surgeon as the words made horrific sense. "What do you mean, gone?"

"I'm sorry. He died about half an hour ago. We notified his family, and they're on their way. They'll make funeral arrangements."

"No!" I wept, pushing my way past the surgeon as an orderly tried to hold me back. I twisted my way free to the surgical bay doors. Locked. I pounded on them. I yelled Calhoun's name.

"We're his family, all of us," Dumont shouted. "You should've told us. You should have told us!" He jabbed a finger toward the surgeon's chest.

The orderly kept me back. My knees turned to water, and I dropped to the floor, sobbing. "I need to see him. Please. He's stronger than this. You don't know Calhoun. He's not dead, he can't be. Please tell me he's not dead."

"His body is already at the morgue."

"No!"

The surgeon stood aloof. "There was nothing we could do." He swiped an ID card, and the surgical doors opened, and he disappeared as they closed behind him.

Dumont knelt next to me, put his arms around my shoulders, and sat with me until I could cry no more. A cold numbness crept in, hollowing out the space where joy had lived.

"Calhoun gave this to me for safekeeping," he whispered, handing me a box. "He loved you."

I lifted the top. It was a ring.

There, on my knees, before the doors to the surgical suites, crying, I held the ring to my forehead, trying to will all of this to be a bad dream.

The air was gone. I loved him, too.

I loved him, too. God, why would you take him? Why now?

CHAPTER 60

By Oregon standards, becoming a police officer could take a year to complete, and a detective, many more.

I graduated that month. By commission.

Chief Dumont brought me Calhoun's belongings and filled in the blanks. Calhoun had found my identity. My name had surfaced with Homeland Security. Turned out I worked for them.

The background check and the skills Calhoun found in me helped me graduate from the academy. Nothing like Homeland Security's blessing. Jerry died in prison from a severe bacterial infection of his face and arm. Probably a gift from Calhoun. Both the corrupt FBI agents died in a fiery car crash. Tragic, yes. Accident? Maybe.

My real name was Beatrice Bodner, daughter of General Weston Frye and Olivia Bodner-Frye. Didn't like its sound. Once Calhoun, who knew all my aliases, said he favored Catherine Marie Cade. I made it legit.

My folks lived in Norfolk, Virginia, and with a prearranged trip to Boston, I planned to get to know them again. The Who Donut's employees took the keys for me when I left.

Not everything came back, but I remembered my parents, and they filled in more blanks. My birthday was on May eighteenth, 1983. My father joked that I interrupted the Pentecost service at church.

Later, they told me I graduated from a prestigious Catholic high school at seventeen, then joined the Navy and became a corpsman the next year. Served in Afghanistan after nine-eleven, "green side" with the Marines, and worked in the operating theater as a surgical assistant. That explained my medical background. Vetted by DHS in 2004. Some, I remembered. Most, I didn't. But surprised to find out that my mother worked for DHS as well.

Everything was there, my old life, my folks, a job. It was impossible to explain, as much as I loved them, that it wasn't an option to move back East. In a few small ways, he would always be here, because as long as I took a breath, he'd never leave. I'd keep my promise to Calhoun. Whiskey River was home.

I had only hoped it would be with him.

When I returned to Whiskey River, his house was on the market. I couldn't bear to see it go to strangers, so I bought it, kept his clothes, even his stupid toothbrush. I figured this would be my next thousand years until God took me home.

When numbness took hold, I'd sit on the bed often, and cry into his coat or his shirt, taking in his scent, listening to his voicemails on my cell. Better heartache than nothing.

Swearing in on graduation day, I saw Zoe, Chief Dumont, Mike, and Tristan from the bleachers, as they waved, taking pictures. Jules forgave me, and here, waving a hanky, she sat with my parents. Dumont saluted. Mike gave a thumbs up. My parents and Zoe cried. Tristan dabbed his eyes, too.

I raised my eyes to scan the stadium and imagined I could see Calhoun there. But knowing he was not, part of me wanted to die. But what would he tell me? *Suck it up, cupcake.* So I did. With French braided hair tucked under itself, standing in my blues, white gloves, cap, and shiny black shoes, I saluted.

The valedictorian turned out to be me, and the speech was tougher than I thought. I choked out the words and told the class about Calhoun, how he inspired me and pushed me. I reminded the graduates to honor the man or woman who had inspired them, whether here or gone, whether spouses, parents, or friends. I told them to remember all of those who had sacrificed to the point of death with little or no thanks for their efforts. And I repeated the statement to them.

They had no idea.

I straightened with my promise, and voice cracking, I saluted. "Detective Rick Calhoun, I pray I'll do right by you."

The tears streaming down my face weren't because I'd made it. They were for the man I loved.

He'd be so proud.

Today was another day, a passage of time, and I still marked each tick-tock since Calhoun died. I daydreamed about a first date we were destined never to enjoy.

On this dreary, cold day, Mike was on a call, and Zoe, quiet, understood my grieving hadn't stopped.

I figured it never would.

Another bunch of Mike's bandits and misfits came through the door. I entered their information onto the computer and saved the data onto a thumb drive. Mike went back out on call, leaving Zoe and me to process his ruffians. A few we sent to Juvie. Two, we released to parents, with one straggler left.

Zoe turned. "Want me to process him? Shelter?"

An elderly man with a walker bent over even as he sat, shaking with the symptoms of Parkinson's. He had stringy gray hair, a long beard, and wore mismatched clothes. Temperatures were predicted to drop below freezing. It was already cold and slick outside.

"The cells are empty. He can stay overnight until tomorrow. It's too late for the shelter. I'll have to grab dinner, anyway. I'll order for him, as well."

Zoe led him to a cell, chatting with him. The door clanged, and I checked my watch.

She returned. "Okay, door's locked, but he's free to run about back there. Don't want him running the station when we all go home."

"Heaven knows we need the help."

She grabbed her coat and umbrella. "See you tomorrow, Detective."

"'Night, Zoe."

Another half hour passed as I pushed on a cold case, when I realized I'd clean forgotten our guest. With extra blankets in hand, I went to him and said, "We need to eat. Two choices, Mister. You come along with me and keep me company, or I'll bring something back."

The tremor in his hands and head gave his condition away.

"No, ma'am, you shouldn't be seen with the likes of me. I can git something in the morning. And it's warm in here."

"Nonsense. What do you want to eat?" I fiddled with my necklace, the one Calhoun called a "hog's tooth," the one my Marine sniper father gave me years back. A bullet.

"Pizza?"

My hands now stuffed in pockets, I said, "Sure. Come with me. Company around here is sparse."

The pizza delivery man knew me by name and brought a giant pie to the counter for me to pay. I thanked him as he left and grabbed napkins and paper plates.

My dinner mate sat at the desk across from me, hunched over, trying to hide his trembling as we ate, apologizing when his tremors increased.

His shoes were brown, scuffed, and worn, matching his dark eyes. A tired, wrinkled face gave away his harsh life. He needed a shave. His slacks were too short, showing off old socks. His coat and mittens where threadbare, not much help in this weather. He gave me a yellowed, toothy grin. His dark eyes played with the light overhead.

"What's your name?"

"John. John Smith."

I chortled at the absurdity. "John Smith, I'm glad to meet you. I'm Detective Cade." I stretched a hand across the desk and wiped tomato sauce from his mouth. He sat back in his chair.

Mortified, I said, "I'm so sorry. A habit. Guess it's not gone."

"It's okay." With his head bobbing with the Parkinson's, he continued, "Can I go back? Be nice to settle in to sleep in a warm spot fer a change."

"You're sure you don't want company?"

"No, Miss. Thank you, though." He tugged on the bill of his cap. My eye lingered, remembering how Calhoun would pull on his hat.

"Okay. I'll be out here for a while if you need something. I'll let you know before I go home."

He thanked me for the pizza, then turned and shuffled toward the cells with his walker. He opened the door and closed it behind him.

Paperwork pushed me to stay, but I couldn't keep my eyes open, and soon—nothing.

"Cade."

I opened my eyes and blinked. Bad enough dreams filled my nights. Now my waking moments at work, too. My eyes closed again, and my hand slid off the computer. Should go home. Gotta go home.

"Move your butt, Cade!"

I snapped my head up, I clutched my chest, and ran into the hall leading to the cells. I flung the door open. No one but the old man, seated and hunched over.

"You okay?" he asked in a halting voice.

"I dozed off. Had a dream. That or I'm going crazy." I stood there, twisting the ring I'd worn since that awful day, the ring Calhoun never had the chance to give me.

"You engaged?"

"None of your business," I snapped. "Sorry, jumpy, I guess. Yes, sort of, well, no. I'm not engaged, but I'm spoken for. It's complicated."

"Thinkin' you could explain." He coughed. "We got time."

I took a seat in the cell across from John Smith. "His name was Rick. Homicide detective Rick Calhoun. He was the only one who saw the real me—besides God, that is—and he loved me in spite of it. He's gone. Died. I was selfish, never there for him. Found out he planned to propose. The day he died, we both did. Died, that is." I buried my head in my hands as my soul crumbled again. My patient dinner partner let me pull myself together.

"You can move on, you know. Ya don't look so much dead to me."

I handed him a small smile. "I moved on, became a detective because of him. He's not dead. At least—" I teetered on losing it. "They gave me his flag at the funeral, so I guess you could say I'm engaged to a dead man. Moving on. My way."

"Sounds like you're clingin' to someone who's not coming back. Ain't no life for a lady like you."

My hand covered the quiver in my chin, and despite my best efforts, I pulled my knees to my chest and cried. "My dreams at night with him are more real than my days without him." I wiped my sleeve across my face. "Um, why don't you tell me about yourself?"

"They took me, you understand. Abducted me right off, they did."

I lifted my chin. Oh, no. I just broke bread with an alien abductee and told him about the worst moment of my life. "Really?"

"One minute, I was in a hospital, and the next, spirited away." His head bobbed with his tremors. "I escaped, though."

If I had a dime ... Nodding, I swallowed. "Go on."

"Someone told her I died. I didn't. Die, that is." His voice had stopped its quavering. His eyes glistened with tears, and he stretched a gloved hand my way.

My world stopped. *What did he say?*

At that moment, gravity turned upside right, and everything I believed plummeted, because it was *his* voice.

Calhoun.

I grasped the man's outstretched hand, and he tugged on mine. I didn't dare look into the octogenarian's face, because, desperate to be right, I might be wrong, and that would be just weird.

John Smith. My stomach quaked, and my voice caught. I knelt before him. "Calhoun?" I whispered, removing the man's funky old mittens. I ran my fingers over his hands. He curled his fingers around mine, his tremor gone.

"Calhoun," I choked.

He straightened and raised me to my feet. Ran his thumbs across my cheeks. I buried my face in his chest.

"Catherine."

I turned him around, yanked his shirt up, and ran my hand along the old scar. "I knew you weren't dead! But the surgeon said you died." I sobbed, both relieved and angry.

"Near enough. Nobody expected me to survive, so they moved me out of there without telling anyone. I was in a coma for a week, and when I woke, the chances were still slim to none. They made the surgeon cover for them, so you'd believe it was over. Your mom didn't want to put you through the likelihood of a second death."

"My mom?"

He nodded. "She's my real boss. I work for Homeland Security."

Information scrambled my brain. "She came to the funeral, and she *knew*? How could she?" I sat. "You tried to tell me before they took you. I thought you couldn't talk about your work."

"No secrets between us, never, not anymore. I wanted to tell you."

I halted my tears, not wanting to relive the horrible moment. Part of me wanted to lash out at him even though he wasn't at fault. Every day had been an abyss, as I dreamed of the face that I would never see again this side of eternity. Now my grief came flooding back in one last torrent as I re-lived his death, his funeral, his absence—and now, his presence.

Moments passed, my tears dried, and still I clung to him as though he was the source of gravity.

Rick touched the tip of my nose. "Can I kiss the woman I love?"

"You look like someone's great-great-grandfather. I don't want long-term psychological therapy."

He removed the disguise and the brown-tinted lenses.

"You're wearing the ring I bought you." He dropped to one knee. "Catherine Marie Cade, will you do me the honor of being my wife?"

I stood, dumbfounded, unable to think of anything other than, "I don't know, John Smith. I'm engaged to this certain dead guy I know."

We smiled. Then we clashed in a flurry of kisses. He pulled back. "Do you remember anything more?"

"Some." I twisted the ring again. "Not everything. I couldn't handle Beatrice. I don't even think my mom likes it. She fumbles over it all the time."

"It's your grandmother's name. And I lived on Martha's Vineyard." He wiped tears from his face.

An image came to mind of a home on Oak Bluffs. "No. Did you and Melanie live there? I swallowed and searched his eyes, aching to see something that made sense. "Oh, no. I'm going insane." I rubbed a fist against my chest.

He waited, quiet.

"Wait. Wait." I closed my eyes. "We danced, I laid next to ..." I pressed my hands to my head. "You lived there with Melanie, but ... you and me. Oh, no. I was a homewrecker."

He shook his head, and I worried my thumbnail between my teeth, wishing my memory hadn't taken flight.

"If I'm not a homewrecker, but I remember us together, and the time is right, that would have to mean ..." I stepped back. "Melanie didn't die. She didn't die. You lost her—me. When the accident happened."

"It was no accident. You were in a hit-and-run all right, but Jerry meant to kill you. I thought you were dead. There was so much blood. Your DNA matched, but your body was gone." He struggled to keep tears back. "After the search ended, I looked everywhere. I ended up putting an empty coffin in the ground. I never stopped looking for you.

"Later, rumors surfaced that you were alive. Every lead I had evaporated, until that day in the clinic when I came looking for a signature, and instead you took me to school on proper procedure."

He grinned, sheepish. I gave him a sour look. "Why didn't you say something?"

"I came close more than once. But I wanted to know if Catherine Cade loved me for myself, not out of a sense of obligation."

I was his wife. Everything clicked into place. Married long before I met him at the clinic. No wonder he'd kept Mike at bay and lit into McCloud.

I'd never seen him weep until now, and standing, we held each other, our bodies wracked with sobs. Ten minutes later, we were a mess, out of tears, and quiet.

He buried his head in the crook of my neck. "I've always loved you. Always."

"I love you, too. Always." I stopped. "But what about my name?"

He frowned. "Hush, woman." We swayed together. "I'd like to take my adorable, crazy, amnesiac wife home tonight."

He stopped, and a tiny grin appeared as he sighed. "Gonna be a lot of work, though. Before you lost your memory, you were an obedient wife. Catherine Cade, however—"

My eyes widened. "Obedient, my—"

He laughed and stopped my mouth with a kiss.

ABOUT THE AUTHOR

Claire O'Sullivan is a retired nurse practitioner. A member of Sisters in Crime, she writes primarily in the genre of romance, which bleeds into other genres such as crime, police procedurals, inspirational, military, medical, forensics, mystery, thriller and comedy.

When she is not dusting the house for fingerprints at midnight, she enjoys plotting mayhem with a good cup of cocoa—and extra whipped cream. You can find her on Facebook Claire O'Sullivan https://www.facebook.com/claire.osullivan332. On Twitter, find her at @authorclaire1.

Projects after *How to Steal a Romance* in Whiskey River include three sequels—romance/thriller, *While I Was Dead*, romance/comedy/noir/inspirational/forensics, *Glass Slipper,* romance/mystery—*The Corpse in the Cupboard*, as well as *Alex and the Very Dead Doxy* and *The Voodoo That You Do*. Her current work is *Rules of Engagement*, a military thriller. She also has an international spy trilogy, no name as of yet, and last, a romance/psychological thriller, *Night Terrors,* in the works.

Made in the USA
Middletown, DE
21 July 2021